ANCHORED BY LOVE

Sons of Ishmael
Book 2

UNOMA NWANKWOR

KevStel Publications

KevStel Group LLC

Lawrenceville GA 30046

ISBN 978-0-9890738-8-2

ISBN 978-0-9890738-9-9 (Ebook)

First printing December 2015

Printed in the United States of America

www.kevstelgroup.com

Praise for Unoma Nwankwor

Unoma delivers a satisfying "truth is stranger than fiction" tale every time with her plot twists, plus some godly interventions. Romance isn't a fairy-tale in Unoma's **Anchored by Love**. It's real! **~Pat Simmons, award-winning author of Carmen Sister series**

Unoma has woven a compelling story of regret, forgiveness, love and God's amazing grace in this beautifully written novel. Poignant. Engaging, a great read -that cleverly demonstrates how God is able to use the most horrific situations and turn them around for his grace. Five stars! **~Abimbola Dare, Author of The Small Print and When Broken Chords Sing**

This sexy romance weaves forgiveness and love into a warm blanket rich with comfort. Nwankwor writes a well written story with several universal themes of family, forgiveness and love **~ Readers Paradise on A Scoop Of Love.**

"Unoma sets up each scene in **When You Let Go** with an emotional punch that will keep your heart racing to the finish line. Warning: You will lose sleep trying to get there!" **~Pat Simmons, award-winning author of The Guilty series.**

"**When You Let Go** is a true testament of the power of God within ourselves and our marriage. Although, we are tested every day, it is up to us to lean on our faith to get through those difficult times and offer forgiveness to those who may have hurt us in the process. Amara and Ejike's faith was tested throughout this novel but once they learned to put God at the forefront of their household, they were able to weather the storm." ~ **Diva's Literary World**

"I love how Unoma Nwankwor weaves the distinctive, spicy flavor of West Africa into her novels. I feel right at home with the food, pidgin English, quirky expressions, and cultural norms. I'm also enjoying watching her grow as an author. **~Sherri L. Lewis, Bestselling Author and Missionary**

Nwankwor adds more depth with the cultural nuances that could be a roadblock or a gateway to understanding. She expertly intertwines all of these elements, including faith lessons, to make a tightly woven story for a reader's enjoyment.~ **USA Today Review of An Unexpected Blessing.**

"In **An Unexpected Blessing**, Unoma Nwankwor has penned a sweet romance with an important message about love and acceptance. She's definitely a writer to watch." **~Rhonda McKnight, Black Expressions Bestselling Author of What Kind of Fool and An Inconvenient Friend**.

"What woman hasn't felt the pangs of unfulfilled desire? In **An Unexpected Blessing**, Unoma Nwankwor weaves deception, cultures and the intrigue of love for a romantic journey that spans two continents and challenges the cornerstone of faith."~ **Valerie J. Lewis Coleman, best-selling author of The Forbidden Secrets of the Goody Box TheGoodyBoxBook.com**

"I read **An Unexpected Blessing** and I must admit I

loved it very, very much. I look forward to reading your next novel."~ **Diane Ndaba, reviewer Africa Book Club**

"Unoma's writing reads effortlessly. There is the perfect infusion of faith and international flavor. Readers are quickly swept up on a romantic literary adventure. **The Christmas Ultimatum** is a great read for anytime of the year"~ **Norma Jarrett Essence Best Selling author of Sunday Bruch**

"I loved it. **The Christmas Ultimatum** is my first read from Unoma and it won't be my last. I enjoyed the international favor she gave to the story. There is nothing sexier than a Christian man who goes after who and what he wants. Kudos!" ~ **Pat Simmons Award winning author of the Guilty Series**

*To my husband Kevin, and my kids—Fumnanya & Ugo.
Their support is immeasurable.*

Acknowledgments

To my Lord and Savior Jesus Christ. I thank you for paying the ultimate price that I may have life and for your grace which I do not deserve. Thank You for the gift of writing and I humbly pray I continue to be a vessel in this journey.

To my family, my husband Kevin who is my number one fan, cheering me along every step of the way. I love you and thank you. To my kids Fumnanya and Ugo, my gang, my pookies, my munchkins they keep me sane when insanity sometimes abound. I love you both more than words can express. I pray for God's continued protection over you.

To my parents and mother in-law, *Daalu*. Thank you for your constant prayers and words of life, courage and hope upon me.

To my readers, author friends and sistah writers thank you, thank you. Sometimes support doesn't always come from the people or places you expect but trust in God and He will send the right people to you.

Note from the Author

The Sons of Ishmael series tells the story of three brothers who should have been sons of favor, but their lives took an unexpected turn when their father made a decision that molded their future. Or so they thought.

Just like Ishmael in the Bible, our circumstances in life can change quickly, and sometimes for the worse. That is when we should draw near to God and seek His wisdom and strength.

We may be tempted to become bitter when bad things happen, but that never helps. Only by following direction from God can we get through those valley experiences.

Follow Rasheed, Jabir & Kamal; the Danjuma brothers as they try to live in the present still harboring pain from the past and the ladies that will finally make them see that it is best to let go

There are some questions at the back of the book, so you could discuss them with your friends or just read through by yourself. If you have more questions, you can reach me at www.unwankwor.com

In book one, you meet Rasheed & Ibiso, catch up with them as you step into the world of Jabir & Damisi.

He pulled her into his arms once they entered her hotel room. He closed the door with his foot and kissed her deeply. After all this time, he was back in the arms of the one who got away. His head tugged at him to leave; his libido commanded him to stay. He was tempted to be the voice of reason, but this was where he had dreamed of being for almost seven years.

She returned his kiss with an eagerness that surprised him. The passionate exchange ended when there became the need to breathe. He thought a break in the moment would make her come to her senses—make her realize that if she kept looking at him like this, they'd go to a place of no return.

The air was filled with sexual tension and the added mixture of her light, flowery perfume, and his cologne. Rays of the Abuja city skyline slipped through the light curtains. It struck her face at an angle that gave her the appearance of an angel.

"Are you sure?" he whispered.

She looked down at her bare feet for a moment. His breath caught as he awaited her response. She stood on the tips of her toes and wrapped her arms around his neck. Her eyes taking his hostage, she didn't flinch. Something must have happened because the person who stood before him wasn't the one who walked out on him several years ago.

He gave her another chance to back away. "We can't go back."

"So are you just going to stand there?" she challenged him.

He lifted his hand and placed a wayward strand of her dark, black hair in its place. Words to describe her beauty failed him. Her bare, mocha shoulders were exposed through the hip- hugging red dress she had worn to the wedding earlier.

In one swift motion, he swept her up in his arms and walked toward the bed. He knew the dynamics of their relationship were about to change. *Again.* Change was inevitable, however, whether this change would be good or bad was yet to be seen.

Chapter 1

Two Months Later

How did I allow this to happen again?

Jabir Chike Danjuma frowned and slowly sat up in his king-sized bed. Women weren't allowed to sleep overnight in his bed. He placed his interlocked fingers on his head and peered at the woman by his side. The annoying sound of his alarm clock jarred him from his irritated state. He reached over to silence the unwanted noise when his hand brushed up against her soft body. It was 7:00 A.M., and the soft rays of spring sunlight had begun to make their way into his bedroom. The room was quiet except for the soft snores coming from his left and the light humming of the heating system.

The woman who lay beside him wasn't just any woman, but a coworker. Angela Smith was a neonatal nurse at Mercy Stone Hospital. When she arrived at Mercy two years ago, she had made her interest in him known. From experience, there were two things he never did—date women younger than thirty or anyone from work. He broke both rules. He had justified his actions with the fact that he was in the Department of Surgery, and she looked older than her twenty-five years, so he took the bait. Throughout their off-and-on eight-month relationship, he had made sure she never slept over. He knew when women started to share a man's bed overnight, they began to have ideas and fantasies about forever after, neither of which he was ready to entertain or fulfill.

He looked over at Angela again and shook his head. He vaguely remembered boarding the charter jet they hired to return from Vegas the previous night. Angela had been complaining about his lack of attention, so after a lot of persuasion, Jabir had agreed to the double date with a fellow doctor and his girlfriend. If he had known that while in Vegas, Dr. Leo would propose to his girlfriend and get married all in one night, he would have declined the invitation. There was no way he would willingly go to a wedding with Angela, but it was too late. They had had a lot to drink and eat and even tried their luck at the casinos. It was time to get back to his normal.

Impromptu weekday trips to Vegas, drinking, gambling—his life was spiraling out of control. This wasn't him. Granted, he had been working for six days straight, covering his shifts and Dr. Bradman's, but he should have been more alert. He had to find a way to end this relationship for good before he went on his missions' trip with Doctors in the Skies the following month. He didn't want any attachments. He wiped his face with the back of his hand, reminding himself to be tactful. The last thing he wanted was drama at work.

After he got back from Nigeria two months ago, he felt his life had no meaning, was out of control and anything was game, but he had to get it together. Damisi, the only woman he wanted more than anything, even after all these years, had rejected him—again.

"Good morning, Jay darling." Angela's voice interrupted his memory. She sat up and brushed her cool lips on his cheek. Her jet-black hair fell to her side. Its wavy nature and length were a result of her mixed Indian and African American heritage.

He hated it when she called him Jay and had told her that several times. Jabir meant "comforter," and he wanted to keep it that way. His mother often told him he had always shown compassion at an early age. He liked to think his name was the reason he turned out to be a doctor. "Jay" distorted its meaning. However, Jabir knew the real reason he disliked the name. His late father used to call him "Jay Boy." The man and the name both got on his nerves.

"Morning. I see you didn't leave."

"No." She rubbed his chest. "You were out cold when we got back from Vegas last night, so I decided to fulfill my new role and take care of you." She rubbed her hand gently across his chest and winked.

Her sexiness was his downfall. He closed his eyes, trying to focus on what he should be doing—letting her down easy. Before he could gather his thoughts and speak, she scooted to the edge of the bed, put on his shirt and made her way to the bathroom. His eyes followed the sway of her hips until she was out of sight. He shook his head and exhaled.

"What role? What are you talking about?" he murmured to himself. "This has to end." There was a time and season for everything. Angela's time was up.

Jabir swung his legs over the bed, put on his robe and walked out of the bedroom. Today was Sunday, his first weekend off in two weeks, and he planned on doing absolutely nothing. He walked into the kitchen and opened the blinds. He placed a Robust Joe cup, his favorite brand of coffee, into the Keurig machine and waited for it to brew. Through his kitchen windows, he could view the magnificent Detroit skyline. Michigan had been home to him since he moved from the United Kingdom after his sophomore year in college. He had come over as an exchange student, then decided to make his stay permanent. He had built a whole new life for himself. Different from the one he left behind in the United Kingdom. A life that was filled with painful childhood memories.

At six years old, when his father decided to walk out on him, his brothers and his mother, Jabir learned a valuable lesson. No one could be trusted. If his father, who had made so many promises about always being there for them, abandoned them without a backward glance, then anybody could leave. He could only rely on himself.

Commitments left people vulnerable, and that he simply wouldn't do again. He always walked away before he was walked out on. Why he didn't remember that lesson when he met Damisi Odinga was beyond him. How on earth could he have let his guard down? Damisi's abrupt decision to end their year-long relationship and move to Nigeria six years ago had been a bitter pill to swallow. The way she tossed away what they had should have been enough to teach him a lesson, but he couldn't let it be. She was the one woman he had never been able to get over.

Jabir shook his head to clear it of the bittersweet memory. He leaned against the marble counter and lifted the cup to his mouth to savor the aroma when his heart stopped. He placed the hot liquid on the counter and examined what looked like a ring on his finger. He turned around swiftly and saw Angela leaning against the doorframe with a smirk on her face.

"What the hell is this?" He lifted his hand and pointed to his finger.

"Jay, darling, I wondered when you'd notice." Angela sauntered into the kitchen holding up her left hand, smiling.

The bands looked similar. What in the world? "Stop calling me Jay. Notice what?"

"We got married," Angela announced excitedly.

Jabir put one finger in his ear and shook it to make sure there was nothing blocking it. He could not have heard her correctly. He advanced toward her. "You say what? You and who are married?"

Angela backed up. "Hold on. Give me a couple of minutes to explain."

"You've got sixty seconds."

"Yesterday was so crazy. We were all drinking and having fun. After Leo and Sasha got married, we were all drunk and happy. In the chapel, I asked you if you thought we should do it. I mean we've been dating almost a year—"

"So, what the hell are you saying?" Jabir seethed. He walked into the living room and headed for his cell phone. If she was saying what he thought she was, he needed Ashton on the phone now.

Ashton McDermott was his lawyer. Apart from Jabir's brothers, he was also his closest confidant. He dialed, but after several rings he got no response. He tossed the phone on the couch, remembering that Ashton and his family were probably at church.

"Who are you calling?" Angela was freshly showered, and her wet hair was wrapped in a towel on top of her head. His white terry robe swallowed her five-foot, one-inch frame. What he formerly saw as attractive was now the biggest mistake of his life.

"You knew I was drunk. And you just admitted that you took it upon yourself to get us married. Who do you think I'm calling? My lawyer, of course."

Angela walked over to him with mischief in her eyes. She took the towel off her head and rubbed it on her wet hair.

"I asked you and you said sure, whatever. Those were your exact words," she said. "Besides, we've been dating for a while now."

He looked at her incredulously. "You really can't be serious." He paced. "I was drunk for goodness' sake, and eight months, off and on, is not a while."

She frowned. "The first three months and the last two months have been pretty steady."

A matter of semantics, but she was right. And the only reason that happened was he was tired of Damisi and her games. He remained silent.

"What are you getting at?" He sat on the arm of the couch.

"This could work. And it's a natural next step," she whispered, but not low enough that Jabir didn't hear her.

"You're joking, right? I don't do next steps." He got up from the chair and picked up his phone again. "I told you that from the beginning."

He turned around, and Angela had occupied his spot. She was quiet. He had counted on her temper rising and her stomping out of the room. This calm Angela was strange to him. She began to whimper. He shook his head. Her anger he could deal with, but crying was a different thing. Jabir walked over and touched her shoulder.

"Angela, we can't be married. We have to get an annulment. Please stop crying," he begged.

"How can you be so insensitive? I love you…"

"Love? Whoa! Hold on. Where's this coming from? Some dates and tosses in the sheets…"

His words were cut off by a slap across his face.

His daze lasted a few seconds. Jabir gently massaged the area where Angela's hand had connected with his face. The pain from the sting went straight to his head.

This was the Angela he knew. She placed her hands on her hips. "Is that what I am? A toss in the sheets?" She turned to stalk out of the room. He grabbed her upper arm.

All his relationships ended well, and now the stakes were higher. He couldn't afford the drama. His reputation at work was clean, and he wanted to keep it that way. He wasn't going to allow any woman to tamper with his career. It was his life. All he had.

"Angela don't be like that. I'm sorry. This whole thing caught me off guard." He cupped her face.

She hesitated for a few moments. "I thought we had something good."

"We did, but obviously you want more, and I can't give it. We can't be married."

She jerked away. "We'll see about that…"

Jabir's heart thudded against his chest. "What are you saying?"

"You're a dog, Jay. I always knew it, but I was carried away by your charm."

"I never promised anything. Let's just get this annulled, and we can both move on," Jabir said.

Angela rolled her eyes at him. "Whatever. Come to think of it, you should be glad to have all this." She spread her arms and twirled.

Jabir remained silent, trying to conceal the excitement in his eyes. She was finally beginning to see reason. Besides, he did have all that, but no longer wanted it. "So, it's my loss."

"Don't think you can use that reverse psychology on me. I have no one to blame but me for thinking you would see my worth and change your mind." She stomped back into the bedroom.

As he watched her, he felt a pang of regret for the hurt he saw in her eyes. He had no one to blame but himself for letting this relationship continue for so long. Maybe that's why she thought he would change his mind. If only he had stood by his decision to forget Damisi, none of this would have happened.

Angela stomped back into the room and sized him up for a moment. He opened his mouth to speak but closed it again. Nothing he could say would be what she wanted to hear. The silence in the room was saturated with unspoken words.

"You are one of those types who can have any girl you want and also discard them without a second thought. Well, mister, I have news for you. If you want this annulment, you're going to have to work for it." Seconds later, the front door slammed.

Jabir had the sinking feeling he was going to pay for this for a couple of months to come.

Chapter 2

Damisi clamped her hand over her mouth, propelled herself from the bed and raced into the adjacent bathroom. Seconds later, she was hugging the commode, spewing the contents of her stomach into it. She dry heaved until she was sure nothing else was coming up. She flushed, splashed water on her face and brushed her teeth thoroughly. Exhausted from the effort, she staggered back into the bedroom. She plopped down on the bed, let out an exaggerated sigh and then fell on her back.

She placed her hand on her forehead. "My life is over."

Staring up at the familiar ceiling, Damisi remembered the first time she slept in this bedroom. She was six, and it was her first summer vacation to Kenya. Well, the first one she could remember. At the present, it served as her hide-out for the last couple of days. Give or take a day. She didn't know anymore. The days had begun to run together as she became more depressed over her situation. She placed her hand over her stomach. It was still flat with no movement. But then at nine weeks, she couldn't expect anything more.

She was desperate for any indication that the plus sign displayed on the little white stick some weeks ago was a false positive. The thirty or so other little sticks she had also used must have been flawed from the manufacturers. She remembered lining the sticks along the sink of her bathroom. They all said the same thing, not one minus sign in sight. The final confirmation from her gynecologist got her a plane ticket to Kenya. She felt safe here.

This has to be a dream. This can't be happening to me. The sound from a cockerel that crowed in the distance wiped away the possibility of this being a dream. She was very much awake, and this was her reality. What was she going to do? What would happen to her job? She was supposed to be the face of single women who were waiting on the Lord for their Boaz. As one of the most popular and well-paid television personalities at Kingdom Television Network, the largest Christian network on the continent of Africa, it had been her job for the past six years to encourage and uplift women waiting on their husbands while carrying out their God-given purpose. Something she did weekly on her *Becoming Ruth* show. She looked down at her stomach. *So much for that.*

Choices you make have consequences. Damisi could hear just hear Eno's high-pitched voice in her ear. Eno Ikpe, her friend and producer, was currently in South Africa for training.

The thin, white curtains that separated the balcony from the bedroom danced under the early morning, mid-April breeze. The refreshing wind was a result of the rain that fell the night before and the fact that her Kenyan childhood home was built on elevated land.

She sat up and tears she hadn't been able to stop for weeks began to stream down her cheeks.

"Jesus, I'm in so much trouble. I'm sorry. Please tell me what to do..." She began to contemplate that fateful night. Her mind flashed back to the events that led to her acting as though she had no sense. Before she could settle in that memory, another wave of nausea began to rise. She covered her mouth and ran back into the bathroom.

An hour later, Damisi walked into the kitchen. She had showered and changed into lounging pants and a fitted tee. The kitchen hadn't changed a bit. The black appliances, light vinyl-covered floors and granite countertops were just as she remembered them. She glanced at the breakfast nook in the corner, and the memories of her early years flooded to the forefront. Bittersweet memories.

Damisi's mother, Sola Odinga, had passed away when she was ten, and Damisi's world fell apart. It was a traumatic period. The woman who was her everything left her all alone, and she was forced to live with a man she had only stayed with during summer vacation. Her parents had been estranged for most of her childhood until they finally divorced when she was eight. Her mother had told her that although she loved her father, their marriage couldn't survive family pressure, but that was all she would say. As her mother told it before she died, it was for their safety that she took Damisi and ran back to her home country, Nigeria, when Damisi was a baby.

She walked over to the sink and filled a pot with water to make *ugali*. Her dad would be up soon, and she wanted to have breakfast ready. He still preferred his cornmeal over an English breakfast any day. She started the coffee maker, and within seconds, the aroma of the caffeinated beverage began to fill the kitchen. Damisi looked around the kitchen and located the chopping board and the spice rack. Madam Paulina, her father's longtime housekeeper, had a knack for not putting things in their place.

Damisi cracked some eggs, whisked them together and set them aside. As she cut up the spinach and tomatoes to go with the dish, she hummed to the melody of an old classic hymn. A tear streamed down her face. She had not only let herself down, but was certain God was disgusted. How could she disappoint Him so? When had she sacrificed her relationship with Him on the altar of her career? That was why she was in this mess.

Minutes later, everything was set up in the breakfast nook. She turned to get some napkins, and her eyes caught the picture in the corner of the other room. Damisi went over and stared at it. No matter how many times she saw it, she still couldn't believe it. Her parents looked so happy. What could have caused her mother to give it all up?

"Ah, my darling daughter, you're awake already. Paulina would have made breakfast. I thought you were here on vacation." Her dad's voice interrupted her thoughts.

"Good morning, Daddy." She walked over and kissed him on his cheek.

Age had been good to her dad. At sixty-nine, Victor Odinga still looked as vibrant as ever. His frame was lean and toned as a result of his daily exercise routine. He often got up before dawn and walked the expanse of the compound. According to him, his motivation for keeping fit was twofold. One, his health and two, if his staff thought he was an old man, they would think they could cheat him. Damisi always thought it ridiculous he could care about his health but didn't give up snuffing tobacco.

"Sit. Breakfast is served." She took him by the hand and led him back into the kitchen.

After he was seated, she poured him some coffee and served his food.

"Damisi, I'm not handicapped, you know."

"I know, Dad. I just like doing things for you." Damisi poured herself a glass of juice and sat next to her dad. She couldn't stomach *ugali,* so decided on baked beans and eggs. She hated beans, but figured the baby had started making its demands because she suddenly had a craving for them.

They joined hands and said grace over their meal. Damisi could barely say, "Amen." Guilt pangs stabbed her heart.

Her father took a sip of the hot coffee and paused. Damisi met his gaze. His eyes seemed to gloss over as he gave her a faint smile. "I know you like doing things for me. Once upon a time, so did your mother."

Damisi reflected on his statement. "Dad, I'm now twenty-eight years old. Isn't it time you told me what happened between the two of you?"

"You look more like her with each passing day." He smiled, stretched his hand and rubbed her cheek. "Your mother's hair was jet black, too, and she liked to wear it long as well. Your hazel-brown eyes, those cute dimples on your right cheek, even the way you crack your knuckles when you're nervous. Just like her."

"Dad, I know what I look like. You're stalling."

"It's best to let the past stay there."

Damisi knew that would be his response. It always was when she brought up the topic. Now, however, she wouldn't force the issue. It was best to let it go. She had more pressing problems.

"It was late by the time you got back last night. Busy day?" Damisi took a spoonful of her baked beans.

Her father owned one of the most successful poultry farms in Kisumu, Kenya. He had built it from the ground up, and she couldn't have been more pleased, but wished he would have slowed down by now.

"Not that bad. I had a meeting with some potential buyers. They opened up a supermarket in the city and want the farm to supply eggs." He took a bite of his vegetables.

"I'm so proud of you, Daddy. God is faithful." She toyed with the eggs in her mouth. For some reason, they refused to go down her throat. She quickly knew why—something was coming up. Damisi covered her mouth, pushed her chair back and raced to the bathroom down the hall.

Moments later, she slowly walked back into the kitchen. She picked up the chair that had fallen in her haste and sat back down. She needed to lie down, but her dad's piercing eyes demanded an explanation.

He pushed his empty plate forward. "So, are you ready to talk?"

"Dad, it's nothing." She stacked his plate on top of hers and drank the rest of her juice.

"Really?" He folded his arms and leaned back into his chair. "My daughter, the ever busy and well-known TV personality, suddenly leaves her job in Nigeria and appears at her father's doorstep all the way in Kenya. And it's nothing."

Damisi lowered her eyes for a second.

Her dad leaned forward. "Do you think I don't hear the weeping at night? I've given you time to tell me what's going on."

He was right.

She cracked her knuckles. Her throat started to close as emotion began to ripple to the top. Her stomach felt uneasy, and her eyes began to blur.

"Dad, I'm in trouble."

Chapter 3

"No jokes, man. I'm in deep trouble here," Jabir said. He had tried to contact Ashton for hours the previous day with no luck. At dawn, he was up from the most fitful night of his life. All the nights cramming for exams in med school were nothing compared to the previous one. Not being able to get a hold of Ashton, he had researched every website he could find on divorce and annulments in Nevada. Some of the information he found gave him hope, but Angela's threat scared him.

"I know you're in deep trouble. I confirmed it, remember?" Ashton got up from behind his desk and walked over to Jabir, who was standing by the file cabinet.

"I *cannot* be married. So what now?"

Ashton placed his hand on his shoulder. "Relax. I was just trying to rattle you. I'll do my job while you go about your normal business and pray to whatever you worship that Angela won't contest the annulment." He smiled.

"I'm glad one of us thinks this is funny."

"Don't blame me. You're the one who agreed to a proposal by saying…what was it again? Oh yeah, "sure, whatever."" Ashton laughed.

As much as Jabir wanted to strangle his friend and lawyer,

it really was laughable. How did he allow Damisi to mess him up so badly that he'd become so careless? "Very funny. So you'll take care of it."

"Yes. This morning I'll go file the papers. Hopefully the P.I firm I work with can get the tapes of the ceremony where you were slouched over, and we can prove fraud."

"So, what about Angela?"

"That's where it becomes dicey. We really need for this to be quick. If we don't have her, that's still okay. It would just take longer. The real problem comes if she contests it. Then, we'd have to go to trial."

"This is just great." Jabir ran his hand over his head and glanced at his wristwatch. He had to get to the hospital.

"It'll be okay. I'll go to the courthouse this afternoon, and I'll call you later." Ashton walked back to his car. He stretched out his hand. "Go save lives, man, and let me start working on saving yours."

Jabir placed his hand in Ashton's for a firm handshake and left the office.

Forty minutes later, Jabir exited the elevator on the fourth floor of Mercy Stone Hospital to make his rounds. The facility located in the heart of Detroit was known for having one of the best heart centers in the state of Michigan. Since he graduated from medical school, it had been a dream of his to work at Mercy. After his residency in St Josephs, Ann Arbor, he got permanent employment in the twenty-year-old hospital. He had worked hard, and it had paid off. Not God's favor—as his mother loved to attribute all his success to—but hard work got him to where he was. Jabir believed in God and knew He did some things, but there was no way He was involved in every little detail of his life as his mother swore He was. He—Jabir —made things happen.

The move to Detroit was more than welcome. With it, he left behind memories he desperately wanted to forget. He turned the corner and stopped. He needed to get to Room

408 to check on his patient, but Angela and another nurse stood outside Room 407. She wasn't supposed to be here. Maybe she was visiting someone. He hadn't heard from her since she left his house Sunday morning, and he wanted to keep it that way.

Jabir heard footsteps behind him and turned around just in time to prevent the head nurse from speaking his name aloud.

"How are you, Valerie?" he asked.

"Fine…" She eyed him suspiciously. "I thought we were headed to Room 408?"

Valerie Johnson was an elderly lady who had worked at Mercy for the past ten years.

"Erm…yeah, right." He couldn't stall any longer. Taking the chart from her, they proceeded down the hall. He acknowledged Angela with a nod. She returned the gesture with daggers in her eyes. Not sure if she was going to make a scene or not, he quickly entered the patient's room with Valerie following closely.

"So, how's my patient doing today?" Jabir walked over to the bed and jotted a note in the chart he was holding.

The sixty-five-year-old man gave him a faint smile. "Better than I thought I'd be."

"I told you everything would be fine. You just had to have a pacemaker put in—nothing major."

"You're the doctor. It's easy for you to say." The man placed his hand over his upper chest.

Jabir moved over and inspected the incision, then removed his stethoscope from his neck and listened to the patient's lungs. Everything was as it should be.

Jabir chuckled. "What did you think would happen?"

"We don't know, doctor. Just glad that Jesus used you as a tool to help my Eddy here," the patient's wife said.

Amused, Jabir sucked in air. Another one of those. Just shoot to the moon all those nights he had spent studying and learning his profession…everything was still attributed to God.

"Do you have questions for me?" Jabir asked.

They both shook their heads.

Jabir informed the couple he would observe Eddy again overnight, but they should be able to go home in the morning. He engaged in a little small talk before he left the room.

By afternoon, Jabir had seen all his patients and was back in his office writing some notes. He hummed to the *Flintstones* theme song. He did that whenever he was having a good day. The cartoon took him to a happy place—a time when everything was normal in his world. Really normal and not what his older brother, Rasheed, and mother tried to make it after his father, Zayd Danjuma, suddenly decided he no longer wanted his wife and three sons. He had abandoned them in the United Kingdom and started a new family in Nigeria. Funny thing, they didn't even know about it until his mother and Rasheed paid the man they called dad a surprise visit.

Jabir shook his head and mentally tossed the thoughts that brought him pain. He continued typing his notes. Now this was what brought him joy. He loved what he did. Making people feel better was his number one priority. Ever since he could remember, he'd wanted to be a doctor. Cardiothoracic surgery became his desired field when his childhood friend had died from heart disease. His love for it, however, was beginning to take on a new form. He wanted to do more.

In the United Sates, people had the luxury of getting the best medical attention they could afford and bank on it being right. The odds were even better with President Obama's new initiative. But in other parts of the world, that sadly wasn't the case. One of the reasons he belonged to the volunteer program Doctors in the Skies was that it gave him the opportunity to give back. He had to admit the perk of visiting different countries was worth it. The itch to give back was one of the reasons he had so willingly invested in his closest friend Bernard Nano's clinic in Lagos.

Jabir and Bernard or Benny as he was fondly called, had attended medical school together in the U.S., but a year ago, Bernard had decided it was time to move back to Nigeria. The idea he had for a clinic had been brewing for a while, and he finally decided to do it. Benny had emptied his account to get the dream off the ground, but he still needed an investor. Jabir, who had recently inherited a hefty sum from his late father, was only too willing to support his friend's dream.

The idea of moving back to Nigeria was looking more appealing to Jabir. He had always dreamed of opening a dedicated clinic for people with heart issues—a clinic he already had a name for, Helping Hearts. Early last year, his brother Rasheed moved back to Abuja from the United Kingdom. The forced move was not so appealing to Rasheed at first, but meeting and marrying his wife, Ibiso, had made being blackmailed into running their late father's company worth it.

There was a light knock on his door, and Dr. Bradman poked his head in the office. "Hey, Danjuma. Thanks again for last week."

"Not a problem, man. Hope everything is okay now." Jabir reached for the small jar of green M&Ms he kept on his desk.

"Yes, it is. You coming?"

"Where?"

"Didn't you get the memo for the department meeting?"

"It's time? Okay, I'm right behind you."

"Cool."

Several minutes later, Jabir sat at a table with seven other doctors. At the head of the table was the chief of staff, Dr. O' Reilly. He was flanked on the left by Dr. Gary, head of general surgery and Jabir's mentor. Dr. Gary and Dr. O' Reilly were men Jabir respected. They were pure geniuses, and he admired their dedication to the medical field. No one had anything negative to say about them.

Seated with them now, his mind reached back to his quiet encounter with Angela earlier. He couldn't afford for her to make any trouble for him. He was up for the prestigious Tony Forster Rookie Surgeon of the Year Recognition Award later this year. The award was given to surgeons who exhibited outstanding exemplary surgical contributions within the year. The ceremony would be the week of his thirty-third birthday, and he would be the youngest recipient. What was he thinking, jeopardizing his name and career?

He wasn't, and that was the truth. He was blinded by his broken heart and rage.

"Ladies and gentlemen, we've finalized our volunteer assistance with the Hearts Foundation of Africa." Dr. O' Reilly paused and surveyed the room for attention. There was applause as this would be Mercy's first year on the mission.

The Hearts Foundation of Africa was headquartered in New York and every year participating hospitals around the United States signed up for the pro bono mission to certain hospitals around the continent of Africa. They would provide services to those in need of cardiac procedures. Anticipation filled the room as everyone wanted to know their assignments. Participation was a good look on any doctor's résumé.

"We'll be going to five African countries in staggered two-week intervals. The beneficiaries of the program have already been lined up." Dr. O'Reilly passed out sheets of paper for each doctor.

Jabir looked down at his sheet. His assignment was Egypt. The other countries on the list were Nigeria, Namibia, Tanzania and Ghana. Jabir wondered why he wasn't given Nigeria since everyone knew it was his home country. But then again, it was just as well. He really needed a new experience. He had had enough of Nigeria for a while. He needed to stay as far away from Damisi as he could. What happened between them two months ago had left a mark he didn't expect, but also made her loathe him. When he remembered the look on her eyes the morning after their rendezvous, he cringed.

For the next half hour, updates on the department were made. Different doctors spoke on challenges or special cases they'd had since the last meeting. Final instructions on the partnership were given. The group going to Namibia would kick off the mission, followed by the Nigeria group. With that schedule, Jabir knew he wouldn't be in Egypt for another month and a half. The meeting was then adjourned.

———

IT WAS 6:00 P.M. BY THE TIME JABIR EXCHANGED HIS WHITE coat for his oyster-colored Jos. A. Bank jacket. One thing Jabir didn't skimp on was nice clothes. The adage "you are addressed the way you are dressed" had stuck with him ever since he was a little boy. It was something the mentors at the boys' camp he attended back in UK drilled into his mind. Thoughts of his childhood years made him remember he hadn't spoken to his twin, Kamal, in two days. He took out his phone and FaceTimed his brother.

"I thought you had forgotten about me," Kamal said as soon as he appeared on the screen.

"*No vex*. But not even if I tried."

There was a pause.

"I had a bad dream. Are you in trouble?" Kamal asked.

Jabir sneered, then contemplated how much he should tell his brother of what took place the last couple of days. Kamal, the younger twin, was a trained architect until he decided the hustle wasn't for him. He then used his talent to make himself millions as an international soccer star. After a few years with a premier league in the United Kingdom, the Sun Side Soccer club in Los Angeles decided to sign Kamal. A deal he took without hesitation. It was nice to have his brother in the United States with him.

Jabir decided to come clean. When he was done with the story, Kamal was silent at first.

"Say something?" Jabir urged.

"Are you crazy?"

"Look, I really don't need this. I've beat myself up enough," Jabir said.

"I can imagine, but I still deserve to knock you out. I told you that chick was way too young and ditsy for you the moment I met her."

"Ashton is handling it…" Jabir filled his brother in on the meeting with his lawyer earlier.

"You better be careful, man. You're about to be up for an award. You can't afford any work drama," Kamal said, after he was done snickering.

"I know that." Jabir waved good-bye to the nurses at the front desk and walked out to the parking garage. He took the short stroll to where he parked his car that morning. Kamal filled him in on the game he had this Sunday.

As his brother rattled on, Jabir remembered how Rasheed was against Kamal playing soccer instead of using his degree. Rasheed was ten when their father left. He had big shoes to fill and never complained. He was the best big brother there was, but that also meant he felt he had authority over the way they lived.

"So when are you going to Kashmir?" Kamal asked.

Jabir noted the concern in his brother's voice. This would be his second trip to the flood- ravished Indian area. Kamal was the only one in his family who knew the extent of Jabir's travels. It would only worry their mother, and although he would never admit it, Rasheed, too.

"With this Hearts Foundation of Africa thing, I'm not sure."

"Choose one, Egypt or Kashmir. This constant travel worries me."

"It's all part of the job and volunteer work. I like it."

"You and I know that's crap. It just keeps you busy so you don't have to deal with what's been eating you for years now… Damisi. I can't stand that chick."

"Watch it. We're *not* going there," Jabir said. "Besides, you and I know although it started off that way, a lot has changed, and I can't see myself not doing the work I do."

He got to his car and stopped in his tracks. "You've got to be freaking kidding me."

"What's wrong?" Kamal asked.

Jabir turned the phone's screen around so his brother could see. He ran his fingers across the damage as he walked around his car. "Someone just keyed my convertible and slashed all my tires."

This car had been his gift to himself after he cashed in on part of his inheritance when his father died the year before. It was barely a year old, less than thirty thousand miles. There was only one person responsible: Angela. He knew she was too uppity to do it herself, so she would have gotten someone to do it. He could prove it by asking security to pull the tape, but that would open up an investigation and draw unwanted attention. He rocked with rage as he decided to chuck it up and take care of it himself. He disconnected the call and dialed the tow company.

Minutes later, Jabir walked back into the hospital. His night just got worse. There was a backup on the interstate and the tow truck wouldn't get there for about another three hours. As he walked back the way he came barely twenty minutes ago, Jabir hoped that this wasn't a sign of worse things to come.

Chapter 4

Damisi stood and cracked her knuckles. Her dad picked up his snuff box from the middle of the table and walked into the living room. Damisi trailed behind. The space was warm and had very little color. Just like what one would expect for a man who hadn't been married in more than twenty years. The only thing that had changed from her childhood was the furniture. The oversized, dark gray sofa had been replaced with a more modern, lighter shade of brown, three-piece set with coordinating black pillows. She sat on one end of the sofa and her dad sat at the other. She clutched one of the pillows over her stomach and a tear escaped from her eye.

Damisi took a deep breath. "I'm pregnant."

Her father stared at her, then scratched his head. His expression didn't show the surprise she'd expected. He opened his snuff box and proceeded to perform the ritual she knew so well. He took a pinch of the tobacco, placed it on the back of his hand and sniffed in one nostril. Then he performed the same action for the second nostril. Next, he wiped his nose with a handkerchief.

Damisi shifted in her seat. *Did he really have to do this now?* "Aren't you going to say anything?" Her father had never been one to pressure her into or about anything. But she didn't expect him not to have any reaction.

"There's nothing I'm going to say that you haven't already told yourself." He scooted forward.

She wrinkled her nose. "Daddy, when are you going to let go of this tobacco thing?"

He chuckled. "In my old age? I stopped smoking when the doctor complained. Allow me this please." He put the snuff box away and continued, "Where is the young man? Does he know?"

"No." Damisi knew there was no way she could tell him. To what end? He had made it pretty clear that commitment wasn't his thing. It was just going to be her and the baby.

Damisi used the next couple of minutes relaying to her father the quick version of why she was in this mess. He remained silent for a couple of moments.

"This is a disaster," she declared.

"But it has happened. So we have to think of the way to get through. You need to tell this young man."

"Hmm…I don't think he'd want to know. He is not that kind…"

"Tell him, and then let *him* decide what kind of man he is. Don't make that decision for him," he said firmly.

"I don't want sympathy." She folded her arms in defiance.

"The minute you became pregnant, it stopped being about you." He paused. "You don't want that baby to suffer the same fate we did."

Damisi knew he was referring to all the time they spent apart while she lived with her mother in Lagos. She had resented her mother for keeping her away from her father. Sometimes she still did. Even at a tender age, she could tell how much her mother still cared for her father. So why didn't she stay? Her dad had spent many days, weeks and months trying to convince her that "she wouldn't understand" but never took the time to explain it so she could try.

"Your mother and I loved each other. Things happened in our marriage from which we just couldn't recover. The separation still cost our family dearly," her dad said. "You do not want that for your child."

She put her head in her hands as fresh tears rolled down her cheek. "Daddy, I could lose everything."

"That might be true, my daughter, but that baby will start to reveal itself very soon. It's better to prepare yourself. You can start by telling the man who's responsible."

"What have I done?"

Her father took her hands in his and rubbed them. "My daughter, as much as I love having you here with me, you can't run from your life."

Damisi continued to whimper. *Me? The face of* Becoming Ruth *and the spokesperson for the Right Time…how am I going to explain this?*

A couple of days before she left Lagos, Damisi had done the first photo shoot for the Right Time foundation, which catered to single women who had escaped pre-arranged marriages to men old enough to be their fathers.

"How am I going to get through this?"

"By the grace of God. Lean on Him. It'll all work out."

Her mother had raised her in the church just as her father did when she moved to Kenya. She had kept the teachings of Christ with her, but somewhere along the line in trying to do the work of God, she neglected to do the things that pleased God—spending time with Him.

Damisi hadn't been to church consistently in about five months. She wasn't even sure where her Bible was until she found herself pregnant. Right before she travelled, Eno had tried to warn her.

"You're not going to church again this week? You missed the last four Bible studies, and this is the fifth Sunday you're missing church," Eno had said. "When you leave your front door wide open, the enemy will come in and occupy your house." Her dad wiped the tears from her eyes. "You'll be okay."

She had lifted her head. "I hope so, Daddy. I hope so."

Two days later, Damisi made up her mind to stop running and boarded a flight back to Lagos. She smiled at the flight attendant as she handed her a glass of orange juice. Damisi took a sip and reached for her purse in search of the mixed nuts Madam Paulina had packed for her. Next to the snack bag was a prayer booklet. Madam Paulina must have put in there. She rubbed her palm over the booklet titled *Restoration*. She was hesitant to open it. How was she going to pray herself out of this? She placed one hand over her stomach. With the other, she slowly opened the booklet. When she read the title of the first chapter, her gut tightened— *Wrong Choice: 2 Samuel Chapter 11*.

She knew the story of King David and Bathsheba very well. She also knew God was forgiving and merciful. Still, it was no secret forgiveness didn't wipe away the consequences of sin. She had made that choice, even though she knew better. Her only prayer was that whatever lay down the road, she would be able to handle it. She leaned her head back, and the face of the man she had thought she'd never have to see again appeared in her mind. She closed her eyes and began to communicate with God in silence. She needed special help if she was going to tell Dr. Jabir Danjuma, he'd be a father in seven months.

———

Eleven hours and one stop later, Damisi gathered her bags from the baggage claim area of Murtala Mohammed

Airport in Lagos. She turned her luggage trolley toward the exit when she thought she heard her name. She turned but didn't see anyone she knew.

"Damisi!"

When she heard her name again, she paused, turned and the person came into focus. It was Ibiso, the newest Mrs. Danjuma. Behind her was her husband, Rasheed. Her breath caught. He looked like his brother, Jabir. But one could tell he was older, especially with the mustache and thin beard he kept. The older Mrs. Danjuma accompanied them. Damisi had nothing against them, but they were the last people she wanted to see. Conjuring up a smile, she waved.

"Ibiso," she said as the Danjumas approached.

It wasn't uncommon for them to come to Lagos since the logistics part of the Danjuma Group, run by their baby half-sister Halima, was located in Lagos. But it was strange that the older Mrs. Danjuma was with them.

"Good evening, Ma," Damisi greeted the older woman.

"Good evening, my dear. How are you?" Jabir's mother pulled her in for a brief hug. Something about the way she held Damisi felt weird. Even after she released her, Damisi could feel the older woman's eyes roam over her body.

"Hey, you." Rasheed acknowledged her with a nod.

"Rasheed, nice to see you again," Damisi said. When she met him many years ago, he was hard as rocks. He never smiled. The phrase *he who finds a wife, finds a good thing* must indeed be true.

"You, too." Rasheed curved his arm around his wife's waist. The love the two-month newlywed couple shared was visible even to a blind man.

Damisi had the pleasure of interviewing Ibiso last year where she shared their love story—how they met when Rasheed unexpectedly found himself in Nigeria running their late father's company, the Danjuma Group. During that time, Jabir had come to see Damisi in Lagos. She had skillfully avoided him for the last six years and would have that time, too, if not for her cousin Moji's interference. She still loved him after all these years, but her heart still hurt over what he had done to her…to them…then.

Jabir was in Lagos just one day, and they had lunch. It was then he told her how their late father's will literally forced Rasheed to take over the company after his death. The consequence of not doing so would have meant the company would go to their uncle. Then it all made sense, because she of all people knew the only person the Danjuma brothers hated more than their father was their uncle They were of the opinion Uncle Musa was the brain behind their father leaving them at such a young age. So according to Jabir, as much as Rasheed hated the idea of running his father's company, he would die before his uncle ran it.

"Thanks again for coming for the wedding. Also, the piece you did on me…loved it." Ibiso paused and looked up at her husband.

"Oh, it was my pleasure. Congrats again on the wedding. I wish you guys nothing but blessings," Damisi said. She needed to get out of there. The way Jabir's mother was looking at her was beginning to get on her nerves.

"What are you doing at international?" Damisi asked. The local airport and this one were different, so unless they were travelling out of the country or picking someone up, they shouldn't be there. Her heart skipped a beat. *Oh God, no! Jabir can't be coming to Nigeria. I can't see him now.*

"Halima is out of town, so Rasheed had to handle some business with international cargo the Danjuma Group was sending," Ibiso said. "Mama and I are just along for the ride."

Damisi let out a breath she had no idea she was holding. She had a lot to sort out before she came face to face with Jabir, so it was a good thing he was tucked away in the United States

"Why don't we get together for lunch while we're in Lagos?" the older Mrs. Danjuma asked.

"Oh yes, that would be great. Rasheed has other business, and although I want to check out a potential Bisso Bites location, which shouldn't take up a lot of time," Ibiso said, while her husband checked his phone.

Bisso Bites was the restaurant Ibiso owned. It had been her dream, and as a pre-wedding gift, her husband opened up a larger restaurant in another Abuja location for her.

"I just got back from Kenya. I'm going to need a few days."

"That's fine." Ibiso dismissed her protest. "We'll be here for a week before heading back to Abuja."

"How is your dad?" Mrs. Danjuma asked.

"He's fine, Ma."

Damisi displayed a smile that had no root in her heart. These ladies were so sweet, but lunch really wasn't a good idea. She couldn't be around the Danjumas. There was one Danjuma she had to see, and after that, she was done.

The group walked out of the airport. The car that Moji hired for Damisi was waiting. The driver got out and started loading her luggage into the car. Damisi was about to speak when two young women came up to her and asked for a picture and an autograph. It was something she would have had no problem doing ordinarily, but nothing about her life now was ordinary.

The Danjumas looked on, impressed while Damisi obliged her fans. The group of two turned to a gathering of four as the two ladies beckoned their friends to join in. After the group left, Damisi turned to the Danjumas. "I'm sorry about that."

Rasheed smiled at her. "We're used to it with Kammy."

"Okay, so it's settled. Let me make sure I still have your number." Ibiso quickly checked her phone, nodded, then confirmed with a smile.

They said their goodbyes, and Damisi got into the car. But not before she saw what the umpteenth suspicious glance from the older Mrs. Danjuma.

Chapter 5

"I think you're making a big mistake." Moji leaned on the dresser in Damisi's bedroom and took another sip of her tea.

Moji was her aunty Bola's only daughter and the sibling Damisi never had. During the separation and consequent divorce, Damisi's mother moved in with her widowed sister, Aunty Bola. The sisters had raised their daughters as twins, although Moji was a year younger. They did everything together. Moji even followed her on occasion to spend the holidays with her father in Kenya. Even after her mother died and Damisi moved to Kenya permanently, their close bond remained.

Damisi had a hard time adjusting to her mother's death, getting to know her father and relocating to Kenya, so to make things easier, most holidays, her dad would invite Moji to Kenya or send Damisi back to Nigeria. Both women were schooled in the United States. While Moji obtained her finance degree from Georgia State in Atlanta, Damisi got her degree in journalism from the University of Michigan in Ann Arbor. After Jabir's betrayal, Damisi took the job with KTN and moved back home. Moji followed.

"And you figure that how?" Damisi slid her feet in her barely six-month-old BCB Generation black heels. *Very soon I'm gonna have to give these up.*

"How can a sane woman just walk in and tell her employers something she knows will get her fired on the spot?'

"You don't know that, and neither do I. But I have to tell them before they find out." She slipped on a large orange and white sweater over white her pencil skirt. Damisi walked to the mirror and gently nudged Moji to the side. She studied herself for a moment. Her breasts were becoming heavy. She adjusted the sweater again, then opened her compact to apply her makeup.

"Hmm…*dis kian* oversize sweater in this Lagos heat." Moji began to laugh. "You won't have to tell them anything. They'll know something's up with you wearing that."

Now in her tenth week, Damisi knew her baby bump was barely visible. However, she couldn't shake off the strange feeling that came over her when Jabir's mother stared at her a couple of days ago. Thinking of the Danjumas reminded Damisi she had a lunch date with them later in the day. Her first thought after she got home that night was to come up with an excuse, but she knew that would only raise more questions.

"Don't you have a job to go to?" Damisi asked her cousin.

"No, I don't. I'm on vacation, remember?" Moji must have seen her confused expression because she continued, "Don't you dare blame my unborn niece or nephew for your memory loss."

"Oh yeah, I forgot. Okay, since you don't have anywhere to go, get out of my room and let me finish getting dressed. I should've been at the station fifteen minutes ago."

"Look, cuz, I like Jabir. What happened between you guys was too bad. I'm still rooting for both of you. Please don't go and commit career suicide just yet. Call him." Moji made her way to the door and paused. "Please don't tell me it's about Jesus…"

"It's all about Jesus, my dear. God's grace is available, but there's also the need for true repentance. I signed an integrity agreement with the station. They deserve to know."

"Whatever. Just wait a bit. Tell him and see what he says. He might marry you." Moji leaned against the doorframe.

"Why does everyone keep saying that? I don't want him having pity on poor knocked-up me." First her dad, now Moji. She only feared what Aunty Bola would say. She wouldn't have to wait long because in a few days at family dinner, she was bound to find out.

Damisi knew about Jabir's reputation even before she met him. He didn't do long-term relationships, but everything about their year-long affair was the total opposite of what she had heard. He was caring, attentive and fun to be around, but he also had an air of arrogance about him that she loved and hated.

But everything came crumbling down when she got saved. She changed, and so did he. Maybe she was a fool for trying to change him or thinking their love was strong enough to survive no sex. She had learned the hard way she couldn't trust him with her heart, so marriage was definitely not an option.

"*Na you sabi.* Just wait before you say anything." Moji lifted the mug to her lips and emptied the remaining contents down her throat. She then studied her cousin. "You look cute. When you start waddling about, all these clothes are fair game." She turned and left the room.

Damisi chuckled then picked up her keys, shoved her iPad in her purse and left. On her way out, she picked up the lunch bag Moji had prepared for her. She inspected the contents and smiled—fruits, spaghetti and mixed nuts.

"I love you, cuz," Damisi yelled, headed toward the door.

"Right back at you. Have a good day. And please…wait oh, before you say anything."

Damisi shook her head. What was she waiting for? The earlier she got this over with, the sooner she'd know where she stood. She started her car and turned out of the complex.

Her station manager, Mrs. Kofo's calendar was unpredictable, but Damisi knew she had to fit in there somehow.

She rubbed a protective hand over her stomach. She had a new life growing in her that would make its appearance very soon. She activated her Bluetooth and dialed the doctor's office. It was time to set up her prenatal visit. There was no going back now. She had to get used to her existence.

———

"Excuse me, everyone," Mr. Donte said.

It was about thirty minutes into the daily production meeting when Mr. Donte, the West African division manager, entered the room. The writers, reporters and assignment editors were all convened to hash out ideas and stories for the evening news. The chatter in the room ceased. Everyone including Mrs. Kofo turned their attention to him.

Mr. Donte looked over to Damisi and said, "Ms. Odinga, glad to have you back."

Damisi nodded and acknowledged his greeting with a smile. "Glad to be back, sir."

"I see everyone is hard at work, so I won't be too long. I just got a memo from our affiliates in New York that the Heart Foundation of Africa will be sending doctors to different countries in Africa." He paused and smiled.

Applause erupted, and there were murmurs of "praise God" heard across the room. This was primarily because this had been a hot topic in the Christian media circles for a while. The Hearts Foundation of Africa was met with a stumbling block this year because of terrorist activity in some African countries. The foundation normally would do their outreach mission at the beginning of the year. It was now the end of April.

Damisi was just glad they had finally reached an agreement. People who genuinely needed help shouldn't have to suffer because of the senseless acts of others.

"That is fantastic news," Mrs. Kofo said.

"Yes, it is," Mr. Donte replied. "I don't mean to hijack your meeting, but we need to work on getting a story together for the evening news. Ms. Fey, I want you to anchor it."

"Yes, sir," Mrs. Kofo and Ms. Fey, who was normally the morning news anchor, said in unison. Damisi understood why Mr. Donte wanted her. Enitan Fey was a recent returnee from England, and her following was steadily growing.

Mr. Donte turned to leave, then paused. "Oh, by the way, I don't have all the details yet, but Ms. Odinga, they're holding a gala to welcome the doctors to Nigeria next month, and you've been selected to host it." He left without waiting for a response.

Damisi pressed the tip of her pencil so hard on her writing pad that it snapped. All eyes turned toward her direction. She gave a faint smile and shrugged. Being the well-known face of the station, part of her job description included hosting a variety of high-profiled Christian events. It was sometimes tiresome, but the benefits were worth it. She got to dress up and watch people having a nice time while fellowshipping with one another. At the moment, however, she wanted some invincible force to transport her to a faraway island. How could she get up and speak on Jesus as she normally did at these events when she felt as filthy as a hog.

"Paul, I want you to take this on. Get on the phone and let's see who we can get Enitan to interview for the 6:00 P.M. news special. George, I need a write-up on my desk in two hours. Both of you can be excused from this meeting." Mrs.

Kofo punched in information on her iPad as she dished out orders.

After the gentlemen had left the room, the rest of the team continued with the agenda for the day. Damisi was half listening as her mind wandered from the life growing inside her to the scandal that awaited her in the future. The anxiety caused beads of sweat to form on her face and her bladder needed emptying. Excusing herself, she left the room. She wished so bad she could go home, but she still had to endure another meeting and a late lunch with the Danjuma women.

———

By the time Damisi walked into the restaurant, Ibiso and Jabir's mother were already seated. Ibiso waved to get her attention, and Damisi made her way to the table in the corner. She was hungry and tired and almost half an hour late. The only thing that propelled her forward was the thought she didn't have to go back to work until tomorrow.

After the production meeting, she spent the rest of the morning working with the crew for the Hearts Foundation of Africa taping. Enitan had a last-minute emergency, so instead of pulling in another anchor, Mrs. Kofo insisted Damisi do the special interview. Paul was able to secure a Skype session with one of the directors of the Foundation. Despite the late request, he was gracious about answering a few questions. By the time the interview was over, George was done with the script and the segment was taped.

Damisi set her bag and attaché down on the chair next to the one Ibiso pointed to. "Good afternoon, Ma. I'm so sorry you had to wait."

"Good afternoon, that's okay, my dear. How was work?" Jabir's mother said with a smile. The resemblance between her and her middle son was uncanny.

"Fine, Ma," Damisi said.

Ibiso stood and stepped toward Damisi, drawing her into an embrace. "Hey, lady. How are you?"

"I'm good, *jare*," Ibiso said.

The ladies sat down, and the waiter appeared. Damisi was thankful because the aroma from the food was doing a number on her senses.

"Good afternoon. Are you ready to order?" the waiter asked.

"Erm…" Damisi scanned the menu. She had been to Ajole's Assorted so many times and always ordered the curry chicken and white rice. However, today she wanted something different.

Ibiso's phone buzzed. She glanced at the phone and smiled. "It's my honey."

"Just get us something to drink first," Jabir's mother said.

Ibiso looked up from the text she was typing. "I'll have a Fanta orange."

"Please get me water with lemon," Jabir's mother said.

"Let me have a Sprite. Oh, and can you bring me ice in separate glass?" Damisi asked.

The waiter nodded and left. Moments later, he returned with their drinks, and the women placed their orders. They talked about everything from the weather to their jobs to Jesus. When the waiter arrived with their food, Jabir's mother said grace, and the women began to eat.

After a couple of spoonfuls, Damisi signaled the waiter. "Please, can I have some red chili pepper?"

The waiter nodded and went to do her bidding.

"Did you find the location you wanted?" Damisi asked Ibiso.

"No, I didn't see anything," Ibiso replied. "Maybe I wasn't looking hard enough. I just wanted to be with my bobo, *jare*." She playfully nudged her mother-in-law. "And I dragged Mama along."

The waiter came back with the chili pepper, and Damisi

took a spoonful and sprinkled it over her jollof rice. Any other time, she'd think something was wrong with her. She'd never really liked pepper, but the doctor had told her it was a common craving among pregnant women. Damisi looked up from her food and caught Jabir's mother and Ibiso staring at her.

Ibiso giggled. "Do you think you have enough pepper there?"

Damisi put a spoonful of her rice into her mouth and relished the taste. She nodded. "Yep. It's all good."

Ibiso dabbed the corners of her mouth with a napkin. "You're good, oh. I love heat, but I can't eat that hot for anything. At the restaurant, Amina constantly has to remind me I'm not cooking for myself."

Damisi chewed her food slowly then lifted her glass to drink. She had met Amina, Ibiso's chief chef while she was in Abuja last year. "It's new for me as well, but I like it."

Jabir's mom who had remained relatively silent all this while finally spoke. "That's funny because that exactly how I was when I was pregnant with the twins."

Damisi spit out the Sprite that was in her mouth and began to cough. Both Ibiso and Jabir's mom stood and began patting her back. She drank some Sprite and finally the cough subsided.

"Are you okay?" Jabir's mother asked, peering at Damisi.

She nodded.

Jabir's mother who was studying her keenly asked. "Are you sure you're okay? We could go if you need to lie down and rest."

Something about the way the woman said the word *rest* made Damisi crack her knuckles. The older lady knew something. Of that, she was convinced. When Damisi was in her teen years and would visit Nigeria, there would be at least one girl in the neighborhood with an unwanted pregnancy. Aunty Bola used those opportunities to have the pregnancy prevention conversation with her and Moji. On those days, she and Moji would get a twenty-minute lecture on their worth as young women. Aunty Bola's method of prevention was abstinence. Damisi remembered how those speeches always ended: Aunty Bola would sniff like a dog and say, "Don't think you can deceive me. I can sniff out any sign of pregnancy."

Damisi suddenly found herself gasping for air. She needed to get out of there. She slowly pushed back from the table. "On second thought, I am a little tired—still jet lagged from my trip."

Ibiso looked at her with concern, her eyes searching for answers Damisi was not ready to provide. Next to her, Mrs. Danjuma stood and just nodded.

"Okay. You go rest. We leave for Abuja in the morning." Ibiso picked up her purse. "I have your number, so I'll call and check on you later."

"Make sure you rest, my daughter, and I'll tell Jabir we had lunch."

Damisi grunted. She was sure that was another way of saying, "I'll tell my son you might be pregnant."

"I'm so sorry we had to cut this short. We'll definitely do it again." Damisi gathered her purse.

Ibiso summoned the waiter and paid the bill. All three women left the restaurant, hugged one another, and got into their prospective cars. Damisi waved as the car carrying the Danjuma women pulled out of the parking lot and merged into traffic.

She got in her car and placed her head on the steering wheel. She wasn't ready to deal with Jabir at the moment. The plan to tell her employers was delayed because of the upcoming gala. She had hoped to get it done before having to confront Jabir. She couldn't deal with him and the fallout from her job at the same time. It would be too much stress for her.

"Be a lamp unto my feet, oh Lord. Amen," Damisi prayed.

She shuddered when she remembered the morning after their night together. What devil made her invite Jabir into her room was still a mystery to her. She had been a ball of emotion at Ibiso and Rasheed's wedding ceremony. It was the most beautiful and intimate one she had ever attended. No one else in the room seemed to matter to the couple. They only had eyes for each other. Once upon a time, that was how she and Jabir had been. For a year, it was only about them. After his betrayal, she had spent a lot of energy hating him, but her heart and love were only for him. She did date, but no one could compare, and that made her dislike Jabir more.

For just that night in Abuja, it was as though they were back in Ann Arbor, when their relationship was still new. She was a ball of emotion, and as usual he was there. The next morning, however, she was emotional, ridden with guilt and angry. She said some things she shouldn't, but still, she didn't expect the loathing in his eyes.

"You can't just cast me aside anytime you grow a conscience. I'm done. Goodbye and trust me, we'll never cross paths again," Jabir had said, then he walked out of the room.

Damisi rubbed her stomach. Fate had indeed played a good one on them because they were about to be bound together for the next eighteen years.

Chapter 6

The gym in his condo complex was always overcrowded on Saturdays. Jabir planned to beat the rush by being there by 6:00 A.M. As he strolled into the facility, the huge clock on the wall told him he had missed his goal by thirty minutes. He located the treadmill closest to the window to give him a view of the city he loved. He put in his ear buds and set the speed and gradually got into a rhythm.

The threat that Angela posed seemed to increase as the week went by. He got a call from Ashton a few days after the car incident, and it wasn't good. The sheriff couldn't find Angela to serve her with the annulment papers. Jabir remembered the gut-wrenching feeling he got when he was told by her boss she was out on leave. So that had been her plan, to disappear so as to drag out the process. With her previously living with her sister and just recently moving out, Ashton said they had no choice but to petition the court for permission to publish a motion to serve in the local newspaper.

Jabir wanted to kick himself. That process would take several weeks. He needed to get this done with before he travelled. Ashton had assured him not to put his life on hold. The fact she wasn't around to contest was a good thing. Jabir swore this was the last time he would be so irrational because of Damisi. Not even she was worth his career and name. Damisi had made her stand clear—twice—and he would be a fool to allow thoughts of her to ruin his reputation or his life. She had had her fun, and just like before, she felt she could change the rules when it suited her. The Damisi fantasy had turned into a harsh reality of rejection. That was now over. She wanted to be left alone. He'd leave her alone. He increased the speed on the treadmill and commanded his mind to focus on the present.

The ringtone he assigned to calls from Nigeria began to play. He lowered the speed on the treadmill and looked at the caller ID of his phone. It was Rasheed. Jabir hadn't talked to him in about a week, and Kamal had given him a heads-up that he was irritated. Jabir smiled and answered the phone.

"Hey, bro," Jabir said.

"*How far now?*"

"Work, work, work. You know I gotta earn that paper." Jabir wiped off his forehead with a towel.

"You and I know you don't have to work for your paper, thanks to your late father. But then we all work, so you could pick up the phone once in a while, especially when you get back from those mission trips," Rasheed said.

Jabir grunted. He only thought of his inheritance as backup. "My bad. I'll do better."

He then heard Rasheed smacking his lips. Jabir couldn't believe he had the nerve to be making noise in his ear this early morning.

"I hope you're not calling to brag about what type of meal your wife prepared today," Jabir said.

"Do I ever do that?" Rasheed smacked louder, then laughed.

"Err...yes. Ever since you got married. All of a sudden, you think you're all that."

"I am all that. Have you seen my wife? No scratch that, I have the joy of the Lord."

Jabir laughed hard. "Here we go again with the Lord. I can't believe how much you've changed."

His brother had indeed changed. Rasheed's guarded, almost angry-all-the-time personality had given way to a more accommodating and tolerant one. Jabir hadn't still come to terms with how happy he always seemed. As a child, he always wondered why Rasheed and his mother changed after that trip to Nigeria. That journey changed things for them—they lost any hope of their father coming back—and Rasheed took it the hardest.

"So how is my sister-in-law?" Jabir asked.

"She's good. Have you heard from your knucklehead twin? I've tried to reach him twice today."

"That's your brother, but no. He hasn't returned my calls either. I don't know what's up with him. Anything?"

"Not really, but what do you mean? You don't know what's up with him? Aren't you guys supposed to be *sensing* each other?"

Jabir laughed. "I know a graduate like you didn't just say that. That's not how it works."

"If you don't hear from him in a couple of days, please make a trip to LA," Rasheed said. Jabir could hear the concern in his voice.

Kamal's sudden silence worried him, too. Even with their busy schedules, the brothers never went without talking to each other every couple of days. Jabir made a mental note to call him again once he got off the phone with Rasheed. If there was no reply, he wasn't going to wait until the following week.

"Did you hear me?"

"Huh? What did you say?" Jabir asked.

"I said now that your cat-and-mouse game with Damisi is finally over, what are you going to do?"

Jabir stopped the machine and wiped his face with a towel and made his way to the door.

"What are you talking about?" Jabir asked. He leaned against the wall and waited for the elevator.

"What I don't understand is why she wasn't wearing a ring. After all the grief she's given you—"

The elevator opened and Jabir stepped in and pressed the button for the tenth floor.

"What in the world are you talking about?" Jabir couldn't explain it, but there was a sudden constriction in his heart at the words *ring, finger* and *Damisi* in the same sentence. His irritation grew at his reaction. A few short minutes ago he had vowed never to let her ruin his life, so why did he care? He had opened his arms to her twice, and she had voluntarily walked out each time.

"You mean you don't know?" Rasheed asked.

"Look, bro, say what you gotta say or get off the phone. I'm sure Ibiso needs help with something." Back in his condo, Jabir kicked off his sneakers and went into the bathroom to start the shower.

Jabir listened attentively as Rasheed narrated the events of the previous week—from the airport meeting to the lunch Damisi, Ibiso and his mom had together. Good for them. He meant what he said when he told her good-bye two-and-a-half months ago, so any alliances his family was building were solely for their benefit.

"So what's this about a ring?" Jabir found himself asking.

"On our way back to Abuja, Mama swore that Damisi was pregnant."

Jabir felt his brain sway from left to right. *Damisi pregnant?* He turned off the water and leaned against the sink.

"You know what a pregnant lady looks like...Was she pregnant?" Jabir knew his voice sounded more forceful than it should, but he had to know.

"Calm down, bro. It wasn't visible if that's what you're

asking. Mama just kept saying how silly you were to let a good woman slip away," Rasheed said. "What happened anyway? I thought when you guys came to the wedding together you had finally reached an agreement."

Jabir's jaw tightened with anger as he recalled their first meeting years ago. It was during the first year of his residency program when Damisi was in her junior year of college. The attraction was instant. He wanted her and she wanted him, too. Their romance was swift and passionate. They spent every minute he could spare together. Everything was great until she was invited to church by some of her friends.

She became saved and strange. She cancelled dates, was always in church and worst of all, she cut him off. Cold turkey, just like that—she made a vow of celibacy. Then she became one of those types. The type who admitted they liked a guy, but demanded he meets certain conditions. In his case, he had to be born again. That to him was blackmail.

Things grew tense between them. Jabir wanted the old Damisi back, and she wanted to change him into something else. They spent the little time they had together arguing. The last fight they had was major, but he hadn't expected her to break things off. He'd never forget her speech that day in front of the restaurant where they'd had an early dinner. He tried convincing her that if she left him, he would never get to know God.

"Well, that's a shame," she had said. "Having faith in God is a personal thing and requires a commitment—something you're incapable off."

He was too stunned to react. His pride was wounded because he had fallen in love with her. An emotion he had never let himself feel before. What was she talking about? But then he decided that he didn't need that kind of stress in his life. He had his residency to complete. He needed to stay focused, so he did what any sane man would do—let her go.

She moved and they lost contact, until he went to Nigeria last year.

"Are you there?"

Rasheed's question transported Jabir back to the present.

"Damisi is not a topic I want to discuss. Whatever she's doing is no longer a concern of mine." Jabir propelled himself away from the sink and walked to the massive shower and turned the water back on. "Look, bro I have to go. My love to Ibiso."

He disconnected the call before his brother had time to ask anything else. He peeled off his clothes and stepped under the warm jet stream. The soothing pellets of water had a relaxing effect on his tense muscles. The new Rasheed had the tendency to want to talk more and end with one kind of prayer or the other. Jabir was was no longer in the mood to talk. He just wanted to be left alone.

———

"WHO AMONGST YOU THINKS THIS MAN AND WOMAN shouldn't be married? Speak now or forever hold your peace."

He struggled to get up. He couldn't. Some sort of weight had him pinned down. Then he decided standing was not the only way to stop this travesty. He opened his mouth to speak. His voice had been muted. Sweat filled his brow as the minister proceeded to pronounce the couple as man and wife.

"Nooooo!" Jabir woke from his nightmare.

He sat up in the bed and looked around his room. Despite the coolness of the room, beads of sweat formed on his forehead. He sighed. Since Rasheed had told him about Damisi's supposed pregnancy, every time he closed his eyes, the dream came to him. There was no way she wouldn't have told him by now. If his calculations were right, she would be almost three months along. It had to be his, because no matter how angry she made him, he knew she couldn't have slept with somebody else in that time. She had too much character for that. His blood boiled just thinking about the possibility of her sleeping with someone else.

Jabir detangled his legs from the bedding. He knew it was useless trying to go back to sleep. He put on his robe and walked into the living room. He had just finished the book he was reading and wasn't in the mood to start a new one. He picked up the remote and sat by the window. The clock on the wall told him it was 2:00 A.M. He began surfing channels. He stopped on ESPN when he caught a glimpse of Kamal.

"Breaking news: Just moments ago, the star midfielder for the Sun Side soccer club in Los Angeles was involved in a bar brawl that injured five people. One of the people is in the hospital, we're told in critical condition. More details will be given as this story develops."

Jabir's mouth hung open as the anchor went to commercial break, promising to be back with a panel to discuss athlete discipline. He couldn't get over the shock of what he'd just heard. Since when did Kamal go to bars and become involved in a brawl?

He picked up his phone to dial Kamal but got no response. He stood and began pacing the length of his living room. Something was not making sense in this scenario. Throughout the night, Jabir made a couple more calls to Kamal's friends he knew and to Kamal's girlfriend Brittani, but nobody was answering. And no one had the courtesy to call him back.

Jabir wasn't supposed to travel again until Egypt, but nothing came before his family. He walked to his room and dialed Dr. Bradman who was on call. He owed him a favor. Jabir was headed to LA.

Chapter 7

Sunday morning, Damisi and Moji slid into the vacant pew near the front of the church. Damisi had been a member of He Is Able Ministries since she moved to Lagos years ago. Her eyes welled up as the praise team sang its rendition of Ghanaian gospel artist, Pastor Sonnie Badu's "Let It Rain." Damisi fell to her knees as tears glided down her cheeks. The lyrics of the song sank in, "If this is Your presence, let it rain all over me" and the tears flowed more. She desperately needed God's presence to rain all over her. Confusion, fear and guilt weren't letting her think straight. Some days, she walked in the grace and mercy she knew He had given her. On other days, she couldn't help but feel like a hypocrite and unworthy to be in the presence of God.

She wiped her eyes with the back of her hand. She knew emotions didn't move God. What He wanted was true repentance from the heart. She placed her hand on her stomach. She now had to stand in her truth and depend on her faith in Jesus to handle what lay ahead.

"Are you okay?" Moji whispered.

Damisi looked up at Moji and nodded. Her cousin's

confused frown told her her face must be a mess. She quickly smiled and took out a Kleenex and wiped her face.

The choir faded out the music as the pastor stepped onto the podium. He closed his eyes and lifted his hands. Pastor Dede always delivered his sermons, even the most serious ones, with a touch of theatrics. The congregation had come to expect conviction in the Word as well as entertainment. "Yes, Lord, rain down Your glory. We need your presence in our lives."

His eyes were still closed when he called on someone to read from Romans 8:38–39. Almost immediately, several voices from the congregation started to read. Moji turned to her and shook her head. Damisi smiled. It always amused them how the single ladies jumped at the widowed pastor's requests. He was light skinned with hair that was cut close to his head. He wore stubble, which gave him a rugged look, an image he contradicted with form-fitting tailor-made suits. Granted, he was easy on the eyes, but in church though?

The loudest voice won out and began to read. *"For I am persuaded, that neither death, nor life, nor angels, nor principalities, nor powers, nor things present, nor things to come. Nor height, nor depth, nor any other creature, shall be able to separate us from the love of God, which is in Christ Jesus our Lord."*

"Amen, somebody!" the pastor shouted.

"Amen," the congregation replied.

"For those of you who have young kids—I'm not talking about the older ones because they can be a case sometimes— those young kids, their love for you is pure, and they crave to always be in your good graces and stay there.

There was laughter and murmuring in the congregation.

"Same with God. Once you have accepted Jesus, your love for Him should keep you on the right path." The pastor folded up his sleeves and strutted down the stairs of the stage.

He began asking random members whether they understood what he was saying. When he got the answers he wanted, he walked to the middle of the aisle, dabbed his forehead with his face towel and continued. "But just like teenagers, you and I know we don't always do what we're supposed to do. *Abi*, I lie?"

"No, Pastor, *na* true you talk," someone shouted from behind.

"Although Paul had it correct that nothing can separate us from the love of Christ—" He let out a long sigh, scratched his head and looked around, then he pointed to the congregation— "your actions can." He then ran back up to the podium and took a drink of water.

"You see, my God changes not. He remains the same. He loves us. If we truly repent of our sins, forgiveness is ours, but if we can't accept his grace and mercy, that's where we start having problems because you begin to separate yourself from Him. Your sin will eventually win the day, and you will find yourself moving farther away from God."

"Preach, Pastor" and "Amen" were some of the shouts that came during his silence.

The pastor further illustrated with Adam in the Garden of Eden. He narrated the story they all knew, but this time from a different angle. He explained how after Adam and Eve ate of the forbidden fruit, he went into hiding. God was still there and available. But the shame from his sin made him hide and separate himself from God.

By the end of the service, Damisi felt exhausted. The word seemed to be tailored specifically to her. It encouraged and gave her the confirmation she needed, that she was headed in the right direction by coming clean. However, be that as it may, she was also weighed down by regret that her professed love for Christ wasn't enough to constrain her that night.

———

"Tell me you're joking?" Aunty Bola shouted.

Damisi knew this conversation wouldn't be pleasant but hadn't expected this level of outrage. She and Moji had come over right after church to dinner. While they lived on the island, her aunty lived on the mainland area of Lagos.

Aunty Bola's Ikeja home was located in an exclusive part of the area. It was where the cousins had grown up. Since her aunty lived alone, except for a housekeeper, they always made it a tradition on Sunday to go over for dinner right after church. It was during the preparation of the meal that the older woman got to catch up on the lives of the younger ladies--at least the part they wanted to share. On the menu for today were peppered snails, plantains, fried rice and salad.

"Damisi Titilola Odinga, tell me you're joking."

Damisi walked over to the sink of the modern kitchen and turned on the faucet. The kitchen had been remodeled some years ago. Its dark antique features had been replaced with a lighter contemporary style. She ran the water over the raw snails and began scrubbing them with alum, a stone-like scrub that got rid of the sliminess and dirt.

She looked over to her cousin for help. Moji shrugged and continued to cut up the carrots, peas and liver that were going into the rice. When Aunty Bola went on like this, they always thought it best to remain silent. Her mood passed faster.

"Aunty, please—" She turned around with the alum in her hand.

Her aunty raised her hand and shook it in the air. "Don't 'please' me! Ha! My sister would be turning in her grave now." Aunty Bola stood and paced the length of the kitchen. She put the side of her index finger between her teeth. Damisi's late mother used to make that gesture as well when she was distressed. "Everything you've worked for, down the drain."

"Mummy, she's pregnant, not dying," Moji said.

Damisi gave her a look of gratitude.

Her mother remained silent.

Moji continued, "Think about it this way, that grandchild you've been pestering us for, you'll get sooner rather than later. There's always a bright side."

"Aunty, it's done. I can't change it, but you've been my mother since mine died. I need you, Aunty, because I don't have a clue about what to do," Damisi pleaded.

"That's what's wrong with you young people. Always leaping to the next stage of life without mastering the stage you're in. You of all people should know that, Damisi. You teach it." Aunty Bola shook her head and left the kitchen.

Grateful for the breather, the ladies continued to prepare the meal in silence. Damisi sincerely hoped that by the time they sat down to eat, Aunty Bola would have cooled down.

An hour later, they were seated at the formal dining table. Extending her arms, Aunty Bola joined hands with Damisi to her left and Moji to her right. They said grace and began to eat. The tension was thick until Moji broke it by talking about the latest political scandal to rock the nation. A well-known politician had collapsed from exhaustion in a gym. Ordinarily there wouldn't have been anything to it, but he was there with his mistress. When she was interviewed by the police, she said that they were training for a marathon. He was going to express his love by running the 5K with her. His wife, on the other hand, on hearing the news ran to the hospital and her rant was caught on tape. She claimed her enemies were after her seventy-year-old potbellied husband.

"If not, why would he think he can run? He barely walks. Chai! My enemies o…" Moji, Damisi and Aunty Bola chanted the woman's response that went viral around Lagos.

The laughter that filled the room was welcoming. After lunch, the young ladies joined Aunty Bola in the living room.

Damisi knelt down in front of her Aunty. *"An ti mi,"* Damisi said, using the Yoruba version of the term "my aunty." She always considered herself blessed to be fluent in Yoruba.

her mother's native language and Swahili, her dad's native language.

Her aunty, who never could stay mad at her for long, placed her hand on Damisi's back.

"*E ma bi nu.* I'm sorry." Damisi placed her head in her auntie's lap. Aunty Bola had always been good to her and to know she had let her down was heartbreaking.

"Titi, you know I always want what is best for you. And I can never turn my back on you. I'm upset at what this might cost you."

Damisi smiled that her aunt used her middle name. That meant she had forgiven her. Her anger had subsided, and they were on to the advice and problem-solving mode.

"Aunty, I know. I have some savings. My plan is to go back to Kenya and come back after the baby is born. As unplanned as it is, even at three months, I can't wait to see him or her."

Her aunty helped her up and patted the cushion next to her to sit down. Moji remained glued to the television, only turning around once in a while. Aunty Bola placed her hand on Damisi's stomach. She smiled and looked up.

"*Olorun oshe o.* Thank you, God. This may not have been how we wanted it, but this child is a gift from God. He or she will bring you blessings, joy, and happiness. You will never have cause to cry over it, in Jesus name."

"*Amin* o" Moji and Damisi said in unison.

"Now where is its useless father?" Aunty Bola asked.

Damisi laughed. "He's not useless, aunty."

"He is useless and irresponsible," her aunty reiterated.

"*Ah ah,* Mummy, didn't you just finish praying? Why are you using the same mouth to curse?" Moji asked.

"I will curse because I don't know how a man can leave a woman, knowing her condition." Aunty Bola headed to the toilet down the hall.

When Aunty Bola was out of earshot, Moji whispered. "You better tell her that you haven't told the poor man before she uses insult to scatter him." She changed the channel and continued, "He's that baby's father and you don't want my mum's curses to follow him, oh."

They heard flushing and Aunty Bola reentered the living room and resumed her position.

"*Ehen*, so where is the——"

"Aunty, he is not any of those things you called him. I haven't told him yet."

"*E gbami.* What are you waiting for? Remember how your mother left your father? I pleaded with my sister that a child needs its father, but she never listened until they got divorced. Do you want the same for your child?" She placed her hand on her hip and continued. "The way you modern women operate is amazing. I know you're old enough to handle yourself and whatever went on with this young man, but listen to me – do not let next weekend and you haven't told him," Aunty Bola said with a tone of finality.

Damisi nodded. Sitting back on the sofa, she covered herself with a blanket. She surprised herself just now by defending Jabir. Where did that come from? In fairness, Jabir hadn't done anything wrong. He hadn't abandoned her, nor lured her into the hotel. She was just as much to blame as he. In defending his honor right now, she had allowed herself to see that. He wasn't useless or irresponsible. In fact, he was kind, attentive, funny and nurturing. If only he wasn't so afraid of one thing—commitment. To Jesus or to her.

Chapter 8

Two days later, Jabir walked through LAX and caught a taxi straight to Kamal's apartment. Looking out of the cab window, Jabir now understood why Kamal often compared the May weather in LA to London in December. It was gloomy with overcast skies. However, the temperature couldn't be compared, as Londoners would kill for the 75-degree temperature.

He had finally gotten in touch with Kamal who told him he only had a sprained wrist. But Jabir felt that he was leaving something out. He couldn't understand the sudden change in his brother, so he decided to go to LA to find out what was going on.

With a confused look on his face, the doorman let Jabir up to Kamal's fifth floor condo. Jabir gave a faint smile. He got that reaction a lot, especially with his brother being famous. As he rode the elevator up, he popped a handful of green M&Ms into his mouth. The elevator opened and he walked to Kamal's door. The noise was so loud that it was fruitless knocking. Luckily, the door wasn't locked. He walked in and headed to the game room where the noise was coming from.

There were six men in the room, including Kamal. Their laughter ceased the minute he entered.

"Jabir, what are you doing here?" Kamal asked.

Ignoring his brother's question, Jabir exchanged handshakes with the men, some of which he knew as Kamal's teammates.

"I told you I was coming. You thought I was playing?" He paused and looked around at the empty beer bottles littered around the room. "It's either me or the old woman."

On that note, the men made excuses and left the room.

"I told you all you needed to know," Kamal snapped.

"I don't think so. What's going on? This isn't you." Jabir pointed to the empty beer bottles and pizza boxes.

Kamal shrugged, picked up his brother's hand luggage and headed to the guest room.

"It's nothing. I had a small scare and the whole day turned out bad, so I ended up in the bar. I told you over the phone."

"About the bad day, yes, but what scare are you talking about?" Jabir followed his brother.

Kamal kept the luggage in the corner of the guest room and leaned against the dresser. In his eyes, Jabir saw the fear his brother was trying to hide.

"I went for a checkup that day and the doctor insisted I do an EKG because of some funny heart sounds he heard when he was examining me. After reviewing the EKG, he called for more tests." Kamal walked over to the blinds and opened them. Rays of sunlight that had broken through the clouds illuminated the room. Jabir knew his brother was stalling so he decided to help him along. "And…"

"And nothing. I didn't go. I know how these things turn out. I've seen it happen to enough players to know that…" Kamal walked out of the room.

Panic seized him. His mind flashed back to his childhood friend. "Are crazy? You need to get it checked out. Don't you remember Jim?" Jabir followed his brother. "Or maybe you don't want to play ball anymore."

"Don't even joke about that. I passed out on the field one day and the next thing you know, the team coach is making a big deal out of it. I've passed all my physicals. It's nothing."

"Again, don't you want to be sure? For your doctor to order more tests, they must be worried."

"I hope you're not like them." Kamal brushed past his brother on his way to the kitchen.

"Like who?"

"Your nosy doctor folk. I know all of you are the same, but please bros, you guys should learn to leave the patient alone when they say no." Kamal picked up a menu and brought out his cell phone. "You want Chinese?"

Jabir stared at his brother, who already had the Chinese restaurant on the line. He decided that now wasn't the time to deal with his pig-headed twin. He was tired and hungry. He'd had very little sleep and had been working non-stop to make sure he saw all his scheduled patients before leaving Detroit. Fatigue was beginning to set in. He needed food, a bath, and sleep. He headed toward the guest room. He'd let it go for now, but if Kamal didn't listen, he would bring out his secret weapon—their mother, Obiageli Danjuma. The last thing Kamal would want was their mother crowding his bachelor pad. One word in her ear and she'd be in the United Sates in a flash.

———

Jabir twirled his pancake around with his fork. Today was his last day in Los Angeles after a two-day stay. They had decided to get breakfast at IHOP before they took the drive to the airport. Just as he predicted, Kamal didn't want their mother anywhere near his condo in Los Angeles. He didn't need the fussing or guilt trips. He agreed to go back to the hospital and get checked out.

Jabir wanted him to do it while he was in LA, but he couldn't wait until next week. He had his own patients to see. So, he made Kamal swear to keep his word. Rasheed had called the morning before, and Jabir's lips turned up in a smile as he remembered Kamal's wild hand gestures pleading with Jabir not to tell him. Those two behaved like a real father and son pair.

"Okay, spill. What's going on?" Kamal said.

Jabir looked up. His brother's plate was empty. "What time is it? I don't want to miss my flight."

"Nice try. We have plenty of time. Once you actually eat, we can get going." Kamal pushed his plate away. Kamal opened his mouth to say something else but was interrupted by the waiter who began packing up his empty plates.

"So, spill, we're twins. We don't keep secrets."

"Said the twin who didn't tell the other about his health issue," Jabir countered.

"Technically, that wasn't really a secret. Now spill."

Jabir needed to talk to someone. The Damisi situation had been bothering him for a while now. "Remember I brought Damisi to Rasheed's wedding?"

"I don't know why after what she did to you. I mean who does that? Ends a relationship and moves halfway around the world without an explanation." Kamal seethed.

Jabir knew his brother's anger came from a good place. Kamal was the only one that knew what it took for Jabir to get himself together and refocus on his residency after Damisi left.

"Focus, bro," Jabir said.

"Okay. I remember how you dangled the chick on your arm all evening. I had no idea y'all were that tight again." Kamal stretched his hand over and took a piece of Jabir's sausage.

"Well, I kinda blackmailed her. She wanted an interview

with Ibiso, but our new sister-in-law didn't have time for that. She was planning a wedding and running her restaurant so kept blowing Damisi off. Damisi needed the ratings to close out the season on her show and Ibiso marrying a Danjuma was it."

"So you conned the poor woman to go with you. But she got her interview, so what's the problem?"

Jabir sipped on his lukewarm coffee and narrated the story of Damisi, Rasheed, Ibiso and their mother at the airport, and filled him in on Rasheed's call a week ago. The nonchalant look on Kamal's face turned to empathy. He was about to speak when two families brought their sons over and asked for autographs and pictures.

It amazed Jabir how they were able to distinguish between two of them. But then he noticed his attire. His dark black jeans and green, button-down dress shirt was clearly a huge contrast to Kamal's sky blue, Nike track suit and the latest Jordan sneakers. Jabir noticed how Kamal's face lit up when his fans were around. He was glad that he and his brother had a chance to do what they loved. Jabir had been worried that Rasheed nearly became the exception to the doing what he loved rule. But he knew now that nothing gave his brother a better thrill than running Danjuma Group.

Jabir looked on as another family joined. Kamal was happy to oblige them. After they left, he turned to him, lifting his teacup to his lips.

"My bad, so where were we? Oh…okay at least now you know that she's out of the picture. The game of "I hate you, I love you" you guys are playing is getting old," Kamal said.

"Look for someone else. Oh, I forgot you're already married." Kamal laughed.

Jabir drummed his fingers on the table. "That's not funny. And that will be history in three months tops."

"Okay, my bad."

Jabir rubbed his eyes.

Kamal frowned. "What?"

"That night, I have no idea what happened. Maybe it was the wedding atmosphere. I dropped Damisi off at her hotel, one thing led to another, and you know…"

Wide eyed, Kamal shook his head. "No, I don't know."

"You want me to draw a picture for you?"

Kamal remained silent; his brows raised.

Jabir let out a labored breath. "We had sex."

———

DURING THE THIRTY-MINUTE DRIVE TO THE AIRPORT, JABIR felt like a disgraced celebrity being hounded by the press. The questions didn't stop until Kamal had to take a phone call. Jabir used that time to collect his thoughts. They were beginning to settle too heavily on how good Damisi felt that night. Just like old times.

"So what are you going to do?"

"Huh?"

"I'm trying to solve your problem and you're daydreaming."

"Nothing. That woman woke me up at 3:00 A.M., yelling and screaming with regret. She was hysterical, and I was mad," Jabir said.

"What did you expect? Think about it. She's one of those practicing Christians who fell under your charm. Her whole career is centered around helping single women wait on their God-fearing husband and all that stuff. Then you, who is neither God-fearing nor husband material come and shake up her world." Kamal chuckled.

Jabir remained quiet. He never thought about it like that. But they could've talked about it. She didn't give him a chance, just like she hadn't given him one six years before.

"*Kai!* For a medical doctor, you're kinda dense." Kamal honked at the car in front of them to move.

"But if she didn't call me, then maybe it's not mine or maybe she isn't pregnant."

Kamal took his eye off the road for a second and looked at him. "After all we went through growing up, you owe it to yourself to see if you've conceived a child. You'd want to be there for him or her." His tone was somber.

Jabir remained silent for a few moments. Kamal was right. "Why do you always have so much sense in solving other people's problems, but can't seem to do right in your own?"

Kamal shrugged as usual.

"Let me find out you didn't go to the hospital, Mama will be on the next flight to LA." Jabir put on his sunglasses and reclined the chair. He had some thinking to do. If there was the slightest possibility that they had conceived a child, he would move mountains to be in its life. His only obstacle was his trip to Egypt in the upcoming week. An idea suddenly popped into his head. He logged on to his work email with his phone. He wasn't going to be like his dad. He was better than Zayd Danjuma.

God help Damisi if she deliberately tried to keep his child away from him.

Chapter 9

S ome weeks later, Damisi walked into the Herbert Lotun Hall in the Sheraton hotel, Victoria Island. The Lagos chapter of the Hearts Foundation chose the prestigious venue to host the welcome gala. The doctors, she'd learned, would be working in Nigeria for the next two weeks. She cracked her knuckles and rubbed her hands down her bare arms. She had on a sleeveless black-and-gold, flirty A-line dress that stopped a couple of inches below her knees. Her feet were as comfortable as they could be in three-inch gold heels. Damisi knew she had to be clever with her clothes. She needed to make accommodations for her increasing bust line while still maintaining the sexy look she was known for. She was glad Moji had been able to help her shop.

As the host for the night's gala, she had the dual job of entertaining the guests and publicizing her station, KTN. Damisi didn't feel like they really needed the publicity since they almost had a monopoly on Christian entertainment. However, as she looked around the room and saw all the other television stations represented, she thanked God for the opportunity.

People had begun to trickle in, and the place was rapidly

filling up. Damisi walked over to the corner of the room and observed as people networked. The gala was scheduled to start in a few minutes. She closed the pamphlet that gave her the order of events for the evening and said the prayer she always said before she went on the air. "Be in my speech, Lord, and articulate my words so that they convey your message. Amen."

"Good evening, ladies, and gentlemen. Welcome to the Hearts Foundation of Africa's kick-off gala," the event organizer said.

Applause erupted in the room.

"We have a packed agenda, and there's no other person to navigate us through it with grace and style other than our host KTN's own, Damisi Odinga."

Damisi inhaled deeply, then exhaled and walked on the stage. She smiled as she waited for the applause to die down. She bowed slightly in acknowledgment of the standing ovation.

"Good evening, everyone. It's a great privilege to be your host for the evening. I promise not to bore you or crack humorless jokes, but we're going to have a nice time. I know you want to get on with what really matters…eating and dancing."

There was applause and laughter.

"So, without further ado, we're going to play a welcome message from the chairman of the foundation, and the voice you hear after that would be Dr. Akintola, the host for our guest doctors." She bowed slightly and walked off.

Thirty minutes later, Damisi quickly introduced a group of dancers that would perform Yolanda Adams and Donnie McClurkin's duet "The Prayer," then she made a beeline for the bathroom. The baby had been sitting on her bladder for a while, and she couldn't hold it in any longer. Several seconds later, she exited the bathroom stall and heard the opening melody of the second and final song for the dancers. She quickly washed her hands and refreshed her makeup. She ran her fingers through her loose curls which she let flow around her shoulders.

Satisfied with her appearance, Damisi walked out of the bathroom and turned back to the hall when she ran straight into a rock-solid chest. She slowly lifted her eyes, but she didn't need to make eye contact to know exactly who stood in front of her. Jabir Danjuma.

Her mind went into overdrive, and her heartbeat accelerated. It couldn't be. She had looked through the doctor list a dozen times and his name wasn't on it. So how could…

"Hello, Damisi," Jabir said.

She met his gaze. Overwhelmed, she staggered backward.

"Running again I see." His brown eyes had no emotion in them.

"W–What are you d–doing here?" Damisi stuttered.

Her heart pounded against her chest, and the butterflies that lay dormant in the pit of her stomach began fluttering around. Her palms began to sweat as a sense of euphoria engulfed her. Everything faded to the background, and all she could see was the man standing in front of her.

His height and posture gave the illusion of someone larger than life. Despite his formal tuxedo, one couldn't miss his well-toned physique. He wasn't a model, but sure could have been.

"Trust me. I wouldn't be here if I didn't have to." His eyes roamed over her. "I have a question to ask that can't wait." His tone was curt. His full eyebrows always showed the first signs of his frustration—or was it anger?

Until she had to speak, she had forgotten she had been holding her breath. The effect he had on her irritated her in the moment. His dark hair cut close to his head, and his well-trimmed mustache and connecting beard showed signs of a recent trip to the barber. His mocha skin was flawless except for the small scar next to his left eye. He was gorgeous.

"Here? What is it?" She cracked her knuckles.

Gone were the warm smile and playful wink he gave her

whenever he showed up in Lagos. In its place...an ice-cold stare. His expression was unreadable as his gaze travelled from her stomach to her face. His jaw tightened as his stride closed the small gap between them. She thought she'd suffocate under his presence.

He stared down at her. "I need a straight answer. Are you pregnant?"

Applause could be heard in the ballroom. *Saved.* "I have to go." She tried to get around him, but he stepped in front of her.

He lightly touched her cheek with the back of his hand. "Go, but we're finishing this tonight."

JABIR FELT HIS INSIDES CLENCH WITH ANXIETY AS HE TRAILED Damisi on the way to her house. He'd had to endure three more agonizing hours before the event ended. He continued to observe her keenly throughout the evening and became convinced she was pregnant. He still knew every contour of her body, and something was definitely different about her. That February night, things had happened so fast that neither of them thought about protection. While they were together, she was on the pill, so he just didn't think of it. A slow, wry smile tipped the corner of his mouth at the most glaring sign of all—her increased bust line. Her breasts, although tightly packed in her sleeveless gown, had increased in size.

He parked under the outdoor garage next to her Toyota and watched her get out of the car without giving him a backward glance. He angled his head with intrigue as he wondered how she could be so beautiful. His loins tightened as his eyes followed the sway of her hips up the three steps to the front door.

His reaction to her angered him. This was Damisi after all. He needed to stay angry with her. That way he could focus better on the issue at hand. Was she or wasn't she pregnant? Was it or wasn't it his? He got out of his car, activated the locks, and followed her into her house.

He couldn't believe he was in Lagos. How he got so lucky amazed him. Before his plane took off from LAX back to Detroit, Dr. O' Reilly had accepted his request for a meeting. During that meeting, Jabir explained to him he had a family emergency and would like to switch places with one of the doctors who were previously assigned to Nigeria.

The assignment would be in Badagry, a town on the outskirts of Lagos, about a ninety-minute drive from the city. He explained he would be able to do his job and see his family at the same time. For the next couple of days, he waited for the request to be approved. Then right before he was scheduled to go to Egypt, one of the doctors agreed to switch places with him. Being a last-minute change, it took some doing to get an emergency Visa, and there was no time to change the roster for both assignments.

For that, Jabir was grateful. From the way they ended things, he couldn't predict Damisi's reaction to knowing he was coming ahead of time.

Damisi held the door open and kicked off her shoes. It was a little after 10:00 P.M. and he could see she was exhausted. Jabir walked into the living room. Nothing much had changed since he visited last year. Damisi's décor was mainly made up of pieces of African artwork. She loved ancient history, and it showed in her collection of Kenyan and Nigerian pieces. Her walls were painted a light greyish color which highlighted the darker crème furniture with Ankara covered throw pillows. He took off his jacket, folded up his sleeves, and sat.

"Where's Moji?" Jabir asked to break the ice.

"She's staying with her mom tonight."

Jabir had heard of Damisi's aunty Bola but had never met her.

"Do you want anything to drink?" She turned around and headed to the kitchen.

Moments passed, and she hadn't returned. Jabir followed her into the kitchen and caught her staring into the refrigerator.

"No, thank you. You're stalling." He walked up behind her and shut the door, trapping her between the fridge and his frame.

She turned around to face him. Her eyes glistened with unshed tears.

"Are you going to give me an answer?" He struggled to remain firm. He couldn't handle her tears, no matter how angry he was at her. His heartbeat against his chest in apprehension.

"Yes," she whispered.

"Yes, you're going to give me an answer or yes, you're pregnant?" He needed to be absolutely sure of her meaning. Now was not the time for assumptions.

Several beats of silence hung between them. He continued to stare at her, and she slowly lifted her eyes to his.

"Yes, I'm pregnant," she said.

He could feel her eyes searching for a reaction. Everything he thought he would feel or say in this moment escaped him. He had nothing. "Is it mine?" The minute the question left his lips, he regretted it.

"How dare you insinuate that I sleep around?" The fury in her eyes was unmistakable. "How dare you?"

She pushed past him and walked back into the living room.

It took a minute to make his legs move. *I'm going to be a father. I'm going to be a father.*

Jabir entered the living room to find her pacing. She was muttering something and cracking her knuckles. She always did that when she was upset and nervous. He had spoken out of turn and had to apologize if they were going to have any chance of ironing things out today.

"I apologize. I wasn't really prepared for your answer."

"How could you be when everything has to be about the mighty Dr. Jabir Danjuma? Have you stopped to consider me?"

"I said I was sorry." He paused and shoved his hands in his pockets. "Are you okay?"

Jabir saw the anger dissipate from her eyes. She studied him for a minute and slowly sat down. He wanted so much to hold her, but something held him back. Fear. He watched her take out a rubber band and gather her hair on top of her head. He itched to tuck the loose strands behind her ears.

"I don't know how I am, and that's the truth."

"Why didn't you call me? How far along are you?" His tone was low.

"A little over three months—thirteen weeks." She bit her lower lip. "I was going to call, but hadn't gotten to it. We didn't exactly part on great terms."

Jabir walked over and sat down next to her. "But you should have known nothing would keep me away from my child."

"Jabir let's not pretend that a baby is the magic glue that would bind us together. But I should have called you earlier." She reached for her purse and brought out something. "Here."

Jabir slowly took what looked like her test results from her. He opened it up and scanned the document. It confirmed how many weeks she was when she visited the doctor and gave an estimated due date. A ball of emotion rose to his throat and made it hard to swallow. Right now, in this very moment, he acknowledged he hadn't figured out what his reaction would be if she were indeed pregnant with his child.

Commitment was never his thing. During their one-year relationship, in the back of his mind, he knew it would end one day. What angered him was the way it did and that he had fallen in love with her. He was, after all, his father's son. He was not about to give any soul a false sense of security then turn around and swipe it from under their feet. Neither was he going to allow anyone to do that to him.

But staring at the image in his hands humbled him. He never thought of having a child. But he always knew that if he did, the child had to be raised in a home with two parents. The absence of his father from his life demanded it. Jabir always vowed never to put his own child through that. For him, a baby automatically translated into a wife.

He straightened his shoulders and sucked in a deep breath. There was no way he was going to father a child and not be in its life every day of its life—even if he had to sacrifice his to make that happen.

"I know we have issues, but we can spend the rest of our lives figuring it out," Jabir said.

She stood. "Meaning?" Her brows scrunched together.

He stood. "Marry me."

I must be out of my mind. Jabir couldn't believe he'd just asked Damisi to marry him when his annulment wasn't final, but he was desperate; his child was involved.

Chapter 10

Damisi blinked a couple of times, reassuring herself this wasn't a dream. She then lifted her finger to her ear and pressed against it. It wasn't stuffed up. Jabir stood in front of her, his expression blank as though he hadn't asked her to turn her world upside down.

"What?" she asked. She couldn't have heard right.

"I asked you to marry me."

"More like commanded," she retorted.

"Do you want me to kneel? I can, but I think we're past that stage." His eyes travelled to her stomach.

"Are you insane?"

"Why? Because I want to marry the soon-to-be mother of my child?" Jabir countered.

She folded her arms across her chest and walked past him. She sat on the bay window and stared into the darkness of the night. She was tired. This was all too much for her. How could one slip-up have so many repercussions?

Jabir walked up beside her and leaned with one shoulder against the windowsill. Beats of silence passed between them.

She looked at him. "You're suggesting I marry you out of obligation?"

He shrugged. "Would it be that much of a sacrifice?"

Her eyes widened. "Are you kidding me?"

She couldn't believe he was acting so nonchalantly—like it was no big deal. Their relationship had failed, so what made him think a marriage wouldn't?

"All you have to do is view it as a business transaction." He smiled.

"With no expiration date?"

"Who says? That can be arranged, but this time I'd have some notice. You won't be able to pull your disappearing act because you would belong to me." Jabir winked.

Damisi seethed. She had never met a more arrogant and cocky man.

"You are the most—" She bit down on her lip.

"Easy now. I know for a fact that babies can hear even in the womb. Watch what you say about its father." He smirked.

"Is this a game to you?" she sighed.

"A game? A game? Do I look like I'm playing?" Jabir paced before her.

She knew he was trying to control his temper, but she wasn't bothered. Let him get mad and leave. Just leave her alone.

"I don't play games. You do." His fiery gaze darkened his eyes.

His accusation hurt. Damisi waved her hand wearily. "I can't rehash this now. We buried the past for six years. Why now?"

"You're carrying my child. That's why." He paused. "I was so eager to be done when you left me in that hotel room. I refuse to be the forbidden toy you toss aside when your Christian conscience kicks in."

"And I refuse to be with a man who knows nothing about loyalty and commitment." She trembled on the verge of tears.

"Accuse me of anything, but while we were together, I was committed to you. You left!"

Damisi had avoided having this conversation for years. There had never been any hope of reconciliation, so there was never a need to broach the topic. Besides, they had each moved on to other relationships. She did leave without an explanation, but he didn't follow her. If he loved her, he would have.

Even before she left, their relationship was already strained. Telling him she saw him at a whorehouse would do nothing but add to their anguish. She had to accept the fact that her then newfound faith would be a constant strain between them until he became saved. Since she couldn't do that for him, she decided to let everything stay buried. Who could have predicted that years later, she'd be single and pregnant for him while parading the name of the Lord? Still, she couldn't marry Jabir. With the way she felt about him and his obvious dislike for her, it would be a painful existence.

"I've made some mistakes, but I'm not about to make another one," she said. She wasn't going to allow him take her down the self-pity route again. She had prayed long and hard to pick herself up. She stood and walked to the front door.

He grabbed her arm. "Why did you leave me? Because I wasn't godly enough?"

"Because you weren't worthy of me…" She regretted the words the minute they escaped her lips. It was a desperate attempt to get out of the corner he was backing her into.

He dropped her hand.

"I'm sorry," she said softly.

It was too late. His jaw tightened. His demeanor had glazed over.

"Marriage or children were never in the cards for me, but considering my childhood, nothing will separate me from a child I conceived."

"We barely know each other anymore."

"According to your Bible and my seed growing in you, we do *know* each other." He smirked.

Her blood boiled. Not only had she let herself down, but had failed miserably at any chance of getting Jabir to walk with Christ. Now he would think that anything goes.

She looked down at her stomach. In a couple of weeks, she wouldn't be able to hide it anymore, but she had made up her mind. It wasn't too late to crawl out of the hole she had dug for herself.

"No," she said.

"What did you say?" he asked between clenched teeth.

"I said no. I will *not* marry you out of some false sense of obligation on your part or mine." She walked to the door. It was time for Jabir to leave. It was almost midnight, and they were hurting each other.

She placed her hand on the door and opened it.

He raised his brow and with purposeful strides reached the door and closed it. "You're kicking me out?"

"Jabir, I can't marry you and that's that."

"Can't or won't?"

"Same thing. You don't have to marry me to be a part of your child's life."

"How do I know you won't disappear with my child? You do have a track record. I won't have an occasional relationship with my child. I intend to be there all the way."

She glared at him. "You don't love me, so why subject you or me to a loveless marriage?"

He was shooting down all of her arguments. Surely, he wouldn't be able to counter this one. Maybe he would let go of this silly idea.

He chuckled. She failed to see the humor in their situation.

"Didn't you tell me you loved me once? But you still ran away. That word means nothing to you, so don't you dare throw it in my face."

Her gut clenched. She closed her eyes trying to suppress the tears that threatened to pour any minute now. She needed to lie down. She was emotionally and mentally spent.

"I think you should leave," she said, softly.

Jabir lifted her head with his index finger. "I'm staying at the Danjuma Group guesthouse, and I leave for Badagry in two days. I'll be in prep meetings all day tomorrow, but I'll call you. I am patient, but don't push me."

Damisi remained silent. She knew about his impatience all too well. There was, however, no more fight in her tonight.

He opened the door and left.

———

The next morning, Damisi didn't feel any better than she had the night before. She tossed and turned all through the night. Just as she finally settled into slumber, the sun peered through the curtains, signaling the sunrise. She propped herself up against the pillows and rubbed her hands over her stomach. The interior decorator told her that the lime green and yellow colors of her room would have a soothing effect. She should feel relaxed and energized every morning. Today, she felt neither. She reached over to her Bible, but something in her didn't allow her to open it. What was the use of reading it if she couldn't follow the instructions in it?

"Lord, thank You for another day," Damisi mumbled and proceeded to recite Psalm 23. It had become a habit of hers when she found it difficult to pray. The good thing though was that she had come up with some semblance of a plan. The bad thing was that Jabir wouldn't like it one bit. Deciding that that would be his problem, she ran the thought through her mind again.

Come Monday morning, she would face her problems head on. She wasn't going to let Jabir bully her into getting married. The way she had it all planned out, her savings could at least hold her over for the first two years while she was out of a job. She'd be able to take care of the baby, then look for another job when ready. She got out of the bed and proceeded to the bathroom. She peed, brushed her teeth, and secured her head scarf. Grateful that today was Saturday, she planned on doing absolutely nothing. It was just going to be her, African Magic Movie channel and her thoughts. She heard the television in the living room. Moji was back.

Damisi walked to the living room. Moji was seated in her favorite chair eating her breakfast and watching an entertainment show.

"You're home." Damisi smiled and walked into the kitchen.

Moji stuffed her remaining *akara* in her mouth and followed Damisi. "Ha! I thought you'd sleep all day. It's 10:00 A.M."

"It's Saturday."

"So? That's no excuse for not waking up early, when you know I'm waiting for *tafia. How far now?* How was last night? Were there any nice-looking American doctors? I hope you checked like I told you to since I couldn't crash the party."

Damisi shook her head and laughed. "So which question should I answer first?" She got a pot from the cupboard and filled it with water.

Moji waved her off. "Whatever. So how was it?"

"It was going good until…" She opened the fridge and got out the carton of eggs and some strawberries. Rinsing two eggs, she placed them in a pot on the stove.

"Until what?"

"Until Jabir showed up."

"*I don die!* Jabir is in town? How? Does he know?" Moji's shocked expression was hilarious.

"Slow down. I'm exhausted from even thinking about it, and this baby is hungry." Damisi reached for the bread.

"*Pele*, sorry. Sit down. Let me make your breakfast while you tell me all about it." Moji pulled out a bar stool for her.

Damisi smiled and did as she was told. Nothing could get her cousin to do something faster than the reward of gist. Moji set a glass of orange juice in front of her. Damisi thanked her, took a sip, and began narrating the vents of the previous evening. She gave her cousin a play-by-play but stopped short of the marriage talk.

"I'm glad you finally talked to him." Moji sliced the strawberries into halves.

"Talk *ke*? It was more like a battle of wills."

"It's better than the game of pretense both of you have been at for the past six years. It was getting old."

"Oh, really now?"

"Before *nko*? Tell the man what he did. Free him and free yourself or get back together. I've been telling you that. Every relationship after him, it's been one complaint after the other. But on the rare occasion Jabir comes to Nigeria and comes to see you, you treat him like a polite stranger, and I have had to watch in silence."

"Wow! Are you siding with a stranger over your cousin?" Damisi rested her chin in her palm.

"Jabir isn't a stranger. He may have a funny way of showing it, but he loves you. Unless there's gold between your legs, I wonder what else would keep him coming back to you after all these years." Moji winked.

Damisi creased her brows. Her cousin said the brashest things sometimes.

"You of all people know exactly why I left Jabir…"

"Yeah, yeah you've told the story a million times, but to the wrong person."

"What do you mean? Never mind. Let's just drop it."

"All I'm saying is now there's a baby on the way. You guys need to talk. You just broke it off with him. No explanation…nothing."

"What's there to explain? We had started arguing a lot because of my celibacy vow. The last fight was terrible." Damisi remembered him threatening something about there being more fish in the sea. So cliché…he couldn't even be original. She hissed at the memory. "He's been with many others after me, so don't act like Jabir has been idle."

Moji laughed. "*Bad belle. Ehen*, instead of fighting for your man, you take the KTN job and escape. And you want to hold it against him?"

The kettle began to whistle. Damisi was hungry and tired of talking about Jabir. "*Abeg*, make my custard, oh."

Moji turned off the kettle. "Even at that, he still keeps in contact."

Damisi laughed. There was no depth to the sound. "That's just because I was the one who got away."

Moji shook her head. "Ha! Self-deceit is not good, oh. All I'm saying is you guys should have talked, but you kept dodging the man until you needed an interview." She placed a bowl of custard in front of Damisi. "You got it and something extra, and it's entirely his fault again." Moji placed her hands on her hips.

Damisi knew Moji was right, but she was not willing to accept it. Not just yet. She couldn't go down that path with Jabir. "He asked me to marry him."

"For real?"

"No, I take that back. He tried to bully me into marrying him."

Moji turned to her and frowned. Damisi knew she owed her an explanation, but she remained silent.

"Meaning? What did you say?" Moji asked.

"What do you think? I said no." Damisi scooped a spoonful of custard and blew on it before she put it into her mouth.

"Why did you do that?" Moji eyes widened in horror. "You have a second chance, and I know you love that man."

"Do I have to list the reasons for you? Number one, he doesn't love me. In fact, after yesterday, I know he hates me. Number two, he has commitment phobia, hence his womanizing. Three and most important, he is *not* going to use my child to make up for some damaged childhood he had." Damisi continued to eat.

She looked up and Moji was shaking her head, obviously not agreeing with her reasons.

"I already feel shame for my actions; why worsen the situation?" Damisi popped a strawberry into her mouth.

Moji sat down next to her "*Na wa o*. All these excuses from a girl who was once so angry with her mother for divorcing her father. Do you wish that for your child? God forbid that at least Jabir is trying not to make the same mistake with his child. Let's crucify him." Moji stood, pushed the chair back in and walked out of the kitchen.

Damisi stared at the plates in front of her. The memories of the early years of adjusting to living in two different countries came back. When she was separated from her mother, she cried. When she was separated from her father, she cried. Nobody won in that situation. She still had no idea what happened. Why had her mother left her father? Why did she go back? Why didn't she stay? Her dad still refused to tell her but didn't seem angry about it either.

Was trying not to repeat the sins of their parents enough reason to get married? Could she be in a loveless marriage because of a child? Damisi suddenly understood what her mother might have had to deal with. Was that why she went back but couldn't stay? The answers lay with her dad. He never liked to talk about it, but now it was no longer about him.

Chapter 11

Monday morning, Jabir walked into the kitchen of the guesthouse where he was staying. The Danjuma Group guesthouses were not your ordinary guesthouse. They were more like a home away from home. Rasheed had decided to expand the reach of the company late last year, so he had Halima buy two guesthouses in Lagos and Abuja. The aim was to provide convenience and comfort to out-of-town potential business associates. It was part of the overall strategy to woo their business by taking care of their accommodations while in Nigeria. They also had drivers assigned to them during their stay. Jabir knew his brother was a savvy business-man, but he continued to surprise him. Jabir and Kamal didn't need to know details of the company's operations. They trusted their brother to do the right thing, but Rasheed always insisted on giving them regular updates.

For the next two weeks, this would be his home. He picked up the cup of Ovaltine he had made earlier. He wasn't much of a coffee drinker, so the chocolate-flavored beverage was his morning drink of choice. Jabir glanced around the spotless kitchen and made a mental note to see Halima sometime during the week and take her out to lunch. When he walked into the place two days ago, he was stunned the kitchen had been stocked with what she knew he liked. She was the little sister he always wished he had to dote over and was glad the strain in their relationship was mended. Their father's decision to leave his mother and marry Halima's mother, Aisha, was no fault of hers. After Rasheed took over the company last year, the strain between the siblings had been resolved. His mother demanded it.

He walked out of the kitchen, grabbed his cell phone and headed out the door. He had to get a move on it if he was going to get to Badagry by noon. The driver Halima insisted he use started the car as he stepped out into the parking lot. He didn't need the additional stress of driving long distance in Lagos, so he willingly took her up on the offer.

"Good morning, sir," the driver greeted Jabir as he slid into the backseat.

'Good morning, David. Thank you for being here so early," Jabir said.

"Ah no problem, sir, *shey na Badagry we dey go now?*"

"Yes, and please call me Jabir."

David laughed, but Jabir failed to see what was funny.

"Did I say something?" Jabir asked.

"No, Oga. You just remind me of your brother, Oga Rasheed. He likes being called by his first name, too. But *me I no f t oh.*"

Jabir shook his head. It was no surprise to him that the driver said he couldn't call him by his first name. Until last year, the only person who called them Oga was his mother's driver, and he couldn't call Jabir by his first name either.

As the driver navigated through the city, Jabir looked out of the window to observe the place he thought was charming. At almost mid-morning, the city had been awake for hours. Lagos's fast pace paralleled that of New York. After relocating from the United Kingdom, his mother settled in Abuja, which had a much slower pace. Like most fast-growing cities, Lagos was enticing, but its increasing population equated pollution and unpredictable traffic gridlocks. He had nothing against the city, but the only reason he ever visited it was Damisi.

His thoughts shifted to the woman who infuriated and calmed him at the same time. Damisi was testing his patience just like he thought she would. She had avoided all his calls on Saturday and Sunday. She sent him to voicemail so many times that he lost count. He almost went over to her house and demanded she give him an audience, but then that would be what she would have expected.

Two things stopped him. One was that he didn't have a moral leg to stand on; he was still technically married. He had given Ashton a call to get a status update. The paper announcements had started and would run for five weeks. The second thing was something she said—or didn't say—when they talked the other day. She was convinced he didn't love her, but nowhere in her tirade did she say she didn't love him. That gave him a glimmer of hope and made him change his approach. He decided he would woo his woman back to him.

She was his, had always been—whether she was mad at him or not. She probably thought he'd allow her to walk away from him again. She was sadly mistaken because she had something of his in her possession. A baby they created out of love. Whatever reservations he had about her would have to be put aside because of that baby. Despite the fact that he loved her, she couldn't know it because he couldn't trust her with his heart. However, he knew she loved him. That was good enough for now.

Jabir speed dialed Damisi.

After three rings, she answered. "Hello?"

"At the station already?" Jabir asked. It was 7.00 A.M. She sounded alert, and there was some background noise.

"Yes. I always have a pre-production meeting by eight Monday mornings," Damisi replied.

Jabir did the mental calculation. In Lagos traffic, that

meant she probably woke up by 5:00 A.M. to be there. Her hectic schedule was something she was going to have to cut back on. He wanted to bring it up, but they would just fight about it, and now was not the time.

"You should take it easy." He found himself saying. He couldn't help it. He worried about her stubbornness.

"Don't worry. *Your* child is okay. I, on the other hand, need to work for as long as they would have me. I need the money."

She was goading him. Jabir forced himself to bite back the remark he had for her. "I take care of my responsibilities." He thought he had made himself clear about his involvement in the child's life.

"Your child is your responsibility. Not me."

So she thought. He checked the time and he had just enough to make a quick stop. He covered the mouthpiece of the phone with his hand and gave the driver some instructions.

"So I take it you haven't given any more thought to my proposal?"

"No, and I'm not going to. My boss will be back from vacation soon, and I plan on telling her, then the chips can fall where they may. But I *will not* marry you out of obligation."

Jabir's jaw tightened and his nose flared. Damisi knew the exact buttons to press to get a reaction from him. Even after all these years. He grunted.

The car came to a stop. "I'll call you back," Jabir said and disconnected the call.

After about ten minutes, he was back out with what he knew to be her favorite pastries and a smoothie. He could bet she hadn't had anything to eat yet.

"David, you know that Christian TV station?"

Jabir received an affirmative nod and was glad when David said it was on their way. Jabir hadn't thought about the implications of going against traffic.

Thirty minutes later, Jabir was in the KTN lobby waiting

for Damisi. He got curious stares from the receptionist and guard. He didn't know whether it was because he looked like Kamal—someone they'd recognize—or because Damisi never received male visitors. He hoped it was the latter.

The space was decorated in light colors, and the walls were decorated with paintings or pictures of guests of their shows. He walked to the one the one that had Damisi in it. She was on the set of her show and looked beautiful. She had a microphone in her hand and was smiling. From the picture, he could see she loved what she did. His eyes saddened at what having a baby out of wedlock would do to her career. If they acted fast, she might have a chance of salvaging it, but she was too stubborn, and his approach wasn't helping either. He had to get her to see reason.

"What are you doing here?" she whispered behind him.

Jabir turned around and marveled at how gorgeous she looked. He smiled inwardly. She hadn't started to really show yet, but the way she crossed her hands over her chest told him she was self-conscious.

"I figured you could use breakfast." He handed her the smoothie and the box of pastries.

She took it from him slowly, her eyes softening with gratitude. "Thank you, but you shouldn't be here."

Jabir frowned. "Why? Expecting someone?"

She grabbed his wrist and tried to pull him to the corner. He resisted at first but caved when he saw the plea in her eyes. "I really appreciate the breakfast, but I thought you were supposed to be on your way to Badagry. I really don't need any rumors started."

He lifted his brow. "Rumors? I'm not doing anything but making sure you're fed. The baby needs to eat."

She looked around in shocked horror. "*Shhhh.* Do you want to say it a little louder?" She rolled her eyes at him, and he chuckled. "Jabir, please you can't be here. In case you forget, you look like one of the most recognizable Nigerian soccer players. I can't do the rumor mill now."

He wanted to dismiss her argument, but he was running late, and she was right. But then he had another idea. "Okay, I'll leave on one condition."

"Really?"

' Really." He smirked.

Some people walked past them and did a double take. Damisi panicked. "What is it?"

"Have dinner with me when I get back."

Damisi hesitated, then someone she knew walked over to say hello to them. By now, he could see the fury in her eyes. The daggers in them were aimed at him. He raised his eyebrow.

'I can't believe you. Okay. Go," she said hurriedly and turned away. He watched her go, but smiled when she walked back his way. "Thank you, and please drive safe."

Yep. This new approach just might work. There was hope.

Chapter 12

Damisi put the last morsel of her cinnamon roll in her mouth and washed it down with her strawberry smoothie. She closed her eyes and thanked God for the baker and Jabir. She had planned on getting something to eat at work. In fact, she was on her way to the network cafeteria when she was told a Jabir Danjuma was there to see her.

Shock, curiosity and fear were the emotions to best describe her feelings. The effect he had on her wasn't what she expected. He was dressed to stop the heart of any woman. Underneath his ash-blue blazer was a gray shirt tucked into dark jeans. The way his jeans fit his muscular thighs almost made her lose her mind. She had spent years training herself in a life of celibacy, but that vow didn't kill her yearnings when it came to Jabir. He was one sexy man, and time had done nothing to change that.

She smiled and pulled out her phone. Her finger hovered over his name for a few seconds as she tried to make up her mind on whether to call or to text. Deciding she wanted to hear his raspy voice, she dialed. He wasn't a smoker, so his voice was a sexy mystery to her. His British and American mixed accents made her think about things she shouldn't.

Jabir answered on the first ring.

"Have you finished eating?" he asked.

Damisi rolled her eyes as though he could see her. His obsessing over her all of a sudden was getting old, then she remembered his real concern was for the baby. She shouldn't get too carried away. Coming to terms with that, however, was disappointing. Suddenly she became annoyed. She should have sent him a text instead.

"Yes. I wanted to call and say thank you."

"You said that already. You miss me?"

She could tell he was smiling. He really did think she was at his mercy.

"Please. Don't you have enough people lying down at your feet? Why do you need one more?" She heard him grunt and knew she should stop but she couldn't. "Or is it because I'm carrying your child that brings me to the front of the line?"

An awkward silence ensued. She should apologize. And she was about to when he spoke.

"I'll be back from Badagry in a week. I suggest you give some serious thought to my proposal." His voice was tight. "Damisi, I'm being nice here and offering you a sweet deal. Marry me. You'll have your precious reputation, and I'll have my child and its mother in my life."

The way he said "its mother" angered her. "No. So what is the big, bad Jabir Danjuma going to do now?"

"I'd drag you through every court in Nigeria. I don't have to tell you you won't recover from the damage to your reputation, not to talk of the fact I might be awarded custody."

She gasped. "You wouldn't dare."

He snickered. "You know almost anything goes in Naija, and I'm a Danjuma."

"I really hate you."

"Are you sure about that? You know what they say, there's a thin line…"

Damisi tried to respond, but no sound came out.

"Have a good day, sweetheart, and I'll talk to you later."

She disconnected the call without a response. She bowed her head on her desk and cried. She was not prepared for this battle. She had underestimated the two sides of Jabir Danjuma.

Three hours and two meetings later, Damisi was back at her desk. She had fixed her makeup and joined the team for preproduction and a screening meeting for potential guests for the new season. She needed someone big to be on the August season opener. Although she knew the future was uncertain, concentrating on work was the only way to keep her from focusing on her situation.

She still couldn't believe Jabir had threatened her with a lawsuit. As if she didn't have enough to deal with already. The sad part about it was deep down she knew she had pushed him. However, the realization he could even utter those words instilled a fear in her she hadn't dared to think about. He was a Danjuma, from one of the richest families in Nigeria. She wasn't ready to gamble if the judge would rule in her favor.

"I can't let that happen," Damisi said to herself, rubbing her stomach.

"Can I come in?"

Damisi swiveled her chair around, and Eno stood in the middle of her office. She had gotten back from South Africa the night before, and they really hadn't had a chance to talk. All morning, she had been looking at her funny. Now in the privacy of her office, she wondered which Eno to expect. Damisi hoped it was Eno, her friend and not pious Eno, the producer. As mad as she was, Damisi would throw the latter one out of her office in a heartbeat.

"I'd say you're already in," she said, irritated Eno never knocked.

Eno walked closer to the desk and pulled out a chair. "Are you all right?"

"No, but I don't want to talk about it."

"You've been acting strange since I got back. What's going on?" Eno inched closer to Damisi's desk.

"I'm fine." Even to her ears, the words she'd just uttered were unbelievable. Damisi felt nausea rising in her throat. She should be over morning sickness, but just like its father, this baby insisted on punishing her. A protective hand went over her stomach, and she rushed out of the office to the ladies' bathroom.

Moments later, she exited the stall and saw Eno waiting for her with a questioning stare.

"Tell me what's going on now!" Eno whispered.

Damisi remained silent. She rinsed out her mouth, washed her hands and ran her fingers through her hair. She grabbed Eno's hand and dragged her out of the bathroom. Once they got to the comfort of Damisi's office, she closed the door.

Damisi paced, then stopped in the middle of the room. She looked at Eno but unlike before, she couldn't find comfort in her friend's eyes. Her expression was blank, but Damisi knew Eno probably already knew what she was about to tell her.

"I'm pregnant."

"Jabir?"

"Yes. How did you know?"

"When a fine, caramel-colored man comes to visit the princess of abstinence, tongues wag." Eno shook her head. Then as though something struck her, she began to pace. "Do you understand what you've done? Everything you've worked for?" Her voice rose.

"Shhh," Damisi said.

"Don't shhh me. *Be...co...ming Ruth!*" Eno stopped abruptly and looked at her watch. "It's almost lunch time. Let me get my purse. We can't talk about this here." She walked out without waiting for a response.

Damisi stood there for several seconds before following Eno. "My God is bigger than my mess." She repeated the words over and over to prevent herself from slipping back into despair.

Several minutes later, both ladies were seated in their regular booth with their meals in front of them. The restaurant was a couple of streets from the studio, and they had lunch there at least twice a week. More if their schedules permitted. Many brainstorming sessions took place in this booth over bowls of goat meat pepper soup, fried plantains, jollof or fried rice, peppered snails or anything they had a taste for.

Damisi took a spoonful of her *Banga* rice and bit into her roasted chicken. Eno's shocked stare was not stopping this baby or her from wanting to consume everything in sight.

"*Banga* rice? You used to hate that," Eno said.

"You'd be surprised what happens when you're pregnant."

On the way to the restaurant, Damisi had given Eno the rundown of events, starting from Ibiso's wedding and ending with her present situation.

"Normally, I wouldn't say I told you so—"

"Since when?" Damisi asked.

"Whatever. We've always told each other the truth. When you started focusing more about the cares of the works of God than God Himself, I told you this could happen," Eno said.

"Don't you think I know that now?"

"Apparently, but at what cost? There's a reason the Bible tells us to guard our heart and put on the armor of God daily."

Damisi knew Eno was right, but she was in no mood to listen now.

"Would you please allow me to eat this food in peace? You scolded me all the way from the studio to the restaurant." Damisi took a sip of water.

She had been through this already. In the weeks since she'd returned from Kenya, it had been a constant struggle with her conscience. Sometimes when she tried to pray, words failed her. Sometimes when she could pray, in her head she knew God heard her and forgave her, but her heart couldn't conjure the faith needed to give her peace.

Any time she looked at her stomach, guilt stabbed her heart. Guilt over the love she had for her unborn child, despite the circumstances under which it was conceived. Damisi finally realized there was no use crying over what couldn't be changed. So she accepted for herself His grace and mercy. She was picking herself up and wouldn't allow anybody else to put her down. She needed solutions and not chastisement.

"I know those scriptures, remember? We quote them together. This wasn't my intention. It just happened," Damisi said.

"Sis, sin does not just happen..." Eno's face expressed her regret the minute she uttered the words.

"Enough. I feel dirty enough as it is. You're supposed to be my shoulder to lean on."

"I know. I'm sorry. I guess I'm just angry at all the work you put in going down the drain." Eno signaled for the waiter to come over and ordered additional food for them to take away.

"You're not going to be mad at me forever, are you? I really need my friend." Damisi pouted.

"Of course not, and I'm sorry I made you feel like I'm not here for you. The baby is here to stay, and I'm glad you didn't compound the issue by having an abortion before I got back." Eno paused and eyed her friend. "Please don't tell me the thought even entered your mind."

Truthfully, it did, but only for a fleeting second when the pregnancy test was positive—when the thought of all she stood to lose crossed her mind. But the Holy Spirit whispered, *"What does it profit a man to gain the whole world but lose his soul?"* That knocked her thinking back into shape. Too bad she didn't remember any of the scriptures when she was with Jabir.

"Never mind. Don't answer that. If I wasn't in J' burg, all this wouldn't have gone down. I'd have gone to Abuja with you." The waiter brought their boxes of food, and Eno paid.

"Part of this is my fault. The first time I saw you with Jabir, I knew there was a lot of unfinished business between you two. But instead of listening when you wanted to talk, I dismissed you with scripture. Iron is supposed to sharpen iron, but not just with scripture but understanding and tolerance. I'm sorry."

"Now you make me sound like a two-year-old." The friends shared a bout of laughter. Although strained, it felt good.

As they walked out of the restaurant, Damisi had a moment to her thoughts. She couldn't be mad at Eno. She was just being herself. But by tomorrow, she'd want to go shopping for the baby. Eno always kept it real with her, and she respected that.

"Oh no," Eno exclaimed.

"What is it?"

"When do you plan on telling Mrs. Kofo?"

"When she gets back. Why?"

"As your producer, and coworker, you know I'm supposed to report any known violation of the integrity clause."

Damisi felt bad. She had just jeopardized her friend's job by telling her. "Don't worry. I'll report it as soon as possible. Then I'll tell Gary," Damisi said.

"*Oh wee,* your agent is going to give you an earful. If anything happens to your endorsement, you know he'll starve," Eno laughed. "Don't let him swear for you, oh."

The friends laughed and strategized on next steps as they rode back to the studio. The next day, Damisi had an interview with a well-known prophetess who was visiting Nigeria from Liberia. She needed to leave work early so Moji's could help her come up with something to wear. The clothes at the studio were becoming a little snug now.

When they got back to the station, they headed straight to Damisi's office.

'Let's pray," Eno stretched out her hands. Damisi placed hers in them.

"Father God, please soothe Damisi's aching soul and restore peace in her world, in Jesus' name."

"Amen," they said in unison.

"It's going to be okay." Eno pulled her friend into a comforting embrace for a couple of moments.

Damisi lifted her head. "Okay, go. I know taping for Suzy's show starts soon. I'll be fine." Shifting on one foot, she grabbed her purse. "Gotta go, gotta go. It's like this baby sits permanently on my bladder."

As Damisi scurried to the bathroom, she thought about Eno's comments during lunch. She had let her ministry become an idol and she was now trying to dig herself out of the hole of her consequences.

———————————

Chapter 13

———————————

Jabir walked into the rec room of the hospital and poured himself a cup of coffee. It was almost 10:00 A.M. and he had been in Badagry for two days. Sleep tugged at him, but his adrenalin level was too high to succumb to it. Maybe he would tonight when he finally made it back home. He had been sleeping in the hospital quarters since he arrived. He and the other doctors had been swamped from the first hour of the first day.

His mother had complained that he had spoken to her only twice since he had arrived in Nigeria. Rasheed, Kamal and Halima had all called to check on him. It wasn't surprising, however, that Damisi hadn't called and had sent all his calls to voicemail. He sighed. What did he expect when he had virtually threatened the woman with taking away her child? Their child.

The last forty-eight hours had whizzed by. Jabir had just come from the office he shared with three other foreign doctors on the mission. They had been evaluating patients for the last day. The foundation had already pre-qualified patients that would be the beneficiaries of the free procedures. However, as was always the case, when the doctors arrived, they also did their own evaluations. They made their decisions based on the severity of the ailment and the patient's physical ability to undergo the procedure.

The qualifying patients on the list ranged from twelve to sixty-five years of age. The host chief medical director had made sure he and the other doctors were comfortable. The welcome was rousing. They had all kinds of continental and local delicacies waiting on them in the cafeteria. They all sat to eat that morning and they were introduced to the staff that they would be working with.

Later, he and the others were taken on a tour of the facility and introduced to some of the patient's families. Jabir hadn't been ready for the look of hopelessness he initially saw on their faces, then how those faces shone with joy and hope when they were assured they would be helped soon. For him, this was what it was all about. Providing hope for those who thought all hope was lost. The medical attention or expertise was not lacking, but the fact that these families couldn't afford the procedures made them the perfect candidates for the foundation's help. Some of the patients had been waiting for months; some had had some kind of intermediate procedure done and the last group was new patients.

Jabir whipped out his iPhone and checked it again. His jaw tightened in annoyance as he didn't see what he wanted to. No text. No missed calls. How could she not even send him a return message? He had sent her several "I'm sorry" texts. The woman's stubbornness incensed him, but he loved her. Emotions he knew where dangerous for his peace of mind, especially when it came to her. He had to remain focused. He wanted to be in his child's life—in her life— but he was afraid to show his feelings too soon. She had become good at trampling over them.

His mind flashed back to her accusation of infidelity. At first, he didn't think anything of her "incapable of commitment" comment, but she'd repeated it again the other night.

She had been throwing infidelity in his face for a long time and quite frankly he was tired of it. When he got back to the city, she would explain once and for all what she meant because he had never been unfaithful to her. Ever.

"Not what you expected, huh?" Dr. Kwame Nsofor said, bringing Jabir out of his reverie. He walked over to the coffee pot.

Kwame, a native of Ghana had joined the mission from a hospital in Atlanta. He and Jabir had become quick acquaintances since they had been on a different assignment with Doctors in the Skies some years ago.

"Man, I wasn't sure what to expect. You never know on these trips. I'm just glad we're able to help," Jabir said.

"Well, they got the backup generators running now, so we should be ready to go into surgery in the next hour." Kwame walked over to the wall and checked the roster.

The lack of constant electricity was one of the stumbling blocks they ran into when they arrived. Although the hospital had a generator, Jabir and the other doctors had been worried about its sustaining power. Their host chief of medical staff had wasted no time in taking their concerns into consideration and got a new backup generator from town. Now that it was installed, they would be able to see and perform as many procedures as they could in the remaining days and weeks of the mission.

"Great. You have the stent procedures and an angioplasty?" Jabir asked, not really expecting an answer since he remembered what was discussed in the meeting earlier.

"Yep, they're prepping my first patient now, so I better get to it. See ya." Kwame left the room and Jabir was close behind.

His first procedure was a coronary bypass grafting procedure. He had familiarized himself with Mrs. Camilla Ojo's case. He had been to her room earlier in the day to calm her fears and explain once again to her husband and teenage children what was about to take place. According to her chart, she had tried the less invasive procedure, but it had had little effect. In Jabir's experience, that was not uncommon. Sometimes those worked and at other times they didn't.

Jabir stopped at the nurses' station where the two local doctors who were going to assist him were waiting. They compared notes one final time, and he turned the corner to the patient's room. He walked in, and the scene was no different from before. Her husband was kneeling down in the corner praying and her teenage sons stood at her bedside.

He frowned for a moment. Despite how many times he had tried to ease their fears, the family acted like they were never going to see her again. Jabir empathized. They didn't know who he was. He wasn't arrogant, but he was good at what he did and this—making hearts new—was what he did. What he had devoted himself to. He knew everything would be okay. He just had to remind the Ojos of that.

He cleared his throat and stood at the foot of the patient's bed. She smiled up at him and he returned the gesture. According to her chart, Mrs. Ojo was a fifty-two year-old teacher at the local primary school. Her soft-spoken words when he first met her reminded him of his mother. Jabir thought she was lucky to have a family who cared so much they hadn't left her side. He was especially impressed with her husband. He had refused to go home or sleep since Jabir met him. He was an example of what a true husband should be and not the sorry excuse God had given his mother. He mentally kept himself from going down the road that was filled with thorns.

"It's time. Are you ready?" Jabir asked.

"Doctor, are people ever ready for these things?" Mrs. Ojo sighed.

"Doctor, with God we know everything will be okay, so yes we are ready," the woman's husband said, squeezing her hand.

Jabir looked at her sons who were quietly observing the

exchange. The scene felt like *déjà vu*, reminding him of the day his mother had to have appendicitis surgery many years ago. The only people by her side were him and his brothers.

"As I explained to you before, this will be an open-chest procedure. Don't be afraid. All we're doing is connecting a good blood vessel to the blocked one. The new blood vessel passes the blocked artery to increase blood flow to your heart," Jabir explained. He usually tried to oversimplify the procedure so as not to alarm the patient, unless there was reason to alarm them. In this case there wasn't, although he wouldn't actually be sure until they were on the table whether she would require just one graft or multiple. His hope was one, but he would wait and see.

The family used the next few minutes to ask questions they had already asked before, like length of the procedure and time to stay in the hospital after and side effects if any. Jabir was patient and answered them, giving them the level of comfort, they needed.

———

Ten hours later, Jabir reentered the rec room. The surgery for Mrs. Ojo had gone better than he had expected. He only had only to perform two grafts, and the surgery was over in about six-and-a-half hours. Mrs. Ojo was in the intensive care unit, and if everything went as he hoped it would, she would only be there for a couple of days and back home in about eight to ten days.

After surgery, Jabir consulted with two patients he had to operate on in the next couple of days. His plan of going back to the city was shot. Jabir had given David money for public transportation and asked him to go back to Lagos, not wanting to keep him from his family. And now he was too tired to make the one-and-a-half-hour drive.

He filled his paper cup with water from the cooler and

drank. His eyelids were becoming heavier, and he was losing the battle to keep them open. He discarded the cup and walked back to the ICU. His plan was to check on Mrs. Ojo again and call it a night.

A couple of hours later, Jabir had an actual meal prepared by the cook. He then showered and retired for the night. No sooner had his head hit the pillow than he heard a buzzing sound. He rubbed his eyes and reached for his phone. The display told him it was 1:00 A.M. and that Damisi was on the other end of the line. Panic shot through him. Sleep suddenly disappeared.

Taking a deep breath, Jabir answered. "What's wrong?"

"Wrong?" Her voice conveyed her surprise.

"It's 1:00 A.M. and you haven't so much as answered my calls or bothered to reach out." Now that he was almost positive nothing was the matter, his earlier irritation with her resurfaced.

"The last time we talked, you threatened to take my child away, so forgive me if I'm not feeling chatty or friendly towards you."

Jabir let out an exaggerated sigh and sat up in the bed. "And I apologized…a million times." He was tired and had to be up in less than six hours. He needed to sleep.

She remained silent.

"I don't want to fight with you. Is the baby okay?" he asked.

"The baby is fine."

"Are you okay?"

"Why do you care? All you care about is the baby."

"Look, woman, I'm tired. It's been a busy day. I told you I don't want to fight with you." He paused. "State your mission or let's continue this argument when I'm mentally capable."

"When will you be back?" Damisi asked after a while.

"She misses me."

"And I see even in your tiredness, your ego is alert."

"I've told you, there's a difference between ego and confidence. You're allowed to miss me. It's okay."

She giggled, and the sound teased him. It had been way too long since he'd heard the melodic sound. Her laughter always indicated she was at ease with him. He couldn't believe the thoughts that were forming in his head, but he had craved the sound of her voice. He joined in her amusement.

When the laughter faded, they proceeded to have a decent conversation—the first one they had had in a long while. They talked for the next several minutes. She grilled him about the mission. He told her about Mrs. Ojo. He, in turn, asked about work and her family. Their conversation flowed as freely as it had when they dated, the same way it did that night in Abuja. He didn't ask her about his marriage proposal because he didn't want to spoil the mood.

He frowned, however, when he asked about her job. There was something about the way she responded that made him aware work was the reason for the call.

Jabir decided to find out what was wrong. "I'm enjoying this talk, but I have a feeling there's something else. You wanna talk about it?"

She remained silent.

"Damisi," he persisted, "have you given any more thought to my proposal?" He hadn't wanted to ask but couldn't help himself. He wanted to know. He needed to know.

She exhaled. "That's the reason I called."

Jabir rubbed his forehead. Part of him told him he wouldn't like what she was about to say.

"I've been thinking…"

"And?"

"Tomorrow, I'll put in my resignation at work and go to Kenya for a while."

Jabir couldn't describe the shock he felt. The words she just spoke felt like a jab to his throat.

"Why would you do that? Is the idea of getting married to me so repulsive that you would lose everything over it?"

"Jabir, we can't just get married because of a baby, and getting out of the public eye for a while is the right thing to do—"

Jabir shot up from the bed. "People have done stranger things. And in what world do you think I would let you to go to Kenya with my child? I guess you didn't hear me correctly the last time. I'll fight you for him or her if I have to. Please don't make me."

"Please don't do this. You'll have access to the baby. I wouldn't deprive you of that, but I can't marry you. Not like this," Damisi pleaded.

Jabir detected a hint of emotion in her voice. As angry as he was, he couldn't stand her tears. He had to make it back to Lagos the next day. "You're trying to be a martyr for no reason at all. If you want to throw away everything, okay, but don't go anywhere until I get back into the city."

"I can only wear so many oversized sweaters and shirts before I'm noticed."

"Just hold on. I'll be home tomorrow. Please."

Her "okay" was faint, but he was grateful.

Without another response, she disconnected the call. Jabir stared at his phone for a few minutes. An array of emotions ran through him, starting with frustration at Damisi's insistence on being a martyr.

There was not only love between them, but a deep attraction. He had always known it, and the way she responded to his touch the night of the gala confirmed it. So why she was fighting him so hard was frustrating. Maybe if he told her he loved her, it would change her mind—make her see things differently. But sadly, that was no guarantee because he told her he loved her six years ago, and she still walked away. He felt empathy toward her dilemma, but in the end, the determination to make her see things his way won.

The last emotion forced a sigh out of him. He couldn't carry her over his shoulder to the altar, and he really didn't want to take her to court. He looked up to the ceiling. It had been a really long time since he needed God's help. Things had been going fine. He—Jabir—had been making things happen just fine. He shook his head. No need to bother a God who was probably busy with people who were more dependent than he was.

He rested his head on the pillow. He'd sleep now, and by morning he knew he would be focused enough to come up with a solution to his problem. He was going to get Damisi to agree to his proposal. His child's future was at stake.

Jabir had pushed to the back of his mind the teasing and ridicule that went along with not having his father in the home, especially when the news broke of his other family in Nigeria. If it had not been for the youth camp his mother sent him and his brothers, things would have been different. Jabir was well aware some children who came from divorce, separation, or even abandonment turned out okay, but he had a chance to make things different for his child. He wasn't going to rely on the odds. Besides, he couldn't bear sharing its mother with some other man as they raised his child in happily-ever-after land.

It wasn't until after seven the following evening that Jabir got into his car and headed to Lagos. He had performed two stent and one angioplasty procedure. He then checked in on Mrs. Ojo. She was still in ICU but was stable. His plan was to make it to Lagos, see Damisi and come back early the next day. He pulled out of the parking lot and headed toward Ajeotu road when his pager went off. He pulled out the device he had been given the first day he got to the hospital. He glanced at the screen, then found a spot to park the car. He pulled out his phone and dialed the nurse on duty.

"Dr. Danjuma, I know you're on your way to Lagos, but

you said to call you if anything changed in Mrs. Ojo's condition…"

"What is it?"

"She stopped breathing, sir."

Jabir felt a clamp squeeze his heart. What could have happened? He just saw her. He disconnected the call and turned the car around, speeding back the way he came.

Chapter 14

I'm on my way. ~J

Damisi paced the corner of the waiting room of her doctor's office. She checked her watch again, 4:24 P.M. Jabir should be here by now. She had gotten that text nearly two hours ago. It was because of him that she took the late doctor's appointment. She had tried calling him, but he wasn't answering. She knew he wasn't so used to driving in Lagos, but because of her, there hadn't been time to call David his driver. A pang of guilt and a wave of fear overtook her. Was he okay?

After her late-night call to him two days ago, he had called her early the next morning to check on her. By evening, when he was supposed to be back in Lagos, she got a call from him about some complication with his patient. Damisi was surprised at how disappointed she was.

Barely a few days ago, they wanted to kill each other. They spent almost all night talking about his patient. She could tell how passionate he was about what he did. She always found that trait about him really attractive. He was a true comforter. The only issue was he didn't want anyone comforting him.

Jabir rushed into the doctor's office, and she let out a sigh of relief. He rushed toward her, and she surprised herself by opening up her arms to welcome his embrace. She held on to him for a few minutes longer than she should.

He studied her and caressed her cheek with the back of his hand. "You okay? I got here as fast as I could."

She nodded, not trusting herself to speak. She saw the skeptical look in his eyes. She couldn't explain it either. They weren't in a good place with so much between them, but she needed him. The last two days had left her feeling vulnerable and afraid.

"Are they ready for us?"

"Yes." She turned and looked at the nurse and nodded, signaling she was now ready.

The nurse showed them to a room in the back. Damisi handed Jabir her purse while she followed the nurse to give a urine sample and have her vitals done. Soon after, she reentered the room followed by Dr. Leonard. She made the introductions. He and Jabir exchanged greetings. On being told that Jabir was a cardiac surgeon, Dr. Leonard's eyes lit up, and his smile grew wider like he had found his long-lost brother. His look of surprise though was the funniest. That was the reaction of most people because of Jabir's young look but he was so smart he had skipped one grade in elementary school and another in middle school.

Jabir helped her get on top of the examination table and placed the pillow under her head. He held her hand and smiled at her.

"So how's Mummy doing?" The doctor placed his hands on her stomach and began examining her uterus.

"I'm doing okay. I just feel heavy." Damisi gave a weary smile.

Dr. Leonard smiled back. "You're measuring a little bigger than fourteen weeks, so I'm going to order a sonogram."

"Okay, doctor," Damisi said. Jabir helped her up.

Dr. Leonard looked up from her file and asked more questions about her general well-being. "Let me get the nurse to check on the room and we'll take you back."

"Okay," she and Jabir said in unison.

Soon after, Damisi lay on her back in another room. Her fingers were interlocked with Jabir's, who was standing beside her. She could feel him tense up in nervous anticipation. She used her thumb to caress the back of his hand. They hadn't said anything to each other, but their silence spoke volumes. He smiled at her with his eyes glazed over. She had always loved his tough "I am man, hear me roar" persona, but his sexiness was in those rare occasions he bared himself to her. She wished she could capture the emotion in the room in a bottle. She'd want to relive this moment over and over.

"It's gonna be okay," Damisi reassured him.

He nodded. She searched for another comforting word when the cold gel hit her stomach. The nurse technician spread it across her mid-section. Damisi turned her head to the right toward the screen.

"You ready?" the nurse technician asked.

Damisi looked at Jabir. They both nodded. He bent and kissed her forehead.

"Okay, here we go…"

Damisi's heart thumped against her chest as she heard the baby's heartbeat. She had heard it before, but not with Jabir. She peered at the screen. She blinked. She looked up at Jabir who had an equally confused look on his face. They both turned back to the screen and were met with the technician's sheepish grin as she nodded.

"Is that…"

"Yes, it is. You're having twins, the nurse said. "I can't really tell what they are…but definitely two babies."

Damisi began to sob as Jabir reached down and kissed her repeatedly. He kissed her on her lips, eyes, nose and finally her forehead. The words *thank you* accompanied each kiss. Damisi sobbed some more—tears of joy, something she never thought she would experience again. But in the hands of the Potter, her imperfection had been made perfect. Aunty Bola said it best—children are gifts from God.

After she had cleaned up, Damisi and Jabir sat in Dr. Leonard's office. They were still shocked and reeling with excitement while the doctor explained the potential risks of multiple births. She couldn't believe she was having twins. It wasn't impossible—she just couldn't believe it.

"Damisi, I know you have a hectic schedule, but remember what I said about multiple births. They come with risks. You have to slow down some," Dr. Leonard said.

"Oh, she will, trust me." Jabir looked at her. The way his brow rose, she knew he was daring her to counter.

"But everything is okay, right?" She heard the panic in her voice. Jabir squeezed her hand.

"Better than okay, but still read the pamphlet I gave you. If you have any discomfort of any kind, call me." Dr. Leonard stood, and so did they. They set her next appointment, and she and Jabir walked out of the doctor's office.

Jabir walked her to her car and got in with her. "Have dinner with me. I have to get back first thing in the morning. Please."

The calmness in his voice warmed her heart.

"Okay, what did you do to with the real Jabir?" She tried to laugh, but he looked serious. She lifted a hand to his cheek. "Hey, what's wrong? Don't tell me because you're having twins, you're now a big softie." Although the nurse had said she wasn't sure of the sexes yet, she secretly wanted girls, but more than that, healthy babies.

"Don't tease me when I'm tired and hungry, woman."

"Tomorrow is Saturday, so I guess I can stay up late, but I can't go out."

"Yeah, I know…celebrity struggles. Okay. Your place or mine?"

"Mine."

It was his turn to laugh. "Home turf advantage?"

"Smart man." She was so happy at the news of healthy babies that it was okay to pretend with their father that everything was okay. She just had to remember where pretense ended, and reality began.

"Funny. I'll see you in an hour with take-out."

"Please call your driver to drive you. You look really worn out."

"Well, I'll be…the lady cares about me." He winked and got out of the car.

———

Dinner was a good thing. It would give them a chance to talk. Talking was good. It was about time. Maybe she could get him to see marriage was not an option for them, especially just because of a baby—even if there were two of them.

Fresh out of the shower and moisturized, Damisi slipped on the pink-and-white caftan Moji had approved of. She wasn't in the mood to dress up, but neither did she want to look like a hag. Despite her pleas, Moji had left the house five minutes earlier with a flimsy excuse. Damisi secured her hair atop her head, put on some lip gloss and exited the room when she heard the doorbell ring.

Dressed in a simple violet polo and some jeans, Jabir looked and smelled good enough to eat.

He smiled down at her. "Hey you."

"Hey yourself." She stepped aside for him to enter. He headed straight for the kitchen with aromas of curry, pepper and thyme following him. Her stomach growled. She couldn't believe her eyes when he began removing the contents of the bag. He brought out grilled fish, plantains, stewed goat meat, honey chicken, two kinds of rice and fruit.

"Are you feeding an army?"

"I didn't know what you wanted. Besides, my girls have to be feed." He wiggled his eyebrows.

She frowned. *His girls?* Well, that didn't take long for him to remind her this was about the babies. She tried to give him a smile. None came. She turned to the cupboard and retrieved the plates. He dished some food for her and himself. Next, he put some fruit in a bowl then took the plates to the table.

"Let's eat in the living room," she said.

They threw down all the sofa pillows to make a cozy fortress, then moved the center table so they would be able to rest their backs on the sofa and face the television. She said grace and began to eat. For the first couple of minutes, they were both silent.

"I hope you like the meal. It's from that place you took me to last year," Jabir said, breaking the awkward silence.

She swallowed. "It's fantastic. Thank you."

They discussed safe topics for the remainder of the meal, and Damisi was grateful for the attempt he made at easing the tension between them. He cleared the dishes and came back to join her in the living room.

He moved the fruit bowl closer and picked up a kiwi with his fork and twirled it in the air before eating it.

"That doctor, the nurses...do you trust them?" he asked.

"Yeah. I only see a particular nurse and Dr. Leonard, and both of them have earned my trust. How long I can keep this a secret, I don't know." She had to believe they wouldn't leak her story to a gossip blog, but knew money could do anything.

"So what happened the night you called me wanting to go to Kenya? You sounded shaken up."

Damisi contemplated telling him. She looked into his eyes. They seemed sincere, but she was concerned he might use the information as ammunition to push his "marry me" agenda.

Maybe she was just being paranoid. Feeling she could trust him, she told him of the scare she had. After the interview with the prophetess, Gary, her agent, had reminded her of her photo shoot for The Right Time foundation. It was the same day, and she had completely forgotten. With Eno tied up, she had gone there alone. While Damisi was changing, a stylist had walked in on her. Her pregnancy-swollen breasts and the small baby bump she usually hid with large clothes had been in plain view. In the young woman's defense, Damisi wasn't supposed to be there at that time. She was supposed to be in makeup, but had gotten the times mixed up. It was a mistake that could have cost her dearly, and it rattled her. She needed to resign before she was exposed.

Jabir's expression was unreadable. Then he said, "This is why you should consider my proposal."

"Not again, please. I've seen you three times in six years, twice in the last year alone."

"So, what's your question?"

"Why are you so intent on tying yourself to me when I didn't matter to you all these years? When the babies grow up, what happens?"

"You assume you didn't matter."

"You have a funny way of showing it if I did."

"Don't you dare." He narrowed his eyes and turned his body toward her. "You left me…why?"

"You know why."

"That's crap. Oh yeah, I remember you saying something about me not knowing the meaning of commitment."

"Well…"

"Give me a break. We had been dating for a year. You changed. We had our differences, but that didn't mean I wasn't committed to you!"

"Forgive me for giving my life to Christ. You made me feel like I had betrayed you. You were no longer first in my life, and you couldn't deal with it." She furrowed her brows. "Why are we even talking about this after all this while?"

"Because…I admit, it bothered at me."

"Then why did you not fight for me? Come after me? You

just let me go. You made your decision so don't act like the victim now."

He stood.

Damisi stood as well. They stared each other down. Passion, anger and hurt were just some of the emotions she could see in his eyes—the same things she felt. Her first thought was to shut down, but that was part of the problem. They didn't talk.

"Sammy Modu," he said.

She placed her hands on her hips. "What? What does Sammy have to do with anything?" Damisi asked, her eyes searching his. The mention of her ex was a curve ball she didn't expect.

"You started hanging around him just days later. You left me for him."

"No, I didn't. My heart begged for you to fight for me, but you didn't. He was just a friend." She paused. "But you wasted no time in replacing me. I saw you."

He looked at her, confused. "What do you mean *saw* me?" He walked toward her.

She held out one hand to stop him. "After our fight… remember, the one where you threatened to find better fish in the sea. Well, I saw you with your fish, and might I add, she was ugly."

"How mature. But I still don't know what you're talking about."

"Remember that night I told you I was going for an outreach program with my church group at the homeless shelter? Well, instead they changed the venue, and we ended up in the hotel downtown to pray for runaways and prostitutes." She cracked her knuckles. "I walked up and saw you were dragging this lady out of the hotel. I froze and watched, hoping no one else saw you, but they did. Back at the church center, our relationship was the topic of the sermon: the danger of being unequally yoked."

She saw fury creep into his eyes. *Where did he get off getting angry?* "I came over to see you the next day. I asked you about your evening, and you lied to me. You told me you were at home, but I saw you," she yelled.

"So you broke up with me, took the job with KTN and ran away." He fumed.

"Is that all you have to say?"

"Sweetheart, you don't want to hear what I have to say." He plopped down on the chair and bowed his head. Damisi saw him shaking, trying to control his temper. "I don't freaking believe this. You mean you broke up with me because of something you saw and your church friends drummed into your head?"

"Your reputation preceded you, and I've seen heartbreak before. It's not a pretty thing…"

"So you decided to do the honors without even giving me a chance after all we shared?" He rubbed his hand on his head. "Do you have any idea what you've done? The years you've cost us…why couldn't you just ask me?"

"I did!"

"I mean come right out and ask about what you saw?"

"Why didn't you fight for me?" she asked, ignoring him.

"Oh, no you don't. You will not wiggle your way out of this one. You're the one who sat on your high horse and decided both our fates." He walked over to the mantle and leaned against it.

Damisi let out an exaggerated breath and walked toward him. He glanced over at her and turned away.

Damisi spoke softly. "I can't turn back the hands of time. I was young, as were you. The attraction and love we shared was fierce, intense and the strongest thing I've ever felt. Quite frankly, it scared me. When I became saved and we started having problems, things got out of hand."

"You think?" His sarcasm wasn't lost on her, but she ignored it. Jabir turned and looked at her. The fire in his eyes was still burning bright. "You 'Christians' amaze me. All of you sat in judgment of me that night. Not one of the so-called brethren advised you to check with your man and see what happened. Instead, they crucified me when they had no clue." He let out a mocking laugh. "Well, look at us now. The single Christian woman, pregnant for the still unsaved man. I wonder what the brethren would say about that." He walked away, leaving her standing there, and headed for the door.

Damisi was speechless until he opened the door. "Where are you going?"

"Home. After all, I'm not worthy to be in your presence."

"That's not fair." She went after him.

He turned. "Go to bed. Oh, by the way, that woman was Yvette, my friend Bernard's wife. She used to be an addict. That day, she was at the wrong place and needed me to get her before Bernard found out, so I did."

Damisi's eyes widened. She was sure her shock was written all over her face.

"How's that for an unsaved man?" He walked out, slamming the door behind him.

Damisi wanted the ground to open up so she could disappear. She dragged herself to bed.

"Oh Lord, I've made a mess of things. Please show me how to fix it," she whispered. She couldn't help but think of the irony of Mathew 7:2 *For with the judgment you pronounce you will be judged, and with the measure you use it will be measured to you.* Shortly, she'd get to feel what it was like to be judged. She wrapped her arms around her body and got in as much of a fetal position as she could. She then drifted off into a restless sleep.

Chapter 15

"Did you see *Tafia Central*?" Eno threw a copy of the gossip rag on Damisi's desk. Damisi looked at her friend and down at the paper. She scanned it quickly, but didn't see her name or face anywhere on it.

"No, why? What's going on?"

"Where is Jabir?"

Damisi's heart and head hurt at the same time at the mention of that name. She hadn't heard from him since he walked out of her house. All weekend she had tried to call him to talk, but he didn't answer the phone. The only correspondence she got from him was when he left Lagos and when he got to Badagry.

"In Badagry, I suppose. His mission won't be over 'til the weekend."

"Okay. I know you two still have issues…"

"That's an understatement."

"Well, whatever. You need to do something fast. Page six has a picture of the two of you with the caption, 'Couple Alert.'"

Damisi rushed to page six and saw a picture of them at

the gala and another of Jabir leaving KTN. "Who could have taken this picture of him coming out of the studio?"

Eno shrugged. "It wouldn't have been a problem, but then I went online and most of the comments speculate you have a baby bump."

Damisi froze. The week before, it was the scare with the stylist, this week a gossip rag. She had done what he said and waited for him to come back, but instead of talking about their next course of action, they ended up fighting and he now wasn't speaking to her. She couldn't keep it any longer.

"You need to do something before the media eats you alive." Eno sat down.

"I know," Damisi whispered. "Mrs. Kofo is back. I'll see her today."

"Today? I thought you'd marry the man instead. He's fine, and you obviously love him."

"Looks will fade and see where love has gotten me." Damisi flipped through the magazine again. She nodded. "I'll soon be fifteen weeks. I need to tell her today."

"Please call Jabir first. Whatever the reason for your fight, let him in on what you're about to do." Eno looked at her watch. "I gotta go…Suzy's show."

Damisi called Jabir all morning and afternoon, but his phone was off. When she called the hospital, she was told he was in surgery. She wanted him to know of her decision to tell her boss and take a leave of absence. Immediately after she made the announcement, her pregnancy would become public knowledge, and she didn't want him to be blindsided. It would be better for her to disappear for a while on her own terms rather than be called out by the media. She was one of them and knew exactly what would happen if anyone leaked this but her. She called Jabir again. No response. He would be upset, but she'd prefer to deal with him than the whole country.

Her shift had been over for hours, and the deed could've

been done by now, but her appointment with Mrs. Kofo kept being moved. Damisi cracked her knuckles and adjusted her new multi-print top and matching flared skirt and left her office.

Damisi walked up just as Mrs. Kofo was escorting her previous appointment out. Damisi's heart pounded in her chest. Her throat went dry.

"I apologize for keeping you waiting, my dear. Any time you get back from vacation, the whole world has an emergency." Mrs. Kofo ushered Damisi into the office. The space always felt so welcoming—probably had something to do with its tan tones.

Mrs. Kofo had run the Lagos station since its inception fifteen years ago. She used her degrees in journalism, marketing and business to elevate the station to the heights it was known for. Damisi admired her professionalism and doggedness, especially in a business where the women were often only the pretty faces in front of the camera, while the men were in the boardroom. Mrs. Kofo showed she could do both and made fifty look like thirty while doing it.

Her dark brown hair was cut in a short bob and complemented her milk-chocolate skin.

"We haven't talked since the gala. Good job. The hosts are still raving about you. But then again, you're the best at what you do, so no surprises there." Mrs. Kofo smiled and pointed Damisi to a seat by the windows.

Damisi smiled. "Thank you, Ma."

"The trip to see your dad must have left you well rested. You seem to have gained some weight." Mrs. Kofo chuckled.

Damisi held back a gasp and gave a weary smile.

Mrs. Kofo studied Damisi for a moment and continued. "You're lucky, being able to gain weight and lose it whenever you want."

Damisi giggled nervously at the off-handed comment, but that was the confirmation she needed to know what she was about to do was right. With Mrs. Kofo back, it was only a matter of time before her secret was out.

"So what can I do for my number one presenter today?"

"Err…Ma, I'd like to thank you for the opportunity you've given me at this station. The *Becoming Ruth* show has been my dream come true." Damisi knew she was rambling, but it was the only way she could hold back the tears that were threatening to fall.

Mrs. Kofo frowned then placed her hand on her chest. "Damisi, please don't tell me you're resigning. Are you going to another station?"

Damisi shook her head vigorously. "Ah no, Ma! What I was trying to say was that—" *Why did I just say no? That was the perfect opening.* She silently prayed for strength.

"Child, say what is on your mind, or we're going to be here all day. Dinner and homework won't do themselves." The older woman checked her phone.

"Okay, Ma, I need to tell you something. You see…" Damisi began.

Mrs. Kofo raised her brows to usher her along. Damisi opened her mouth to speak when her phone rang. Luther Vandross's "Dance with my Father" ringtone told her it was her father. She wanted to ignore it at first. She'd call him on her way back home. That way she'd have something to tell him about this meeting.

It stopped and started right back again. She couldn't ignore it. She panicked, then quickly figured answering the phone would buy her more time. She wasn't ready for this, after all.

"Madam, may I take this? It's my father."

Mrs. Kofo nodded.

"Daddy, hold on." Damisi muted the phone when Mrs. Kofo stood and walked to her desk. "I'm sorry, Ma."

"It's okay, my dear. It's late, so you're going to have to reschedule this. I have a father in the village, so I know they can be needy, but I also have a husband and kids I need to get back to." She began gathering her things.

Damisi nodded and placed the phone back to her ear. "Hello…hello?" The line was dead. She frowned. "Ugh, network issues."

Mrs. Kofo strapped her handbag on her shoulder and held her portfolio and keys in the other. Damisi stood and gathered her things as well. Her father had hung up, but Mrs. Kofo had already told her to reschedule, so whatever her father had to say was going to be said once she got in the car and called him back. A few more minutes, and she would have said what she needed to say. Now she had to wait until the next day.

Minutes later, Damisi strapped herself in her car and started the engine. She then placed her Bluetooth in her ear and dialed her father. After a couple of rings, someone answered the phone, but there was silence.

"Hello?" Damisi pulled out of her parking space. Her heart raced.

"Daddy, please talk to me. What's wrong?"

"*Binti yangu,* how fast can you get here?" Madam Paulina asked.

Her breathing stopped. Why was Madam Paulina calling her on her dad's phone? Something was not right. The older woman always called Damisi "her daughter," but something about the way she said "*binti yangu*" this time, was scary.

"Madam Paulina, what's wrong?" Damisi pulled her car over when the tears that had begun to fall blurred her vision.

Madam Paulina sniffed. Damisi had never known the woman to cry. She always seemed so strong. "Your father had been complaining of headaches. I begged him to call the doctor. He said he was fine." She paused and drew in a breath.

"You're scaring me. What happened?"

"Your father had a stroke."

"What?"

"Calm down. Remember your condition. The doctors want to speak with you." Madam Paulina sighed.

Tears began to stream down her face. Her head began to hurt. She couldn't think. After a couple more questions that Madam Paulina couldn't answer, Damisi hung up the phone.

She had to go to Kenya. She dialed Jabir. Still no answer. She yanked off her Bluetooth and flung it across the passenger seat. She gripped her steering wheel tighter than usual. Why had she thought he would now be available? Nothing about her concerned him but the babies. It was a fact he had made clear, and she chided herself for not getting the message yet.

Later that night, she talked to Moji and Aunty Bola. Both of them were worried and agreed she should travel immediately. Next, she called Dr. Leonard on his private line. Having twenty-four-hour access to her doctor came with her celebrity status. It was a privilege she tried not to use, but this was an exception.

After a brief conversation, he told her she was safe to travel. By the time she had sent Mrs. Kofo an email telling of her need to travel urgently and purchased a ticket, Damisi was exhausted and hungry. After a quick shower and a meal of leftover yam porridge, she lay down in her bed. Sleep came quickly, but she didn't indulge it until she had read Psalm 25, concentrating on verses 15 to 18. *My eyes are continually toward the Lord, For He will pluck my feet out of the net. Turn to me and be gracious to me, for I am lonely and afflicted. The troubles of my heart are enlarged; bring me out of my distresses. Look upon my affliction and my trouble, and forgive all my sins.*

She had let go of God's hand once. She was not about to do it again.

Chapter 16

The mid-June heat was becoming unbearable, but it was nothing compared to the last couple of days. It was about 7:00 P.M., and Jabir was speeding down the Lagos-Badagry expressway. His sole focus was getting to Damisi. He still couldn't believe she had thought so little of him—that he'd been in a hotel picking up prostitutes. Her misconceptions and his pride and lie about that night had kept them apart for six years. He hadn't meant to lie to her, but they were already having problems, and he saw the judgment in her eyes.

When she left him, he relived his issues with his father's abandonment. Just like his father, everything was going great, then their whole life was turned upside down. Zayd Danjuma had kissed them good night, and by morning he was gone. But this departure was like no other. He never came back.

The more Jabir thought about it, the closer he came to the conclusion that even the truth of his whereabouts that night wouldn't have saved them. The only thing left to do now was to concentrate on the future.

He turned his car onto the highway leading to Damisi's house. He had allowed his anger to get the best of him, and he had neglected to respond to her messages. Part of it had to do with his schedule, but he really knew anger was at the root.

The previous evening, on getting back to the doctor's quarters, he reached for his phone. Despite his anger, he had missed her. It was then he noticed his phone was missing. To get a new phone in the rural area proved to be a chore. When he finally got one, he realized he didn't have any of his contacts. He had sent Damisi an email, but got her out-of-office message. No information, just saying she was currently out of the office. The uncertainty of his present situation was driving him crazy.

Jabir exhaled when he drove into her complex and saw her car and Moji's car parked outside. She was home. He found a parking spot and walked up to the door. After the third ring of the doorbell, the door opened. Moji stared at him with what he thought was fear in her eyes. She looked like she had been crying.

'Moji? What's wrong? Is Damisi okay?" Jabir asked.

He thrust his hands in his pocket to hide his trembling fingers. A thousand negative thoughts passed through his mind before he heard her say, "Yes, she's fine. Come in." She sniffed, opened the door wider and let him through.

Seated in the living room was a woman whose hair was laced with gray.

"Where's Damisi?" Jabir whispered, glancing back over Moji.

"She's not here."

"Is home?" His patience was wearing thin.

"Moji, who is that?" the older woman asked. As Jabir came to face her, he knew immediately who she was. She was Moji's mother, the woman Damisi affectionately called Aunty Bola.

"Good evening, Ma," Jabir said.

The woman studied him from over the brim of her glasses.

Why is Moji crying? Where is Damisi?

"*Eh hen,* good evening. Have a seat." Aunty Bola instructed.

Jabir hesitated for a moment before obeying the woman's command. His eyes shifted to Moji. "Where's Damisi?"

"Are you her friend?" Aunty Bola asked.

"Mummy, this is Dr. Jabir Danjuma. Jabir, this is my mom," Moji said.

Jabir nodded his head. "It's a pleasure, Ma. Now I see where Moji gets her looks."

The woman blushed, then the smile on her face quickly disappeared. She stood and began pacing. She placed her index finger between her teeth, then stopped and shook her head. When she looked back at him, there was anger and disappointment in her eyes.

"So you're the man that lured my poor Titi and got her pregnant?"

"Mummy, please," Moji said.

Jabir sat in shock. His mouth flew open, but no sound came out. For one, he didn't lure anybody and two, he didn't know any Titi.

Aunty Bola faced Moji. "Don't beg me. That's what's wrong with you young people. You're always hiding your evil." Then she turned to Jabir, "*Oya* young man, are you the one?"

"With all due respect, Ma, I didn't lure anybody, and I certainly don't know who Titi is."

Moji looked like she was trying not to laugh.

Aunty Bola raised her hand and shook it vigorously. "Don't say it again. So you mean you people can sleep together without knowing each other's full names?"

Jabir eyes caught Moji's. He clenched his jaw. What had he just walked into? Then it occurred to him that the woman called Damisi by the abbreviated version of her middle name. He looked for Moji to help him out, but she shrugged. *I have bigger problems than this. Where is Damisi?*

"Err, Ma—" Jabir began.

"So what are you going to do about my niece's pregnancy? Are you just going to leave her like that? With all she is going through."

Since Moji was being of no help, he was going to have to get this conversation back on track before it geared even farther off course.

"Damisi and I are making plans. Could someone please tell me where she is?" Jabir demanded. He knew the bass in his voice was evident, but he needed answers.

"She had to go to Kenya. Her dad had a stroke," Moji said.

"Stroke? When? Why didn't she tell me?" He fumed.

How could she just leave the country and not say anything? She's pregnant for goodness' sake.

"Jabir, she tried calling you—" Moji started.

He rubbed his head and closed his eyes, trying to banish the thoughts going through his mind. "My phone is missing. Long story." He sighed. "Do you have a phone number?" he asked. His eyes shifted from Moji to her mother. He didn't care who answered as along as someone did.

"Oh, so now you're showing concern? When you ran off and left her, you weren't concerned then?" Moji's mom asked.

Jabir knew she didn't really want an answer because she turned and walked to the kitchen. It was just as well because he was becoming irritated with her judgmental attitude. The only things that kept him from responding to her were Damisi and the home training his mother had given him.

"Sorry about that," Moji said.

Jabir shrugged.

Moji spent the next few minutes filling him in on the events of the last couple of days.

"All this happened in a couple of days?"

"Yep. We dropped her off at the airport this morning."

Jabir paused. He tried to come up with his next course of

action, but came up blank. He had two more days to the completion of the mission. He couldn't just abandon it, but he was worried sick. Had she seen the doctor before she left? Why had he been so stubborn and shut the door of communication? There was no telling how pissed she was at him.

"Can I get an address or a phone number?" he asked.

Moji shook her head. "Not until she gets there. She never uses her Naija number when she gets to Kenya. It's a good thing 'cause if I had a number, I would give it to you although she would kill me."

He smiled. "I'm glad you're in my corner."

"Hmm…. the last time I stood up for you, she nearly killed me. I had to make it up to her by buying maternity clothes." She giggled. "By the way, you owe me ten thousand naira."

He grinned at the thought of Damisi in maternity clothes. He liked the caftan she wore the last time he saw her. "I'm good for it. That's if your cousin doesn't run me to an early grave."

"Funny, she could say the same thing about you."

"I should leave before your mom comes back out." He walked to the door, then paused. "If Damisi calls, please tell her to call me. Good night."

Jabir had no idea how he got to the guesthouse that night. His mind had been preoccupied with thoughts of Damisi and what she must be going through. He knew she was close to her father and hoped everything was all right. If it were up to him, he would be in Kenya the next day, but he still had an obligation in Badagry he couldn't abandon.

He unlocked the door and looked around the empty house. For the first time in his life, it seemed like he had no control over his situation, and that wasn't a good feeling. He plopped down on the large leather sofa and rubbed his hands on his head. He tried to think, but no thoughts came.

Restless, he picked up the remote and turned on the television. He had no idea what channel showed what, but needed some distraction. Not finding anything, he left the channel on an infomercial and walked into the kitchen. He came back shortly with a drink of water and then a man appeared on the screen.

It was one of those televangelist people. Jabir mumbled, "I'm not in the mood." He picked up the remote to mute the sound when he heard the man say, "God has placed you where you are at this moment for a reason. Trust He is working everything out."

"Yeah, right." Jabir powered off the television. He definitely wasn't in the mood.

Chapter 17

Damisi pressed her fingers against her eyelids. It was all she could do to stop the tears from flowing. She looked at her father sleeping on the bed in the middle of the hospital room. She had been in Kenya for a little more than five hours, and he hadn't said a word. Her male cousin Ita picked her up from the airport. Ita, an architect based in Nairobi, was the son of her father's deceased brother. He was like a big brother to her. They were close growing up, but didn't communicate as much when she went abroad to study. Although they kept in touch, their closeness waned with distance. However, any time they saw each other, it was like they were never apart.

She continued to stare at her father She had lost count of how many times she had uttered the words *Thank you, Jesus* since she arrived.

Madam Paulina found her father just in time for him to be rushed to the hospital and operated on. The doctor came in earlier and told her they were very lucky. The small artery that had ruptured only had a small leak, so the damage wasn't that bad. The operation was a success, and all bleeding had stopped. His prognosis was good, but Damisi needed him to open his eyes. She lifted her hand and caressed head. She rubbed gently, and the tears she had been holding back fell.

"Daddy, can you hear me? Please wake up."

She got no response. Not even a stir or flicker of his eyelids. She pulled up one of the two chairs in the private hospital room at Kisumu General and sat near his bed. She rested her head on the bed and prayed. She prayed for Jesus to cover her father with His precious blood. She asked forgiveness for all the times she had missed Christmas with him when she was busy with work. She even missed calling him this past Easter being so wrapped up in her own problems. Finally, she prayed for healing.

She lifted her head and saw that Ita and Madam Paulina had entered. She tried to form a smile, but couldn't.

"My daughter, you came here straight from the airport. It's been more than five hours. You have to go home. You have to eat and rest," Madam Paulina said. Her eyes travelled to Damisi's stomach and pleaded at the same time.

"I'm fine. I had something from the cafeteria." Damisi glanced over to Ita, expecting some kind of support. He shook his head and walked toward her.

"*Cuzo, howayu?*" He patted rubbed her back.

"I'm fine," Damisi answered. Ita hadn't changed. Despite his two advanced degrees, he often spoke to her in *sheng.* He often teased that he liked speaking to her in *sheng,* so she wouldn't forget the Kenyan slang language entirely for Nigerian Pidgin English.

"Let my driver take you and Madam Paulina home. I'll stay with *mdosi,*" Ita said, referring to her father.

"I don't want him to wake up and not see me."

"The doctor said with the sedation, he'll likely be out for a while. Come back when you're rested."

Damisi opened her mouth to protest, but he continued, "You're pregnant, and you don't need the stress."

On their drive from the airport earlier, she had given him the brief version of her story. He had questions, but she wasn't in the mood. She promised they would talk later. Her father was foremost on her mind. She hadn't even had time to call Jabir. She called Moji when she arrived and was told about Jabir's phone being lost. She could only imagine his anger at her being gone and having to deal with Aunty Bola's cold reception.

"*Tafadhali*. Please." He spoke in Swahili and stretched out his hand to help her from the chair.

Madam Paulina remained silent. Damisi could see the fear in the older woman's eyes. She went to her. The two women held each other in a long embrace, drawing strength from each other. Damisi broke the embrace first, and in silence, both of them made their way to the door. Damisi looked back and saw Ita had taken her place in the chair.

"We'll soon be back," she whispered.

———

THE NEXT DAY, DAMISI SHIVERED AND SECURED HER THROW around her body. The temperature in the room was colder than she was used to, or maybe it was just her raging hormones. She looked down at her sleeping father. He woke up about two hours ago. She had never been so excited to see his eyes or hear him call her name in all her life. The excitement didn't last long as he fell back asleep shortly after. The doctor said that pretty soon, he would be able to stay awake for longer periods at a time. She was relieved, though. He was going to be okay. Over the last two days, she had prayed hard and cried harder, and God had answered. The road to recovery might be long, but she felt good about his prospects.

Ita left for Nairobi on urgent business after they had talked to the doctor. Madam Paulina was running some errands, so

Damisi was left to her thoughts. She walked toward the window and stared out of it. There were some decisions she would have to make that she wasn't looking forward to. Her dad's illness changed things for her. She was going to have to stay in Kenya a little longer, and her babies weren't going to stop growing.

She placed a protective hand over her stomach and rubbed. This meant that the option of coming clean about her condition to her employers before her condition was visible was now out of the question. It wasn't something she wanted to do via email or over the phone. She wasn't as well known in Kenya as she was in Nigeria, but the risk of being outed by the media still scared her. Should she go back to Nigeria, resign properly, and then come back to take care of her father? Her heart ached. She felt alone.

Her father stirred from his slumber. Damisi rushed over to him.

"Daddy, you're awake?"

He nodded. His eyes glistened, and his lips quivered. He looked tired and groggy. He opened his mouth, but no sound came out. The effort seemed to make him weak.

Damisi ran out to get the doctor, praying this time her father would stay awake longer. When she returned, she smiled because he was still awake and seemed aware. She kissed his forehead and cheeks repeatedly.

"Thank you, Jesus. Daddy, you're going to be fine."

He managed a smile.

There was a slight knock on the door, and it opened to the physician on duty and a nurse. Damisi stepped aside for them to examine her father. She kept rubbing her hands together in supplication. There were series of hand and facial motions the doctor asked her dad to do. She walked back and forth waiting on some more news.

"Let's take him for some tests. It shouldn't take long," the doctor said.

One painful hour later, Madam Paulina had arrived, and the nurses wheeled her father back in.

"You came," her father whispered to her.

Damisi went over to him, but was careful not to get in the way as the nurse worked to situate him in a comfortable position.

She walked over to the doctor, concerned edged on her forehead. "Did something happen to his memory? He saw me the last time he woke up."

"No, nothing is wrong. He was heavily sedated then. Remember, he's not such a young man, so he's bound to get forgetful sometimes." The doctor smiled at her.

"So how is he?"

"Your father is doing miraculously well. Everything looks good."

Her eyes widened in excitement. "Really?"

The doctor nodded. "His speech will be impaired, but with speech therapy, it should correct itself." He looked over at her father, then turned his attention back to her. "He would also need physical therapy and may end up walking with a cane."

She gasped.

"He's a very lucky man," the doctor said, leaving her and Madam Paulina to be alone with her dad.

"I was so worried and scared," Madam Paulina said with tears in her eyes.

Damisi held her father's hand. His eyes went to her stomach, which was now clearly visible with her babies.

"How…you?" he managed to speak. He took a deep breath. "Baby…grow." He smiled.

"You're going to be the grandfather to two babies" Damisi shared her news.

Madam Paulina squealed and came around to hug her.

"I…happy." Her father frowned. "What…father?"

She knew he was trying to ask about Jabir. That was the

one person she had tried hard not to think about, but he invaded her thoughts regardless. She hadn't talked to him, so she really didn't know, but she didn't need her dad worrying about her.

"Daddy, just rest so we can get you out of here."

____

Chapter 18

____

By Friday afternoon, her father looked much better. He had just woken up from a nap. While he was asleep, she had sent a message to Madam Paulina to prepare him something to eat. She didn't want him eating hospital food.

"You're up. I have something for you. Just hold tight." She busied herself serving him some *matoke* and rice. She knew her dad loved the plantain stew, which she always made extra spicy, so she told Madam Paulina to do the same. She propped her father up and sat on the edge of his bed. She spooned the food, blew on it and began to feed him. Her father ate slower than usual, but she was patient, making sure he drank enough water at intervals. When done, she cleared away the disposable plates and tidied up, then she came and sat back beside him.

"I'm so happy you're doing better."

He nodded.

To Damisi, he looked happy, but behind his eyes, she noticed what looked like fear and worry. "Daddy, what's wrong? Are you in pain?"

He shook his head. "Worried…you. Babies…where father?"

"Daddy, please don't worry about me—"

He frowned. "You…my daughter."

Damisi knew he had a point. She also knew the more she evaded the issue, the more he worried. She exhaled.

"I'm fine. Did I tell you I'm having twins? Jabir is a twin, so go figure." She paused, then rambled on. "He knows about the children, and he wants me to marry him. I said no." She noticed the questioning look in her father's eyes, but continued. "He doesn't love me, and I don't want to be tied down because of the babies to a man who doesn't love me."

"Job?" he asked.

"They don't know yet. I was going to tell them on Tuesday…"

"Day…Paulina…called you?" Her father nodded in understanding. "Where…young man?"

"He's still in Lagos. I haven't talked to him yet."

There was a long silence between them. Her father took a deep breath.

"Your mother…and me. My fault…stubborn."

"Daddy, please, not now. Later."

"You need…hear this. Grandchildren."

She nodded, seeing as he was intent on having this conversation she'd wanted to have forever. Damisi folded her arms across her chest as if she was trying to shield herself from what she was about to hear. His tone was laced with regret.

"Your mother…me. In love. So…in love. Divided by me… pressure from family."

"Why, if you were so in love. What happened?"

"In 1980's…new president…Kenya. Things changed. Corruption and crime…high."

Damisi wished he would leave this story alone for another day. She filled in the blanks for him so he wouldn't have to strain. "Yes, Daddy. They taught us in history about Daniel Arap Moi."

Daniel Arap Moi was the vice president who succeeded

Jomo Kenyatta who was the first president of Kenya. According to the history books, under Moi's rule, there was nepotism, corruption, arrests of dissidents, censorship, the disbanding of tribal societies, and the closure of universities. History showed him as an autocratic leader and one who advanced his own agenda, leaving Kenya in debt.

"Me…politics. Your mother…no like. One day…raid in the house." Her father shook his head.

Damisi raised her brows in surprise. She never knew her dad was into politics, but knowing her mother and the fact she had loved a quiet life, it made sense she didn't like it.

"There was a raid in the house? Hired men?" Damisi asked for clarification.

Her father nodded.

"So what happened?"

"Mother…" He shook his head. A tear escaped.

"Daddy, what is it? What happened?"

"Your mother…that night…raped."

Damisi pressed her unsteady hand on her temples. Her heart raced in confusion. Her body shook at the five-letter word. She tried to make sense. *Was she a product of rape? Was that why her mother left? Why the marriage couldn't work?* Rape in African culture, especially in those times, was something that was looked upon as the woman's problem. Her poor mother… Tears formed in her eyes.

"Am…I?" Damisi asked the question, but was so scared of the answer.

He father wiped down his face with his hand. "No…no… no." He paused. "At the time… did not know."

"So she became pregnant with me after the rape and you didn't know if it was yours or the rapist's?" Damisi had seen this scene so many times in African movies and in real life. The woman was made to feel as though she had somehow brought it on herself. The woman's husband did little or nothing to comfort her. Often, he asked for the pregnancy to be aborted. She couldn't wrap her head around her father doing that, but considering the times, his political career and the ten-year age difference between her parents, she knew he probably had done worse.

He nodded. "Family…and I… treated her bad." He reached for her hand. "Didn't know… you… mine when born…" He lifted her sleeve, then lifted his.

Damisi eyes widened. She had never noticed that she and her dad had the same odd shaped birthmark inside their left arm. It was tiny, but noticeable.

"No…see this…until…you…one."

Damisi sobbed. "When I was born, I looked so much like Mummy, so you weren't sure I was yours. Then Mummy couldn't stand the pressure and ridicule, so she left when I was almost one?" Damisi filled in the story for him. The only reason she knew it was because she often overheard her mother and Aunty Bola when they talked. Her memory reached back to when she was eight, right after the divorce was final.

"I should never have told him," her mother had said. "He never stood by me."

"But you did. Allow him to have a relationship with his daughter. It's sad that even though you went back to him, it still didn't work," Aunty Bola had said.

"The damage had been done, and you know his family never liked that I was Nigerian," her mother had whispered.

Now it all made sense to Damisi. Between staggered breaths, she asked. "So how did you know I was yours?"

"Your mother…took picture…birthmark…and sent to me in letter."

"So you came to Nigeria and brought us back to Kenya, but the damage had already been done?" She raised her voice. How could he have been so cruel? Her mother died of a broken heart. It might have officially been complications from diabetes, but it really was a broken heart.

Damisi stood up from the bed and paced, trying to process it all. She rubbed her stomach. She had suffered because of her father's lack of compassion and her mother's inability to forgive him. That couldn't happen to her children. She and Jabir couldn't remain at each other's throats. They had to talk and really listen to each other. They had to come to some kind of agreement. She would do anything to shield her babies from pain that could be avoided.

"I'm sorry...sorry." Her father's voice interrupted her thoughts. He stretched out his hand toward her. She wanted to stay angry, but he looked tired. And he was her father.

She hesitated for several seconds. He dropped his hand and lay his head back. He winced in pain. It was time for him to take a nap. She pressed the button by the bed for the nurse. Once his medication was administered, he would be out for probably the rest of the night. Before he did that, she needed him to know she had forgiven him.

She went to him and lay her head on his chest. "It's okay, Daddy. It's in the past. Thank you for telling me."

"Your...young man...talk." Her father closed his eyes and the nurse entered.

Damisi stepped back as the nurse checked his vitals and administered his medication. She watched as her daddy fell asleep. Her thoughts went to Jabir. What if he got so angry with her disappearance that he went back to Detroit? He wasn't the most patient person. She had to call him.

She checked her watch—5:40 P.M. which was 3:40 P.M. in Nigeria. His mission would be over the next day. She would leave the call until then. That way, she would have his undivided attention.

LATER THAT NIGHT, DAMISI TOOK A QUICK SHOWER AND crawled under her comforter. Ita had returned and agreed to sleep at the hospital. He wouldn't hear of her doing it. She needed a bed to stretch her back. It had been a long day, and she was still reeling from the aftermath. As she lay there, her thoughts journeyed to her next move.

Too restless to sleep, she sighed and picked up the remote control. She sat up and surfed through channels before she landed on KTN. *Bedtime With God* was on. She leaned over to the dresser and picked up her Bible and turned to the verse the female televangelist referenced, Hebrews 4:16. Damisi flicked the pages with speed until she got to the verse. She then read along, "*Let us then approach God's throne of grace with confidence, so that we may receive mercy and find grace to help us in our time of need.*" She hugged the Bible to her chest, turned to her side and closed her eyes. Her eyes remained closed as though she was soaking up God's presence—mentally allowing herself to stand on His promise.

Then the woman said, "So therefore my brother and sisters, no matter your situation, sleep well by standing on the promise of Hebrews 4:16. Until the same time tomorrow, good night."

Damisi turned the television off. "Amen."

At that moment, she felt movement in her stomach. One of the babies had kicked. She rubbed her stomach. Through her child, she believed God was telling her it was going to be okay. With a smile on her face, she drifted off to sleep.

Chapter 19

Friday evening, Jabir walked through the double doors of the hospital and turned right. Mrs. Ojo was being discharged, and he wanted to see her before she left. Over the last few days, he had become attached to the older woman. Maybe it was because she reminded him of his mother or the fact that she had a close call with death.

He had been working nonstop since he got back from Lagos to keep from going crazy. He never knew it was possible to worry about someone so much. He still hadn't heard from Damisi three days later. The only thing keeping him in Nigeria was his commitment to the Hearts Foundation. That commitment, however, would end the next day with a closing ceremony.

He had mixed feelings as he had become fond of the people. Right after the ceremony, he would get on a plane to Abuja. His mother was about to have his hide. He also needed a sit-down with Rasheed. Jabir thought he could work this thing out with Damisi, but he was losing ground. He needed advice. He couldn't trust Kamal's opinion on this. His twin was totally against him proposing to Damisi. He still believed she couldn't be trusted with Jabir's feelings. He was scheduled to be back in Detroit soon, but couldn't go until they got things sorted out.

Jabir knocked on the door and entered when Mrs. Ojo answered.

He smiled at her. She looked better. He could tell she had showered, put on a change of clothes and combed her hair.

"I see somebody is ready to go home," he teased her.

"Yes, oh. Thank you so much, Dr. Danjuma."

"Call me Jabir, and the pleasure is mine." Jabir read her chart. Satisfied, he looked around. "Where's everyone?"

"My husband and the boys went to get some things from the market." She giggled. "I think they want to try and cook. Greg says he wants me off my feet."

"Smart man. I knew there was something I liked about him." Jabir shoved his hands in the pockets of his lab coat.

"He's a good man. Very caring." She grinned. "God has been so good to me."

"I'm sure," Jabir said, not enthused.

She frowned at him. "Doctor, don't you believe in God?"

"I do." Jabir was not about to elaborate on his theory on God.

"Oh, okay. I'll always be indebted to Him—for my salvation and my family."

"The boys are lucky to have a father who cares about them and their mother." His tone turned somber.

She shook her head. "Oh no, Greg is not their father. Not biologically anyway. Their father—my first husband—died, then I remarried, and the man left me. The boys were too much for him. Just when I was giving up, God sent me Greg." She became reflective. "We've been married now for fifteen years."

Jabir couldn't reconcile how she had been able to put herself out there so many times after such disappointment and pain. He couldn't believe what he said next. "I'm curious. How could you bring yourself to trust again after all that?"

She let out an exaggerated breath. "Doctor, it wasn't easy at first. I gave Greg a rough time in the beginning, but I found my faith again. I began to trust that God wanted the best for me. My pain and previous disappointment was a set-up for where I am right now." She shrugged. "Besides, life is a risk. It's better to take a risk with the chance of experiencing something good, than to be safe and be guaranteed of missing out on a lifetime."

"Wise woman," Jabir said, just as the doors opened and her family walked in. After exchanging greetings, Jabir went over her discharge instructions. He then summoned a nurse and a wheelchair. Several minutes later, he watched as her husband wheeled her out.

Jabir contemplated her words. The internal struggle between his mind and heart began. Was he ready to trust completely again? Could God work this out as Mrs. Ojo said? Maybe part of the reason Damisi was proving so difficult was because she didn't trust him as well. What was it his mother always said? "You get what you give." Was he at the point where he could give more? Open himself up to the risks of love?

Damisi's beautiful face came to his mind. She and his mother were the most important women in his life. His anger had kept him away from her. Surprisingly, she'd stayed single. He couldn't believe no man had snatched her up. Maybe Mrs. Ojo was right—God did have a way of fixing things. He finally acknowledged his second chance. Damisi was going to be his wife, and not because he pressured or bullied her. While he waited to be untangled from Angela, he was going to work earnestly to be the man Damisi fell in love with the first time.

———

THE FOLLOWING AFTERNOON, JABIR STARED OUT OF THE window of his brother's Range Rover. He had arrived in

Abuja some minutes ago and Rasheed was at the airport to pick him up. The day he found out he and Damisi would be having twins, he had put in for a one-month leave of absence from work. He still hadn't heard from Damisi, except for the coded vague message she passed through Moji, saying she'd call him soon. It had been a week since they'd talked. Five days since she disappeared. Ibiso couldn't help him since she only had Damisi's Nigerian number. Patience was not his thing, but he was determined to try. So far, it was torture.

Earlier that morning, he said a prayer for the first time in years. It was really short, but he knew from his mother that verbose prayers didn't mean a thing. He prayed for Damisi's dad's healing and for her heart to soften up enough to reach out to him. The rain continued to fall from the gray skies as they approached Rasheed's home. He needed a full stomach when he saw his mother later. She would suffocate him with questions he didn't have answers to, especially since he hadn't spoken to the woman in question. What was there to tell?

"She still hasn't called?"

"Huh?"

"Damisi...your runaway baby mama. She still hasn't called?" Rasheed laughed.

"Ha ha. I'm so glad you think this is funny. Look, I still got pictures of your face when you ran away to London after Ibiso dumped you." Jabir pulled out his phone and began to scroll. He remembered that night last year when he had called his brother. Rasheed sounded awful, but claimed he was okay. So Jabir insisted he take a picture of himself and send it. It was the saddest thing he had ever seen.

"Give me that." Rasheed reached over to get the phone.

Jabir yanked it out of his reach. "Behave oh, you're driving. Besides all of you have been to church recently. I haven't. If anything happens, I'm not ready to face God."

"For real? I'd never have guessed you thought about judgment and living right."

"Why wouldn't I when it's all Mama, you, Ibiso and Damisi talk about? Even Bernard is now getting on my nerves." The last time he talked to his friend, he was trying to badger him with a Bible study invitation.

Rasheed laughed as he pulled into his compound. "Hmm, better get with the program now before it's too late."

"Stop it. I don't scare easily. Besides, I don't have time now. My life is in shambles."

"His job is to help you clear it up. Seek Him. Trust Him to fix whatever you've got going on."

"Just like that?" Jabir's tone was sarcastic.

Rasheed gave him a stern look and parked the car. "Sometimes, but that's where the trusting part comes in. Believing where He'll take you will work out in the end."

"Dang. Oh man, I thought it was just like that." Jabir snapped his finger, got out of the car and ran to the front door.

He turned around and saw Rasheed still staring at him. Jabir laughed and pressed the doorbell.

Seconds later, Ibiso opened the door for him. Jabir wrapped his arms around her small frame and rocked her from side to side. They hadn't seen each other since her wedding. After she helped him out with Damisi's request, he and Ibiso had gotten a lot closer. She was so perfect for his brother. She was the one who broke down those walls he had erected around himself.

"Get your hands off my wife." Rasheed entered into the house.

"Be nice, honey," Ibiso said.

Jabir let go of Ibiso, but kept his arm draped across her shoulder. He studied her.

"How far along?" Jabir asked. Rasheed had shared they were expecting.

Ibiso walked over to her husband and stood on her toes to give him a full kiss. "Two months."

"Wow. You guys work fast." Jabir took off his shoes and stepped on the cream shag carpet. He sat on the maroon couch, which was decorated with multi-colored pillows.

"You should talk. Aren't you approaching fatherhood already?" Ibiso giggled and walked into the kitchen.

Jabir smiled. "You're not funny."

"Yes, she is," Rasheed countered.

Ibiso laughed and walked into the kitchen. His stomach rumbled. He was in for a treat. With a chef as a sister in-law, the possibilities were endless.

Moments later, they were seated at the table with a spread that looked too good to eat. Jabir didn't know what he wanted to take first. Ibiso had pounded yam, fried rice, African salad, goat meat and snails sautéed in stew. She also had egusi and okra soup. Then for dessert, she had fruit salad and a small pound cake.

As though she sensed his confusion, she said, "Don't worry. I'll put a little of everything."

Rasheed frowned and shook his head. "Stop spoiling this man. Even Kammy doesn't behave this needy."

Jabir laughed out loud. "Whatever, man. You're about to burst a vein." Jabir laughed harder knowing it would irritate his brother more. *"Bad belle."*

"He's just teasing. He knows I spoil him all day every day," Ibiso said, placing a plate of pounded yam and okra soup in front of her husband. She then bent and kissed him. Rasheed placed his hand in her hair and deepened the kiss.

Jabir coughed. "Some of us are trying to eat, oh."

"Don't hate." Rasheed glanced at Jabir then winked at Ibiso.

They said grace and began to eat. They talked about the Hearts Foundation mission, the expansion of Bisso Bites and the latest happenings at Danjuma Group. He noticed they stayed away from Damisi, and he was grateful for it.

They finished eating, and Jabir and Rasheed worked

together to restore the kitchen and dining table to its pristine state. Ibiso sat on the couch and stretched out her legs in front of her. Soon after, the men joined her and began watching a game show on the television.

A few minutes later, Ibiso's phone rang. She eased away from her husband's protective arm, but not before Jabir caught the frown on her face. She walked into the kitchen. There was something about her whisper that made him tune his ear to her conversation. He knew he shouldn't be eavesdropping, but what if it was Damisi? He knew they talked. His thoughts wandered when he felt a tap his shoulder.

"Damisi," mouthed Ibiso.

His nose flared as he jaw set. His breathing accelerated. He flew up from his seat. So did Rasheed.

"Calm down, bro." Rasheed placed his hand on his brother's shoulder.

Ibiso placed the phone on her chest to cover the mouthpiece. "Jabir, she's very upset and wants to speak with you. Go easy. Remember, she's pregnant."

The tightness in his chest eased. Was her father all right? How did she know where to find him? Moji must have told her. He nodded and took the phone from Ibiso then walked toward the study. So many questions he wanted answers to *now*, but no matter what was going on, one thing he did know for sure, was that they'd face it together.

Chapter 20

"Damisi, what's wrong?" Jabir sat on the sofa and placed the phone to his ear. He could hear her sniffing.

"It's…my father," her voice was as shaky as his nerves.

"Please tell me what's wrong. Why are you crying? Is anything wrong with your dad?" He turned the phone over to look at the caller ID. The 254 country code told him she was still in Kenya.

She began to cry.

"I'm worried sick out of my mind. Please, talk to me." It took a few seconds for her tears to turn into tiny sniffles.

Silence filled the distance between them. He knew they had a lot to talk about, and he didn't want to hold Ibiso's phone hostage or be interrupted by an incoming call.

"Lemme return Ibiso's phone. Hang up, and I'll call you right back so we can talk."

When she acknowledged his request, he hung up. He put her number in his phone and hurried back into the living room. Ibiso was nowhere in sight.

Rasheed stood up to meet him. "Is she okay?"

"I don't know yet. I came to return Ibiso's phone." Jabir handed Rasheed the phone.

"I already called you a taxi to take you to Mama's, but if you'd rather stay here, that's fine," Rasheed said.

"No thanks, bro. Let me head out. I already have one crying woman on my hands. I can't add Mama's tears of negligence to it."

There was a honk outside. Jabir gave his brother a hug. "Tell Ibiso thanks."

"We'll talk in the morning. Behave yourself," Rasheed said.

The taxi driver loaded his bags into the trunk. Jabir settled in the back, gave him instructions and dialed Damisi back. No answer. He hung up and dialed again. She answered on the second ring.

"Had to see about my dad," she said. Her voice was barely audible.

"No worries. Talk to me."

For the next few minutes, Jabir listened in astonishment as Damisi relayed the events of the past days. Her current tears were a result of her father's sudden loss of mobility on his left side. Jabir reiterated what their doctor had told her. It was probably temporary, especially since it occurred almost a week after the stroke. She seemed calmer, but that didn't stop his emotions from raging. Why hadn't she called him sooner? This amount of stress wasn't good for her. But now was not the time to tell her that. She needed his comfort. At that moment, he decided the phone was not going to do it.

"So how is your dad now?" Jabir asked.

"Apart from slurred speech and now his left side, he's okay. We're still in the hospital." She paused.

Her silence made him uncomfortable. There was something else.

"I think I'll stay here for a while," she said.

Jabir scooted forward in the seat. Panic set in. "What's a while?"

"As long as it takes. To take care of my dad."

"You can't do that…"

"Why not?"

"Do you really need me to spell it out? You're pregnant with twins. You're in no position to be taking care of anybody. You need to be taken care of!" Jabir's eyes blurred with frustration. Was she out of her mind?

She let out a defiant sigh. "Jabir, I don't need to be taken care of…" her voice trailed off.

Jabir struggled to get a hold of his anger. This wasn't just about her father. There were nurses who helped stroke patients rehabilitate. This was about running away from him and her problems, and he wasn't going to allow it. Not this time. She was carrying his children.

"Listen to me. I understand your dad's health is paramount, but there are nurses you can hire to do this stuff," he pleaded.

"Those nurses are expensive, and I need all the money I can save up. I'll probably be out of a job soon, and we have two babies on the way."

"Oh, so you remember them?" Frustration laced his tone.

"Of course I remember them. I'm saving my money so I can raise them," she yelled.

"You raising *our* children alone was *never* an option."

The driver turned around and gave him a curious stare.

Damisi was silent. He was tired. This was not going according to plan. The clock on the dashboard told him it was 6:32 P.M. which meant it was 8:32 P.M. in Kenya. He needed to let her go and rest. He had calls to make and things to do. He was headed to Kenya.

"Give me your address?" Jabir asked.

"Why?"

"Woman, we're not arguing about this." Jabir was losing patience with her stubbornness.

She grudgingly recited her address.

"Get some rest. I'll see you soon."

"Jabir, there's no need for you to come. I can handle this, and we'll talk about the children soon."

"You are *not* doing whatever *this* is alone." He paused to let his message sink in. "Don't test me. Good night."

After she wished him a good night, he disconnected the call. It was then he noticed the driver had come to a stop in front of his mother's house. Jabir got out, paid the man and gave him a generous tip.

Damisi could kick and scream all she wanted, but their lives and what they did had ceased to be about both of them. He protected his own. The minute she became pregnant with his seed, she became his own. It was his duty to protect her and his babies from anything within his power. He just had to get her to understand that. Never again would she have to do or go through anything alone.

———

THE NEXT MORNING, JABIR BLEW ON HIS HOT OVALTINE AND took a sip. He sat on the bar stool in the kitchen and opened his laptop when his mother walked in. He beamed.

"Mama, I was wondering when you would get back." He went over and hugged her tight.

She tried to fight him off in feigned annoyance, but he wouldn't let her go, then he broke the embrace and studied her. She had on a turquoise native wrapper that matched her headgear and a violet blouse. "Looking good, Mama. Good morning."

"I don't know if I should be talking to you." She set her purse down, opened the deep freezer and looked inside.

"You know you can't do without talking to me. I got in late last night. You were sleeping. By the time I got up this morning, you'd left for Mass."

"Since you've been in Nigeria, I'm just seeing you?" She set a frozen bowl on the counter and exchanged her shoes for house slippers. She filled the kettle with water and set it on the burner.

"*Haba*, Mama. I came for work." He closed the laptop. "Are you cooking yourself? Where is Nkechi?" Nkechi was his mother's right hand. She was a hired help and companion for his mother. Being alone in Nigeria was not easy. In years past, he and his brothers came home often, but only to visit. He was happy Rasheed now lived in Abuja with her, and Ibiso was the daughter she longed for.

"My hands aren't broken. Didn't I cook for all of you until you left my house?"

He smiled. She sure did, and it was good, too.

"She went to visit her parents in the village. She'll be back later today." When the water boiled, his mother poured it into a large bowl and placed the frozen smaller bowl into it.

"Let me go get out of these clothes." She left the kitchen, and Jabir reopened his laptop. He logged on to his email inbox—something he hadn't been able to do in the last couple of days. He browsed through the sales pitches for new drugs and quickly transferred them to his junk box. He then checked for anything that might need his urgent attention. He had been covered for the past two weeks, but since he might be in Africa a little longer, he needed to make sure he didn't have any patients scheduled for surgeries.

If everything went well, he planned to be back in Detroit soon. With that thought, he composed an email to the head of surgery and requested an extension to his leave of absence. Jabir wanted to make sure it was in Dr. Gary's mailbox by the time he gave him a call Monday morning. He read over the brief email and hit the send button.

He then constructed another one to his office manager and head nurse, telling them he'd give them a call the next morning. He sipped on his beverage again and was about to close the laptop when an email popped up from one of his doctor friends, Lyle Jenkins. He and Lyle met at a conference years ago, and they became close acquaintances when he found out he consulted at Mercy in pediatrics. When time permitted, they also played tennis together. It was through him he met Angela.

Hey Man!

How's the motherland treating you? When you getting back into town? By the way, what happened between you and Angela, man? You married? Congratulations. Holla at me when you get in.

Be easy!

L

Jabir blinked and reread the email. Was she back? Had she started telling everybody? He looked down between his legs. "I knew you would get me in trouble one day." He took a deep breath.

The truth of what happened was irrelevant. It was a perception that ended up being the conceived reality. People already thought he had more women than he actually had, but that was his fault. He needed to shut this down. Now it wasn't just his career and the Rookie Surgeon of the Year Award that could be in jeopardy, but his chance at happiness. He constructed an email to Ashton for an update. By Jabir's calculations, by the time he got back from Kenya, the annulment should be final. For the umpteenth time, his heart tugged at him to tell Damisi. Jabir shook his head. He knew her too well, and she wouldn't understand and would run in the opposite direction. He'd just fix it, and she would never have to know.

He reread his email and sent it to Ashton, then shut his laptop just as his mother reentered the kitchen. She had changed into one of her lounging Ankara *bou bous*. She pulled on his cheek and walked to the counter.

"Ouch. Mama, I'm not a kid anymore." He rubbed the spot. From old pictures, one could see he and Kamal had humongous cheeks when they were babies. His mother apparently didn't mind that those cheeks had long disappeared. She still pulled on them any chance she got.

"Hush now. You'll always be my baby. All of you." She measured rice from the bag and washed it. "Speaking of children, do I have to ask about Damisi, or are you going to tell me?"

Jabir thought to stall, but then his mother was going to bug him to death until he gave up the information she wanted.

"Your hunch was right. We're having twins." Jabir said.

His mother dropped the pot on the burner with more force than necessary. The water splashed on the fire. But she obviously could care less about the sizzling sound it made. She stood in shock. Then she broke into a dance and crooned the song *"Imela,"* which meant "God has done well" in her native Igbo language.

"So where is my daughter? What have you two planned? When is the wedding?" his mother asked without taking a breath. She leaned against the counter.

"Mama, easy. She's in Kenya." Jabir told his mother what was going on with Damisi's father's health. She then insisted they say a prayer for him right then. After the prayer, she looked at him. He saw the intensity in her eyes.

"My grandchildren cannot be born out of wedlock."

"Mama, she has to agree to marry me first, *abi?*"

"Did you ask her?"

"Err…yes. Kind of."

His mother frowned. "What does that mean? Chike?"

"Oh Lord Mama, not the Igbo name…" his mother always called them by their middle names when she was angry, disappointed or wanted something they couldn't give.

"Jabir Chike Danjuma, did you ask her, or did you throw your weight around?" She placed her hand on her hip. "See, I know each and every one of my sons and what they are capable of doing."

He remained silent.

"The moment I saw that child I knew she was carrying your baby. She's such a nice young lady, and I could see she loves you."

"Mama, your glasses must have superpowers?" Jabir teased.

"I'm serious. I saw the pained look in her eyes when she saw us at the airport. During your brother's wedding, I got to spend time with her, so I know." The rice boiled. His mother lifted the pot to the sink and ran cold water in it to wash it the second time.

Jabir sighed. "So much has happened between us. She's putting up a fight."

"From the looks of it, you are, too. Does she know you love her? That's a start."

"Huh?"

"Don't 'huh' me. It wasn't just your ego taking you to Lagos every time you visited Nigeria, although you won't admit it to yourself," she said.

"And how do you know that, Mama?"

"What I see sitting down you'll never see standing up."

Jabir chuckled at the adage she always used to tell them she was wiser as an old woman than they were as young men.

"I know growing up without your dad made you cautious, but for the short time that young woman was here in Abuja last year, I could see something deep between both of you." His mother set the pot of rice back on the stove.

She walked over to him and cupped his face, a feat that was made possible since he was seated and she was standing. "You don't just turn off that kind of love because you're angry or hurt."

"I don't know if I can be what she wants. I don't even think she knows what she wants."

His mother smiled. "She's a woman—a pregnant one with raging hormones. You can't throw your weight around and hope she bends."

She turned back to the stove. She lowered the stew and rice to a simmer. "Go to Kenya. Make her see the man I raised you to be, then bring my daughter-in-law back to me." She walked out of the kitchen.

"Yes, ma'am," he whispered.

Chapter 21

Damisi couldn't sleep. Despite how tired she was, thoughts of Jabir made it impossible for her to rest. He hadn't been as angry as she'd thought—more like disappointed and hurt that she hadn't reached out to him. But there was something else in his voice, something she dared not think about in case it was a figment of her imagination. Could she dare? Love.

"You're *not* doing whatever *this* is alone." She remembered the words he spoke to her two days ago. His protectiveness made her feel wanted and safe, but was also overbearing. During their relationship, he was always ready to take over and fight her battles. They had gotten into arguments about it, but she accepted that she couldn't change that part of him. It was the way he was wired. If she admitted the truth to herself, she loved that about him. She smiled, secured the sash on her night robe and sauntered into the kitchen.

She opened up the fridge and pulled out a container of milk. She then set a small pot on the burner and poured some in it. Warm milk should help her sleep and make the babies happy. She leaned against the Formica countertop and rubbed on her very visible stomach.

"There's no hiding you girls now." She sighed. Her mother would have been thrilled to become a grandmother. Although the circumstances were not the most ideal, she just imagined her buying a bunch of yarn and knitting for the babies. Knitting had been their thing. Her mother taught her to do it when she was growing up. Lately, Damisi hadn't knitted anything, but she figured it was time to get started. Very soon, she would have a lot of time on her hands.

She thought about her job. As of now, she was still on vacation. All those vacation days she hadn't used over the last couple of years came in handy. Her show was still showing reruns, and she wasn't needed for promos until early August, which was in about six weeks. By then, she would be well into her six month of pregnancy.

Damisi turned off the burner and poured the warm milk into a mug. She looked in the cookie jar and retrieved two *mahamri*. Madam Paulina was simply the best. She knew her dad loved the cardamom-flavored mini donuts, so she always made sure to make a fresh batch. However, he was allowed only one per day.

Her father had regained some movement in his left arm. His leg was still not quite there, but there was hope. It had been a long week, but there was progress. Ita, her cousin, had been her rock, alternating hospital overnight stays with her. Tonight, was his night.

She bit into the *mahamri* and closed her eyes to savor the flavor.

"I'm glad you like it."

Damisi opened her eyes and smiled at the new occupant of the room. She nodded, finished chewing, and drank some of her milk. "You know I do."

Damisi glanced at the timer on the stove. "It's late. Why are you still here?"

Madam Paulina poured herself a glass of water and

pulled out a chair. "I didn't like the way I saw you in pain earlier. I stayed in case you needed me."

Damisi's stomach gave her a little discomfort earlier in the day, but she hadn't meant for Madam Paulina to see that. She knew it would worry her. She was fine. Besides she had made an appointment with a doctor that Dr. Leonard recommended when she called him earlier.

"Oh no. I'm fine, really," Damisi said.

"*Ni sawa*. It's okay. It all worked out because by the time I would have left, Kwaba road had been shut down. I forgot there was a curfew because of the recent unrest."

Damisi smiled. She still didn't understand why her dad hadn't asked Madam Paulina to marry him. They were comfortable together and Damisi could see his illness was really taking a toll on the woman. She had been with them forever and anyone could tell they cared for each other deeply. "Oh, I'm so sorry. So you're in your old room, right?"

Madam Paulina nodded. She had been given a room in the house when Damisi first came to live in Kenya permanently. The adjustment wasn't easy and her dad had no clue what to do. Madam Paulina was the glue that kept them together.

"You couldn't sleep? How are the babies?"

Damisi looked down at her stomach. "They're fine. At least they aren't angry with me." She and Madam Paulina hadn't really talked about her unexpected pregnancy. Unlike Aunty Bola, all she said was, "It is well." Then she hugged her and prayed for her. Damisi remembered Madam Paulina praying specifically for her to stay in God's presence despite her mistake. Then, it didn't make sense, but now as the months had rolled by, it did. The older woman knew that the shame and guilt of what she had done was bound to send her away from God instead of running to Him.

"Their father is angry with you?" Madam Paulina asked, although her eyes told Damisi she already knew the answer.

"Yes." She took another bite of her snack. Needing someone to unburden to, Damisi began to open up to Madam Paulina. Moji was too biased, Eno was too sanctimonious, and Aunty Bola wanted blood, while her father didn't have a solid opinion one way or the other. The older woman sat in silence while Damisi talked. She nodded from time to time to indicate she was following the story. When Damisi was finished, she waited for a comment. None was forthcoming so she asked, "So what do you think?"

"Child, I can't tell you what to do, but you seem to be asking everybody but the One who will never lead you astray. God.' Madam Paulina took a sip of her water.

"God is not speaking."

"Are you reading your Bible?"

Damisi remained silent. She did read her Bible, but not as regularly as she should.

"Stop trying to act like a Christian and be a Christian. Remember, nothing you did made you good enough to be where you are as a television woman. The undeserving grace and favor of God did. So instead of trying to do things to get you back into His grace, accept His grace and mercy and work on obedience." She walked over to the sink and rinsed out her glass. She leaned against the sink and folded her arms across her chest. "As for this young man, the father of your babies…you obviously love him. Every woman prays for a good, godly man, but you don't choose who your heart loves."

Damisi remained silent.

"Is he a Muslim?" Madam Paulina asked.

Damisi frowned. "No."

"Is he that type who doesn't believe in God?"

"Atheist?" Damisi shook her head vigorously wondering where she was going with this.

"So, he's just not saved? *Kuelewa*, I understand that, but you should have thought about that before getting into bed with him. Now the deed is done. You can't change him, but you can teach him. *Show* him why and how good it is to love Jesus. He might want to listen, but your methods haven't been right." Madam Paulina walked over to Damisi and placed her hand on her protruding stomach. She smiled and kissed Damisi's forehead. "*Kupata mapumziko baadhi.* Get some rest, my child."

Damisi watched the older woman walk out of the kitchen. She finished her milk, washed out the glass and emptied the remnants of her *mahamri.* "I guess she told me. Lord, help me be the witness you called us all to be."

She walked back to her room to get some sleep. In less than ten hours, Jabir would be here in Kenya with her. She was excited and anxious. This could be great, or it could turn out very bad.

———

LATER THAT EVENING, DAMISI STOOD AT THE ARRIVAL GATE OF the Kisumu International Airport. Jabir had arrived at Nairobi's Jomo Kenyatta International about two hours ago and took another flight from there to get to Kisumu. It was either that or a five-hour road trip from Nairobi. She cracked her knuckles and rubbed on her stomach. Her heart rate quickened when she saw him a few minutes later. In spite of herself, her heart leaped as he walked toward her. Dressed in a simple polo t-shirt, jeans and leather sandals, he looked nothing like the millionaire he was. His simplicity was another one of his endearing features.

There was smugness about his swagger that always made her weak at the knees. He was a very handsome man. The problem was he knew it. His dark stubble showed signs of having been freshly groomed. His eyes had a twinkle in them, telling her he was just as happy to see her as she was him. All the fights they'd had in the past weeks seemed to disappear in the moment.

Her lips formed a smile as her babies kicked. She rubbed her stomach in a circular motion to calm them down. They must know their dad was around and didn't want to be left out of the fun.

Jabir quickened his pace. Once he got to her, he wasted no time in pulling her into his arms. Damisi didn't fight the embrace. She needed the comfort he provided. She missed him and was tired of maintaining the front she had put up for her father. She sobbed against his chest. *Why am I crying? I have to do something about these tears.* She felt the welcome rub he gave her back. Without words, he told her it would be okay soon.

"I haven't done anything. Why are you crying?" Jabir joked when her sobs quieted. She knew he was trying to lighten the mood.

She wiped her face, trying to restore some order to it. It was already a little swollen from her pregnancy and she didn't want to look a total mess.

"I'm sorry. How was your flight?"

"Seventeen-plus hours of torture, but I'm glad to finally set eyes on you." Jabir brushed her hair back from her face.

"You must be tired. Do you have any checked bags?"

"No."

"Okay, let's get you settled. By the way, welcome to Kenya." Damisi led the way to the parking lot where her dad's driver was parked.

Jabir draped one arm around her shoulders as they fell in step. "How are you and my babies?"

Damisi felt the heat of his eyes roam over her body.

"We're fine. As you can see, we're getting bigger." She pointed to her stomach.

"I wasn't going to say anything, but since you said it..." He chuckled when Damisi playfully swatted his stomach. "Ouch."

"Serves you right for making fun of us."

Some minutes later, Damisi and Jabir arrived at Kisumu

General. He'd insisted on seeing her father at the hospital and taking her home afterward before he settled into his hotel. He held her hand as she led him down the hospital corridor. She pretended not to notice the curious and admiring stares the nurses gave him. She burned with an unfamiliar feeling. She didn't know whether he acknowledged them under his dark shades. She didn't look up for fear of finding out he did. This time, ignorance was bliss.

Damisi opened the door to her father's room. She stepped in, and Ita stood. He was supposed to have gone back to Nairobi earlier, but waited until she got back from the airport. She walked over to him and hugged him.

"*Asante*. Thank you," she said.

He shifted a wayward strand of hair from her forehead. "*Ni sawa dada.*"

Jabir cleared his throat and walked up to her. She felt his possessive hand slip around her waist. Ita raised an eyebrow, challenging him. Damisi now knew why Ita spoke to her in Swahili. He wanted to get a rise out of Jabir. She had given him Jabir's story earlier, and he wanted to wring the man's neck. But then, he scolded her for running from Jabir instead of talking to him. Men.

Her father was coming out of his slumber, and she needed to diffuse whatever this was before it got out of hand.

"Jabir, this is my cousin Ita. Ita…Jabir."

The men held each other's stare. Neither made an attempt to greet the other. She rolled her eyes and went over to her dad.

Her father stretched out his right hand, and she hugged him. She felt Jabir stand behind her. *I guess their testosterone contest is over.*

"Daddy, this is Dr. Jabir Danjuma. Jabir, this is my dad, Steven Odinga."

As comprehension dawned, her father gave him a once-over.

Jabir extended his hand and bowed slightly. "It's nice to meet you, sir."

After a long pause, her father stretched out his hand. "Welcome."

"I'm sorry about your health, Mr. Odinga. How are you feeling?"

"Better than some…days ago."

Damisi smiled, thankful for the effort he was making on his speech. He didn't need therapy after all. It was gradually correcting itself.

"You…a doctor?"

"Yes, sir. I'm a cardiac surgeon."

Ita grunted, then walked over, said his goodbyes and left.

"Pay no attention to my cousin. He's very protective," Damisi said.

Jabir grinned, and Damisi winked.

Her father then pointed to Jabir's shirt. "You…play…tennis?'

Damisi looked and saw the crest at the top left-hand corner of Jabir's t-shirt. It was of a tennis racket and ball. She smiled. He father was the only African of his age she knew who loved tennis. At least that was something they had in common. The awkward silence in the room was deafening.

Jabir's eyes lit up. "Yes, I play."

Damisi needed to pee, but she was afraid to leave the men to themselves. She tried to hold it, but her bladder was threatening to spill its contents on the floor.

"I have to go to the bathroom. I'll be back." She gave Jabir a warning stare. He wiggled his eyebrows and made the sign of a cross on the corner of his heart. *Behave,* she mouthed. She didn't need him feeding her father any falsehoods about their relationship. She needed him to keep his ideas to himself until they talked.

Chapter 22

"My daughter didn't...tell...pregnancy?" The older man pulled himself up to a sitting position.

Jabir, who stood at the end of the bed, stared at the older man for a few seconds. He hadn't expected him to come right out and broach the subject of him and Damisi. He knew she didn't want him saying anything about them to her father, especially when they hadn't had a chance to talk, but what was he to do?

"Yes, sir. I didn't know. At least not at first."

A spark of curiosity lit the man's eyes, and Jabir waited for the next question. "Now...you...know. Your intentions?"

Jabir paused. He knew Damisi had made her stand about marrying him perfectly clear. The next few days or weeks were meant to change her mind. However, when he did ask her again, he wanted to have her father's permission. He figured why not get it now.

"With your permission, sir, I intend to marry her." Jabir heard the tremble in his voice. He was never afraid of anything, but with the way the man was looking at him, he didn't know what he'd say.

"Damisi has money...I...money. No marry...baby or money."

Jabir shook his head vigorously once he understood what the man was saying. "No, sir. I know she can take care of them herself and money is not an issue. I want to take care of them because they're my responsibility. I care for her and my babies."

"My daughter...means a lot..."

"Yes, sir, I know that. She means a lot to me, too."

"Stubborn...but good girl."

Jabir chuckled. He was glad it wasn't just him who knew Damisi could be stubborn.

"Take care of her...my grandchildren."

Jabir smiled, clasped both hands together and bowed. "I will. Thank you, sir." He had her father's blessing. Now it was time to work his magic. His plan was to leave Kenya a *real* married man. Before he left Abuja, he and his mother had another long chat. He told her of what he planned. Although she was not happy that she would be deprived of a wedding, she understood he had to do things his way. He prayed to God his annulment was finalized soon.

The door opened, and Damisi walked in. She gave both of them a curious look. He smiled at her and pulled out the chair near the bed for her to sit on. The trio chatted for a bit more. Jabir resisted the urge to examine Damisi's father himself, but he did ask the doctors questions he felt the family should ask when he came to check on Mr. Odinga. Damisi fed her father with the food she brought with her earlier. They talked about sports, Damisi's well-being and America. When her father's eyes began to droop, they decided leave.

Damisi promised their housekeeper would be by later to spend the night. She kissed him, and they left.

Settled in the backseat of the car, Jabir pulled Damisi closer to him and was glad she didn't resist. She rested her head on his shoulder and exhaled.

"Tired?"

"Yes."

"You've been stressing yourself out. You have to be more careful." He wanted to scold her more, but the moment they were in made him feel peaceful, so he let it be, hoping she didn't put up a fight.

"He's my father."

"I'm not disputing that, but you're delicate right now."

"So I guess you're my knight in shining armor coming to rescue the damsel in distress…" The tone of her voice was not lost on him. There was an edge in it he didn't like. She continued, "How many of us have there been over the years?"

"What?" He stared down at her.

She sat up straight and scooted away from him. She stared at him. "How many of us have there been? Six years…let's see…yeah, I remember the three-month rule, so what is that, twenty-four?"

"You want to do this? Now?" His forehead creased in confusion. What had he said? How could she go from sweet one minute to this the next?

"We might as well. All this pretending we're all good is making my stomach sick."

He sighed. He wasn't going to take the bait. Besides, she really didn't want the answer. She just wanted to find a way to not let him into her heart.

"Answer me. How many?"

"No."

"No?"

"N-O. No." He lay his head back and put his hand on his forehead. He was tired and hungry, and now he had to deal with this. He peered over at her. She had turned away from him and was looking out of the window. He wanted so much to drag her toward him, but he didn't have the mental energy to deal with her right now. Silence overtook the atmosphere, and it stayed that way until the car came to a stop minutes later.

Jabir walked her up to the front of the massive bungalow. She still hadn't said a word, but didn't object when he took her hand. Once inside the house, he turned her to face him. He then lifted her head with his index finger.

"Dami, I'm trying here. Please meet me halfway. Let me be here for you. We'll talk once your father comes home."

There was a twinkle in her eye. He knew she was surprised when he called her the pet name he had for her. He hadn't spoken that name in years, but it felt right now.

She nodded.

"Let the past stay in the past."

She tried to turn her head away from him, but he wouldn't let go.

She gasped and held on to her stomach. He put his hand on her stomach and rubbed. The babies calmed down.

"They love kicking me," she said.

"No, they just don't like their parents arguing. Do you have a doctor here?"

"Yes. I see him tomorrow morning. Do you want to come?"

"Nothing can keep me away."

They stared into each other's eyes. He raised his hand to the nape of her neck and caressed it. He didn't break eye contact, and neither did she. The atmosphere became charged, and his heart slammed against his chest. He lowered his head and whispered in her ear, "I'm here now."

He heard "thank you" escape those red lips he'd longed to take since he first saw her in Nigeria. He hadn't let himself think about it for fear of giving into temptation. In the present moment, however, his reasoning seemed to escape him. They were standing so close. He rubbed his forehead against her. His eyes landed on her parted lips. He needed to taste her. Was he right when he thought she still loved him? The way she kissed him never told him a lie. Would he dare? He pulled her close, his hand dropped to the small of her back, and their lips met.

The kiss was powerful, amorous and too short for his liking, but it was long enough for him to get his answer. Yes, she loved him. Despite the anger, pain, guilt, she loved him. Now he needed her to say the words, and the only way to do that was for her to feel he loved her, too.

"Don't ask me to apologize because I won't," he said.

"I wasn't going to." Damisi cracked her knuckles. "What hotel are you staying at?"

Jabir supplied the name of the hotel, and she frowned.

"That's about forty-five minutes from here. Why so far?"

"'It was short notice."

She hesitated for a few moments, and then said, "We have a guest house at the other side of the compound. You could stay there."

His wiggled his eyebrow. He pulled her to him. "You want me close, huh? I told you it's okay to admit these things."

Damisi chuckled and stepped out of his embrace. She then moved a couple of steps to the door. "Your ego is so big, it needs to be named."

"Confidence, baby." He winked.

"Come on, Mr. Confident. Let's get you settled in."

Chapter 23

A week and a half after Jabir arrived in Kenya, Damisi's father was discharged from the hospital. He had spent the last few days in therapy, and his speech was much better. He was walking, but with the use of a cane.

If she thought it was impossible to love Jabir anymore, Damisi had been sadly mistaken. He took over the care of her father as though he was actually her husband. Some nights, he had stayed in the hospital overnight with her dad, relieving her and Ita of the responsibility. He also hired an in-home nurse that would stay with her father and Madam Paulina for at least the first month of him being at home.

He hadn't brought up the marriage idea, but catered to her every need. He had taken care of the arrangements, and she was instructed to follow his lead. Over the past week, he had hired a car and a driver that took them everywhere. She initially objected, since her dad had one, but then for a moment she forgot who she was dealing with...Jabir Danjuma. It was a miracle he agreed to stay in her father's guesthouse. But then she suspected one of the reasons he did was so he could be close to her in case she needed him. He took her to her doctor's appointment and stayed up with her massaging her feet when they became swollen. He even followed her to church once for mid-week Bible study and prayer. That stunned her.

Damisi remembered Jabir asking about her plans for that evening and she said church. She wanted to invite him, but hesitated. To her surprise, he invited himself. She didn't go to her regular church, but another one close by. They sat at the back and listened to the man of God. Once everyone was dismissed, she stayed on to pray. She needed clarity and instruction from God concerning where her life was going. Surprisingly Jabir did the same—he prayed.

Damisi smiled and looked at her barely clothed reflection in the mirror. She had used the black soap and cocoa butter Madam Paulina recommended for her stretch marks. She lifted her freshly curled hair and put it in a loose bun and proceeded to do her makeup. A shiver washed over her body as she applied her lipstick. She had chosen a dark color to go with the smoky eye effect she had on. Tonight, she and Jabir were going out for dinner and dancing. It would be their first real date in years.

Her lips had been teased by Jabir so many times in the last couple of days that they automatically longed for him when he wasn't around. His kisses weren't urgent like the one they shared five months ago, but they were tender. He caressed her lips like they were prized possessions. It was a good thing the kisses never lasted long. With her hormones, there was no telling what would happen. She had already slept with him, which was the reason she was in this mess in the first place. She was determined to do things right going forward. The James 4:17 verse made its way to her mind: *If anyone, then, knows the good they ought to do and doesn't do it, it is sin for them.*

She tried to make sense of all that had happened between them in the past week. Was it more than lust and concern for his babies that she saw in his eyes? Was there a possibility he really cared or—dare she say—loved her? She blinked in awe of how they got here. She finished her makeup and picked up the flared blouse she'd bought a couple of days ago. It was an off-the- shoulder lace, royal-blue top. It stopped mid-thigh and had a sash that formed a bow at the back. She slipped on her jeans and struggled to zip up her blouse, but it was useless— she couldn't. As though she telepathically sensed her frustration, Madam Paulina knocked and entered.

She smiled at her. Damisi could tell she was pleased. She walked over and zipped the dress and tied the sash at the back. Damisi let down her hair, and the loose curls fell to a just beyond her shoulders.

"*Wewe ni mzuri.* Beautiful." Madam Paulina lifted her hand to fan out Damisi's hair across her shoulders.

"Thank you. How's Daddy?"

"Sleeping. Don't worry about him. He's happy. I'm happy, too. You're giving yourself a chance at happiness. No more crying."

Damisi slipped into her light blue ballerina slippers.

Madam Paulina folded her hand across her chest and smiled.

"What?"

"You're as giddy as a school girl. Why are you fighting so hard when you obviously love the young man?"

Quiet hung between them. Damisi shrugged and picked up her matching clutch.

"You know your problem?"

"Err…no, but I know you're going to tell me."

Madam Paulina waved her hand dismissing Damisi. "Your problem is you think that your refusal to marry him is penance to God for your 'mistake.'" She made air quotes at the word *mistake.*

Damisi twisted her lips. "Before you and I talked, yes. However, he hasn't asked me again. I guess something has changed."

"No, it hasn't. Open you heart."

———

Jabir picked her up twenty minutes later. He refused to tell her where he was taking her. To her surprise, they ended up parked in the VIP spot of one of the most happening spots in Kisumu—Samba Marina club. At first, she frowned at the idea. How could he take her to somewhere that would be rowdy and have loud music? Happening or not, she wanted to be in a quieter environment, especially in her present condition. She protested, but he told her to trust him. She was glad she did.

When they entered the establishment, they were escorted to a secluded part of the club—a private lounge that had mood lighting and was decorated in hues of violet. It was the most romantic thing she'd seen in a long time. There was a snack and wine bar in the corner and a view that allowed one to get lost in the beauty of the city's skyline. They could still hear the music and be part of the fun, but it wasn't noisy. As soon as they were settled, their private waiter came and took their orders. They dined on seafood.

She opted for a whole red snapper. It was perfectly grilled and laid on a bed of boiled potatoes, tomatoes and slices of giant limes. She had asked that they set the rich and creamy coconut-tamarind sauce to the side. Jabir ordered a shrimp dish. He spent more time eating off her plate, though.

"I like it when you smile."

Jabir's voice penetrated Damisi's thoughts. He held out his hand to her. She took it, and he helped her to her feet. "Let's dance."

He held her close to him as the opening chords of "No One" by Alicia Keys began to play. A tear escaped her eye as he gently rocked her back and forth. The beat was faster, but they danced to their own rhythm.

"How?" She was confused as to how he was able to pull this together without her help. She knew he had done a mission in Kenya once, but that was in Nairobi and not Kisumu. The place, food and getting the deejay to play the 2008 hit?

"That's my secret." He smiled at her and kissed her forehead. "Do you remember?"

She was choked with emotion, so she nodded instead. This was their song. The night they declared their love for each other, this song was playing in the car. They had just made up after a fight, and he was taking her back to her off-campus residence. They had been arguing about the nature of his emotions for her. Just like now, it had taken him a good while to admit his true feelings for her. She had been insecure because he did have a track record with women. On that snowy day in Ann Arbor, he crooned to the song as it played on the radio. He couldn't sing then, and he couldn't sing now. She giggled as she drew her head to his chest.

"You and me together through the days and nights..." he sang.

"I don't worry 'cause everything's..." she joined in.

"Gonna be alright."

She remained silent as the next verse played. He hummed, then did the worst Alicia Keys impression ever, shaking his head and singing, "No one, no one, no one, can get in the way of what I'm feeling."

She laughed. "Stop before they chase us out of here."

They both laughed and enjoyed the rest of the song. When it was over, they continued to sway together. She looked up at him. "Is it?"

"Is what, baby?"

"Is everything going to be all right?" she asked.

His gaze was intense. He stopped dancing. "Come here." He took her hand and led her back to the lounge chairs. He put her feet in his lap and took off her shoes and began to massage them.

"You've perfected this knight-in-shining-armor thing, haven't you?" She giggled.

"As long as there is a damsel in distress…" As he said the words, she could see immediate regret in his eyes. "I didn't mean that the way it came out."

"Your reputation with women is—"

"Is made up. I'm a one-woman guy. I'm sorry I lied to you that night. Things were weird between us, and I spoke without thinking."

She dropped her eyes and took a sip of her drink. The cranberry and Sprite mix was Jabir's idea, and she loved it. "I agree things were weird, and I think I made them worse by thinking the worst even before I asked you a thing."

"We can make this work again," he pleaded.

Damisi's breathing hitched at the possibility of giving her heart to Jabir again. Who was she kidding? He already had her heart. The question was, should she let him know it?

"You've had all these women over the years—before and after me. What makes you think you can settle down? You never wanted to get married, remember?"

"I admit marriage was never on my radar, but things and people change."

"Marriage is not a game."

"Do I look like I'm playing? Now listen to me carefully." He turned her face toward him. Damisi stared at him. Even with the dim lighting, the intensity of his gaze held her captive. It was those same mesmerizing eyes that got her every time. It was as though he could read her thoughts because she tried to look away, but his hold was firm. "I've never been, nor will I ever be unfaithful to you."

"How can I be sure of that? How can you be sure of that?"

"I told you, I protect what's mine. When you become my wife, your heart will belong to me, and I will protect it."

His words slay her resistance, but this was the time to lay

all the cards on the table. "I have a firestorm waiting for me when I get back to Lagos. I'll be in every tabloid and blog. My reputation will be tarnished and questioned. Are you ready to be in that kind of spotlight?"

He held her hands. "Maybe I haven't made myself clear. I'll be right there by your side."

"You live in Detroit, I live in Lagos. It can't work." She withdrew her hands. Any time he held her, her insides danced to a melody of their own, and her heart did backflips. His touch—his comfort—made her weak. This was serious business, so she needed to be focused.

"If you have your heart set on Lagos, I can always work anywhere or build my own clinic for cardiac patients. It has always been a dream of mine for the future. Or you could move to Detroit. You liked Michigan when you lived there."

She placed her hand on her stomach. She and the babies needed stability, but she couldn't fault his commitment to them. She yawned. Her head was spinning, and she needed to lie down.

"Come on. It's time to take Mommy home," he said.

She stretched out both her hands, and he pulled her up. The force slammed her right into him. He held her close. Warmth filled her. It was bound to happen, and she was ready when he claimed her mouth for a brief kiss.

He smacked his lips and chuckled. "You taste good."

"*Kuishi mwenyewe.*" She walked ahead of him.

"What does that mean?"

"Behave yourself."

"*Lafiya.*"

She raised her brow.

"Means 'okay' in Hausa." Jabir smirked.

Chapter 24

Jabir opened his eyes and squinted. His irises adjusted to the darkness while he searched the small table beside him for his phone. He looked at the time. It was well past midnight, but he couldn't sleep. He was so wired from the evening's events he couldn't get his thoughts to quiet down.

Ita really came through for him, and the night was great. After their initial awkwardness, he and Damisi's cousin were able to come to an agreement. They both cared about her and wanted her to be happy. Jabir made it very clear that although Damisi was Ita's cousin, she was his woman, and there was a difference. Ita was the one who told him about the club.

He counted the night as a win—not a total win, but one nonetheless. Especially since he couldn't make a move until his lawyer gave him the go-ahead. He detangled his legs from the sheets and pulled on a shirt over his bare chest. He slipped his feet into his flip-flops and walked out of the room. He headed for the window and drew the curtains Damisi had opened earlier for ventilation and sunlight. The guesthouse had an extra-large porch, which reminded him of his maternal grandfather's compound in Enugu.

He and his brothers had been there only once. About a

year after their father left, money became tight, so their mother took them on a trip to her home in the eastern part of Nigeria, hoping to get some help. Although he offered assistance later, his grandfather maintained his stance that their mother had no business marrying a Muslim man behind her family's back.

His anger didn't prevent him from showing his grandsons a good time during their one-week stay. Every night, they would spread a mat while he told them folk tales. It was the first time Jabir had lain on the hand-woven fabric made out of dried grass. In that week, he had heard so many lion-and-tortoise tales that he'd be glad to never hear of the animals again.

Jabir opened the door leading to the front porch. The cool, fresh breeze was tempting, but he also didn't want to be eaten up by mosquitoes. He walked back into the room and sprayed the Off mosquito repellant he brought from the States. Satisfied he had covered all the exposed areas of his body, he took a bottle of water and walked out of the house. The surroundings were calm and serene. It was a sharp contrast to Lagos. There was no way Lagos could ever be this quiet, no matter the time of the day. He loved Kisumu, but knew it wasn't somewhere he could live for an extended period. He needed to stay busy.

He looked up at the stars and smiled, remembering one of his mother's favorite sayings when he was a kid: "It's okay, my sons, the God who holds the stars in the sky will take care of our needs." Jabir shook his head and took a sip of his water. He grew up in the church. His mother made sure they all did, but later in life, his faith had given way to logic.

The special ringtone assigned to his family started to play. It was Rasheed.

"Hey, bro," Jabir greeted.

"Hold on."

There was silence, then a click. Someone else had been conferenced in. Jabir rubbed his temple.

"Jabir, are you there?" Rasheed asked.

"Err…yeah. Why are you guys calling so late?"

"Kammy called me, so we decided to call you," Rasheed explained. "Kammy, you there?"

"Yep," Kamal answered.

Jabir had called Rasheed the day before to fill him in on the latest developments. Although he had said he was happy for him, Jabir could tell Rasheed was still worried. He really couldn't blame him because up until six months ago, Jabir had always sworn never to settle down. The result of that conversation was this intervention at 3:30 in the morning. He'd listen to them, but his mind was already made up. He and Damisi were getting married. He loved her, and he knew what he was doing.

"Please don't tell me this call is about Damisi," Jabir said, although he knew the answer.

"Bros, all I told you was to go see if you had conceived a child. How did *marriage* enter into the equation?" Kamal chimed in.

Jabir knew the way Kamal stressed the word *marriage* was code for, "You're not out of one, how can you think about another?"

"We just want to make sure you're not doing this out of guilt or obligation. Those are not reasons to get married," Rasheed said.

"Guilt? Why would he be guilty? It takes two to do the deed. Weren't both of them in that bed?" Kamal asked.

"Shut up, Kammy," Jabir and Rasheed said in unison.

"I can't believe you're getting hitched after all your talk," Rasheed said.

Jabir was not about to tell them it would all be a bust if he didn't hear back from Ashton soon. He didn't need the added pressure.

"So have you been delivered? Or is it because she's pregnant that you're good enough to be with? All these fair-weather church girls," Kamal said.

"Kammy, I swear, if you say one more thing…" Jabir began.

"Kammy, be quiet. The woman is about to be his wife," Rasheed scolded.

"My bad," was Kamal's response.

"Look, I know what I'm doing." Jabir lowered his voice. "I'll not be like that man who fathered us and shrank from my responsibility."

"I get it. Honestly, I do, but I've heard words like *fond of, care a lot* and *like* in your vocabulary, but never love."

"That's because with love comes trust, and you know Jabir doesn't do trust." Kamal laughed.

Jabir shook his head. His knucklehead twin could never be serious. Everything was a joke to him. He either joked, or he remained silent. There was no in between with him.

"Just like you told me, by trying to be so unlike our father, you're being just like him. If he loved Mama as he should, he would have stayed and trusted their love could conquer his family's evilness," Rasheed said. "So the question is, can your marriage last without love?"

"Yeah man, after the baby, then what?" Kamal asked.

"I love her! Always have. We hurt each other, and I was angry, but there's hope, and I'm going to cling on to it—for my kids."

There was silence. Then Kamal spoke, "Kids?"

"Yes. We're having twins."

Jabir removed the phone from his ear as his brothers roared their congratulations.

"Does Mama know?" Rasheed asked.

"Yes."

"That woman, and she kept quiet. If she has a complaint, she'll remember my phone number," Rasheed said.

"Don't mess this up, man. You guys have a second chance," Kamal said. "Be good to her."

"I will," Jabir replied. That support meant a lot coming from his twin.

Before they disconnected the call, Jabir informed them that after the wedding, they'd honeymoon in Nairobi before they went back to Nigeria. If everything went according to plan, he'd be a married man—a real married man—soon.

With that thought in mind, Jabir checked his emails. His heart raced as he clicked on the one he was looking for. All Ashton said in the email was, "Call me in the morning." As his mind raced on why his lawyer just didn't tell him what he wanted to hear, Jabir dialed his number, not considering the time difference.

"Hello," Ashton answered after the fifth ring.

"It's Jabir. I'm sorry to wake you, but I got your email…"

"Do you know what time it is?"

"Please put me out of my misery…" Jabir felt his heart tighten. He didn't want to even think of what would happen if the news wasn't favorable.

"It's over. The judge signed, and I took it to the court to be filed. You're free," Ashton said like it was no big deal.

Jabir's mouth fell open as he knelt to the floor. How he had longed to hear those words. He pumped his fist in the air. "Yes!! So I'm good to do what I need to do?"

"Yes. I'll send you the judge's signed document."

The men talked a little more then hung up.

Jabir ran into his room to retrieve the tiny velvet box. He had purchased the five-carat, white princess-cut ring in Abuja. It was a rush job and turned out great. He hoped Damisi would like it. He sent up a prayer to God. *I want my woman back. Please let her agree to be my wife. I have no idea about the future, but as long as we're together, things will work out.*

He couldn't wait until morning. He was going to propose.

———

Late the following morning, the door to the guesthouse opened after a brief knock. Damisi walked in. His stomach clenched at her beauty. Her hair was in a bun atop her head with loose tendrils hanging down around her oval face. The floral gown she wore covered the swell in her stomach and stopped right below the knees. His need and want for her grew with intensity each day. All the emotions he thought had been locked up were all jumbled in his head, but his loins were very clear of what he wanted.

"Hey, beautiful."

"Sleepyhead, you're finally awake." She smiled and opened up the curtain for light to enter the room.

"My brothers called, so we had a late session."

She frowned. "I hope they're okay."

"Yes. Now wipe that frown off your face." Jabir walked over to her. He held her and twirled a strand of her hair. "It's Saturday. What's up? How's your dad? I should go check on him."

She patted his chest. "Yes, you do that. Then I'm taking you somewhere."

He grinned. "I love it when my woman takes charge."

"You have an hour. Move," she warned as she left the house.

True to her word, she had given him one hour to dress and chat with her dad a little before she instructed his driver to take them to the Kisumu Impala Sanctuary. Jabir had never been that close to nature, and he was enjoying every minute of it. The sanctuary was one of Kenya's smallest wildlife preserves. Hippos that came out of the lake used the grounds for grazing.

They ate the light lunch Damisi packed on one of the picnic tables. After eating, they stretched out on a blanket, enjoying a perfect view of Lake Victoria. She positioned herself between his legs and laid her head on his chest. Jabir caressed her stomach as they idly watched tourists pass by. He caught her smile as he placed his chin on the crown of her head. The sun shone brightly, but they were protected from its rays by the shade of the tree. It was almost a crime to interrupt this perfection by real talk, but they had to do it.

"It's so peaceful here," Jabir mumbled.

"Hmmm, yes, it is."

"So this is the famous Lake Victoria. I've only read about it, but to see its magnificence…amazing," he said.

"Its port is right here in Kisumu, and I've only seen it once." She paused, then turned her head to look up at him. "Did you know that Kisumu was a sister city of Boulder, Colorado, in the U.S?"

He twirled her hair. "Nice. Look at you. You know your Kenyan history. I guess I need to brush up on *Naija* so you won't outshine me."

She laughed. "You forget I'm half Nigerian, too. I can probably teach you about Nigeria too…you British American man."

"I'm going to get you for that." He tickled her and enjoyed seeing her wiggle and squirm while begging him to stop.

"I'm going to pee all over you, and it won't be funny. Stop." She laughed and sat upright.

"Don't mess with me again," he warned playfully.

A warm look passed between them. He put his hand in her hair and drew her parted lips to his. The kiss was sweet and intense. He savored the minty taste of her mouth. He broke the kiss, and she lowered her eyes.

"You *cannot* be shy. Look at me," Jabir commanded softly.

Damisi slowly lifted her eyes. He cupped her face with his palms, warding off loose tendrils of hair that were obeying the commands of the wind.

"I want to look into your eyes when I say this."

She nodded.

"You're right. I do have commitment and trust issues. I'm trying hard to work through them. When you changed on me back in school, I equated that to my father leaving and not being worthy of his love either. I did *not* cheat on you, but I admit to pushing you away. Then when you left, my anger raged. I've been holding on to that anger for six years." He looked down at her stomach, then lifted his gaze again. "I never thought I would get married, then after you left, I was sure I didn't want to, but like I said, people change."

She smiled, and a tear spilled onto her cheek. He wiped it away.

"I may not be worthy since I don't have the faith in God you have, but I'm committed to you and my babies. I love you so much," Jabir said fervently.

Her eyes widened. "I love you, too."

"I need you in my life. I'm ready to have the babies in my life. I know I can have that without being married to you—" his raspy voice was full of emotion— "but please don't make me wake up every day without you."

He reached inside his pocket and retrieved the velvet box. He removed the five-carat diamond, moved her to the side and knelt. "Damisi Titilola Odinga, will you do me the honor of changing your last name to mine? Marry me."

She closed her eyes, inhaled deeply and exhaled. Tears misted her eyes, and she vigorously nodded. "Yes...yes...yes."

He slid the ring on her finger, helped her stand up and lifted her into his arms. "Thank you," he whispered into her ear. Once he put her down, she wrapped her arms around his neck.

"*Upendo wangu. Ife mi. Masoyina.*" She giggled at his confusion. "That's Swahili, Yoruba and Hausa for 'my love.'" A beat of silence passed between them. "I've learnt so much about grace that I didn't know then. I went about my faith by the reward for my works and not by the grace of God. If I operated from a place of grace—that none of us are worthy and we all come short everyday—then maybe your love for me would have made you willing to find out why I loved God so much." She kissed him.

"Okay, I have no idea what you just said, but I got my yes and I'm happy."

She laughed joyously. "I'll teach you, my love." She pulled him back down to the blanket. "Come. The best part of this spot is watching the sunset over the lake."

They resumed their former positions and fell into a comfortable silence. Minutes later, the sun set. The sight was enchanting.

Damisi held up her ring. "I can't wait to tell Daddy."

He kissed her hair. "I already told him." She turned her head to him, shocked. He kissed her forehead and smiled.

"Oh, I forgot one. What's 'my love' in your mother's language, Ibo?" She placed her hand over her stomach and snuggled closer. "Never mind, I'm sure you don't know… American man." She chuckled.

"*Ihunanya m.* You see, that I know." He began tickling her. "But I told you not to mess with me, didn't I? Now you pay." The sound of her laughter delighted his soul. He made a vow to make her laugh every day as long as it was in his power.

—————————————————

Chapter 25

—————————————————

Damisi settled into her business-class seat on Kenya Airways and adjusted her body toward her new husband. They were headed to Nairobi. She looked down at the white princess-cut ring and matching band Jabir had placed on her finger twenty-four hours earlier. They had exchanged their vows in the office of her father's pastor—Pastor Aneja. The elderly man had pronounced them as husband and wife with her father, Madam Paulina, and Ita as witnesses. Damisi noticed the frown on the man's face when she waddled in pregnant. His silent opinion and judgmental glances were just a small piece of what waited for her back in Lagos. At least for the weekend, she would pretend she and her husband existed in a vacuum.

She looked over at Jabir who had his nose buried in a mystery novel. She smiled. Reading was what he was doing when they met. She would never forget it. He had been reading *A Simple Plan* by Scott Smith, and he didn't realize the coffee line had moved. She was running late for her class, so she called out to him. He was so engrossed, he didn't hear, so she nudged him. While they were making his coffee, she asked what he was reading. A budding friendship ensued from there.

Needing his warmth, she raised the armrest between them and put her head on his shoulder. Jabir absently draped his hand around her shoulder and pulled her closer. While she was packing the previous night, she heard God whisper, *"Let your light shine."* She opened up the Mathew 5:16 verse: *Let your light shine before men in such a way that they may see your good works, and glorify your Father who is in heaven.*

After packing, she had stayed on her knees in prayer. Madam Paulina had told her saved or unsaved, Jabir now had authority over her, and her job was to pray for him and let God do what He does best. Right before they boarded, Madam Paulina had pulled her to the side. She prayed for her and said, "My child, remember patience attracts happiness. It brings that which is far near. Your husband might be the head of the home, but you're the heart. Pray for him constantly. It shall be well with you, my child. *Chunga.*"

The two women had embraced. Damisi would forever be grateful to the woman who stepped into her mother's shoes and raised her to adulthood.

"Are you comfortable, baby?" Jabir asked, breaking her out of her trance.

"Yes, *mpenzi.*" She smiled up at him.

He grinned and planted a series of kisses on her face and neck before stopping at her lips. His kiss was tender and sensual. His grin told her he was pleased she had called him "darling" in Swahili. That was what she called him all those years ago, and it never felt right using it on anyone else.

"What was that for?"

"Do I need a reason to kiss my wife? Besides, your Swahili sounds so sexy. So let's just say you asked for it." He placed his hand over her stomach. "We'll soon land. Are you ready?"

"I don't know since you won't tell me where you're taking me. All I know is we 'll be in Nairobi for two days then Abuja." Damisi pouted.

He kissed the bridge of her nose. "That's all you need to know. Trust me.

"I'm excited."

She was going to play her part in making this trip magical. They'd go back to the real world soon enough. "I can't wait to meet your family again. I'm glad Kamal will be in Abuja by the time we get there."

He frowned.

"What is it?"

He hesitated for a few moments.

"You can tell us apart, right? I don't want to have to fight my twin because you mistook him for me."

She lifted her hand and touched the small scar right above his left eyebrow. "He doesn't have this…"

"You're kidding me. So without that, you wouldn't know?" He looked alarmed.

Damisi enjoyed teasing him. "Relax. I can tell the difference." She wasn't about to tell him that the hair at the back of her neck stood any time he was close and made her aware of him. Or that her skin became goose pimple ridden when he was near. Jabir could be dangerous with that kind of information, so that answer would have to do.

He seemed pacified and relaxed back in his seat. He pulled out a packet of M&M's from his pocket and tore it open. He offered her some, and she took a few, then just as she knew he would, he began separating the green ones from the others. He'd had a thing for green M&M's as far back as she could remember.

"Sooooo, you're the twin who eats only the green M&M's?" She snapped her fingers. "I thought it was Kamal."

He gave her a warning look. "Careful, woman."

She fluttered her eyelids. "*Mpenzi*, I was just teasing. Lighten up."

———

AFTER A FIFTY-MINUTE FLIGHT AND A THIRTY-MINUTE DRIVE, they arrived at the Villa Rosa Kempinski in Nairobi. A bellhop waiting on new arrivals came to help them gather their luggage. Jabir paid the driver and took her hand, leading her through the revolving doors. Damisi knew the European-originated hotelier had villas worldwide, but those were things she'd only read about. During her travels to Europe or around Africa, she'd stayed in some pretty good hotels, but none compared to this one. The place oozed elegance. To actually be in one on her honeymoon caused butterflies to dance in her belly.

A very beautiful young and slender receptionist checked them in. Damisi noticed her smile was extra wide when she was addressing Jabir. Damisi rolled her eyes in annoyance. She looked down at her protruding belly then caught the reflection that stared back at her from the mirrors on the wall. She felt aggravated and irritated. She tried to remove her hand from Jabir's at least to straighten her hair, but he frowned and held on tight.

"Welcome again, Dr. Danjuma. Mrs. Danjuma. The gentleman here will take you to your suite. I hope you enjoy your stay," the woman said, looking at Jabir the whole time. He smiled at her. *Why is he smiling?*

Jabir swiped the key to their eighth-floor suite, and the bellhop set down their luggage and left as soon as Jabir tipped him.

Damisi walked to the window and opened up the curtains. The sun was just about to go down, and the view of the city was beautiful. She felt Jabir behind her. He placed his chin on her shoulder.

"You like?" he asked.

"I love," she replied.

He turned her around. "Good, and I love you."

"Am I fat?"

"What?"

"Am I fat and ugly?" she repeated.

"Why do you want to get me in trouble? We haven't been married two full days yet." He smiled. "And the answer is no."

She walked into the bedroom. There were rose petals strewn all over the bed. There were several bottles of grape juice and Sprite in an ice bucket by the corner. Tears began to fall from her eyes. Why was she crying? She sat on the bed, but couldn't get the tears to stop. She bent her head and wiped her eyes with the back of her hand.

Jabir appeared a few moments later with a warm washcloth and sat beside her. He wiped her forehead and face. She stopped crying. He took the washcloth back to the bathroom and handed her a Kleenex.

He knelt in from of her. "You ready to talk to me?"

"It's silly, I know. I'm pregnant. I'm supposed to be fat, even if you won't say it."

"What happened from the plane to here to make you think that?"

"It's nothing."

"What happened?" he asked again in a sterner voice.

She felt embarrassed she'd have to repeat the foolishness to him, but he wouldn't let her go until she did. She hated she was spoiling their honeymoon. She told him about the receptionist and her feeling when she looked at herself in the mirror.

He smiled at her, cupped her face and kissed her. "I fell in love with your spirit before I even noticed your body."

She deadpanned him. "You're such a liar." She smiled.

He caressed her cheek. "There she goes. That's my girl." He raised himself to his feet and pulled her up to him. "You're my world. I have eyes only for you. Don't ever doubt that."

He walked toward the bathroom. "Let me run you a bath and feed you, then we can decide what to do later."

Her heart swelled with love. "*Mpezi*, all I want to do is stay in tonight. Let's watch old movies."

He frowned. She pouted.

"Do that often and you'll get anything." He winked and walked into the bathroom.

———

HOURS LATER, DAMISI AND JABIR HAD SHOWERED, CHANGED and eaten. Somewhere in between, they both had a nap. It was a little after midnight, and they were cuddled up on the sofa in the living area and unable to sleep. They had just finished watching their final movie of the night. The credits rolled, and a tear glided down her check

Jabir reached over and flicked away the stray tear. "You remember you cried the first time we watched *Pretty Woman*?"

"It's so touching." She sniffed.

He shrugged. "It's a'ight."

Pretty Woman was the first old movie they watched together when they started dating. The fact that he remembered after all these years made her heart explode. *Pretty Woman* always reminded her that love conquered all and overcame all odds.

"You know what I love about *Pretty Woman*," she asked.

He fed her a piece of red velvet cake. "The romance."

"Before, yes, that's all there was, but now I see it from different eyes."

"And?"

"Who would have thought a prostitute would end up with a rich man who loved her? But this is the thing, he fell in love with her just the way she was. His love for her made her want to do better. She cleaned up and made something of herself."

"Love makes us do things we never would have imagined," Jabir said.

She laid her head in his lap and looked up at him. He stroked her hair.

"*Mpenzi*, that's the same thing with Jesus' love for us. His blood paid the price for our sins while we were still sinners ourselves. He died just because He loved us. It's that love and grace that should make us want to do right."

There was a long period of silence between them.

"I'm probably out of a job, but what made me so ashamed and angry was that I failed God."

"Out of a job?" he asked.

"When you work for KTN, there's a code of integrity you must abide by as an employee—one of which includes upholding their values, i.e., no babies out of wedlock."

"You can't tell me that every single person abides by this clause."

"No, I can't, but I knew better. My morning segment is called *Becoming Ruth* for goodness' sake." She turned to her side.

"Won't being married lessen the damage when you tell your boss?"

"How do you know I'll still tell my boss?"

He caressed her face with the back of his palm. "Because that's who you are. You wouldn't be at peace until you've gotten it off your chest."

She smiled and sat up.

"So, won't it help?" he asked.

"I don't know."

"How can you be so calm? Medicine is my life. If anything interfered with it, I wouldn't know what to do." He looked at her, concerned.

"Because God gives me peace, and I trust Him."

"Must be nice."

"It is, darling. There'll be fallout, but I trust God to take care of me—of us."

"Good. Now let's go to bed." He stood and lifted her up.

———

JABIR AWOKE WHEN HE FELT A SET OF LIPS PRESSED AGAINST his. He opened his eyes to see Damisi leaned against him. He felt a stirring in his loins as his eyes travelled to her slightly exposed breasts.

"Good morning."

"Good morning," she replied. She smiled and rubbed her hand across his chest and kissed him again, this time, long and hard.

He raised his hand and caressed her back. They broke the kiss when it was time to come up for air.

"Will I be awakened like this every morning?" Jabir smiled and pulled himself into a sitting position on the bed.

Damisi laughed and sat up. "Depends…"

"On?"

"If you're a good boy the day before."

"Hmm. Hope you're ready for today. I have the whole day planned."

"So, what are we doing?"

"First, we'll visit the Massai market. We need items to pacify Ibiso, Halima, Moji, Aunty Bola and Mama."

"Ah, yes. I've been so scared to call. They'll be furious they didn't get to plan a wedding," Damisi agreed. "It's a good thing we'll have another one after the babies are born."

"I think next we'll see the Bomas of Kenya and end with twin massages and dinner."

She clasped her hands together. "Nice full day. We need to get back early though so I can pack for our trip to Abuja in the morning."

He grunted. Her clapping motion revealed more of her naked chest. His eyes darkened. "Come here." His gaze raked over her body. He peered at the clock in the corner. It was 8:00 A.M.

She looked at him skeptically. "What?"

His brow shot up. "Really?" His hooded eyes dimmed. He coaxed in a low voice, "I said come here, woman."

Damisi bit her lip and winked at him. She was playing with fire. He loved it. Her eyes told her story. She slowly crossed the bed. He reached out and brushed his knuckles against her face. She trembled. He loosened the clasp she used to hold her hair. When the black mass fell, he immersed his hands in it and drew her face to his, then he slanted his mouth for a kiss and started the journey of rediscovering his wife.

———

"You owe me another trip to Kenya to see the Bomas," Damisi said the next morning as she folded the last piece of clothing into the suitcase.

"You forgot you were the one who kept begging for more." Jabir chuckled and folded the ironing board. He walked past her to return it to the closet. He spanked her bottom on the way back. "It was amazing…I'm not complaining. I've heard of pregnant women and their libidos but man, I'm worn out." He stretched in mock tiredness.

Damisi balled up a piece of clothing and threw it at him. "Shut up."

Jabir laughed and put on his newly ironed shirt. Their flight to Abuja was in four hours, and they needed to check out and have breakfast before heading to the airport.

They had stayed in bed for longer than they planned the previous day, so they only had time to go to the market and get their massages. Damisi was so tired afterward that they ordered room service and talked most of the night. Although talking was an integral part of their night, it wasn't the only thing they did. Damisi shared more with him about the grace of God and salvation. Most of the examples she gave were from stories he knew, but she told them differently. He understood what she said, but he still didn't understand why suffering and perseverance should be part of the Christian package.

Damisi zipped up the last of their bags, and Jabir called for the bellhop. Minutes later, they walked out of the room hand in hand. The honeymoon had been nice, but it was now time to head into the real world.

Chapter 26

"Mrs. Danjuma," the sales girl said.

"Yes?" all three Danjuma women answered.

Damisi, Ibiso and their mother-in-law were in an upscale boutique shopping for baby items. The store sold only baby clothes ranging from newborn to twelve-month sizes. Damisi was impressed. The store owner thought about everything an expectant mother would need. One part of the store had a green and yellow theme for those mothers that didn't want to find out the sex of their child. The second part was decorated in the traditional pink and blue themes for a girl or a boy. Each area had light-colored sofa chairs for comfort and snack and beverage tables. There were also attendants assigned specifically to each section.

All three of them laughed, and the sales girl indicated she was referring to Ibiso who had told her to bring out baby booties in every color they had in stock.

"Thank you, my dear. Leave them here. We'll look at them and choose," the older Mrs. Danjuma said, ushering Damisi to a chair nearby. She gave her a warm smile.

Damisi hadn't lacked loving motherly figures in her life, but Jabir's mother took it to a whole new level. The woman had welcomed her almost to the point of suffocation since they had arrived in Abuja the previous day. She made it her mission to wait on Damisi hand and foot. She had asked the housekeeper to prepare catfish pepper soup for her. After she was fed, Jabir and his mother ganged up on her and made her lie down. Damisi was too tired to protest. The babies had been kicking, and it was a long and tiring flight.

Her call to Aunty Bola didn't go as smoothly. Only the promise of allowing her to throw an *Owambe* party after the baby was born pacified her. Damisi had laughed at how the promise of a block party quickly quenched the anger of not attending her niece's wedding.

"Damisi, sit down here. I saw you frown in pain earlier. Is everything okay?" Jabir's mother asked.

"Do you need some water? Or should we go back home?" Ibiso asked.

They both looked worried, and Damisi knew she couldn't have wished for a better family.

"Mama, I'm fine. Just tired." Damisi smiled in the direction of her mother-in-law. She turned to Ibiso, "I'm good. You should sit down, too. You're not far behind me."

Ibiso giggled at her. "Ha! Don't compare us, oh. You're carrying twins, remember? Sorry, sis, but at almost nineteen weeks, you're huge."

Jabir's mother cut Ibiso a side eye.

"What, Mama? I'll be where she is very soon. So you both have permission to tease me then," Ibiso said.

They all laughed and proceeded to select the booties they wanted. They shopped around for Ibiso a bit more. Damisi didn't want to buy too much since she was still headed to Lagos. Besides, Moji and Eno would have her head if she did all the shopping without them.

Their husbands' mother paid the bill, and they headed toward the exit. Before they opened the door, Damisi pulled down her hat and put on her sunshades. In Kenya, it had been okay to walk around freely as people rarely recognized her, but this was Nigeria. Even though it wasn't Lagos, she didn't need any attention until she made it to the office in a couple of days.

Later that evening, Damisi sat on the huge bed in Jabir's room of the Danjuma residence. After they had left the boutique earlier, the three women went to Ibiso's restaurant, Bisso Bites, for lunch. When the women got back to the Danjuma house, they watched some Nigerian movies, and Ibiso introduced Damisi to her favorite program, *Super Story*. On the other side of town, the Danjuma brothers spent the day golfing and having drinks.

Damisi picked up her wristwatch to check the time. Jabir had called a while ago to say he was on his way back. His mother had gone to bed early since she always went to first Mass. It was also her Sunday to usher, and she wanted to be back to see them before they left for the airport. Damisi slipped on her night dress, wrapped her hair and tied it with a silk scarf. She had toyed with the idea of cutting her hair, but quickly tossed it aside. Jabir loved her hair. She turned down the comforter and entered into the king-sized haven. Reaching for her bag, she retrieved her Christian novel and searched for her page. Her plan was to read until Jabir got back, then as had become a nightly ritual, she'd insist they pray together. Seconds later, nature took over and she drifted off to sleep.

Jabir and Kamal walked into the house an hour later than they should. Jabir had wanted to talk to his twin without Rasheed present. He and Damisi would be off to Lagos come morning, so this was the only opportunity he'd have face-to-face time with Kamal for a while.

"Bro, with the rate you're going, you'll get into some real

trouble soon," Jabir said once they were seated in the study of their mother's home. "What's going on with you?"

"Are you Dr. Phil now? I'm good. What are you talking about?"

"I read about the DUI you're being charged with. Not too long ago, I was in LA because you were involved in a brawl."

"Are you checking up on me now? *Abeg* chill *jor.*" Kamal stood and walked to the door.

"Wait. I'm not checking up on you, but I'm worried." Jabir was not going to tell his brother he had set up a Google alert with his name or remind him that as a star footballer, news got out.

"Well, don't be. Everything is good. Those were trumped-up charges. My lawyer promised to get them dropped."

"I know what happened, but I'm trying to ask why all this stuff is happening."

"I'm stressed, okay? Let it rest." Kamal raised his voice. He paused and bowed his head. He then looked at Jabir and continued. "My game is off, and I overheard talks they might trade me. That would mean me starting all over, and at thirty-three, I don't have very long in this sport. So like I said, I was just stressed."

"Okay, relax, but allowing yourself to be stressed and acting up is the wrong way to go." Jabir stood, walked over to his brother and patted him on the back. "Just concentrate and get your game together. God will take care of the rest."

"Huh? Did you just drop a God quote?"

Jabir shook his head. He couldn't believe it himself. His wife and Rasheed were to blame. He of all people knew the hard work you put in was what created results. "Man, whatever. I'm going upstairs to see my wife. I haven't seen her all day."

"See you in the morning."

"Good night."

Chapter 27

"Good morning, *mpenzi*."

The sultry voice caused Jabir to stir in his sleep. He slowly opened his eyes and his wife came in to focus, standing next to his side of the bed.

"Good morning, baby." He raised his head from the pillow and gave her a kiss. "I hope you slept well."

"Yes, I did, but your children didn't let me rest much toward morning." She rubbed her stomach. "I think they're early risers."

Jabir pulled himself to a sitting position, then placed his feet on the floor. He widened his legs and positioned Damisi between them. He kissed her stomach through the polyester-and-cotton fabric of her dress. That light, flowery perfume that made him go insane teased his nostrils. He rubbed her stomach, and it occurred to him she was showered and dressed.

"Where are you going? Our flight isn't until evening." He looked around the room. She had packed and laid out something for him to wear. He turned back and looked at her.

She gave him a blank stare and placed the towel in her hand across his bare shoulders.

"I guess wherever you're going, I'm going too, right?" he asked.

"You're such a smart man. Ibiso and Rasheed are on their way. We're going to church, then brunch."

"Huh?" He lay back down and covered his forehead with his hand.

She got on the bed and removed his hand. "Don't huh me. Today is Sunday." She walked around to the other side of the bed.

He scowled and frowned.

She quickly blew him a kiss and pouted. He gave in. He recognized he really didn't have a choice.

"Okay. Stop looking at me like that. I'm going to get ready."

"Good boy. Mama is back from Mass. She said to tell you she stepped out with Mrs. Iheme. Kamal is also getting ready," she said, looking past him.

Jabir followed her gaze to the bed and the outfit she laid out. The sky-blue button-down shirt, dark blue jeans and a black blazer complemented her gray-and-blue dress.

"Kammy is going to church?"

"Yes, but only because I told him we'd be going for brunch afterward." She giggled, nudging him toward the bathroom. "Hurry up. You have thirty minutes. They'll be here soon."

Hours later, Jabir wrapped his arm around Damisi when they were instructed to sit down by the man who just stepped on the podium. Ibiso and Rasheed were seated to their right while Kamal was seated to their left. Jabir smiled knowing Kamal couldn't wait for this to be over before it even started. He wasn't any better since he was in the sanctuary of Over-comer's Chapel because he wanted to make his wife happy. He had no false notion that he would hear a life-converting word from God.

He ran through all the things he had to do once they left the church. They'd be headed back to Lagos in a few hours, and he needed to make sure he did everything to protect her from the storm she was so sure was coming. He also needed to check his emails. He had gotten his half-sister, Halima to tell their real estate agent to line up some houses for them to look at. He should have gotten some houses to check out by now. Jabir also needed to see is if Lyle had any update on the rumor mill concerning his fake marriage to Angela. He was also expecting a call back from his friend, Bernard. Jabir had left him a message offering help at the clinic since everything was up in the air until Damisi checked in at work.

"So brethren," the pastor's voice brought Jabir's mind to the present, "as I wrap up this message…"

Wrap up? How long has the man been talking and I haven't heard a word? Jabir focused. He didn't want to look like a complete idiot if Damisi wanted to talk about what pastor said later.

"According to John 15:5, Jesus tells us that without Him, we're nothing. There's no long story or complicated formula to it. Everything minus Jesus is nothing. Simple. *Shikena.* Finish. Stop trying to do everything yourself. Nothing you have is by luck or chance. It's all due to God's grace and favor, so trust Him. Stand to your feet. Let us pray."

The service ended soon after, but not without a call to the altar, offering and some announcements. After the service, while the women went to freshen up, Rasheed introduced them to some members of the men's ministry and the pastor. Soon word spread that *the* Kamal Danjuma was in the church. On their way out of the sanctuary, people came up to him wanting autographs and pictures with him. Jabir and Rasheed glanced at each other knowingly and took a step back for Kamal to do his thing. Their brother was well known in America and Europe, but his fame skyrocketed in Nigeria when he played for the national team during an international competition. After the crowd died down, the Danjuma brothers left the church.

Jabir smiled and put his hands in his pockets when he saw

Damisi approach. She curved her arm around his waist, and he draped his arm over her shoulder. Rasheed brushed his lips against his wife's.

Kamal let out a sound from his throat. "Please let's go and eat. Once I'm fed, you guys can continue with the sickening PDA."

"Are you okay?" Jabir whispered to Damisi as they walked to the car.

"Yes," she said. "Very."

He took her hand in his. He felt her ring finger, it was bare. "Fingers still swollen? We can get the ring resized."

She looked at her fingers and frowned at him. "No, the rings are fine. They are in my purse. I'll put them back on when the swelling goes down."

Jabir grinned at her then winked.

During the prayer, Jabir watched as Damisi's mood turned melancholic. He had drawn her close and whispered, "It's going to be okay."

She had given him a faint smile, but her mood didn't change. In fact, a tear fell down her cheek afterward. Left to him, no matter what happened, she'd never have to work a day in her life if she didn't want to. However, he knew her job, especially the *Becoming Ruth* program she had started from scratch, was everything to her, so he understood but didn't share her anxiety. Jabir didn't think anything would happen. If only he could get her to believe it.

Ibiso must have talked to her when they went to the ladies' room. Jabir raised his head. His gaze searched for Ibiso's. Instinctively, Ibiso turned around and he mouthed, "Thank you."

She nodded.

Some hours after, the five of them were fed and enjoying conversation at a restaurant near the airport.

"So while you're in Detroit, who'll take care of my new

sister?" Kamal asked Jabir, then he nudged Damisi with his shoulder. "Or are you moving?"

Jabir pointed to his mouth and shook his head as he finished chewing the dessert he'd ordered.

"Excuse me. I'm capable of taking care of myself," Damisi protested.

Ibiso, who had her head on Rasheed's shoulder, laughed. "Tell them, oh."

"You think that's funny, huh?" Rasheed playfully tugged his wife's cheek.

"Of course it's funny," Damisi said and high fived Ibiso. Her eyebrows were raised toward Rasheed as though she was waiting for him to say something.

"Detroit is off the table for now," Jabir finally answered.

He drank his fruit juice and set his glass down. "Halima or her cousin Moji would have been glad to stay with her, but I wonder how my business became your business."

"Don't mind him," Rasheed said.

Damisi waved her hand in the air. "I'm sitting right here."

They laughed, and Jabir planted a kiss on her cheek. "We know, baby."

After a few moments Kamal asked, "You guys ready to go?" He checked his watch. "I leave in two days, and as the favorite son, I wanna make sure I spend enough time with Mama."

Kamal removed some bills from his wallet. "I didn't know you took delusion courses in school."

Laughing, the group exited the restaurant. Outside, Damisi hugged Kamal and kissed him on the cheek. "Thank you for lunch."

Kamal draped his arm around her shoulders "I'll feed you anytime."

Jabir grinned, pleased his wife and twin were getting along. After all his resentment, Kamal decided to be supportive of him and accepting of Damisi. When they became of dating age, the twins always had the final say about the other's relationship. If one of them didn't like the other's lady, there was little hope of it lasting. The day Jabir found out he was going to be a father that tradition flew out of the window. If Kamal hadn't liked Damisi, that would have been too bad since Jabir had her for keeps.

Just as they got to the car, two men with women who seemed like their girlfriends approached them.

"Excuse us, please. We're big fans. Can we get a picture?" one of them asked. His question was directed at Jabir.

"I'd love to, but I think you want his picture, not mine." Jabir pointed to Kamal.

The group did a double take with confused expressions. They chuckled and walked over to Kamal.

Kamal removed his arm from around Damisi's shoulder and held out his hand to shake the man's hand. Damisi moved to the side when they heard a scream come from one of the women.

"Ha! Ha! I knew I recognized you, Ma." She dragged the other girl. "Ify, this is the woman that does *Becoming Ruth* on Channel 151."

The two women seemed happy to see Damisi, and her face also reflected their excitement. Jabir had never seen her around her fans and relished in her joy. Seconds later, he noticed the glee on Damisi's face disappear. His eyes caught the disparaging look one of the women gave her stomach, then he followed as the woman's gaze landed on Damisi's finger. She nudged the other woman with her shoulder. Soon after, the party of four hurried away.

Jabir walked up to his wife and pulled her away. "You okay?"

She trembled and shrugged. "Might as well get used to it." Her voice was shaky.

He took her hand and led her to the car where Kamal was already waiting. The couple gave Rasheed and Ibiso hugs and said their good-byes. Jabir opened the back door of the car and Damisi got in. He slid in and drew her to his side. She rested her head on his shoulder.

Kamal turned back and looked at Damisi. "I'm so sorry, Damisi. Sometimes I forget I have people out there who want a picture of me. I should've declined."

"It's not your fault. People want to take pictures with me as well. They look up to us as role models and people they admire," Damisi said.

Then Jabir heard her mumble under her breath, "Too bad I turned out to be a hypocrite."

He and Kamal exchanged knowing looks. No words were necessary as they decided to change the topic.

Jabir's heart ached at her words. Damisi said she had no regrets being with him, but she regretted how they came about. He knew her values. He knew what and who she was, but he pursued her relentlessly. Her pain was in a huge way his fault, and he was going to move mountains to take it away.

———————————————

Chapter 28

———————————————

Two days later, Damisi got up earlier than she normally would. Anxiety and overactive babies deprived her of the rest she needed. She sat up on the bed, moved the covers to the side and got on her knees. Jabir was still fast asleep. They spent the majority of the last couple of days talking about the future. She was so proud of what he had accomplished. The surgery award was a big deal to him, and she added him getting it to her prayer points. Later, they spent some time rearranging his things in the guesthouse to accommodate the little she brought over.

Damisi reached across the bed and placed her hand over his outstretched one. She prayed in silence. She then sat back on the bed and looked over at the timer on the dresser. 6:42 A.M. She had to be at the station in a little more than three hours. She walked into the closet. She still couldn't believe it was so big. Danjuma Group had spared no expense with this guesthouse. It looked and felt like a real home. Some of the furniture looked contemporary like the dresser, the lamps and the drapery while the king-sized poster-and oak-bed screamed tradition. The sheets were crisp white; a sharp contrast to the delightful green color of the walls, which provided warmth.

Seconds later, she was still staring into the closet. "What to wear? Decisions, decisions." She reached for the pink-and-black striped maternity dress she had purchased in Abuja. At first, the dress didn't appeal to her, but now, she was grateful Ibiso had forced her to buy it. Damisi's mind travelled to the conversation she'd had with Ibiso in the ladies' room of the church some days ago.

"Dami, you need to stop beating yourself up. These babies are a blessing, and Jabir is a good man. You didn't want it this way, but it happened," Ibiso had told her.

"Soso, I know that. I just feel so bad sometimes that I sinned against God. I knew better."

Ibiso had grabbed both of her hands. "Stop letting the devil steal your joy. The God we serve has forgiven you, now forgive yourself and enjoy your husband. Whatever happens with your job, His strength will not depart from you."

Damisi was deep in her thoughts and didn't notice her husband had woken up until he wrapped his arms around her. She rested her head on his chest. He kissed the crown of her head.

"Good morning, *mpenzi.*"

"Morning, wife. What are you doing up so early?"

"Early? It's 7:10."

"Hmm…come to bed." He started to retreat backward, dragging her with him until he sat on the bed. He drew her down to his lap and nuzzled his nose against her arm. Then he began to place light kisses all over her arm and neck. Her insides turned to jelly. He was the master at seduction. Damisi moaned when she remembered how he had made sweet love to her the night before. He was gentle and caring as always, asking if she was okay because of the babies. She, on the other hand, was hungry for him to satisfy her need.

"You're tempting me…"

"That's the idea, woman." He looked at her. "I don't want to hurt the babies, but I want their mama now."

She laughed. "You're a doctor. You should know the babies are protected."

"In my head I do." He rubbed her stomach and kissed it, "but I just want to be careful."

At that point, she knew she had to take charge of this moment or her husband would kill it with worry.

And she did.

———

A LITTLE WHILE LATER, DAMISI HAD SHOWERED, CHANGED AND was making breakfast. She smiled when she remembered the satisfied look on her husband's face after their earlier rendezvous.

"You look nice," Damisi complimented him on his dark blue khakis and Ankara short-sleeved shirt. Today was a first for him as well. He was going to consult with Bernard in the clinic.

He winked. "Thanks, baby. So how long will you be at the station?"

She took a sip of her juice. "Not sure. You know I've been gone for a while."

Jabir nodded and took the glass from her and drank. Her phone rang. She looked at the caller ID. It was her cousin, Moji.

"Are you okay?" Moji asked as soon as Damisi answered the phone. "Have you seen it yet?"

"Huh? Slow down. Seen what? Why wouldn't I be okay?" Damisi asked. She stood from her seat and shrugged at the unspoken question in Jabir's eyes.

"Turn the TV to Channel 6," Moji commanded. "They mentioned something about you and a scandal coming up next."

Damisi scrunched her eyebrows in confusion. "Turn on the TV to Channel 6." Jabir did.

Damisi dropped the phone as the images on the screen came into focus. Jabir rushed to her side and ushered her to the sitting area. She paled, raising a hand to cover her beating heart as she took in the scene in front of her. On the screen were her and Kamal and the headline read. "The Abstinence Princess, Damisi Odinga, Pregnant for Famed Footballer Kamal Danjuma." She recognized the picture immediately. It was of them coming out of the restaurant in Abuja. Kamal had his arm around her.

The anchor, who Damisi knew for her sensationalism, sported a big smile as she read, "Today we're talking about the mystery of an abstinence princess, a baby and no ring. This weekend, famed footballer Kamal Danjuma was spotted with his pregnant girlfriend, Damisi Odinga, in Abuja. The abstinence princess who is the host of *Becoming Ruth* on the Christian news station KTN was seen very pregnant and without a ring. Many are asking, was there a secret wedding, or is this another case of the preacher not practicing what they preach? Stay tuned as we bring you up-to-the-minute information. For our fans on Twitter, follow our hashtag, #DamisiCarryBelle.

Damisi sat speechless. The words she wanted to say refused to string into a coherent thought. It was as if her brain short-circuited and needed to be rebooted. Around her, everything was in slow motion. *How could this happen?*

"How can she read such nonsense with so much confidence?" Jabir thundered. He picked up his phone and dialed. After a couple of seconds, he hung up.

Damisi assumed whoever he was trying to call was not there. Her phone began to ring. It was Eno. She sent the call to voice mail. She wasn't ready to talk to her right now or anyone for that matter. Tears streamed down her face. She held her face in her hands and prayed. *This is it, but Your grace is sufficient for me, O Lord.*

Her husband began to pace. "I can't believe some idiots sold that picture to the press."

She looked at her wedding ring. Why hadn't she remembered to put it back on? It would have made the story less hurtful—or would it?

Jabir got on the phone again. After several rings, he said, "Rasheed, call me back," then he hung up.

He walked over to Damisi and cuddled her in his arms. The tears refused to stop. The music had begun to play; now it was time to dance.

Chapter 29

"What do you mean by we should let it be?"

Jabir and Damisi were seated in the backseat of the car. Jabir had called Halima to send over one of the company drivers to take them to the station. They had received several calls from their families and assured them Damisi was all right.

Damisi turned to her husband. "I'm not ready to fight the press right now. I don't have time for it. Very soon, they'll find another story, and I'll be old news. Now I just have to weather the storm."

"I don't understand how you can be so calm about all this. That news report was a straight-out lie." Jabir's tone was defiant.

"I have bigger problems. Eno said the sponsors of my show have bombarded the station with calls ever since the news broke."

Jabir sucked in air. It was the only thing he could do to remain calm. This doing nothing was killing him. She said something about being still, but that had never been his style. He wished he could whisk her away to Detroit, but also knew she wouldn't go for it. Not now.

"My show is my primary concern and the fans that looked up to me." Damisi cracked her knuckles. Jabir placed his hand over them.

"Baby, I'm so sorry, but we'll get through this. I know how hard you've worked to get to where you are. Say the word and we'll be in Detroit tomorrow. We can come back when this is all over." His heart thudded in his chest waiting for her response.

She shook her head. "Jabir, I can't run from my mess." She paused. "If you break a glass, you're sorry, but you're still left with the clean-up."

"Huh? What does that mean?"

"I messed up. I've been forgiven, but there are still consequences," Damisi explained.

Jabir studied her for a minute, hesitant to affirm her analogy. Damisi moved closer to him and rested her head on his shoulder. He wrapped his arm around her. They remained silent, drawing off each other's strength.

They got to KTN minutes later. The front of the station had photographers, so Jabir instructed the driver to drive to the next street. Damisi picked up her phone.

"We're here," Damisi said when Eno answered.

"Okay, drive around the back. I'll be there to open the door," Eno said.

"Driver, please use MacBay Street to drive around back," Damisi instructed after disconnecting the call.

"My baby, the superstar," Jabir said. He saw her as just his woman, but judging from the scene outside and what had happened in the last couple of hours, the country saw her as something totally different.

Damisi gave him a scolding look. "One day we'll laugh about this, but today is not the day."

Jabir knew his joke fell flat, but he was grasping for straws. He longed to hear her laugh again. The pain he saw on her face arrowed into his heart. He had talked to Rasheed earlier about getting the Danjuma lawyers involved, but Damisi refused, insisting it would only prolong the story.

The driver parked the car, and Damisi placed her hand on the door to open it. She spotted Eno pepping out of the back door.

Jabir held on to Damisi's hand. "Wait here."

"No, stay in the car. I don't want them getting a picture of you or dragging you into this," Damisi said.

Jabir's expression froze. "If you think I'm going to sit back and let you take the heat by yourself, then something is seriously wrong." He was pissed at her suggestion. He got out of the car and walked around to help her out. He trapped her between the opened door and his body. He placed his hand gently on her neck and drew her lips to his. After a brief hard kiss, he said. "I protect what's mine. Don't ever forget it."

Damisi managed a faint smile. "I'll call as soon as I hear something."

Jabir turned to leave, but Damisi grabbed his hand. "Don't go fighting any wars. We're going to trust God with this. I love you."

"I love you too, baby, more than ever. Are you sure you don't want me in there?"

"I'm sure."

Her strength and calmness since this started surprised him. She was a strong, independent woman, no doubt about that, but this was different. She was pregnant, and this situation would bring about unnecessary stress. The thought made his stomach clench. He wished she would allow him to be there for her.

"Call me."

Damisi nodded, then turned and walked into the television station.

By late evening, the emergency meeting of the management of KTN had convened. Damisi had spent the day in her office, trying to catch up on emails and to-dos that had accumulated during her absence. It was all she could do to keep from running out her mind with worry. In between warding off various news outlets that somehow got her number, she took calls from Moji and Ibiso who wanted minute-by-minute updates. Eno never left her side until she was called into the meeting.

Damisi stood and walked over to her window. She wondered what the outcome of the meeting would be. *Keep your mind stayed on Me, and I will give you rest.* Damisi repeated God's promise. She hoped Jabir was doing the same. He had been so guilt ridden all morning, blaming himself for the turn of events. It took her quite a while to convince him she was more to blame, and everything would be all right. She had to hold on to hope. That was all she had. Damisi cracked her knuckles and whispered. "Help my unbelief, Lord."

She had received countless texts from Jabir asking for an update and reassuring her everything would be okay. There was a light knock on the door, and Eno entered her office. The somber look on her face caused Damisi's heart to drop.

"That bad?" Damisi wrapped her arms around her body and moved toward Eno, praying for her to show a glimmer of hope.

"I don't know, but it's not looking good. Mrs. Kofo is fighting for you, but as you know, the sponsors pay the bills, and they've been bombarding Mr. Donte and senior management with calls all day." Eno opened her arms, and Damisi walked into the embrace. She held the embrace, but refused to cry. No more.

Letting go, Damisi asked, "Are they ready for me now?"

"Yes. I came to get you."

"All right, let's go."

They made the short walk to the conference room. Along the way, Damisi got stares and heard hushed whispers from other members of the staff. She'd been getting them all morning. Kemi, the anchor for the evening news came up to them, offering her empathy. Damisi took her words at face value. She knew better. The only reason Kemi came up was to get information she could share with any newspaper that asked. Damisi knocked on the door of the conference room and entered. She thanked the Lord their eyes did not carry some kind of infrared beams. On impulse, her hands went to her stomach as the hot gaze of six people settled on it.

"Good evening, Ma. Good afternoon, sirs." Damisi greeted the one-woman, five-man panel.

"Good evening, Damisi," Mrs. Kofo answered. The men simply grunted in her direction.

Damisi sat at the opposite end of the table as though she was there for an interview and not part of the team. *This cannot be good.*

Mr. Donte started to speak. "Ms. Odinga, you must know why we had to convene this emergency meeting, so I'll get right to it. You are aware that when we hire anybody to be part of our team, they have to sign an integrity promise."

Damisi nodded.

"And so you know that when you sign, you *are* promising to represent the station with integrity and uphold the values we represent. In light of the recent events, it is evident you have violated that agreement. The sponsors are threatening to withdraw their naira from a station and a program that doesn't practice what it preaches." He paused. "We can't have an unmarried, pregnant anchor representing us on air...no matter how valuable you've been in the past."

With each piercing word that came out of his mouth, Damisi was surprised she had no reaction. It was as though she was having an out-of-body experience. Her spirit was still.

So calm that she decided to listen to all they had to say without interruption—even the untruths.

"I've always said that that integrity letter is too severe. We have all these people behind that camera doing things we cannot see, which I'm sure are contrary to what we stand for, but because they haven't been caught or are behind the scenes, they go free," Mrs. Kofo said. Her frustration was evident.

Mr. Akpan, a younger member of management turned to Mrs. Kofo and said, "That is left for them and their God. The Bible we stand on says whatever is done in the secret will come out into the light." Then he turned to Damisi and said, "No pun intended."

Damisi nodded.

"This young lady has dedicated the last six years to this company. Her show brings in the most ratings. We can't just let her go," another member of the panel said.

"So we keep her, after tarnishing our image just for the naira?" Mr. Donte replied. "We have to let her go."

"Ha! You want to terminate her appointment just like that? A suspension is fine, but..." Mrs. Kofo trailed off as though she knew she had lost the fight.

Damisi's heart fell to her stomach. She felt the weight of a clamp squeeze tight on her heart as the reality of having all she had worked for go down the drain became imminent. The babies must have felt her discomfort as they kicked her hard. She groaned. "Excuse me. If I may say something."

"Yes, you may, my dear," Mrs. Kofo said.

Damisi felt the burning of all their stares on her skin. She cleared her throat. "I would like to sincerely apologize for bringing disgrace to this station. I love this station and what it represents, but I went astray. I acknowledge that. I've repented for my sin, but I also understand the situation you're in, so whatever decision you make, I accept. But I have one request."

"Which is?" Mr. Akpan asked with disgust.

"That I be allowed to talk to my fans—or those fans I have left—on my show, one last time," Damisi said.

"For what?" Mr. Donte said, his tone harsh.

"To tell them the real truth. The story that's been airing, the one the sponsors are basing their decision on, is not the truth," Damisi said.

Mrs. Kofo perked up. "Really? *Oya* my dear, tell us the truth."

Damisi scanned the faces of the men in the room. From expressions, they could care less. Their minds were already made up. However, she owed it to Kamal to clear his name. He had felt so guilty when he'd called her earlier. He really didn't care about his reputation, but she and Jabir did—for very different reasons. For Jabir, he wanted the world to know she was his and not his brother's. For her, it was the right thing to do. Kamal shouldn't be in her mess.

"The truth is, I got pregnant before marriage, however I'm now married to my babies' father." She waited for a response. None came. "And he is not Kamal Danjuma the footballer, but his twin brother Jabir Danjuma, a medical doctor based in Detroit."

There was silence in the room.

"*Eh hen*, I knew it. Congratulations, my dear. Is he that man you introduced me to at the gala?" Mrs. Kofo asked.

"Thank you, Ma, and yes, he's the one." Damisi watched the men for a reaction. Nothing. They remained silent.

Finally Mr. Donte spoke. "Congratulations on your marriage. While I'm not sure how much this changes things, step outside and let us discuss."

Damisi walked out of the room. Eno was waiting for her right outside the door.

"What happened? What did they say?" she asked.

Damisi quickly narrated what happened to Eno.

"I told you that Mrs. Kofo fought hard when I was there.

They tried to say I knew and didn't report it and wanted to suspend me, but she stood up for me."

"I'm sorry for putting you through that. I should've listened when you told me to say something the first time."

"The thing with your dad interrupted the plan. It's fine," Eno reassured her.

Her phone buzzed, alerting her to a text.

What's going on? I'm worried~ J

She quickly composed a reply. *Almost done. It's fine. Will call soon.* She hit the send button when the door opened.

"We're ready for you now, Mrs. Danjuma," Mr. Akpan said.

Nobody has called her that since Moji the other night. Damisi squeezed Eno's hand, then followed the man back into the conference room. She sat down and the look on Mrs. Kofo's face said it all.

"We'll grant your request to explain your side of the story, but it will be your farewell speech. We stand by our decision to let you go. People look up to you here. We can't have you setting a bad example for them. It'll make them think we're flexible with the values we stand on. We're about righteous living. If you're going to be our face—our spokeswoman—you have to uphold our values," Mr. Donte said.

Damisi kept her emotions in check. Mrs. Kofo shook her head.

"We'll let you tape your speech now, and it will air tomorrow morning," one of the other men on the panel said.

"Mrs. Kofo, see that everything is done," Mr. Donte said. "I just got another call from another sponsor when you stepped out. They want answers."

Damisi was tired. She needed her bed and her husband. The strength to fight had left her. She stood and placed her hands on her stomach. "Thank you for the opportunity to work here. Again, I regret my actions and accept your decision." She walked toward the door, "And also, thanks for allowing to me to get my own side of the story out."

The men nodded, and Mrs. Kofo walked up to her and hugged her. "Come. Let's get you to makeup."

Chapter 30

Jabir removed his stethoscope from around his neck and walked down the hall to the medium-sized corner office Bernard had given to him. The office, painted in hues of blue, was a sharp contrast to the darker color of his Detroit office. He rounded the desk and sunk himself into the large leather chair. He took out his phone again, and there wasn't a text or a call from Damisi. The last time he checked, she told him she'd call him soon. It was now 7:00 P.M. and he had just finished with the last patient. He really didn't want to work after the fiasco earlier in the morning, but he had given Bernard his word, and it was a good way to stay busy to keep him from losing his mind.

"That does it. I'm going to go find my wife." Jabir picked up his blazer and headed out of the office.

He peeped in Bernard's office on his way out. His friend was on the phone, so Jabir signaled to let him know he was leaving. Bernard raised a hand to stop him. After a few seconds, he hung up the phone. Jabir entered the office.

"Man, you sure stay busy around here," Jabir said.

"Yeah, not every day, but most days. See why I've been hounding you about coming to join me?"

"Hmm, I'm just glad to see my investment is being put to good use." Jabir smiled. He looked around and admired Bernard's office.

"I'm so thankful you took a chance on me."

"Me, too. Now, I've gotta go get my wife." He gave Bernard a knowing smile. "Depending on what happens, I'll let you know if I'll be here tomorrow."

A look of compassion overtook Bernard's face. "I understand completely. What should be a happy occasion is turning out to be a media circus. Remember what I told you this morning, this too will pass."

Jabir scowled. All day, there had been constant news updates about Damisi's pregnancy during the entertainment segment of the news. Even Twitter Lagos had trended with #DamisiCarryBelle for exactly three hours. He knew because he tracked it. KTN had made an announcement that they'd release a full statement soon, but still no word from his wife.

"It's crazy, man. Left to me, we would have been out of this country immediately after the story broke, but you know Damisi. She has this 'I must own up to my mistake' crusade." He paused. "As though it was anybody's business what we did."

Bernard walked around and patted Jabir's back. "My guy, to you it might be nothing, but to Damisi, it's everything." He shook his head and folded his arms across his chest. "Tucked away in America, there's no way you can possibly know the impact she has on thousands of young women in this country."

Jabir offered no response.

"Your wife is a true woman of God for what she wants to do. Others would have run away. You should just be there for her because she'll be the top headline for a while," Bernard finished.

Jabir thought about his friend's words. To some degree, he understood better, but still he needed to do everything in his power to shield her mind, body and soul. First thing would be to get her home and hold her tight.

"I hear you, man." Jabir nodded.

His phone buzzed. It was a text from Damisi.

Pls come get me.

The curtness of the text made his heart constrict. Jabir frowned.

"Damisi?" Bernard asked.

"Yeah. I have to go. My regards to Yvette and the kids," Jabir said over his shoulder.

"Will do. Call me."

Jabir got into the car and activated his hands-free device. He had dismissed the driver hours ago. Damisi answered on the fourth ring.

"Baby, are you okay?" Jabir asked before she spoke.

She remained silent, but he heard her sniffles. The thought that she had been crying felt like a knife running through his chest.

"Please stop crying and talk to me. I'm on my way."

His statement only seemed to make her cry more. He stepped on the accelerator.

"I was fired," she said through muffled sounds of anguish.

"What? Hang tight, I'm coming." He disconnected the call.

Jabir's heart sank. He knew they would want to do something, but to fire her? He swallowed bile of guilt. If he had exercised restraint, they wouldn't be in this mess. She wouldn't be losing her career or going through the ridicule she now faced. He blamed himself. He had always known where she stood and her faith. However, his want for her made him disregard all that and pursue her relentlessly. Even in her current distress, she still reassured him of her love. What had he done to be worthy of her?

After everything that had gone down, how could she love him? In the morning, they had said the words to each other, but now that she had lost her career and her name was being dragged through the mud, would she still love him? Jabir ached at the thought of her taking her words back. The idea of her retreating from him emotionally made him sick. It had taken him a while to realize how much he needed her. To lose her again would be to lose a piece of his soul.

———

Jabir reentered the bedroom carrying a breakfast tray. Damisi was still curled up in the fetal position she was in when he got up a while ago. She hadn't said anything since the night before. Throughout the night, all she did was cry. Jabir had carried her from the garage to the bedroom, ignoring her light protests. He had placed her on the bed while he ran her bath. He then slowly undressed her and pinned her hair on top her head. She was visibly shaken, and he was helpless. She was functioning on autopilot. Jabir helped her to the bath and lowered her in it. Afterward, he dressed her and warmed up some milk for her. She drank, mumbled her thanks, lay on her side and closed her eyes.

He had watched her for several seconds, then offered to read her Bible to her. It was something she liked doing. But, she refused and drew the covers over her. His heart was in knots. His anger flared. He wanted to fix it for her, but she wasn't talking, so he was clueless on where to start. He had then remembered Bernard's words. Right now his wife was hurting and would talk when she was ready.

He had taken a quick shower, turned their phones on do not disturb, gotten into the bed and held her tight. Thankfully, he felt her relax as she snuggled close. She needed him, and he was going to be right there.

He had let her be the night before, but it was a new day, and he wanted answers and was determined to get them, even if he had to go to the station.

"Hey, sleepy head. Breakfast is ready."

Damisi stirred, but didn't try to sit up. Jabir walked around to the other side of the bed and planted a light kiss on cheek. She stared, and her eyes fluttered, then she squinted and pulled herself to an upright position.

"Morning. I'm not really hungry," she said, her tone subdued.

"Well, that's too bad because you have to eat." His gaze travelled to her stomach.

Jabir smiled down at her, then walked over to draw the curtains. Sunlight illuminated the room. He strolled back over to the bed and sat on it. She lowered her head, but he raised it with his index finger.

"Baby, I'm so sorry about what happened. Tell me what to do and I'll do it." Jabir pushed back the stray strands of hair that escaped her head wrap. Damisi remained silent.

"I know you have your way of doing things—left to me, this would have gone differently—but let me know what you need."

"Promise you'll never leave me," she said. Her eyes were dark and intense. "I've lost everything I've worked for these past years. I won't be able to take another loss."

Her words knocked the wind out of him. He had expected her to be fuming and blaming him. He deserved it, but she left him speechless.

"Look at me. Never! You and our children are my world."
She blinked back tears.

"Please, don't." He picked her up and placed her in his lap. She rested her head in the crook of his neck. He rocked her for a couple of minutes in silence. She was supposed to be the weaker vessel, but he drew his strength from her.

"You should eat. Moji called. She'll be over soon," Jabir whispered.

Damisi shook her head. "I can't see anybody. Not today. Maybe later." She snuggled closer.

"Are you ready to talk?"

Damisi shrugged. She tried to get up from his lap, but he kept her in place.

"I need to pee."

Jabir loosened his hold. "Hurry back," he said, making sure his eyes and tone carried his meaning. They were going to talk.

Jabir walked over to the breakfast tray and uncovered her bowl of oatmeal. Making sure she had her choice of beverage, he filled one glass with orange juice and the other with milk. He took a sip of his Ovaltine and a bite of his eggs.

Damisi came out of the bathroom some minutes later and climbed back in the bed. He placed the tray on the bed and they began to eat. After a couple of minutes, he took her bowl of oatmeal from her and began to feed her.

"I'm waiting," Jabir said when she had swallowed the last spoonful of oatmeal.

"What's there to tell? The sponsors cried foul, and the station fired me," she said. Nonchalance laced her tone.

She put up a good façade, but she was not fooling him. It did matter, and he wanted details.

"Explain."

Damisi picked up her juice and began to tell him what happened the previous day. Jabir's nostrils flared in anger as he listened to her narrate the panel experience. His mother sometimes said, "He who is without sin, cast the first stone." Jabir wanted to strangle Mr. Donte. How self-righteous could they get?

He bolted from the bed nearly knocking over her glass of milk. "They had no right to treat you that way." He stomped to the dresser. "After all you've done for them?"

"Aren't you going into the clinic today?"

Her question surprised him. Where did that come from? Then he figured out she wanted to get rid of him so she could nurse her wounds in solitude. That was not going to happen. She needed him. He needed her.

"No," he quipped. Irritation that she was trying to push him away took over.

"I don't want to keep you from your patients…"

"Stop trying to get rid of me."

Her expression was blank, but he could see tears bubbling up to the surface. Jabir followed her gaze as she turned to look at the clock on the bedside dresser.

"They allowed me to record a farewell speech that will air today. It's scheduled for when my program would normally run." She picked up the remote and turned on the television.

He placed his hand over hers to stop her. "I don't want you reliving that again. If you'd rather not, that's okay."

"I want to," she whispered, settling on the channel.

He got back in the bed and drew her against his chest. The strawberry smell of her body wash still lingered.

Jabir had watched her program a few times and was always awed by her stage presence and the ease with which she drew her on-set and at-home audience in. There were a few announcements, then she appeared on the screen. Despite the turmoil she had been going through, his woman looked good.

"Good morning. Unless you've been living under a rock, you've heard the story that broke in the early hours of the morning. As a result, I am resigning effective immediately as the host of *Becoming Ruth*. I deeply regret my actions, the disappointment it has caused my fans, and the inconvenience it has caused the management and staff at KTN.

"Before I go, however, I owe my loyal followers the facts. Yes, I got pregnant out of wedlock, however, the father of my babies and I have known each other for seven years and are now married. Despite the media updates, I want to clear the record. Kamal Danjuma is not my husband, but my brother-in-law. I am married to his twin, Dr. Jabir Danjuma.

"In no way do I excuse my actions, but I love my husband and my unborn children dearly and will use this time to concentrate on them and the next steps God has for my life. I might have fallen, but true strength comes from getting up. So this is just so long and not good-bye. Be blessed, my friends. This is Damisi Odinga-Danjuma, signing off."

Neither of them spoke in the seconds that followed. His heart hammered against his chest. Guilt, shame, and anger overtook him that she was subjected to that humiliation. His love for her couldn't be greater in that moment. His hand shifted her head. Tears rolled down her cheeks.

He kissed them away. "I'm sorry. I'm so sorry," he whispered as his mouth sought hers. She kissed him with pure need that lessened his self-loathing for his contributions to her heartbreak. She needed him. Words were not necessary, and Damisi gave herself to her him, and he gave himself to her—both of them in desperate need of comfort.

Chapter 31

Damisi walked out of the bathroom with an oversized towel wrapped around her. The remaining drops of water on her exposed skin quickly dried in the cool room. She walked over to the closet and selected an orange-and-yellow dress and laid it across the bed. She grabbed her lotion off the dresser and squirted some in her hand. She let out an exaggerated sigh as she lotioned her body.

The last five weeks had been worse than she had imagined. At first she and Jabir were among the top five headlines in entertainment news every day. Then just as the news cycle began to change, the Right Foundation dropped her as their spokesperson. With that, she jumped back up to the number one spot.

She got constant calls from Ibiso, Moji and Eno, but the only person she allowed over was her cousin. With Moji, she didn't have to entertain. Sometimes she'd just lay in her lap and cry. One day, Damisi ventured outside her house, but she hadn't gone far when reporters came out of nowhere and had a field day. Then blogs chronicled her fall from grace, adding facts she didn't even know existed. The news entertainment report kept making up stories as they went along. She rarely left leave the house again, so their initial plans of buying a home also stalled. Their lives seemed to be stuck in time. As a matter of fact, almost everything was on hold, including Jabir's return trip to Detroit. Although he had extended his leave of absence from work, she felt bad about keeping him from his life.

Jabir had taken over. He cooked for her, gave her foot massages and catered to her every need. He also shielded her from the public by not allowing her to watch the news or read the newspaper. That wasn't enough to keep her from falling into despair. Her days and nights began to run together. All she did was eat, sleep and watch movies.

Damisi went from despair and isolation to anger. After all the years she had given KTN, they had the nerve to fire her just like that. No telling what went on in their house that was against the integrity clause, but they had made a public example out of her. She was the one who had the idea to start that show. The station had been slaughtered in ratings by the competition in the mornings. People were tired of the same boring teachings and preaching that didn't offer practical applications.

She and Eno had put up a pilot that was widely received, and the show took off. So did the demands on her time and private life. The station wanted more and more of her time, and she was being booked for more events. Nothing they had compensated her with made up for her time and sweat. How dare they discard her now? If it hadn't been for Mrs. Kofo's insistence on her covering the Danjuma wedding, she wouldn't have been in Abuja. Neither would she have had to ask Jabir for a favor.

Damisi stood from the bed and pulled her dress over her head. She looked over and saw plastic bottle of water she had thrown at her husband the previous evening. She gasped as regret took over. The events of the previous night came flooding back. Jabir had become the target of her pent-up anger. She closed her eyes and tried to rid herself of the look in his eyes when he left the room. As much as she tried to eradicate the memory, it insisted on playing itself out.

"I need you to eat something." He set the tray of food on the stool that was next to her on the couch.

She had taken her eyes off the Nigerian movie she was watching and peered at the tray. He had some Jollof rice, mixed vegetables and an orange. She stood and walked to the bedroom. She had gotten into the bed and lay with her back to the door. She had heard him enter a minute later.

"Baby." His tone lowered.

"I'm not hungry. I had some fruit."

"Fruit is not food. It's after eight at night, and you've had just one meal." She heard him draw in a breath. "Baby please, you've been like this for days." He walked over and touched her shoulder.

Damisi flinched at his touch, then she turned to look at him. "Jabir, please leave me alone. I need space. I'll be okay."

He gave her a disapproving glance. She knew she was a mess, but really didn't care. He looked around and began picking up the clothes strewn across the floor. She had followed his actions with her eyes. The room looked like a hurricane had passed through it. She should clean up, but she had nothing in her. Her pain was unbearable, and she just wished it would stop. He put the clothes in the hamper and turned to her.

"Okay, but you have to eat." He stretched out his hand toward her.

She observed him, adjusted her pillow, and lay back down. "Damisi—"

"I told you I don't want to eat!" she yelled at him. Her eyes blazed with anger. "You just have to have your way all the time, don't you?"

He stared at her, speechless, then he smiled. That smile had pushed her over the edge. Did he think her being out of a job and her reputation being dragged through the mud was funny?

"You're the reason I'm in this position," she accused.

"What is that supposed to mean?"

"If you had just helped me with the interview without asking that I go to the wedding with you in return, we wouldn't be here. I would have been on the first plane back to Lagos without any *wahala*. But you just couldn't take no for an answer, so you manipulated me anyway."

His expression was pained and the hurt evident, but she didn't care. Why should she be the only one in pain? So she pushed a little farther. "I just hate you."

The moment the words left her mouth, she felt remorse, but it was too late to take them back. Jabir had looked at her like she had pierced a dagger through his heart. He hadn't given her the satisfaction of an argument. Instead, he turned and walked out of the bedroom. She picked up the water bottle and threw it at the closed door.

The sound from the slammed front door was what jolted her to the realization that she had been blaming everybody but herself. And the one person that put up with her crap, she had finally pushed away. Her stomach dropped and her hands began to sweat as she cried uncontrollably. If she wasn't careful, she could lose the one thing that kept her stable: the love of her husband.

It was no surprise when she woke up earlier, he was gone. He had left her a note that he was going to the clinic and asked her to call if she needed anything.

Damisi walked over to the mirror, applied light makeup to her face and tied her hair in a silk scarf. She hadn't taken care of her appearance in the weeks she had been out of a job. She studied herself in the mirror. She had some visible bags under her eyes she needed to take care of. A trip to the salon was also in her immediate plans. Her nails, eyebrows and hair needed tending to.

It was almost noon when she walked into the living room. She picked up the remote and turned on the radio, then made her way to the kitchen. She opened the cupboards and the refrigerator and started making a list of things she needed to buy. She had to accept her loss and move on. She knew she would have consequences to her actions, but the actuality of it had been a bitter pill to swallow.

"It's a shame people get stuck in their mess. Every time you see them, they're ready to retell the story of how they were wronged," the voice on the radio said.

Damisi half listened as she went around the kitchen. She mentally calculated how much time she had before Jabir got home. She wanted to be back from the salon and make some *amala* and *ewedu* soup for him. Her late mother and Aunty Bola made sure Damisi was well versed in her Yoruba culture. Teaching her to speak the language and cook the food was a priority.

"I know exactly what you're saying. People act like it's the end of the road when they encounter stumbling blocks in life," another guest on the radio said.

Damisi paused. She walked into the living room and stood in front of the stereo. She protectively wrapped her hands over the twenty-two-week swell of her midsection. She thought about the words the radio guest just uttered.

"It's just like a car. If you're travelling down the road and you ignore when the GPS tells you to turn right. If you turn left, stop whining that you got lost. Acknowledge it, stop the car and turn around. When you get off course, what does the GPS say?"

"Rerouting," the other guest said.

Then laughter erupted.

"This is Stephen and Suzie…S & S of *Midday Moments*. If you're just joining us, we're talking about getting your life back on track. The topic is 'Rediscovering Your Path' with our guest pastor, Mrs. Laide, of House on the Mount. Here is

'Mercy Said No' by CeCe Winans. Keep it right here on 197.4. We'll be back."

Damisi's knees began to quiver as the melody of the song began to fill the room. She steadied herself and leaned against the arm of the chair. The words pierced her heart as though Ms. Winans was speaking to her. Strange thing was Damisi had heard the song several times before, but she hadn't paid attention to the lyrics. Despite her shortcomings, grace was indeed all she needed. In her despair, she had almost allowed sin to demand justice for her soul, but for the mercy of God. Mercy said no.

Her lips trembled at the realization that God's mercy and peace had been available to her all this while, but her flesh was content on playing the victim. She had committed the sin, and thought she could choose the consequences, but that was not how it worked. The veil had been lifted, and she realized she didn't get half of what she deserved. God not only shielded her from what she deserved, but He offered her grace, which she did nothing to merit—a chance to start fresh. Closing her eyes and taking a deep breath, she prayed, "Forgive me, dear Jesus. I repent. I truly repent of everything."

The accumulated sorrows of your exile will dissipate. I, your God, will get rid of them for you, the Lord whispered to her from Zephaniah 3:18.

Damisi felt a burden leave her. She walked into the kitchen and got a banana. She took a bite, picked up her list and purse and made her way out of the house. It was time for to recover all that was lost. God's mercy was bigger than any mistake she had made, and it was time for her to stay anchored in that truth.

———

Later that evening, the driver, who also doubled as her bodyguard, pulled back into the garage they'd vacated earlier.

For the first time in weeks, Damisi felt worthy. All her husband's fears turned out to be unfounded. When she'd called Jabir earlier to tell him of her intention to leave the house, she could sense his worry. He'd asked her to wait for him to drive her, but she objected to him leaving the clinic. He caved, then asked to speak to the driver.

Damisi was sure Jabir had scared the living daylights out of the man. Her suspicions were confirmed when she heard David say, "Yes, sir, I'll not let anything happen to her," then he had nodded. "Yes, sir, I know what's at stake if anything happens to her."

Damisi felt sorry for him, so she had made it easier on him by making a huge effort to hide behind her oversized sunshades. After the market, she spent the remaining time getting her hair and nails done. David got out of the car and opened the trunk to help her with some items. She used the connecting door to enter the kitchen. The clock on the stove told her she had barely a couple of hours to cook and have dinner ready.

Her phone rang as she placed the last bag on the granite countertop in the kitchen. She looked at the caller ID. It was Moji.

"Hold on," Damisi answered, out of breath.

"David, thank you so much. Take this." She reached in her purse and gave him some money. He was a Danjuma Group driver and was paid handsomely, but not for being her bodyguard. "Greet your wife for me."

He bowed. "I will. Thank you, Ma."

"Hello?" Damisi put the phone on speaker and laid it on the counter.

"Okay, this is getting ridiculous. It's been five weeks. Why are you still locked up in your house and sounding like a prisoner?" Moji's irritated voice came through the phone.

Damisi laughed. "You're too late for this pep talk. The Holy Spirit already convicted me."

"*Oshe Baba*. Thank you, Jesus. I thought I was going to have to preach. I just finished Googling Bible verses on encouragement," Moji said.

Damisi grunted at the relief in her cousin's voice. "You wouldn't have to Google if you cracked opened your Bible once in a while."

"Google is your friend," Moji replied. Damisi imagined her sticking out her tongue at her. "On a serious note, cuz, I love you and hate you're going through this, but the media has moved on to the next story. I'm glad you've moved on, too."

"I know, and I have."

"You have a gorgeous doctor who is in love with you and two babies on the way."

"God is merciful." Damisi felt shame at her ungratefulness and the way she had been carrying on. It could have been worse. Jabir could have flat out denied her. She had treated him pretty shabbily. Twice. She thought about his suggestion to go to Detroit for a while. Initially, she dismissed it, but now she was seriously considering it. His life was there, and Lagos had nothing to offer her anymore—at least not at the moment.

"My nieces or nephews will soon be here, and we haven't even fixed up the nursery yet. Let's go shopping."

Damisi smiled and rubbed her stomach protectively. "Nieces, and I may not be having the babies here."

"*Duro*, wait. You found out their sexes?" Moji yelled.

"Yes." Damisi smiled. She and Jabir were elated to find out they were having girls last week. "Sorry, cuz, I should've told you. I just wasn't in that celebratory place."

"Hmmm, I guess I forgive you. So, you are considering going back to Detroit with him?"

"Yes. I didn't want to at first. I didn't want to just disappear, but now it's looking more appealing."

"You loved Detroit. The main reason you ran was because

of your breakup. I'll miss you, but he's your husband, and nothing is stopping me from hopping on a plane."

Damisi eyes welled up. She loved her cousin so much. She was her number one fan and supporter.

"I'll let you know when we make a final decision."

"Okay. Let me know. I'll let *momsie* know you're okay now —or at least getting there." Moji chuckled. "We were about to storm over there and pour Holy water on you if I didn't give her a good report after talking to you."

Damisi laughed at the thought of Aunty Bola sprinkling water and gyrating all over her house in the name of prayer.

"Okay, I will. Now get off the phone. Let me cook for my husband."

"Hmm…take it easy, o. What are you now? About ten months pregnant?"

"Very funny. I'm actually about six months, and we're still sexually active, thank you very much." *That is until I started to starve him while blaming him for my problems.*

"Ewww…I did *not* need to know that. Bye."

Moji disconnected the call. Damisi laughed and looked around the kitchen. Now it was time to go to work. She placed her hand over her stomach, bent her head and whispered to the babies, "The art of seduction; step one: good food. Mummy needs to make up for being a pain in your daddy's side."

Chapter 32

I *just hate you.*

Jabir washed his hands and dried them with a paper towel and left the men's room of the clinic. He couldn't get those four words out of his mind. Damisi could have just as well used a knife to sear his heart. The guilt of the whole situation was killing him. In the past month, he'd watched helplessly as Damisi sank farther into despair, a far cry from the feisty, independent and strong woman who had become his wife. The media attention didn't help as they smeared her name on the slightest provocation. He tried to do everything he knew to make her smile, but in the end, that which he feared most was happening. They hadn't been married for more than two weeks and their life was unraveling right before his eyes.

How was he to know that a bowl of Jollof rice would get her to say things he only hoped never crossed her mind? He made his way down the short hall and turned right. Bernard was approaching from the opposite direction and smiled.

"You heading out?"

"Yeah, soon. Just tidying up," Jabir said.

"It's Wednesday, Bible study. After that the men are going out. You want to come with?" Bernard asked.

Jabir saw the anticipation in his eyes. He had accompanied Benny to his church Bible study once before, and although it was not the usual boring men quoting scripture gathering, he needed to get home to Damisi. She had gone out today for the first time, and although he knew he wasn't her favorite person at the moment, she was his responsibility, and he needed to make sure she was all right. The driver gave him no details when he had inquired.

"No, man, but next time. I promise." Jabir turned in the direction of his office.

Once inside, Jabir sat behind his desk and swiveled the chair from left to right. Restlessness got the better of him. He stood and walked to the window. He leaned on the sill and took in the sights and sounds of Victoria Island. The secluded upscale residential area, which was originally surrounded by water, had now been overtaken by an influx of banks, foreign embassies and other businesses. He and Damisi had started looking into buying a house in the area before they found themselves in their current storm—a situation that scared him.

All his life, he'd never allowed anyone or anything to get so close as to scare him, but he admitted to Kamal the night before, this did. Fear seized his chest at the thought of the wife he'd fallen hopelessly in love with despising him for the way her life had turned out. He needed help.

Pushing away from the window, he went in search of his cell phone and dialed.

"*How far now?*" Rasheed answered, his tone low with concern.

His whole family had been worried about Damisi and what the scandal had done to her. In Abuja, they didn't get the real effect of what was happening, but Jabir had filled them in as necessary.

"I don't know. Can you talk?"

"Where are you?"

"Office."

"Give me a second."

For the next couple of seconds, Jabir listened as Rasheed gave his secretary instructions on what to do, then he told her good night.

"Wassup? I'm heading home now. What are you still doing in the office?" Without waiting for an answer, Rasheed continued, "I thought your helping Bernard was just something you were doing until the babies are born. I didn't know it was full time."

"That's what I thought, too." Jabir sat in his chair, "but Damisi needs space. I think she hates me."

"Who? The woman I saw? Not true. You guys are just going through a rough patch." A pregnant pause followed. "It'll be over pretty soon."

Jabir sighed. "If only it were that simple."

"Whatever she's dishing out right now, you need to handle it and not run to the clinic to hide. This is major for her. She and your girls need you."

"Do you think I don't know that? I tried," Jabir said. A beat of silence passed between them, "but it's not that simple. She blames me."

"Why would she do that? Both of you made a wrong decision in sleeping together, but you love each other and got married. You're in this together. What's the problem?" Rasheed asked.

Jabir remained silent.

"Jabir?"

"Yes?"

"Why would she do that?"

Jabir sighed. He knew Rasheed had a scowl on his face. He narrated everything to his brother. Rasheed remained silent as Jabir narrated the real reason why she accompanied him to the wedding.

Rasheed remained silent.

"Say something?" Jabir said.

"You manipulated her," Rasheed said.

"We've established that." Jabir's temper rose.

"Don't be mad at me. This is your mess."

"Whatever, man. If I wanted to hear this, I would've called Mama." Jabir paused. "I love her. How am I going to fix this for her? You need to see what the press is doing to her. I should have never asked her to go with me to the wedding. I knew what could happen. I didn't try hard enough to stop it."

"You can't fix it. Just be there for her."

"Suppose she leaves me? She has nothing to lose anymore." Jabir's head pounded just forming the thought.

"Only one person can help you with the wisdom needed to handle this situation."

"Who? Don't tell me Jesus," Jabir said.

"The One and Only."

Jabir sighed.

"You tried to orchestrate everything yourself, and it didn't work. It's time for you to trust He'll work it out. It makes things a whole lot easier. I almost had to learn the hard way."

Jabir knew Rasheed was referring to the time when he and Ibiso had broken up, and he almost lost her by the time he came to his senses.

"I'm tired…"

"Trying to keep it together and be in control all the time is exhausting."

"Tell me about it." Jabir stood and started gathering his things to leave.

"Look, I need to get to my wife. I suggest you get to yours…trust God. Both of you should pray together. It'll be fine," Rasheed said.

"I hear you, bro." Jabir took a breath. "For someone who

had a stone-cold heart, the new you is scary. Ibiso did a good job."

"My baby introduced me to Jesus, but I'm still getting to know Him. I'm just telling you what has worked for me."

Suddenly Jabir said something he never thought he'd hear himself say, let alone to Rasheed. "Pray with me."

Before Jabir had the chance to think about it, Rasheed began to pray. "Father in heaven, thank you for another day, and the chance to do it right. You know the heart of my brother and his wife. They might have done it wrong, but they are sorry. Please help them forgive themselves and each other as You have forgiven them. Lead them through this valley of darkness. In Jesus' name. Amen."

"Amen." Jabir headed toward the door. "Next time a simple 'Jesus please help them' would suffice."

"Something is seriously wrong with you." Rasheed laughed. "You're welcome.

Jabir joined in on the laughter, then thanked his brother and ended the call. As he walked out of the office, he could admit that for the first time in weeks, he felt peace. He couldn't understand it, but welcomed it.

Jabir took in a breath and exited the car. He had spent the entire drive thinking about what Rasheed said about prayer. He even attempted to say a few words himself. He needed all the assistance he could get to help his wife through this—to get them back on track.

Armed with a new resolve, he unlocked the door and stepped in the house. It was dark. Candles in the four corners of the room provided illumination. He locked the door behind him, and with guarded steps, made his way through the living room. His heart lurched in anticipation of what lay ahead. The house he had left this morning was cold, a sharp contrast to the romantic and warm atmosphere that threatened to overwhelm him with emotion. Then he saw her.

Their eyes connected, and she smiled. She looked frail, but not the sickly kind, more like a sexy, delicate flower he knew he wanted to spend the rest of his days protecting. He didn't know how his legs propelled him forward, but in seconds, they met in the middle of the living room. Their eyes remained deadlocked. No words where necessary as he drunk her in with his eyes. Her perfume played tricks on his mind. He hadn't had the pleasure of inhaling her scent in weeks. The turquoise-blue dress she wore hugged her curves just right, bulging in the places that showed signs of impending motherhood.

"Hey, you," Jabir whispered.

"Hey yourself. Welcome home, *mpenzi.*"

Jabir beamed as he appreciated the full ambience of the room that smelled of apple and cinnamon.

"What's all this? Is everything all right?"

"Yes, silly." She tried to drag him with her.

Jabir didn't move. He drew her closer to him, her stomach crushed against him. He wrapped his hands around her, then he felt movement in her stomach and rubbed his hand over it. "How are my girls?"

"Just fine. Now come on. Let's get you cleaned up. I have a special dinner planned." Damisi tried to break free of his grasp, but he held on tight.

He looked down at her and caressed her cheek. "I'm so…"

She placed a finger on his lips. "Shh…I have some things to say, but it can wait." She broke free and guided him to the bedroom.

Once in the bedroom, Jabir's brow rose in surprise. It was nothing like what he left in the morning. He could actually see the floor. The clothes were neatly stacked in the corner for laundry. The dark wood dressers had been dusted off, and the room smelled of jasmine. He knew because she used the scent in her apartment. While he was still looking, Damisi entered the room. She watched his reaction. He observed her with his eyebrows furrowed. He was happy she busied herself, but worried she'd probably overexerted herself today.

"I'm not a pig. The devil had me down." Damisi laughed cheerfully. "Hope you like it."

He made the sign of zipping his mouth together. "I didn't say a word."

"Smart man. I knew you were more than just a handsome face." She winked and shooed him into the bathroom.

Minutes later, Jabir had showered and changed into a pair of lounging slacks and a t-shirt. He walked back into the living room. The sound of Seal's "Kiss from a Rose" played in the background. He smirked as the memory of that song in the story of their lives came to the forefront of his mind. It was movie night, and he had had a hard time convincing her to watch *Batman*. In the end, she'd hated it, but loved the soundtrack.

Damisi lit a candle and hummed to a tune that sounded familiar. She was a polar opposite of the person he'd left lying on the bed that morning. How or why he didn't know yet, but he was not going to question it.

"I know that song," Jabir wrapped his hands around her from behind.

She rested the back of her head on his chest, and he slanted her head for a light brush on her lips.

"You should. It's only my absolute bestest song ever…"

He chuckled and pulled out her chair for her to sit.

They sat, and Damisi said grace. The aromatic whiff of the mouthwatering delicacy tickled his nostrils. His eyes took in the meal of *amala* and *ewedu* soup in front of him. He smiled. He hadn't had the delicacy in ages—didn't even know she could prepare it. Sometimes he forgot she was half Yoruba.

"I see you've been busy…" He washed his hands in the bowl of water on the table.

"You like?"

"I love." He wiggled his eyebrows, and they began to eat.

They were halfway through the meal when he looked up at her. "Baby, I love this. I was trying to say earlier, I'm so sorry for my part in your pain. What happened today?" He paused. "All of this…"

She dipped the small rolled ball of *amala* into her *ewedu* soup. She lifted the ball and put it in her mouth. She licked the soup off her fingers and swallowed slowly.

Jabir's eyes hooded at her action. He had missed her in more ways than one. He willed himself to focus. They had a lot to talk about. He listened attentively as she apologized for her outburst the previous evening, then went on to tell him about her day and the radio show she stumbled upon. He smiled when she re-told the GPS analogy they had used. That seemed to be just like his life; he had definitely been rerouted. Nowhere in the journey of his life did he think he would end up here. Maybe he hadn't been the one driving all along.

"I knew you were hurting, and I didn't know how to fix it for you," Jabir said.

"It wasn't your place to fix it. My spirit knew what to do, but my flesh was weak. I just needed to be reminded who my God is."

After dinner, Jabir guided Damisi to the couch, elevated her feet and poured her a glass of juice. Once she was comfortable, he washed the dishes. He was drying the last plate when he felt her enter the kitchen.

"You should be resting." He leaned on the sink and pulled her close.

"Why don't we rest together?"

"You're asking for it." He grinned.

"And I want it, but before that, I've been thinking."

"About?"

"Detroit." Her eyes searched his for a reaction.

"And…" He tried to contain his happiness until she finished her thought. He was supportive of her decision to stay in Lagos, but had many loose ends in Detroit. At the same time, he wouldn't leave her. Couldn't leave her. She was his number one priority.

"Lagos holds nothing for me now. In the future it might, but your life is in Detroit, and I want to concentrate on bringing our girls into the world while I wait on the next phase in my journey. I know for sure God is not done with me yet."

He walked close to her. "Are you sure?"

A long pause passed between them. She braced his face in her hands. "Your home is my home. Right now, that is not Lagos. But on one condition."

He beamed. "Name it."

"I'm not staying where Tonya, Alicia, Stephanie, Paula or any of your chicks have stayed, so I suggest you start house hunting." She turned and sashayed—as much as her stomach would allow—out of the kitchen.

Jabir stared at her for a few moments, and threw his head back in laughter. How many women did his wife think he had? He wasn't that bad. Angela flashed through his mind. He shook his head at the ancient memory. He pumped his fist in the air. "Yes!"

Jabir slept better than he had in a while that night. The future was bright, and he was grateful for it. First thing in the morning, he'd call the realtor who got him his present condo. He was taking his baby home, and she would not lack for anything.

Chapter 33

Damisi hummed P-Square's "Onyinye" as she unpacked the last of the brand-new Nate Berkus plate set she'd bought online a couple of days ago. This was her fourth full week in Detroit, and she although she had settled in nicely, she still had pensive moments. Those moments, she shielded from Jabir. He was doing everything to make this place home. The least she could do was meet him halfway.

After a visit to Dr. Leonard who confirmed everything was okay with the babies and Damisi was healthy enough to travel, they had gone into full planning mode. They quickly made their rounds to Aunty Bola and Moji, spent a couple of days in Kenya with her father and Madam Paulina, then ended with a visit to Abuja. A week later after they got to Abuja, she and Jabir boarded a flight to Gerald R. Ford International.

True to his word, Jabir put his condo up for sale, and they bought this five-bedroom house after a brief hotel stay. He didn't want to be bogged down with a mortgage or escrow accounts, so he paid cash. Her eyes had bulged out at the amount he paid. She felt a sting of guilt, but he silenced her concerns with an earth-shattering kiss.

The adjustment hadn't been as easy as she thought. Some days and nights, she found herself crying over her wilderness state. She had lost her sense of purpose, and although she was looking forward to being the best mother possible, she missed making a difference in the lives of others. She knew she wasn't going to be in front of the camera any time soon, but still, she felt like she was wandering aimlessly.

Her husband was her rock, and she was grateful for him. In her depressive state, he held her tight every night whispering words of encouragement about a bright future. Damisi knew it was more her hormones than her heart talking, but she couldn't shake the feeling.

Jabir slowly eased back into his regular schedule, giving her time to get used to being at home alone. He bought her a Chevrolet Traverse to make sure she could go out if she wanted to. In Lagos, she could barely leave the house without a picture being taken. So although hard, the move was a good idea for her mental and emotional state. She just wasn't prepared for it to hurt so much. She looked forward to the daily calls from Moji and Ibiso but most of all, her father.

Damisi placed her hand on her stomach and rubbed. She looked around the kitchen and was satisfied at what she had accomplished. She had a taste for Nigerian food. She had had nothing but pasta, chicken, fish and burgers since she'd arrived. She'd even had pizza, which she didn't really care for. She'd Googled an African store and a Babies R Us that wasn't far from them. She could sure use some retail therapy. She'd stop there first and then make her way to the food store.

An hour later, Damisi parked her car and lifted her sunshades to the top of her braided hair. The month of July had breezed by and ushered in the heat-filled days of August. She had forgotten how brutal the summer months could be in Michigan. After roaming around in Babies R Us for thirty minutes she left with more than she should. She couldn't wait to get home and look at the gorgeous dresses again. She entered the food store and pushed the buggy around the small aisles until she got to the freezer section. In less than no time, she had everything she needed to cook fried rice except shrimp and goat meat. She took out a bag of goat meat and was examining it when a woman's reflection caught her eye.

"Damisi?"

She put the bag in her cart and turned around. Her brows furrowed in confusion, then her eyes widened in amazement. "*Ash?*"

The lady screamed in excitement and pulled Damisi in for a hug.

"Oh my goodness!" Damisi exclaimed.

Ashley McGregor held her at arm's length and examined her. "I can't believe this. Look at you? You look fantastic."

Damisi managed a smile, pained she couldn't tell her the same thing. "I lost contact with you when I left. I tried and tried to reach you, but no luck."

"It's a long story. Are you done here? Starbucks is around the corner. I know you loved you some Starbucks."

Damisi chuckled and lifted her hand to her stomach. "I can't do coffee anymore."

"Girl, come on. You'll get one of those Frappuccinos. Don't tell me big-time African television personalities don't drink Frappuccinos." Ashley rolled her big blue eyes and smiled.

"Okay. Give me a minute." Damisi opened the second freezer, replaced the perishables and headed to the front of the store to pay for her other items, smiling. God had heard her cry and sent a familiar face.

Several minutes later, Damisi and Ashley were seated in Starbucks nursing their drinks. Ashley was one of the few close friends she'd had while attending the University of Michigan. They met in her sophomore year. Ashley was studying mass communications, and they hit it off immediately. They went everywhere and did everything together. Initially, Moji had been a little jealous of their bond, but Ashley being Ashley, soon broke through Moji's defenses with her cheerful, kind and loving nature, and they became good friends.

In their junior year, they got an apartment together. Everyone who knew them called them "light" and "lighter" because of their contrasting complexions. Although Ashley was Caucasian, Damisi could swear she had been African in another life. She loved the clothes, food and music Damisi introduced her to. They made a promise to visit Kenya together, but things changed a little when Damisi met Jabir.

Ashley took their changing dynamic hard. It caused a rift between them as they spent less and less time together. Jabir knew her relationship with Ashley was important to her, so he tried to win her over. Everything was good for a while—until Ashley met Caleb. Caleb took them to church, they accepted Christ, and Jabir blamed Ashley for everything.

"We've got a lot to catch up on," Damisi said, biting into the slice of pound cake she ordered.

"Yep. Almost seven years' worth. All I know is you're this big-shot TV star."

"Not anymore," Damisi whispered.

"What happened to you?"

"I could ask you the same thing. Where is Caleb?"

Ashley paused. The air between them became charged with an emotion Damisi couldn't quite understand. Her friend's bright blues eyes dimmed, and she raked her hand through her unruly auburn curls. "Dead."

"What?" Damisi felt her heart knock against her chest. She had known a few men of God, but none she knew loved God like Caleb. She had a hard time wrapping her head around the news. "How?"

Ashley sighed. "Remember we were engaged when you left? For the first two years, everything was great. We had a small church in Ann Arbor. We were content with preaching the gospel of Jesus, then Caleb was invited for a pastor's conference." Ashley paused and took in a long breath. "Everything went downhill from there. He started comparing our church to others. He became more and more obsessed about the size rather than the lives we touched. To expand, he did things he shouldn't have. When the scandal of his shady business connections became public, he couldn't bear the shame." Tears streamed down her friend's cheeks. She shook her head. Damisi moved closer to her in the booth and drew Ashley's head to her shoulder.

A beat of silence passed between them, then Ashley lifted her head. Damisi saw fury in her eyes. "I promised myself not to cry over him ever again. Despite all the sermons he preached about forgiveness and God's grace, he couldn't accept it for himself, so he selfishly took his own life." She searched her phone and brought up a picture.

Damisi smiled at the brown-skinned, sandy-haired, hazel-eyed boy who stared back at her. He was a true mix of Ashley and Caleb.

"I'm so sorry, Ash. You have a heartbreaker here. How old is he? Why couldn't I reach you?"

"Caleb died when Brandon was two. He's four. The church fell apart, and I couldn't take it. I've been in New York with my dad. It wasn't until he died a few months ago that I moved back here. Brandon needs his grandparents."

Damisi knew Ashley, like her, had lost her mother when she was young. Caleb's parents lived in Detroit, so being around family was a good thing. Family was important, and she suddenly missed hers more. She made a mental note to call her dad and Aunty Bola when she got home.

"I'm so sorry," Damisi said.

Ashley waved her hand as if to dismiss the somber atmosphere. "Brandon will soon be of school age, and I plan to get a job at a paper. I have a couple of interviews lined up.

I'm fine. The Lord is my strength." Her gaze went to Damisi's stomach. "So what's the story?"

Damisi smiled. "You wouldn't believe it if I told you."

"Try me. But hold on." Ashley stood and returned shortly with lemonades and another pastry.

Damisi spent the next couple of minutes sharing the last six years of her life with her friend. She finished, and Ashley was speechless. Damisi chucked. "I told you, you wouldn't believe it."

"You mean after all these years, you found your way back to that arrogant and possessive man?"

Damisi laughed. Years ago, that would have been the perfect description, but Jabir has changed. The change made her marvel sometimes. Her eyes saddened at the fact that although he had changed in so many ways, he still held out on confessing Jesus and accepting Him as Lord. Damisi couldn't understand it.

"He's none of those things anymore. I love him to death," Damisi said.

"I'll believe that when I see it. But anyway, you've always been whipped by that man, so I'm glad you found the one your heart loves. As for the other stuff, what does Pastor Donnie say?"

Damisi smiled, remembering the Donnie McClurkin song they often sang. "A saint is just a sinner who fell down and got up."

"I tried to tell Caleb that…"

"I'm so glad I found you again," Damisi confessed.

"Me too." The friends hugged and talked a little more. Ashley insisted on hosting a baby shower dinner for her. They exchanged numbers before they left the coffee shop.

As Damisi drove down the road, she contemplated everything Ashley told her about Caleb. She couldn't believe what a fool she'd been. God had shown her so much grace and favor, and she kept whining and sulking. Jabir had sent her a text that he was stuck in the office for a little longer than usual. She was tired and in no mood to cook. She took out the Chinese menu from the glove compartment and placed an order. She'd surprise her husband at work with an early dinner. *Thank you, Lord, for everything.*

Chapter 34

Jabir looked at his watch again. Dr. Gary was ten minutes late. He respected the man, but he really wanted to be home with his wife at the moment—especially since she had just spent the day with Ashley. He rubbed his temples. Just what he needed, Ashley feeding Damisi with falsities about them. He knew Damisi had a mind of her own, but he and her friend never got along, so there was no telling what she would tell his wife.

His first order of business when they got to Detroit a month ago was to kill the remaining rumors of him and Angela's affair. He met Angela one day in the hospital cafeteria. At first, she threw a tantrum about his wedding band. She then calmed down and apologized. Her 180 turnaround worried him, but he heard nothing else of the rumors. He got a few nasty looks here and there, but everything was back to normal. He had a new wife whom he adored, a new home, and twin girls on the way. Everything was right in his world.

A knock on the door drew him away from his fuzzy thoughts. He stood, and Dr. Gary walked in. He'd told the receptionist at the front desk to show him to the back once he arrived.

The gray-haired, stocky elderly doctor approached him.

"Dr. Gary," Jabir greeted with a nod.

"Hi, son. I'm glad you're back."

"Glad to be back."

"Is everything okay?"

"Yes. Just a little family business," Jabir said.

"Well, I see that business got you married. Congratulations are in order then."

Jabir smiled and ushered him to a seat. The older doctor sat and crossed his legs at the knees. "I'll be brief. Betsy and I are having guests over."

"Of course."

"As I continue to let you know over the years, I'm so proud of your achievements."

"Thank you for your guidance." Jabir owed the man a lot. Not every white doctor would've willingly taken him under his wings, but Dr. Gary did.

"I just got word that you are the sure recipient of that award next weekend."

Jabir's eyes widened. He jumped up in excitement. Winners usually didn't know until that night, but he knew enough about Dr. Gary to know he was never careless with information. Dr. Gary stood and patted him on his back.

"Congratulations, son. For a minute I thought you blew it with your Vegas marriage to that nurse, but I heard you took care of it."

Jabir's eyebrows creased. *Was nothing secret anymore?*

"These things are based on merit, but at the same time, character matters. Although you did a good job fixing it, you know what they say about perception." Dr. Gary opened the door.

"Thank you for telling me. I'll still act surprised that night." Jabir looked at his phone in his hand. He couldn't wait to tell Damisi. They'd have their own private celebration tonight.

He looked beyond Dr. Gary and realized he didn't have to wait long. His wife had walked up looking as beautiful as ever, carrying a bag of take-out. He smiled and his stomach rumbled. He stretched out his hand, and she walked past the older man. Jabir kissed her on her forehead.

"Dr. Gary, meet my wife, Damisi. Damisi, this is Dr. Gary." Jabir made the introductions. They shook hands and greeted each other.

Dr. Gary grinned. "She is beautiful. Good choice, son. Okay I'll leave you both to eat. See you next Saturday." He left, and Jabir guided Damisi into his office.

He placed the bag on the small table and hugged her close. "So how's my favorite girl? Hope Ash didn't get her claws in you."

She hit him. He chuckled. "Wait 'til I tell you her story."

They worked together to make space comfortable so they could eat. He noticed her brows were creased the whole time. She placed her hands on her hips.

"What?" he asked.

"What did that man mean by good choice? How many other choices did you have?" she asked.

"You're my only choice. He's just an old man. That's how they talk."

She studied him. "Hmm…Good answer."

Jabir slowly released his breath. She was happy, and he needed her to stay that way.

———

The following day, Jabir studied the chart in his hand one last time before walking into Room 592. This would be his third major surgery since he got back from Nigeria. Reverend Father Kelley had been his patient for a while, and he'd done everything possible to manage his heart condition.

Now they had run out of options, and it was time for him to have a bypass.

The procedure was scheduled to take place in a couple of hours. He had two other doctors assisting him and a couple of students who would be observing the procedure.

"Good morning, Reverend," Jabir greeted the man who was turned to his side. The nurse was already there checking his vitals.

"Hello, Doctor." The man of God gave him a smile.

"In a couple of hours, we'll be ready to rock and roll."

"Yes. My prayer is that the Holy Spirit takes control, and everything goes just as you say it should."

Jabir chuckled. "Let's not bother the Holy Spirit. It's a routine surgery. Like I told you, I've done this procedure many times before."

The priest chuckled. "Routine or not, I always need the Holy Spirit. Son, I don't doubt your physical ability, but everything you are and do comes from God."

Jabir managed a smile, handed the nurse the chart, and shoved his hands into his overcoat. He resolved not to take the bait. He'd learned to skillfully avoid these conversations. He had said it before—he studied and learned his profession—so when he was in the operating room, it was all him.

"Yes, Reverend. God gave me the ability to do things on my own." Jabir reached over to help the reverend with a book he was trying to reach. The book turned out to be a Bible. Jabir wanted to walk away, but his mother had taught him to respect his elders. Besides, just like with his wife, Jabir decided it never hurt to listen. He'd indulge any patient to have his spirits up before a major procedure.

The reverend rummaged through the pages and pointed to a verse. "Here, read this."

Jabir took his eyes off the man and looked at were his finger pointed. Psalm 37:5. "Commit everything you do to the

Lord. Trust him, and he will help you," Jabir read and handed it back to the reverend.

The man shook his head. "Now go to John 15:5 and read toward the end of the sentence."

Jabir looked at him in confusion. He wanted to indulge him, not have a full Bible class. Jabir flipped through the pages of the oversized book that had been highlighted in blue, red and yellow. He had no idea where the book of John was. His lack of knowledge must have shown, because the reverend chuckled.

The reverend peered at the Bible. "John is after the book of Luke. Turn over into the New Testament. Mathew, Mark, Luke…there you go. Go to chapter 15 and read the end of verse 5."

Jabir opened his mouth to speak when the man interrupted him. "Oh by the way, the disciple Luke who wrote the book of Luke was a physician like you."

Jabir grinned. "Thanks for the tidbit." He needed to bring this to a close now. "Yes, I am the vine; you are the branches. Those who remain in me, and I in them, will produce much fruit. For apart from me you can do nothing."

The reverend smiled, but Jabir missed his amusement. *Vine? Branches?*

"You get it?"

Jabir shook his head. "No. Maybe it will come to me." His pager buzzed. "Oh, I have to go. The nurse will come in the next hour. I'll see you then, and it's going to be fine." He winked at the reverend and exited his room. He looked at his pager. It was the nurse's station. Saved.

Jabir held his freshly scrubbed hands up and used his body to open the door of the operating room. He gave a slight nod acknowledging the other two doctors in the room. The reverend had been given anesthesia and was out cold. After a nurse had gloved and gowned him, Jabir walked up to the exposed chest and stretched out his hand. The nurse placed a scalpel in his hand, and he began making an incision down the middle.

Over the next hour, the team worked diligently. The nurse patted Jabir's head with a sponge, and he smiled at her in appreciation. He lifted his hand to continue working, but it refused to move. He panicked. He stretched out his hand and shook it. He had been operating for a while. Maybe he was just tired. He tried to lift his other hand, and he felt like he had been handed dumbbells. He could not move.

"Dr. Danjuma, are you okay?" one of the doctors asked.

"Fine," Jabir blurted in irritation. He tried to lift his hands again, but couldn't.

"Doctor, are you all right?" the other doctor asked.

Jabir was as confused as they were. A man's life was on the line. He had spent a couple of moments willing his hand to respond. Nothing.

"Take over," Jabir whispered in defeat and stepped to the side. Maybe it was just stress. He had had been under a lot of pressure lately. As he moved farther to the side, he flung his hands and suddenly they came back to life. *That's what I'm talking about. Strange, but I'm good.*

He walked back up to the operating table. One of the doctors gave him a nod and scooted over. Jabir nodded back and lifted his hand to continue work, but again it felt like lead. Both hands felt heavy. When the doctors glanced at him, Jabir didn't wait for them to ask. He turned from the table. For the second time, as soon as he turned away from the table, his hands came to life. He wasn't going to make himself a bigger joke. He was done. He snatched off his gloves in frustration and left the room. He stopped at the sink and washed his hands.

"How could I have made such a fool of myself in front of doctors who respect me?" he murmured to himself. "And the students. It must be that reverend who jinxed me. I've done this procedure a million times with no problems."

His strides were hurried as he stomped down the empty hallway to his office. He threw his coat off and paced the length of the room. He rolled both arms back and forth as he continued to pace. What could have been the problem? He would have left, but he had to see the reverend in recovery and subsequently ICU first.

Hours later, when he was sure his patient was resting comfortably and he had done his rounds, he headed home.

Later that night, Jabir felt Damisi's eyes on him. He avoided eye contact because he was tired of lying to her. He stretched out on the leather couch in the living room and adjusted his head toward the television. He hadn't been able to talk to her about what happened, but his wife knew something was bothering him. What could he tell her when he didn't understand it himself? Medicine was his life, and the thought of not being able to help his patient today terrified him. More so because he didn't know what brought the immobility in his hands.

"*Mpenzi*, please talk to me." Damisi stood at the foot of the couch.

He stared into her captivating eyes and smiled. "Come here." He pulled himself up. She sat next to him, and he held her head with his palms and drew her to him. "I told you I'm fine. Tired, that's all." He kissed her lips.

She shook her head. "You've been like this for hours. You barely ate."

"I'm fine." He stood and dragged her up. "Let's go to bed."

She rolled her eyes at him but didn't move. "Don't lie to me. Did anything happen to one of your patients?"

"Oh no, baby, trust me." He looked at her intently. Although it wasn't a total lie, he still felt like a fraud. He placed his hand on the small of her back and aided her up the steps. They prepared for bed with light chatter. His mind still wandered at what happened. He dared his mind to even think about those supernatural occurrences his mother often talked about. No, this wasn't anything a doctor couldn't help. First thing in the morning, he'd set an appointment with his internist. Everything would be okay.

Damisi snuggled up against him. He kissed the crown of her head. Yeah, there was nothing mystical about it.

———

A WARM, GENTLE FEELING WOKE HIM UP. HE COULD HAVE sworn he had heard someone talking, but Damisi was fast asleep. As he closed his eyes, this time the voice was real and clear.

"Why do you continue to resist Me?"

Jabir began to hyperventilate as his heart raced. Each breath became a little harder to take. He looked to the side, but he could no longer see Damisi. Everything had become blurry, and it felt as if he was trapped in a foggy haze.

"Why do you continue to resist Me?" The voice was a little louder.

The sadness in the strange, yet comforting voice wrapped around him. It forced his mouth open. "Lord, is that you?"

"I've been with you since before you were born, but you continue to resist Me. I've caused you to find favor in the eyes of men, yet you refuse to confess My name."

Jabir tried to deny what he knew was right. But he couldn't. His lips were clamped shut. The hands he tried to lift refused to obey his command. Once again, they were useless.

Fear forced his mouth open. "Have mercy, Lord!"

"Whoever, then, acknowledges Me before people, I will acknowledge before my Father in heaven."

Jabir tried to move his hands. They were a dead weight. "Lord!"

Nothing. The silence made Jabir's heart race even faster until it felt as if he could hear blood pumping through his veins. As he moved his body across the bed, he continued to plead. "Do not abandon me…do not abandon me…do not abandon me."

Jabir jerked up from the bed. He sucked in oxygen to fill his lungs and exhaled. He took in his surroundings. They were familiar. He was in his bedroom. He tried to lift his arms, but felt discomfort.

Damisi must have felt him bump against her, because she pulled herself up. Her brows scrunched in worry. "What's wrong?" She grabbed his head.

Sweat soaked at the dent his head left in the pillow. He tried to regulate his breathing.

"I don't know. I think…I think… the Lord appeared to me in my dream."

She looked at him in astonishment. He didn't blame her. His mouth felt heavy saying it.

"Tell me what happened," she said.

He did, narrating the events of the whole day. Jabir watched as his wife's face conveyed emotions of confusion, surprise and delight.

"Do you want to…"

"Yes… yes, I confess Him as Lord. I need…forgiveness."

"Then let's ask for it." Damisi stretched out her hands.

Chapter 35

Wednesday morning, a week later, Damisi made her way down the stairs to her home office. She was quickly realizing she had a little interior design bug in her. With Jabir's help, she had changed a few things around from when they first moved in. The white walls now had a timeless gray and cream paint that made the space feel warm. She had bought a "his and hers" matching set of built-in desks that were made of birchwood. She had a contractor remove the carpet and replace it with hardwood, then she bought a Persian rug that lay in the center of the space. She walked in and opened the blinds, turned on the soft music and powered on her iPad.

Damisi rubbed on her tummy. "I need some tea. These girls are not letting Mummy sleep," she murmured on her way to the kitchen. "We got eleven more weeks. Mummy knows it's crowded in there. Bear with me."

A lot had happened in the days after Jabir's dream that she still had a hard time believing. However, she knew when God got ready to do something, He did it. That night, Jabir couldn't go back to sleep, and frankly, neither could she. In her wildest dreams, she wouldn't have believed that would be the way her husband would come to Christ.

Jabir didn't have a church, but Ashley had told her about one they ended up going to that weekend. She was filled with joy when her husband walked up to the front during altar call. They went out to celebrate after church, then his inquisitive nature took over.

He asked her about everything he could think of, and she was glad to answer what she could. They read the Bible every night when he wasn't in the hospital on call. It was during one of those prayer sessions that God revealed what her next step was. It had all come to her as clear as though the Holy Spirit was with them in the room. She was to encourage young girls and women that in whatever place they found themselves in life, they were to live for the purpose for which they were created. She was so excited and could tell her husband was, too when she told him about it.

With all the detours, if she had planned her life herself, it couldn't be better than it was now. It hadn't been easy, but all her trials had been turned into triumphs she would now use to help others. Her platform might have changed, but the purpose for which she was created hadn't. So her blog, Mosaic, was born.

The name had come to her in a dream. She had been carrying a beautiful vase that fell from her hands. Not wanting to discard the pieces, she took it to an artist that made it into a beautiful mosaic. Broken pieces were put back together beautifully.

She walked back into the office, placed her food and beverage on the desk, then settled into her chair. She raised her feet on the footstool Jabir had bought for her and said a short prayer for focus. She opened her task list, but just as she was about to tackle task one, her phone rang. It was her husband.

"Birthday boy." She giggled.

"Are we celebrating early?"

"Next week will be here before you know it." Keeping the surprise she had planned had been the hardest thing in the world. The Danjuma clan would be arriving in exactly a week, and her husband had no idea. She smiled, grateful for a supportive family—especially a supportive family with a private jet. Rasheed, Ibiso, her mother-in-law and Halima would be here. The only person she still wasn't sure about was Kamal. It was still soccer season, and he wasn't sure he could get away.

"How are my girls? I didn't want to wake you when I left."

"We're good. They seem to be hyper this morning."

"Just like their mother. Let me guess. You're in the office and not resting as I begged you to."

She laughed. "You know me so well. Did you check on the reverend?"

"He's recovering nicely." He paused. "I have some time before the next patient, so decided to call my beautiful wife."

"Oh, the flattery; you know very well I'm huge." Then she yelled, "Arghh."

"What is it?"

"One of these girls just kicked me." She rubbed her stomach. "Ooooh, her behind is mine when she gets out." She giggled.

When his laughter ended, he asked, "So what are you working on?"

"I have a couple of pieces to write for Mosaic. Then, like we discussed, Ashley is coming over so we can go downtown to inquire about the first stages of making Helping Hands a foundation."

One night, they had had a long talk, and she found out about Jabir's dream of opening a dedicated clinic for patients with heart issues. He had named it Helping Hearts. They decided to combine their passions and make it a ministry called Helping Hands. She would teach and counsel, while the private clinic he was planning to build would provide high-quality services at a low rate to those who needed them and met certain criteria.

Damisi called Moji and Eno earlier to tell them of her idea. Excitement wasn't the word for their reaction. They hurriedly offered to do some legwork for her in Nigeria. She glanced at the time on her PC and noted that Ashley would be there soon.

"So we're really going ahead with this," Jabir said.

Damisi inhaled and exhaled. "We've been praying about it. Let's just do it."

"Like Nike, right?"

Damisi rubbed the corner of her eye with her finger to halt the tear of joy threatening to fall. She shook her head in disbelief at what God was doing. "Isn't it funny how God can give you more than you could have imagined for yourself?"

"Yeah...I've gotta go, though. Time to get back." Jabir made the smacking sound of a kiss and disconnected the call.

Damisi leaned back in her chair and gazed out the window. The September day was perfect—clear blues skies, the sun shining in all its glory and the slight breeze from the lake moving the trees from left to right. She knew she could get lost in nature's beauty, but the tasks that lay ahead ripped her from her idling.

She opened her WordPress publisher and began to type her first blog: *Getting Back Up*.

THE WEEK HAD PASSED QUICKLY. DAMISI HAD WOKEN UP feeling some discomfort. At their most recent appointment with her new ob-gyn, Dr. St. John, they were reminded of the risk of multiple births. The doctor reiterated a stress-free environment and getting plenty of rest. With a slightly elevated blood pressure, the doctor increased her appointments. She didn't want to alert Jabir to her recent pain. She rubbed her stomach and prayed the feeling would pass. The family was arriving that day, and she had the next couple of days planned out. The award ceremony was also that weekend. She couldn't afford for anything to go wrong. *Father, please let me at least get to thirty-six weeks.* She pulled out the barstool in the kitchen and sat. She continued to rub her hands in a circular motion on her stomach. After a couple of seconds, the babies settled down.

Damisi stood. No pain. She walked back to the stove. Jabir had taken the day off, and she couldn't wait for him to come down. She had prepared his favorite breakfast of boiled yams and egg stew. She was setting the table when the birthday boy joined her in the kitchen. Smiling, she walked up to him and gave him his gift and a card.

He looked at the items, placed them on the counter and turned to face her. She wrapped her arms around him.

"Happy birthday, my *mpenzi*. You're the light of my world and my prayer today is that God continues to take you to heights unknown to do exploits you were called to do." She stepped on the tips of her toes and kissed him deeply.

Smacking his lips together to taste her strawberry-kiwi lip gloss, he rested his head in the crook of her neck for a couple of seconds then raised it. "Thank you, baby. I'm happy I get to celebrate another birthday, for you, the girls and for getting to discover Jesus. Thank you for allowing me to see Him through you."

They stood misty eyed, and he lowered his head so their foreheads touched. She cupped his face. "That's a huge compliment, but you and I know I had nothing to do with that. It's all God." She rubbed her hands together. "The girls and I have a day full of surprises planned."

"You do, huh?"

"Yes, we do. But first, breakfast. Go sit." She nudged him out of the kitchen. "Have you called Kammy?"

"Yes. I think this is the first time we're celebrating apart. It's either he flies to Detroit or I fly to LA," Jabir said.

Damisi noticed the look of regret in his eyes. She really hoped Kamal could make it. She hadn't gotten a confirmation from him. In fact, he hadn't replied to the text she'd sent the day before.

"I'm sorry. I promise the day will be special." She winked and sat at the table.

After they finished eating, Jabir went to the kitchen to retrieve his present and card. He opened the card first and read it. Damisi watched as he beamed. Her heart was full of love for this man. Six years apart, smooth sailings and rocky paths had all led to this place.

Jabir opened the box and gasped. Damisi smiled as he brought out the matching Ankara mix-and-match outfits. From his closet, she could tell he loved those sets. She found the designer online and ordered special designs.

"I love these shirts!"

"I know. You have three matching pairs of shirts and pants in there. Now see what I have at the bottom," Damisi instructed.

He quickly removed the clothes and peered at the bottom. He placed his hands over his eyes and remained still for a moment. Damisi got up and rubbed his back in a circular motion. She could feel the emotion he was trying so hard to contain. He grabbed her hands and kissed them, then he kissed her stomach before reaching into the box and bringing out three orange-and-brown–print outfits—a shirt for him and two tiny dresses for their unborn daughters, with the inscription "Daddy's Angels."

He stood and drew Damisi to him. "I love you with my life. This is the best gift I've ever gotten."

"I love you, too. I'm glad you like them."

They held on to each other. No other words were necessary. Later Jabir shooed Damisi to the living room while he cleaned up. She argued, but he insisted.

"Sit, Dami. I'm serious. You're doing too much and need to rest," he chided.

He was right. Her feet were killing her. She pouted and went to the living room to stretch out and turn on the television. It was almost noon. The family should be landing in a matter of hours. She made sure Rasheed had their new address, and Ibiso was supposed to text her when they left the airport. Damisi had banned all calls.

"I wonder why none of my family has called yet." Jabir said, reentering the living room. "I tried calling, but I think service or reception is bad." He lifted her legs, sat, placed them in his lap and began massaging them.

"Mmm, that feels so good." She closed her eyes and leaned her head back.

"It's strange that on today of all days, I can't reach any of them. Even Kammy."

She moaned again as he continued to massage her feet, releasing the tension in all the right muscles. "What's strange is I'm shamelessly enjoying this massage when you're the one that should be pampered today."

Jabir laughed.

"Seriously that massage is so good. I'm just going to close my eyes for a bit."

A BIT TURNED INTO A FULL-BLOWN SIESTA. BY LATE afternoon, the ringing of the doorbell woke Damisi up. Her husband had disappeared. *Oh Lord, let me not have spoiled this surprise.*

She looked at her phone. Ibiso had sent her three texts. Damisi quickly read through them. They landed. Kammy had met them at the airport. The last text read, I HAVE A SURPRISE FOR YOU.

"That's probably them," she said, easing off the couch.

Jabir came from the study and headed for the foyer. "Don't get up, baby. I'll get it."

She smiled. She would have loved to see the reaction on his face when he saw his family, but she had to make herself presentable. She went into the small bath down the hall and tamed her loose curls with a brush, re-applied her lip gloss and straightened her red wrap blouse, which she had on over maternity jeans. Satisfied with her appearance, she sauntered back into the living room.

The screams and shouts became louder as the family entered into the living area. Damisi heard her mother-in-law ask where her daughter was.

"I'm here, Ma," Damisi said, coming from around the corner.

"Where?" Jabir's mother asked.

"Good afternoon, Ma." Damisi tried to kneel on one knee in respect.

"No, my dear. Get up. Let me look at you." Mrs. Danjuma twirled her around and hugged her. "How are you doing?"

"I'm fine, Ma." Damisi replied

"Mama, you're hoarding her," Kamal said.

Damisi opened her eyes wide and screamed. "Kammy, you made it. Happy birthday." Damisi hugged her brother-in-law.

"Yep. He was waiting at the airport looking homeless." Rasheed chuckled.

Jabir cleared his throat. "Kammy, you've hugged her two seconds too long."

"Don't pay him any attention," Damisi said.

"I never do," replied Kamal plopping down on the couch.

Rasheed hugged her next. "You've turned into an Americana in just two months?"

Damisi giggled. Rasheed enjoyed teasing her. "It's your brother's fault," she replied.

Jabir and Rasheed exchanged knowing looks and joined their mother and brother on the couch.

Ibiso moved toward her, smiling. "Sis, how are you?"

"I'm fine and so happy. Thanks for hooking all this up." The two women held each other's gaze for a moment. "We can't hug because we're huge." Damisi pointed to their stomachs. Her sister-in-law was almost five months along.

The men's laughter was quickly silenced by the disapproving looks the women gave them.

"What? You ladies said it," Kamal said.

"Yes, and only we can. Your job is to counter and tell us how beautiful we are," Ibiso said.

"Hmmm…that for y'alls husbands to do. Rasheed, Jabir… do the needful."

Both elder brothers picked up throw pillows from the couch and threw them at Kamal. Damisi looked puzzled.

"Don't worry about it. Throwing pillows is their thing," Ibiso said.

Halima stood in the corner and Damisi stretched out her hand to her. The young woman who was three years younger than the twins took her hand.

"Halima, I'm so glad you came," Damisi said.

"I'm glad I came, too. But unfortunately, I can't stay for the award ceremony. I leave for Dubai tomorrow evening."

"You're kidding me." Damisi said.

"No, I'm not. My big brother keeps me busy. I have to meet a client on Monday and have a training course for a week." Halima smiled and inclined her head toward Rasheed.

"Lil' sis, don't put that on me. It's not my fault you're so good at what you do." Rasheed winked.

"If you say so," Halima laughed. Then she turned to Damisi. "I'm sorry I wasn't around when you left Naija. Here's my wedding present." She handed her an envelope.

Damisi thanked her. Jabir walked over to the women and hugged his sister and thanked her. Damisi handed him the envelope. He retrieved the card and some tickets.

"Sis, this is too much. Open tickets to the Serengeti National Park in Tanzania?"

Halima shrugged. "It's one of the numerous perks of traveling on Danjuma business."

"Thank you," Damisi said.

"I told you I had a surprise *abi*..." Ibiso said.

"What else? I thought Kammy was the surprise." Damisi scrunched her brows together.

"Kammy *ke*?" Ibiso asked incredulously.

"Hey..." Kamal shouted.

"Sorry. You know I love you, but you're not my surprise." Ibiso threw him a kiss.

Kamal raised his hand to catch the air kiss, but Rasheed knocked his hand down.

Ibiso shook her head. "Honey, play nice."

The doorbell rang. "Right on time," Ibiso said and dragged Damisi to the front door.

Damisi thought she would pass out when she saw Moji in the flesh standing at her door. She froze. She turned to Ibiso and Moji and broke down in tears. Tears of joy.

Chapter 36

Several hours later, Jabir looked at his wife, asleep in the bed. He pulled the duvet up to her shoulders. She didn't stir, a sign of her tiredness and rightfully so. She had made sure their family was fed and settled them into their rooms. The highlight of her day was when Moji arrived. He had to ask Ibiso later how she pulled that off. His wife screamed so loud he took off running thinking there was something wrong with her. He knew Ibiso was a gift to their family, and he was thankful for the sisterhood she had built with his wife.

He knew Damisi had some discomfort earlier, although she thought she hid it from him. He had watched her like a hawk all evening, and things seemed to be better. Jabir had warned Damisi earlier there was a limit to what she should do. And just as he thought, she argued until he threatened she wouldn't be allowed to go to the award ceremony if she didn't rest tonight and all of the next day. His wife was so stubborn, but he knew she would do anything to see his moment. He was happy Moji was there, even if it was just for the next couple of days. She would keep Damisi rested.

He opened the door quietly and headed downstairs. Rasheed and Kamal were waiting for him.

"Hey, I'm back. Do you guys want anything to drink?" Jabir asked.

"Vita Malt if you have it," Rasheed said.

"Heineken," Kamal said.

Jabir turned and looked at his twin. "I don't serve alcohol in my house."

Jabir saw the confusion in his brother's eyes and the question dangling from his lips. Rasheed smiled. Jabir disappeared into the kitchen.

Kamal gaze went from Jabir to Rasheed. "Oh no…don't tell me you, too." Kamal placed his hands on his head.

"Stop with the drama," Jabir said, reappearing with Vita Malt for Rasheed and Powerade for Kamal. He placed the drinks down and opened the jar of green M&M on the table.

"So are you saved, too?" Kamal asked.

"What kind of question is that? I called you and told you what happened to me." Jabir popped some candy in his mouth.

"You won't get it until you experience it," Rasheed said. "I still don't know how to fully explain the feeling."

"Is this thing an automatic effect of getting married, or is it something else?" Kamal asked. "First Stone Cold turned to mush, now I can't talk to him without a Jesus being slipped in there somehow." Kamal took a swig of his drink and turned to Jabir. "Now you are talking about some dream changing your life. Why?"

"Watch it, bro," Rasheed warned. "Being a practicing Christian man doesn't make me weak. Ask my wife and those that work for me. All it does is makes me want to consciously walk in love."

"You—what's your excuse?" Kamal turned to Jabir.

Jabir laughed. "I find it amusing because I was just like you a year ago. But God got my attention through the beautiful woman He put in my life." Jabir popped a couple more M&Ms into his mouth.

"So, it's a marriage thing?" Kamal asked.

"No, the ladies were just instruments, I guess. You're always free to join us," Rasheed said.

"That's a'ight." Kamal picked up his drink and stood. "Lemme go check on my mama."

"Trust—it's not as bad as we thought. Just takes a decision," Jabir said.

"Nah…I'm cool." Kamal headed upstairs, shaking his head as he went.

Jabir occupied the seat Kamal had just vacated. "Whenever God is ready, He'll get him. That I know."

Rasheed chuckled.

The two brothers spent the next minutes catching up on what was going on in their respective lives. Jabir caught Rasheed up on the Helping Hands project.

"Wow, that's huge, bro…you know our father left you a wide piece of land in Abuja. Why don't you use that?" Rasheed asked.

"Good idea. Abuja or Lagos."

Jabir felt Rasheed staring at him. "What?"

"Nothing. You're just different, and I can see the change all over you."

Jabir laughed. "Change? I don't feel it. After they dunked me in that water, I came out as though I could walk on air. But I looked in the mirror…didn't see a halo."

"Shut up, man. You know what I'm talking about. You don't change physically, but your spirit does."

"Just teasing. I get you. Damisi is helping me with this whole thing. She teaches me the meaning of love and faith in Christ," Jabir said.

"Ha! *Chineke n'eluigwe. Daalu. Ekele diri gi o.*" Their mother's voice entered the room before her body.

The brothers shook their head as their mother made her appearance and sang a native hymn about "Thanking God in Heaven."

"Mama, you're up?" Rasheed stood and hugged her.

"Yes, I needed some water. To hear you boys talking of Jesus, *chai!*" She lifted her hands.

Rasheed flung his arms in the air and waved them from side to side. "Alleluia! God be praised. Let me go and check on my wife you and Jabir can have church."

Rasheed escaped up the stairs before Jabir could stop laughing. He draped his arm around his mother and led her to the kitchen.

"That Rasheed is just a joker," Jabir's mother said.

"Don't mind him. Let's get you some water." Jabir smiled.

As she stepped into the luxurious warmth of the Fergus Banquet Hall, Damisi felt like all eyes had turned on her. A live band provided jazz melodies as people socialized and formed new relationships. This was her first evening out as the wife of Dr. Jabir Danjuma and she wanted to make a good impression. They had been to church, plays, and out shopping, but she hadn't made it around his colleagues except when she stopped by his office. She felt a need to crack her knuckles, but Jabir refused to let her hand go. He looked down at her and squeezed her hand. Still, his unspoken reassurance did little to calm her nerves. As she gazed back at the curious female faces in the room, she wondered how many of them wished they were her. How many of them had previously walked into a room with her husband?

With his hand at the small of her back, Jabir navigated them through the hall to their table. He smiled at her and winked. She smiled back. This was his night. He had worked hard and deserved this recognition. Her job was to be the supporting wife.

"Did I tell you I'm proud of you?" she said.

"For about the thousandth time. Thank you, baby." He

pulled her close and pressed his lips against her forehead. "Let's go find the others."

On the way to their table, they were stopped a couple of times and Jabir made introductions. They were congratulated on their pregnancy. The surprise on many of their faces wasn't lost on Damisi. Whether they were surprised he was married or that they were having a baby so soon, Damisi couldn't tell. Sometimes it was downright awkward, but Jabir never let her feel out of place. He asked her questions in an attempt to make her feel like a part of the conversation.

Damisi searched the room for their family and smiled when she and Ibiso made eye contact. The past couple of days had been so blissful that she wished the family would move to Detroit with them. Rasheed nearly bit her head off when she suggested it. After Ibiso threw a warning look his way, he promised she'd be back to visit sometime.

The couple moved through the crowd and finally ended at their table where the family was seated.

———

"THAT WAS A GREAT SPEECH, BRO." KAMAL TOOK THE AWARD from his brother's hand.

"*Nna m,* my heart is so full that I can barely speak. I can't believe my blessings and that God has allowed me to reap what I sowed in tears all those years ago," Jabir's mother said.

Damisi and Ibiso wrapped their arms around their mother-in-law, who was now sobbing. The women knew from their husbands how their mother had struggled in the years after their father's abandonment. Long before she got to know her mother-in-law, Damisi had admired the woman's strength.

"Mama, we thank God. This is a happy occasion. No tears," Rasheed said.

"Jabir, we're proud of you," Ibiso said.

"Yes oh, and you just had to rub it in by calling Damisi to the stage with you," Moji said.

Jabir winked and brushed his lips against his wife. "If you have a good thing, flaunt it."

Dinner was over and the servers replaced their plates with a variety of dessert options. The live band picked up its tempo. Jabir stood and stretched out his hand. "Come on, pregnant lady. Let's dance."

Damisi smiled up at her husband and put her hand in his. They walked to the dance floor and Ibiso and Rasheed followed. No words could capture what she felt in the moment, so she laid her head on her husband's shoulder and swayed gently to the rhythm. Although she knew she was huge at thirty weeks, she felt sexy.

The day before, she and the other women had made it a day of pampering. They went to the spa, did their nails, and went shopping. She and Jabir's mother moved through the mall slowly while Ibiso and Moji acted like the energizer bunny. Damisi was so grateful that the first dress she saw, she liked. There was no need to go from store to store. The A-line, off the shoulder, purple chiffon dress fell loosely around her stomach. Its length swept the floor, covering her ballerina flats. Her hair was pinned up with a few loose tresses.

"I'm so glad you're here to share this with me," Jabir whispered.

"We've come full circle." Damisi smiled.

"I can't wait to have you all alone tonight."

"I don't know what for. No more hanky panky until these girls arrive."

"You mean nothing for me?" Jabir winked.

Damisi shook her head. "Nothing at all." She raised herself to the tip of her toes and kissed his lips.

"Keep doing that and I won't be held responsible for…"

"Hold that thought. I need to go to the ladies room.

"You want me to walk with you?"

She frowned. "No, thank you, *mpenzi*."

As she walked into the ladies' room, a glimpse of their life flashed before Damisi's eyes. She loved it. Her husband had seen one of his numerous dreams come true tonight. She was living out hers, even if it wasn't in the way she previously thought. She would probably do television again, but right now, she was content working behind the scenes. That way she would be able to make the home that her daughters and husband needed. Everything was working itself out. The magnificence of God's mercy and grace kept her speechless.

She walked into the ladies' room, and within minutes she was back at the sink washing her hands. When she was done, she began fixing her makeup. In her reflection stood an attractive woman of medium height with long curly jet-black hair

"Hello," Damisi took a deep breath and turned around.

"Hi. Are you Jay's wife?"

"Who?" Damisi's body stiffened in alarm.

"Forgive me." The woman extended her hand. "I'm Angela Smith a colleague and friend of Jabir."

Damisi felt a surge of irritation. So that's what the women here called her husband − Jay? She remembered a time he took pride in his full name. "Oh…okay. I'm Damisi Danjuma. It's nice to meet you."

The woman's eyes roamed over Damisi's body and she smiled wearily. "I guess congratulations are in order."

"Err… Thank you," Damisi replied. The woman seemed nice enough but behind her smile, Damisi could see sorrow in her eyes.

Angela smiled. "Are you okay? You look like you're due any day now."

Damisi sighed. "Yes, I'm fine, just exhausted. So you work at Mercy?"

"Yes. I've been there for three years now. I'm a neonatal ICU nurse." I hope you and I don't get to meet there."

Damisi rubbed her stomach and giggled. "Yes, I sure hope not."

"I better let you get back. It was nice to meet you. Say hello to Jabir for me," Angela said.

"I'll see you around." Damisi opened the door to the bathroom and came face to face with Moji and Ibiso. They must be coming to look for her. She had stayed in the bathroom a little longer than intended. Her mind went back to Angela. At first, she had thought she was one of Jabir's many conquests coming to feel her out. She wasn't oblivious to many curious stares she had gotten all night.

Ibiso furrowed her eyebrows. "Are you okay?"

Damisi nodded.

"I know you had some pain earlier, so we were worried," Moji said.

"I'm fine. I meet one lady who says she is Jabir's friend and we got talking," Damisi said as the ladies walked back to their table.

"Friend *ke*? What kind of friend?" Moji asked, placing her hand on her hip.

Ibiso laughed. "Moji, don't start."

"Yes, don't. The lady seemed nice. She was concerned about how I was doing," Damisi replied.

"Let that be all that she's concerned about..." Moji snorted.

"She didn't seem like she had an agenda. Besides it doesn't matter," Damisi replied.

"What doesn't matter?" Jabir asked as the women reached the table. He and Rasheed and Kamal stood up and pulled out the ladies' chairs.

Damisi rubbed his cheek. "Nothing, baby, what did we miss?"

Jabir kissed her forehead. "Nothing much. You must be tired. Ready to go?"

"Yes, and I'm sure Mama is too." She looked over to her mother-in-law whose eyelids had begun to droop.

"Okay, let me go say my good-byes. I'll be right back."

———

JABIR TOOK OFF HIS CUFF LINKS AND PLACED THEM BACK INTO the box his wife had handed him earlier that evening. He wondered when she had gotten around to buying them. The evening had been all he had envisioned and more. The best of it all was that he got to spend it with his wife and family. This birthday was undoubtedly the best one he had had in years. All thanks to his wife. He paused and looked to his side. Damisi had taken a shower and was resting. By the time they left the parking lot earlier, Damisi was sleeping. He had carried her upstairs after bidding everyone goodnight.

She looked so peaceful, and he'd do anything to keep her that way. She was the love of his life. After all their trials, they were finally at a place of peace. He furrowed his eyebrow when he recalled the conversation he had with her while she was getting ready for bed. Damisi had told him of her meeting Angela in the bathroom. Damisi seemed to like her. The woman she described was likeable, but he knew Angela and was determined to do his best to keep her away from his wife.

He stepped out of his clothes and entered into the shower. As the jet stream pounded his muscles, Jabir began to relax. Maybe he was being too cynical. Everyone deserved a do-over. If God gave him one, who was he to judge Angela's motives? Minutes later, he climbed into his bed, pulled his wife closer and said a prayer. God had indeed been good to him. However, two things troubled him: What was Angela up to? And why for goodness' sake hadn't he told Damisi of the extent of his relationship with Angela when she asked?

Chapter 37

Damisi opened the door to her husband carrying a Popeye's bag in one hand and a stack of what looked like mail in the other.

Jabir smiled, planted a kiss on her forehead and walked to the dining room. He placed the items on the table and turned to draw Damisi closer.

"How are my girls?"

"Hungry."

Damisi wiggled her way out of his arms and started going through the bag of food. She took a bite of a piece of chicken and moaned.

"We love you," she said and walked to the kitchen. She returned a few seconds later with ranch dressing.

Jabir scrunched his face. "I wonder how you do that…"

"I'm pregnant. I can do anything." Damisi drizzled the dressing on her chicken. Eating chicken with ranch dressing was one of the new cravings she had acquired in the last couple of days.

Jabir raised his hands in surrender. She placed some chicken, mashed potatoes and a hot biscuit on a plate in front of her husband.

"How was your day?"

Jabir shrugged. "One major surgery and a couple of consultations—a normal day."

They sat and ate their dinner while they talked about their day. Damisi gave him an update on the happenings in Nigeria she had gotten from Moji. The family had left two weeks ago. Despite the fact that a day hadn't gone by that she didn't speak to either someone from her family or her husband's family, she still missed them terribly.

Damisi finished off her chicken, wiped her hands and mouth and picked up the stack of papers. "What's this?"

"Old mail. I had the post office place a hold on it while I was away."

Damisi untied the bundle. "Why are they just getting home?"

Jabir finished chewing his biscuit and raised his waved his hand in dismissal. "The day I got it, I had to go back to the office and forgot it there."

"Ha! *Mpenzi,* we've been back for months now. Supposing there's something important in there?"

"If it were, I would have gotten a call by now."

Damisi shook her head and started going through the stack. Jabir finished eating, cleared the mess they made and walked toward the living room.

"Where are you going, mister?" Damisi asked with her eyebrow raised.

"Err…to relax."

"Let's go through this."

"Now? Babe, I need to unwind."

Damisi pouted. "It'll make Mummy happy."

That does it every time. Jabir walked back to the dining table, picked up the mail with one hand and grabbed her hand with the other. He guided them to the living. Jabir helped her sit and placed her legs on his lap.

"I'll tell you what. You go through the mail while I give you a foot rub."

"Hmmm, what will I do without you?"

"You'll never have to find out."

Damisi giggled, inwardly thanking God for her numerous blessings. As time to give birth drew near, she often reminisced on how close she came to bypassing a good thing because of self-condemnation. As her husband began to work magic on her swollen feet, she went through the mail. She saw a furniture store sales flier and began examining it.

"Oh no you don't," Jabir said.

"I'm not. As a matter of fact, I just finished everything today, so the room is ready for our angels." Damisi knew her husband had gotten tired of her changing her mind about the nursery. Finally, she was done. Even if she wanted to change her mind, there was no time. With only six more weeks to go, she couldn't lift a finger.

"Finally." Jabir let out a labored breath.

Damisi balled the flier and threw it at him. "Whatever. All you have in here is junk anyway."

"I told you." Jabir placed her feet on the couch and stood. "Feel better?"

"Oh yes! You spoil me."

"It's my job." He rubbed his hand on her stomach. "Let me go change."

Damisi quickly went through the mail, keeping to the side what she thought was important. She started to stuff the trash in a paper bag when an envelope fell out. She placed her feet on the floor to examine the mail that was addressed to Dr. and Mrs. Jabir Danjuma. It was from the state of Nevada.

She opened it up and for a few moments, her heart froze as she took in the contents of the paper in her hand. Pain filled every part of her being as she lifted herself from the couch. Her body shook as tears fell from her eyes. She let go of the document that seemed to burn a fire through her fingers.

"The nursery looks great…what's wrong?" Jabir asked in panic.

She lifted her eyes to him. Jabir walked toward her. She stepped back.

"Please tell me what's wrong. Are you in pain?"

She opened her mouth to speak, but no sound came out. Her eyes went to the paper on the floor. She raised her hand to her head as the understanding of the information on the 8½ -by-11-inch piece of paper sunk in. Jabir followed her gaze. He picked up the paper and glanced at it. Damisi observed his expression go from worry, to shock before finally settling on fear as what he held in his hand sank in.

He fell to his knees and whispered. "Babe, please let me explain."

Her voice returned, coated with ice. "Oh, good." She nodded. "I'm glad there's an explanation of why you're married to me and…Angela at the same time."

———

FOR JABIR, THE EARTH STOOD STILL. HE TRIED TO WRAP HIS head around what he was seeing and why. Ashton had assured him this was a done deal. He had seen the judge's signature on the annulment papers, so what happened? He had questions he needed answered, but as he lifted his eyes to meet Damisi's, he knew that above everything else, he needed to do damage control now—and fast.

"Please just give me a second." Jabir wiped the sweat that formed on his forehead.

He looked on at his wife who was pacing the length of the room. She had one hand on her forehead and another on her hip. He walked toward her and placed his hand on her shoulder. The way she flinched sent a dagger straight through his heart.

"Don't touch me," she seethed.

"Okay, hear me out. One minute." At this stage in her pregnancy, he knew she was fragile. He had to get her to calm down while he explained. Even if he didn't know what he was going to say, he needed her calm.

"So while you were chasing me up and down in Kenya, were you married?"

Jabir sighed. "Yes and no. It's complicated."

"You've got to be kidding me." Damisi shook her head and began to laugh.

Jabir knew she wasn't laughing because anything was funny, but it was a nervous, sad laughter.

"So all your scheming wasn't really about me, but your warped sense of responsibility to our children to compensate for your messed-up childhood," she shouted.

Her words pierced him, but this wasn't about him right now but getting his wife to give him a chance to explain. He would do anything just to get her to be still.

"Babe, please calm down. Remember your health."

"Calm down? Calm down? You brought me to this foreign land to make a fool out of me, and you're telling me to calm down."

"Don't say that. Just hear me out. I really need you to listen…"

"You have three minutes, and I'm getting out of here."

Jabir panicked. This couldn't be happening. He wouldn't let her to run away from him a third time. A moment of silence passed between them. Their gazes held, but the warmth in his couldn't melt the ice in hers. He never thought he'd see the day his wife would look at him with so much pain and disgust.

"After Rasheed's wedding, I was hurt. You rejected me—"

"So it's my fault? Don't you dare." Damisi leaned against the chair and crossed her arms on her stomach.

"I'm not saying that. I'm saying you rejected me, and it hurt. It hurt like I never imagined—more than the first time—and I did things. I did…"

She raised her hand. "I don't need the details."

Jabir quickly went through the rest of the story. Her expression remained blank while he narrated the events of months ago and remained that way after he finished. There was a long between them. She bent her head. He wanted to reach out to touch her, but he was afraid of her reaction and what effect it would have on the girls. She was in her thirty-third week, and they had prayed and believed God for her to carry to full term.

"Please say something."

Damisi raised her head and shrugged. "What exactly do you want me to say?" Her voice was a mere whisper.

"Anything but silence."

"Ask you why you're a liar? Why you deceived me? How you ever expect me to trust you? Or why you kept me in the dark while I made friends with a woman who now turns out to be your wife?" Her voice grew an octave with each question. She began pacing again.

"In Kenya, I asked you about other women. You said there was none—"

"There weren't and still aren't. You're the only one for me."

"And your wife. Don't forget your wife." She sighed. "You watched me go on and on about that woman like a fool, and you didn't think to mention this?"

"I thought it was over and there'd be no issues."

"Surprise, it's not over." She pulled herself up from the chair. "And we have major issues."

"Please, just calm down. Remember the babies…your health."

"Don't patronize me. I'm angry, I can't breathe. There were ample opportunities for you to tell me. How in the world did you think we could live in this town and your secrets not come out?"

"I wasn't thinking. I was scared." Jabir couldn't believe he'd admitted that, but he was desperate, and it was the truth.

"Scared? Well now you have reason to really be scared. We have no marriage, and I can never trust you." She turned and headed upstairs.

The words she'd just spoken were true. With him still being married to Angela, the marriage to Damisi was null and void.

"Where are you going? Please wait." He cautiously walked toward her.

She placed one foot on the bottom step and stopped. "There's nothing more to say. I can't even think right now. What I do know is I need to get as far away from you as possible. I can't even stand to look at you right now."

"I'll fix this I promise…"

"I'm going to call Ashley. I'll stay with her for a while."

That was the worst thing she could say to him. That woman hated him. Although their relationship was better this time, he didn't trust her with his fragile wife.

"Babe, wait. I was so afraid of losing you again I tried to handle it without involving you. I'm sorry. I'll fix it. You belong here," he said with a mix of panic and fear.

"According to that paper in your hand, you're someone else's husband. I will *not* live in sin with you again."

Jabir discarded the paper in his hand like a plague. He had no one to blame but himself. Kamal had told him many times to come clean, but the possibility of losing the happiness and love he enjoyed with Damisi—the only woman he loved—was something he wasn't willing to risk. Now, as he watched his wife climb the staircase, the reality of what was about to happen jolted him into motion. He located his cell phone on the table and dialed Ashton. He needed answers before the best thing that had ever happened to him slipped right through his fingers.

"Soften her heart, Lord. Help me fix this," he prayed.

Chapter 38

"What do you mean by you can't find it?" Jabir asked.

Ashton tapped his shoulder. "Man, we're in a courthouse. Just relax. I'll take care of it."

Jabir walked out of the office. That was the only way he could keep from wringing somebody's neck and ending up in jail. The last twenty-four hours had been hell on earth. Damisi was as cold as ice and had kicked him out of their bedroom. Kamal wasn't showing him any love either. Jabir knew he had messed up big time, but now wasn't the time to have his twin telling him I told you so.

After mulling over the situation all night and what could have gone wrong, he knew he needed a miracle. He had prayed fervently this would be a little fixable mistake, but it was turning out to be quite the opposite. He had arrived at Ashton's office a little more than an hour earlier, and they made their way to the courthouse, certain he had handed the papers to be filed in the court. Now the clerk was saying they couldn't locate the document. Jabir began pacing and ran his hand over his head. Did Angela know they were still married? If she did, would she now contest the annulment? Would he have to start the process all over? If he did, what would that mean for Damisi and him? He had never seen his wife as emotionless as he had in the last couple of hours. She hadn't said anything, and that scared him.

Jabir turned around when he heard Ashton's voice. "So what's the deal?"

"I have good news and bad news. The bad news is the clerk I handed the papers to for filing didn't file them and they can't locate them."

"You're kidding, right?"

"No. She has since been fired for other stuff."

Jabir cursed under his breath. "The good news?"

"I know the judge. He'll remember and hopefully waive us having to repeat the process."

"And if he doesn't?"

"Let's cross that bridge when we get there," Ashton said, walking toward the door.

"Don't you have a copy of the paper? That one you scanned and sent to me that made me think this nightmare was over." It was that evidence that made him think his annulment was a sure thing. He would never intentionally hurt Damisi. Apart from being the love of his life, she was going to be the mother of his children. She had to believe he would never do anything to hurt her. But she wasn't trying to listen to anything he had to say.

"I do, but they will only accept originals. Come on. Let's go."

Twenty minutes later, Jabir and Ashton walked up to Judge Lockhart's chambers. They were greeted by his staff.

"Is the judge in?" Ashton asked the elderly lady.

She looked at him over the top of her glasses. "Well, hello to you, too."

"Please. This is urgent," Jabir interrupted. He didn't have time for frivolities.

"Everybody has an emergency." The woman rolled her eyes.

Jabir took a step closer, and Ashton got in front of him. His desperation was making way for the volatile temper he had successfully curtailed.

"We apologize. Please. Is the judge in? I really need to see him," Ashton said.

After a brief pause the woman looked up. "No, he is not in. You just missed him. He went on vacation to the Philippines. His first daughter just gave birth," the woman said with a smile on her face after sharing that tidbit.

Jabir stopped listening after she said the word *no*. What was he going to do? He located the nearest seat and sat. He bent his head and sighed, then he said a quick prayer.

"Okay. We need to strategize. Let's go," Ashton said.

Jabir followed him out without saying a word. They drove in silence until they reached Ashton's office.

"How the heck did this happen?" Jabir asked once they were seated. "My once perfect life is crumbling before my eyes."

"Things happen. We just have to find a way to fix it."

"How?"

"The judge will be back in three weeks. We can either wait, or we start the process all over.

"Six to ten weeks?" Jabir roared. "Are you kidding me? My wife won't even look at me. I'm worried about her health, and my kids would be born bastards because legally our marriage is null and void."

"You could get Angela to sign this time," Ashton said.

"That's a risk I'm not willing to take. That woman hates me. Supposing she now decides to contest the annulment? Then we'll end up in court."

"But from what you told me, she likes your wife."

"I'm not putting Dami through that humiliation. There has to be another way," Jabir covered his eyes with his hand.

"I'm sorry, man. It's either we wait for the judge, get Angela to sign another one or start the process all over..."

"Either way, I'm screwed." Jabir stood and headed to the door. "I'll tell you what I decided tonight."

Minutes later, he was seated in his car with his head on the steering wheel. "Lord, I have been so arrogant in my ways. Please forgive me and get me out of this. I love my wife."

―――――

DAMISI EMPTIED HER SECOND FULL CUP OF TEA. AS OPPOSED to too much sugar like she put in the first one, she had put salt in this one. Her mind was a battlefield, and her spirit was being defeated. She knew Jabir was meeting with Ashton that day. The only reason she knew that was because she had read the note he left for her on the kitchen table. She was so angry and hurt she had kicked him out of the bedroom the previous night. She heard his taps on the door that morning but had nothing to say to him.

Surprisingly, she didn't feel anger anymore, but rather confusion and pain over his betrayal. The ache sent her into silence. Not a grudging silence, but a reflective one. At times like this, she missed Moji. They shared everything, but Damisi knew this was one secret she couldn't share. Shame and embarrassment caused fresh tears to fall as she made her way back up the stairs. She still couldn't believe her husband had another life he didn't share with her. They had been through so much. Why couldn't he trust her with this? Without trust, how could there be true love? If the Nigerian press got a wind of this, they would take them to the mat.

Damisi opened her bedroom door. Her bedroom… Was it really? It was strange how she already felt out of place. No matter how many words of reassurance Jabir said to her the night before or texted her that morning, the fact of the matter was he was married to someone else. How could she live with him, knowing he wasn't really her husband after all? Anger rose up in her.

Damisi knew Angela couldn't possibly know she was still married to Jabir, but the mere fact that the woman knew something about her husband she didn't made her blood boil. What if Angela found out and decided to prove difficult? What would that mean for her and the kids? What would a drawn-out process do to Jabir's career? This was too heavy a secret to keep to herself. But she wanted to be careful of whom she shared with. Moji and Aunty Bola would be ready to go to war. The Danjumas and her father would try to pacify her.

Her phone made the familiar sound that told her she had a text. It was Jabir informing her he would soon be home. Just a few days ago, her heart would've fluttered with anticipation of his arrival. Now it ached with anxiety and hurt. Damisi pulled down the covers and released the breath she didn't know she had been holding. She got between the sheets and turned on the television to her favorite cooking show. She had been on autopilot mode all day, not being able to work on her business, blog or rest. *Lord, please open my heart to be able to listen to what he has to say.*

A few minutes later, Jabir entered the room. His walk had lost its swagger. He gave her a weary smile, his eyes conveying his fear. She instinctively knew he didn't have any good news to share. She stared at him for a moment and focused her blank expression on the television. He sat on the side of the bed, picked up her hands and gently caressed them. After asking about the welfare of her and the babies, Jabir bowed his head slightly.

A few moments later, he raised his face. "Baby, you know I love you…"

She shook her head. "Stop it. This is not about love. Love should've made you trust me."

"I do trust—"

"No, you don't. If I was the one who had a husband just show up, would you take 'I love you' from me?"

Jabir remained silent.

"Stop trying to patronize me like this is just a stubbed toe. Tell me what happened."

He rubbed his hand over the lower part of his face, clearly exasperated. "It didn't go well." He looked at her.

"Meaning?" She angled her body. The pain in his eyes almost made her want to reach out for him. *Almost.*

Damisi sat in silence as her husband confirmed her worse nightmare. It was not going to be as simple as he made her believe the night before. Tears began to fall down her cheeks. Jabir gathered her in his arms and rocked her in silence. She couldn't believe he had done this to them. She snapped. Just like in the past, he hadn't considered how his actions would affect all of them. She pushed him away. A fire that wasn't there before shone from her eyes. Her body shook.

"I need to get out of here," she whispered.

"I know I've said this before, but I'm so sorry. I promise I'll fix it," Jabir said.

"Guess what? You can't fix everything. You tried to fix this and see where it landed us."

"I'm a new man. This time I'm not by myself. I have you and Jesus. It'll be okay, but I need you to be calm because of the babies."

"The minute you found out I was pregnant, you should've told me…"

"Told you? Tell me right here, right now that if I had told you, you wouldn't have run in the other direction. I was already fixing my mistake before I knew anything about you or my girls."

Damisi remained silent. She contemplated his words. She knew what he said might have been true, but he took that decision away from her.

"I have never been as miserable as I have been since we were tossed back into my past. The look of pain in your eyes haunted me all night," he confessed.

Damisi remained silent; fatigue racked her body. She hadn't slept a wink, and the girls were wreaking havoc on her back.

Jabir got on his knees near the bed. "I won't survive if you leave me, even for a short period. You have to believe I never meant to hurt you."

"Deep down, I know that, but it doesn't make the pain go away. You hurt me," Damisi whispered. She lay back and winced.

"Are you okay?" he asked in a soft tone.

"I'm fine" was her curt response. Her back ached, but the pain had nothing on the one he'd inflicted on her heart.

Jabir rubbed his hand over his head. "I know you're hurt, but I think—"

"My back, head and heart hurt right now, so forgive me if I care less what you think." Damisi felt another stabbing pain in her lower back.

"Do we need to go to the hospital? How bad is your back pain?"

She rolled her eyes at him. She knew she was being ridiculous, but she hurt too much to care. She just wanted him to leave her alone. She needed to think, to cry and to pray. This aggravation was not good for her blood pressure or their children, so she knew she needed to calm down.

"I just need to lay my head down…you know where to lay yours. Good night." She turned to her side and pulled the covers over her. She knew Jabir was still standing there, and she wrestled with reaching out to him, but she quickly nixed the idea.

"It's going to be okay. I promise, and at the risk of aggravating you more, I'll say it again: Please forgive me."

Seconds later, she heard the door open and close. Damisi drew in a deep breath and felt tears well in her eyes again. In just three words—*please forgive me*—Jabir had shown her he wasn't just sorry the secret had come out as she had assumed.

He had just humbled himself before her with his call to action. Mark 11 verse 25 came to her mind immediately. *When you stand to pray, forgive so you might be forgiven.* How could she pray when her heart was unforgiving? Wiping the tears from her eyes, she stood to go to the bathroom. With all the things she had been forgiven for, how could she deny him the same? She had to find a way to let go of her hurt and pain. He husband had just called her out.

Chapter 39

Damisi made it to her cell phone just in time to answer the last ring. She recognized the ring tone. It belonged to Ashley. She used to talk to her friend every day, but since this fiasco started a week ago, she had sent all Ashley's calls to voicemail. To make up, she'd sent a text later with an excuse. Damisi had forgiven her husband, but the fact that the process for an annulment was taking on a life of its own was making her weary.

With a labored exhale, she tried to sound normal. "Hey, Ash."

"Don't 'hey' me. If you didn't answer me this time, I would have come over. What's going on?"

Damisi pursed her lips together and took the scolding she knew she had coming. She would have done the same thing if it were the other way around. She took the last pieces of clothing out of the washer and tossed them into the dryer and turned it on.

"What's going on over there?" her friend asked.

"Nothing. It's just the dryer."

"Why are you doing laundry? You should be sitting down with your legs up. What are you, a hundred weeks pregnant?"

Both women giggled.

"I'm tired of you and Moji exaggerating how far along I am. I just entered my thirty-fourth week, and I need to stay busy." As soon as the words left her mouth, Damisi knew she'd opened the door for Ashley's Q & A session.

"Stay busy? Why? Don't let me ask you again what's going on."

There was a pause on the other end of the line. Damisi knew Ashley was giving her time to think. Damisi thought about whether she was up to sharing or not. She couldn't talk to her family. She and Jabir had only polite awkward conversations between them, both avoiding the topic looming over them.

"Dami?"

Damisi walked into her prayer room and closed the door behind her. She spent a lot of time in there. It was where Jabir met her when he left earlier for work. With the recent developments, she needed some kind of intervention. She walked toward her chaise and sat on it, covering herself with the blanket. She sighed and narrated the events of the past week to her friend.

At the end, there was silence on the phone, and tears began to fall again. Damisi wiped them. She had vowed she wouldn't cry again.

"Ash?"

"I'm coming over. You better open the door when I get there."

Before Damisi could respond, Ashley ended the call. Her stomach growled. It was lunchtime. Luckily for her, Ashley ate African food just as much as she did.

Minutes later, Damisi opened the front door, and Ashley pulled her into a hug.

"Are you okay?"

Damisi raised her eyebrow. "As much as I can be. Are you

okay?" The Ashley she knew would have come in laying into Jabir.

"Yes," her friend replied and guided her toward the kitchen. "I'm hungry, and this place smells heavenly."

"You're always hungry, but it never shows on you."

Ashley opened the pot and dished some coconut rice and spicy grilled fish onto her plate. Damisi did the same, and soon both friends were eating in the living room. They both ate in palatable silence although Damisi wondered why her friend was so calm. With only a quarter of her food left, Damisi set aside her plate.

"I know you didn't come over here to eat," Damisi said, irritated.

Ashley took a sip of her water. "Calm down. You have nothing to worry about."

"Okay, where's my friend? You can't be on Jabir's side in this."

"I'm on nobody's side, but you already want to kill the man. Why should I join in?"

"Really?"

"What he did was wrong, yes. He should have told you. But really like he said, would you have given him time of day?"

Damisi knew the answer without thinking.

"Sometimes we get angry we don't have something—in your case access to that information. But I'm sure God knew if you did, you guys wouldn't end up together."

"But we aren't together. Our marriage is void with him being married to someone else."

"What's going on with the annulment?"

Damisi filled her in, also adding the fact that two days ago, Jabir informed her Angela was nowhere to be found again, so the process would take longer. The new judge Ashton thought might help them out said too much time had lapsed, therefore they needed to start the process again.

Ashley exhaled. "In America, you're not married, but didn't you have about three ceremonies in Africa?"

Damisi shook her head at the reference to Africa being a country instead of a continent. She knew Ashley knew better and was joking, but now was not the time.

"I don't know about Africa, but in Kenya, yes. We did a traditional and court wedding."

Ashley smiled. "You can't get more married than that." She scooted closer to Damisi and took her palm in her hand.

"Father God, we ask for Your rest in this storm. I pray my sister finds the peace to be still and know that You are God. Thank You because we know You've taken care of it. In Jesus' name. Amen," Ashley prayed.

Damisi uttered a light amen.

"Look, I came over here to make sure you're not planning to take flight. That man loves you. I've seen his transformation. He made a mistake, and so have we all."

"But—"

"No buts. What does it say of you if every time there is a problem, you want to run in the opposite direction? How small is your strength or your faith?" Ashley paused. "You've been in love with the man forever. He's from a broken home, and so are you. It's time to break that generational curse."

Damisi opened her mouth to speak when she felt water pool in between her legs followed by a sharp pain in her back. Instead of words, she let out a scream, quickly followed by another.

"What I said isn't that bad." Ashley rushed to her.

Damisi screamed again.

"My water just broke. Unless you want to deliver…these… babies, we need to get to the hospital now."

———

"So how is she?" Kamal asked.

Jabir adjusted his headset and washed his hands. He honestly didn't know the answer to that question. He and Damisi had been tiptoeing around each other since he gave her the news of the delay in the annulment. He sat behind his desk. He had just consulted with the last patient of the day.

"I don't know how to answer that. She's no longer angry—or maybe she is, but is doing a good job of concealing it."

"I hate this is happening. I've learnt so much from your mistakes, bro. That's why I always tell Brittani straight as it is," Kamal said.

"I'm glad to be your case study. Are you still with Brittani? I thought she was gone."

"Nah, player. That was all you. You were the one who changed women every other month—until you caught the Holy Ghost."

"You don't catch the Holy Spirit, but I'm not even going there with you today." Jabir tapped his pencil on the table. He was all out of options. This must be punishment for his past. Any time he needed Angela, she was nowhere to be found. How many vacations did the woman get a year?

"Seriously, bro, I hate you're going through this. You want me to plead on your behalf?"

Jabir smiled at his brother's offer. "No. What I need is a miracle—that either the judge comes back, or I see Angela and she agrees to sign...no drama."

Kamal laughed. "Recently, you're always talking about God and faith, so pray for your miracle."

Jabir thought about his brother's words. He had prayed, but he was still new at total dependence on God. *Help me do that, Lord.* "You're right."

"Good. Keep your—"

His phone buzzed, alerting him to an incoming call. "Hold on, Kammy." He hoped it was his lawyer with good news. He frowned. It was Ashley.

"Hello, Ash."

"I'm with Dami. We just arrived at Mercy. She's about to make you a daddy," Ashley said, clearly out of breath.

His heart constricted in his chest. He hadn't thought about what this moment would feel like, but it jolted him from his seat.

"I'm on my way."

Ashley disconnected the call.

"Kammy, I gotta go. Dami is in the hospital…" Jabir searched frantically for his keys.

"Is she okay? Is it time?"

"It's not time, but either way my girls are on the way. I'm about to be a daddy. A daddy, man."

———

"You're just in time, Dr. Danjuma," a nurse said to him as he approached Damisi's room.

He was still panting from the run across the parking lot, up three flights of stairs and down the hall. Of all days, the elevators picked this one to run slow. He rushed into the room. Damisi's gut-wrenching scream pierced his heart. He rushed over and kissed her forehead. She glanced up at him with tired eyes. She looked so worn out, and it hurt to know he was a part of what had made her restless for days. He quickly noticed there was equipment ready to take the twins to NICU once they were born.

She started to sob.

"Baby, please don't cry. Breathe," he urged while kissing her forehead repeatedly.

Damisi began blowing in and out.

Several hours later, Dr. St. John walked in with another nurse. "Okay, Mummy, let's see if you've dilated some more."

The doctor sat at the end of the bed and examined Damisi. A few seconds later, she raised her head and winked at Jabir. "I guess the girls were waiting on Daddy because ready or not, here they come. Damisi, on the count of three, I need you to give me a big push."

Damisi nodded and gave Jabir's hand a death grip.

"Okay, here we go…one, two, three…puuuushhhhhhhhhh."

Chapter 40

Jabir was in a trance as he followed the doctor's instruction on how to cut the umbilical cords of both girls. After a several pushes, he had heard the healthy cry of his first daughter. Soon after there was a second wail. And just like that, he thought his heart would burst with love. His girls were tiny caramel-colored beauties, each with a head full of hair. As the nurses took the babies to clean and run initial tests, Jabir leaned his forehead on Damisi's sweaty one.

"Thank you. Thank you. I love you with every part of me," he whispered.

"I love you, too." Her response was faint.

He couldn't believe the strength she had shown in birthing his daughters. At a point, her screams were almost too much for him to bear. Ashley had gone, as she couldn't take it.

"Congratulations, guys. We're going to take the babies to the NICU now," Dr. St. John said.

Jabir saw Damisi's frown and quickly squeezed her closer. "But there's nothing to worry about right, doc? It's just a precaution because they're preemies."

"Yep. There's nothing to worry about, Mummy. Remember we talked about this in the event they were born premature," Dr. St. John answered. "Now rest. Let Daddy take care of you."

Thirty minutes later, the doctor reentered the room. She wasn't smiling and Jabir's heart immediately skipped a beat. Jabir helped Damisi, who had taken a quick nap, sit up.

"Doctor, is anything wrong?" Damisi asked in a panicked voice.

"No, but I'm going to recommend we keep the babies in the NICU until they gain a little more weight. They're breathing on their own, but I'm concerned with how small they are."

"When can we see them?" Jabir asked.

"As soon as they're settled in." Turning to Damisi, the doctor said, "Well done, Mummy."

Damisi began to sob. Jabir suspected it was because she feared something was really wrong, when it wasn't.

"Baby, stop crying. Everything is gonna be okay. They'll gain the weight."

"I hope so. I want to see them. I want to breastfeed them. I only got to touch them for a few seconds," Damisi protested.

"And you will, Mama Bear." He smiled and was relieved when she returned the gesture.

"Your husband is right. Soon." Dr. St. John left the room.

"Ashley is on her way. She went to get her son from after-care. What do you want to eat?"

"All I want to do now is sleep. When I wake up, I want fish pepper soup."

Jabir's eyes widened. He didn't know the first thing about where to get such or how to cook it. She was the one who reintroduced Nigerian food into his regular diet.

Damisi must have read his thoughts because a wide grin appeared on her face. She gave him directions to a new African restaurant she had discovered.

"Okay. Promise me you'll sleep while I'm gone."

"I will. Where's my phone?"

Jabir pointed to the table. "There. Please leave it off and rest. Mine is on." He walked over and kissed her. This was the first time in almost a week their lips had made contact. He missed them. He deepened the kiss, but didn't get too far before Damisi pushed him away.

"Err, we're still in the hospital, mister."

"I've missed you."

"I've missed you, too, but let's not forget you're married." She raised her brow and twisted her lips.

Jabir knew she had forgiven him, but flinched at the reality of their situation. He made a mental note to call Ashton on his way out. The sheriff had tried but failed to serve Angela the summons since she wasn't available. Since she had to be served in person, he and his lawyer decided to hire a private company to try again one last time before they went with the final option: the publication in the paper. It would take forever and was his worst nightmare.

"I'm doing everything to fix that."

"Hmmm. Please let them know that if Ash comes while I'm asleep, she should be let in." Damisi yawned and turned to her side.

———

Damisi sat with her newborns in the special care unit. It had been about thirty-six hours since they made their entrance into the world. Her life already had new meaning. She held both babies to her bosom, leaned her head back and closed her eyes. Words could not express her gratitude to God for turning her mourning into dancing. There was still work to be done, like getting her husband's marriage annulled, but she was thankful in spite of and would praise Him anyway.

The nurse came over and took one of the babies from her, so she could feed the other. The previous day, she had tried to breastfeed, but they didn't latch on. She was tempted to cry, but had read that could happen, so she pumped and fed them instead. Jabir had sat with her in silence as she held the babies skin to skin. Madam Paulina, Aunty Bola and her mother-in-law all encouraged her to do that.

She was now prepared to try again. She held the first twin to her breast. According to their birth order, her dad, mother-in-law and aunt had all given the children names. As she and Jabir expected, each baby had a Hausa, Kenyan, Igbo and Yoruba name.

"Ana, please eat for Mummy," Damisi coaxed as she tried to get her firstborn daughter to feed. Jabir felt their Hausa names, Hassana and Hussaina, were too long, so he shortened them to Ana and Ina. Damisi wondered why he and Kamal didn't have the male version of those names.

She began to sing a song she remembered Madam Paulina singing to her. A few seconds later, she could feel her daughter sucking. She smiled and lifted her eyes to the heavens. She couldn't wait to tell Jabir.

After a while, the attending nurse walked over. "I told you you'd get it."

"Yes, you did. I hope Ina is as kind to me as her sister. I was beginning to feel like a failure," Damisi confessed.

The nurse waved off her comment. "Most mothers feel that way, but sometimes it takes time at first." The nurse extended her arms to take the baby. "Here, let me burp her and put her down, then I'll bring Ina over."

Damisi kissed her daughter's forehead and handed her over. She looked up at the wall clock. It was 6:00 P.M. Jabir should be back soon. He had made a quick trip home, then to his office to check on things. After staying most of the afternoon, Ashley also had to leave. The nurse brought her Ina. Damisi kissed her, positioned her for feeding and beamed. The nurse winked at her and gave her a thumbs-up.

"My shift is almost over, but my replacement is on her way.

Hopefully after tomorrow, you and the girls will be home," the nurse said.

"I pray so."

Like her sister, a few seconds later, Ina began to suck. Damisi grinned when she remembered Aunty Bola telling her the belief behind the twins' Yoruba names. Apparently the second twin, Kehinde, sends the first twin, Taiwo, out into the world to see if it's conducive enough to enter. The response to the inquiry is known by the way she cries.

"Damisi?"

Damisi stilled. She slowly looked up and saw Angela. For a minute, she wondered what she was doing here, but quickly remembered she said she worked for the neonatal unit of Mercy. Before she could acknowledge her greeting, the other nurse walked up to them.

"Angela girl, welcome back. Are you working the night shift?"

"Yes," Angela replied. Her voice was almost inaudible.

In seconds that passed, an array of thoughts bombarded Damisi's mind. There was a time when she felt Angela was a harmless, but with recent events, she didn't know what to believe. Could she trust her with her babies? Her life had changed with the birth of her daughters, and their safety would always be paramount.

"Hello, Angela," Damisi said.

"You two know each other? Good. Okay, good night, y'all."

Damisi and Angela's gaze were still locked on each other, and neither responded to the nurse's goodbye. Something about the way Angela looked at her made Damisi suspect she had found out that she was still married to Jabir.

"You had the babies?" Angela asked, breaking the awkward moment.

Damisi nodded. Angela came closer and peered at Ina, then she walked over and looked at Ana.

"They're gorgeous."

"Thank you," Damisi responded with caution.

Angela walked back to the nursing station, and minutes later appeared with some papers in her hand. There was something about her countenance that appeared humble, almost broken. Her head wasn't held up high like the first day she met her.

"I apologize for my manners. Congratulations to you and Dr. Danjuma."

Dr. Danjuma? What happened to Jay?

Damisi nodded. She opened her mouth to cut to the chase. The small talk made her uncomfortable. Before she could speak, Angela did.

"I'm glad I met you here. I'd like to give you these."

Damisi raised her brow to question her comment.

"No, I don't mean I'm glad you're in the special care unit, but that I saw you and not Dr. Danjuma," Angela hurriedly corrected.

Damisi rested Ina on her shoulder and began rubbing her back. "What are those?"

Ina burped. Damisi walked over and put her back in bed. She looked at her angels whom her mother-in-law had named Onyinye and Onyeka. They truly were gifts from God. She walked back over to Angela and folded her arms across her chest.

"So what are those?"

"Annulment papers."

"How?"

Angela exhaled. "Last night I got back from Alabama where I went to see my mother. The circumstances under which I grew up were not the best, and I hated my mother for being so weak…"

"Why are you telling me this?" Damisi asked and turned to walk away.

"Please hear me out," Angela said.

The desperation in her voice caused Damisi to halt. She turned around and folded her arms across her chest.

"My past shaped my future—or what I almost let my future become. I didn't know my father, and my mother surrounded herself with men who mooched off her and still treated her bad. I vowed to never be that way—take care of a man or let anyone treat me wrong—so I did the opposite. I dated only rich men, and I did them wrong."

"I don't want to talk about my husband with you..." Damisi walked away. She felt her temper rising.

"Please. I don't want to fight. I lost my mother to a terrible disease she caught from some random man. Watching her die made me aware of all the wrong I've done. Coercing Dr. Danjuma into marrying me was one of them." Angela wiped a tear from her cheek. "In her last days, my mother accepted salvation through a hospital doctor. She asked for my forgiveness and encouraged me to do the same."

Damisi's anxiety turned to sorrow and pain. Her heart ached for Angela. She knew what it was like to grow up living your life based on your parents' shortcomings. She also knew what it was like to feel so broken from your transgressions. Angela had been nice to her, so there was no reason for hostility toward her. Jabir had admitted to being with her on the rebound. But her husband was a new creature. So was she and hopefully, so was Angela.

"We've all sinned and fallen short of His glory. Nothing makes my sin bigger or less than yours. I know for a fact that once you accept Jesus, old things have passed away and you are made new," Damisi said.

"That's a difficult concept for me. Before meeting Dr. Danjuma, I have stolen, cheated and lied all in an attempt to be one step ahead of men. I've done so much wrong, but I do want to find the peace my mother talked about. This afternoon, as I was about to leave for work, I got served with this summons." Angela paused.

Damisi didn't have a response. The way God worked stumped and rendered her speechless.

Angela continued, "I wanted to sabotage his efforts the first time, but I honestly didn't think we were still married. This was the out I needed to fix one of my numerous mistakes, so I brought them to work. My plan was to take them to Dr. Danjuma's lawyer when I get off in the morning, but here you are. I signed them."

Damisi paused. She didn't know whether she could handle the documents or not. *But there's no harm in looking.* Her hands shook as she reached out to take the documents that had brought her home to a standstill. She opened the papers and looked through. Angela had indeed signed every page that listed her as the defendant. Damisi put the papers in the pocket of her night dress.

Thank you," Damisi said.

"I'm sorry for causing you any pain or hurt."

"Thank you for saying that, but how did you know I knew about you two being married?"

Angela's eyes widened. "Oh my God! You didn't?"

Damisi smiled. "I do, but I was just curious."

"I just assumed. Seeing both of you at the dinner made me envious—not of you, but of what you two share. It was as though no one else was in the room. I aspire to that kind of love," Angela replied.

The woman before her was in a real confessional mode. Damisi didn't expect her to be so truthful considering the circumstances. *But you shall be a witness for Him to everyone you have seen or heard.* Acts 22:15 popped in her head. "You say you want peace. Jesus died on the cross to reconcile us with God. His blood is the price for our sins. He can give you peace; just ask. Do you want to accept Him?"

Angela stared at her, and Damisi knew she hadn't expected to hear that from her. Damisi smiled. After a few minutes, Angela stepped forward, and Damisi prayed the prayer of salvation. The ladies hugged each other.

"What's going on here?" Jabir's harsh whisper came from the door. His eyebrows creased together in confusion. He walked over to his wife. "Baby, are you okay?"

"Hello, Dr. Danjuma," Angela greeted.

Jabir gave no response, but went over to peer at his daughters.

"Hello, Angela." Jabir eyes questioned Damisi. "Is someone going to talk to me?"

Damisi hooked her arm around her husband's waist. He absently kissed the crown of her head.

"*Mpenzi*, I'll tell you all about it on the way to my room." Damisi tried to move him, but he wasn't budging.

Jabir glanced at Angela, then looked at his wife. "The girls?"

Damisi knew his real concern was like her's. Could Angela be trusted with their daughters? "They are fine," she reassured him.

Jabir didn't look convinced, and Angela's silence heightened his fear.

As though she sensed their discomfort, Angela said, "Actually, I'm heading home. Suddenly, I don't feel so well." She turned to leave, and then paused. "Damisi, thank you."

Damisi smiled and nodded.

Angela left.

"I'm waiting," Jabir said.

"Don't they say the patient dog gets the fattest bone?" Damisi teased.

"No, they say the patient dog goes hungry."

Damisi laughed. "Let's check on the girls, then you can tuck me in for a nap."

Moments later, as Jabir fluffed her pillow, Damisi handed him the papers. "God has made everything perfect in His time."

Damisi watched him as understanding came upon him. She saw his eye glaze over with moisture. She gave him the brief version of what happened with Angela.

He sat on the edge of the bed and brought his hand to her cheek and caressed it. "I am so sorry, baby, for everything. Thank you staying with me and giving me my daughters." He kissed her and just stared at her. "You are perfect."

"I have too many flaws to be perfect." She yawned. "But I also have too many blessings to be ungrateful for my journey—our journey."

He kissed her lips. "When I thought I had messed things up for our family, my world was off balance."

She raised her eyebrow. "Oh really?"

"Woman, you must not know that your love anchors me. I love you with everything I am," Jabir said.

Damisi's eyes began to close, and a tear slid down her cheek "I love you, too, baby. More than you'll ever know."

Jabir wiped the tear away. "Rest, my queen, while Daddy goes spend some time with our princesses."

Epilogue

One Year Later
Abuja, Nigeria.

Jabir's smile broadened with pride as he watched Damisi walk down the aisle. Accompanied by her father, she was the epitome of beauty in a simple lace white gown and a head full of loose curls that hung on her shoulders. Her only requests for their do-over wedding were simplicity and a ceremony that was closed to the press. His job was to do everything within his power to grant her those wishes—a feat that wasn't easy once the press somehow got wind of the news. Initially Jabir was upset, but he couldn't blame them for the frenzy. Damisi Odinga-Danjuma was returning home. Everything they had planned had been leaked. He was tempted to call everything off, but he knew Damisi had her heart set on a real wedding. In the end, Eno came to the rescue. Being a member of the press herself, she knew exactly how to throw them off.

Hence, they had ended up in a secluded estate in Abuja instead of the luxury resort in Lagos. His bride had exactly what she wanted. She deserved it after all he put her through the last year.

It had all worked out, but things could have been so different. Once he took the annulment papers to Ashton, the process was accelerated, and they were free to get married... again. The day after they got the clear, Jabir and Damisi said their vows in front of a judge to get the children legitimized immediately.

Jabir extended his hand, and Damisi put hers in it. She smiled up at him. The joy in her eyes made his heart stop for a moment. He couldn't solely take the credit. It was all the grace of God. During the last year, and with all the changes in their life, they'd come to rely on His strength being perfect in their weakness. He lifted his hand and caressed the side of her face.

"Family and friends, we are gathered here today to join together Jabir and Damisi...again," the pastor said.

Light giggles could be heard from the crowd that consisted of their family and a few friends. Jabir turned to give them a stern look, which didn't work but succeeded in exciting his daughters instead. His world revolved around his wife and his girls who were now seated on his mother and Aunty Bola's lap. Between them, Madam Paulina and the rest of the family, he and Damisi had to fight to get a little time in. They'd all have their feelings hurt when they returned to Detroit in a couple of days. Ana and Ina had captured their hearts.

Once the giggling died down, the ceremony continued. Soon after Jabir heard the pastor say, "You many now kiss the bride...again."

"Now that I can do." Jabir lifted the veil and cupped Damisi face.

"This is a G-rated event," Damisi whispered.

Jabir winked at her and captured her lips.

The song "I Found Love" by Bebe and CeCe Winans began playing in the background. They ended their kiss and stared into each other's eyes. The gaze spoke volumes without a word being uttered.

Their bubble was soon busted by the approach of Rasheed who had his son Yohance on one arm and Ibiso on the other. Kamal, Moji and Halima soon joined them, offering the couple congratulatory and kind wishes. Jabir felt his wife shift from his side. He followed the direction of her gaze, which landed on Ana and Ina. The girls were soon brought over by his mother and Madam Paulina with Aunty Bola and grandpa following suit.

"Kammy," Jabir's mother said.

"Yes, Mama," Kamal answered cautiously.

Jabir smiled because he knew exactly what his mother was about to say.

"You're next."

"For what?"

"To go to the moon. To get married of course," his mother said.

"Mama, we have a better chance of getting him to the moon," Jabir whispered.

Kamal looked around. Everyone was still fussing over the babies and Damisi. He put his arm around his mother's shoulder and bent his head. He then beckoned to summon Jabir closer.

"He's right, Mama. I love my sis-in-laws, but after all the wahala I saw my brothers go through, I'd rather go to the moon," Kamal said.

"Mama, let's make sure when the time comes, we make him eat those words," Jabir said as they walked back over to join the crowd.

Discussion Questions

---

1. What do you think of Jabir's attitude to his own achievements?
2. Do you think Damisi's approach to her problem was the right one?
3. Moji and Damisi's father had a quick solution to Damisi's problem. What do you think of it?
4. Discuss Angela. Her backstory at the end was intriguing. Most of the action of the Danjuma brothers is driven by their childhood. So was her.
5. Damisi found it difficult to accept the grace and forgiveness of God. Do we sometimes allow the fact we can't forgive ourselves count when it comes to God's forgiveness?
6. Talk about other notable people in ministry who fell and had a hard time getting up again.
7. What do you think of Jabir's and Damisi's time in Kenya?
8. Discuss the way the Damisi's scandal broke and the couple's reaction to it?
9. Should Jabir have told Damisi about Angela since it was in the "past"

10. What was your scene?
11. Discuss Kamal.

Final Note

Thank you for reading Jabir & Damisi's story. Please consider leaving a review on the platform you purchased the book from. I greatly appreciate honest feedback. They really go a long way. The number of reviews a book receives greatly improves how well it does.

If you liked this story, I trust you might like some of my other titles. But before we get to those, never miss a sale, new release announcements, or freebies. You can ensure that by joining my mailing list. I'd love to stay connected.

Next up in the Danjuma family is Kamal Danjuma. Order Mended With Love here.

Also By Unoma Nwankwor

Stand Alone Books

An Unexpected Blessing

He Changed My Name

When You Let Go

The Ultimatum Series

The Christmas Ultimatum

The Final Ultimatum

Sons of Ishmael Series

A Scoop of Love

Anchored by Love

Mended with Love

Redeemed Through Love

Mixed Tidings

The Invisible Shackles Series

To Live Again,

To Breathe Again

The DuBois-Arazi Family Novels

A Promise Fulfilled

Destiny Fulfilled

The Billionaire Pact

Vegas Nights

Second Shot

Pretend Bae

Away To Africa

New Year's Kiss (Prequel)

Rent-A-Bae

His Makeshift Fiancée

A Suitable Wife